F
THA   Thayer, Nancy

          Family secrets

DATE DUE

JAN 1 8 2001	JUL 2 4 2006
JUN 1 7 2001	JUL 2 1 2007
JAN 0 6 2003	FEB 2 3 2012
FEB 0 1 2003	OCT 1 8 2012
FEB 2 8 2003	JAN 7 2017
JUN 2 3 2003	
JUN 2 3 2003	
MAR 2 5 2004	
JUN 1 1 2005	

Family  Secrets

Nancy Thayer

Family Secrets

VIKING

VIKING
Published by the Penguin Group
Penguin Books USA Inc., 375 Hudson Street,
New York, New York 10014, U.S.A.
Penguin Books Ltd, 27 Wrights Lane,
London W8 5TZ, England
Penguin Books Australia Ltd, Ringwood,
Victoria, Australia
Penguin Books Canada Ltd, 10 Alcorn Avenue,
Toronto, Ontario, Canada M4V 3B2
Penguin Books (N.Z.) Ltd, 182–190 Wairau Road,
Auckland 10, New Zealand

Penguin Books Ltd, Registered Offices:
Harmondsworth, Middlesex, England

First published in 1993 by Viking Penguin,
a division of Penguin Books USA Inc.

10 9 8 7 6 5 4 3 2 1

PUBLISHER'S NOTE
This is a work of fiction. Names, characters, places, and incidents
either are the product of the author's imagination or are used fic-
titiously, and any resemblance to actual persons, living or dead,
events, or locales is entirely coincidental.

LIBRARY OF CONGRESS CATALOGING IN PUBLICATION DATA
Thayer, Nancy, 1943–
Family secrets / Nancy Thayer.
p.   cm.
ISBN 0-670-84439-X
I. Title.
PS3570.H3475F36   1993
813'.54—dc20   92-50746

Printed in the United States of America
Set in Garamond #3
Designed by Kathryn Parise

This book is dedicated to my sister,
Martha Foshee,
and my brother-in-law,
Chuck Foshee,
with gratitude for their courage
and great generosity,

and to Phil Smith,
who gave us hope and faith.

I would like to thank several people for their help with this book: my mother, Jane Wright Patton; jewelers Sheila Bourgoin and Gary Trainor; my intelligence team—Josh Thayer, Sam Thayer, and Bret Stephens—and especially my husband, Charley Walters.

Family  Secrets

Chapter 1
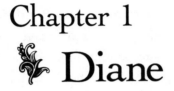 Diane

In the clear light of her Cambridge studio, Diane Randall sat at her workbench drawing the model for an elaborate brooch that had been commissioned by a banker as a wedding present for his bride. The windows were open to the street so that shouts and laughter and traffic sounds drifted in on the cool October air, but Diane didn't notice. As she bent with intense concentration over her sketch pad, she was thinking of love, young love and new love, married love and family love. Sexual love. Her thoughts swirled and twined like her design, until she raised her head and shook it, because her eyes had filled with tears.

Howard Roerson was marrying Patricia Wayne. She must concentrate on that. She had suggested casting the scrolled first letters of their last names in gold, framing and enclosing in the center an emerald-cut one-carat diamond. *R* and *W*. Biting her tongue, Diane returned to her work, painstakingly interweaving the tails of the lovely, curly letters, striving to make them baroque yet distinct. Marriage was like this, she mused, an arabesque coupling, pulling two people into the heart of intimacy and back out again to face the world alone.

She'd send the wax model to Providence to be cast; they'd return it and she would set the diamond herself.

R and *W*. If she'd kept her maiden name years ago when she'd married Jim Randall, this brooch could be hers. But she'd wanted to be rid of the boring White, her family name, and she'd wanted—oh, so passionately—to be with Jim completely. She'd loved him so entirely then, with all the heat and hope of first love, and he had loved her equally, fervently. Then.

Finally, she was ready to carve the wax model. But it was late—she could tell by the slant of the sun across her studio floor. She could hear Lisa, her efficient office manager, bustling around in the front office, slamming file cabinets as she tidied up for the day. Lisa was fastidious to the point of fussbudgetry about the organization of her desk and files; whenever she looked into Diane's studio she was barely able to suppress a shudder of horror at the chaotic glitter in which Diane thrived.

Now Lisa opened the door. "I'm off!"

" 'Bye, Lisa. Have fun tonight. See you in the morning."

"Don't stay too late. You know you don't work well when you're tired."

"Yes, Mother." Diane took off her glasses and smiled. She'd been short-tempered with Lisa recently; she'd felt generally low-spirited. Certainly it wasn't Lisa's fault; it was no one's fault. A fog had floated over her normal cheerfulness, and an invisible virus was sapping her energy. The opposite of spring fever: fall chill.

Lisa shut the studio door. A moment later Diane heard the office door close. She folded her glasses and laid them on the workbench, closed her eyes, and rubbed the bridge of her nose.

Eyestrain. Both she and Jim spent so much time focusing on details it was no wonder they had trouble seeing each other clearly.

Standing, she stretched luxuriously, looking around her. Primitive beauty and state-of-the-art technology met here where beads and charms glittered among small chrome-and-steel machines. She'd been sitting at one of her three workbenches, a jeweler's bench made of solid oak. A cable snaked from a motor suspended from a hook on the workbench to the flexible shaft that operated a variety of hand pieces for precision work. Another cable led down to the foot pedal of her micromatic wax pen; its digital temperature-readout box sat on her workbench, along with the spatulas, round nose, probing, needle, beaver tail, and bent tips, all looking like so many medieval dental tools. Along the back of this workbench as well as the other two grew a metal garden of fluorescent and magnifier lamps, curling and angling their wiry stalks and heads down over her work surface. A counter ran along the back wall holding a double sink, an acid bath in a crock pot, propane and acetylene torches, an exhaust system, polishing wheels, electronic scales, and a steam cleaner. Safety goggles and face shields had been tossed down among her sketch pads and colored pens and pencils.

She was successful in her fine-art and custom-jewelry line, but it was her fashion jewelry she loved most. Playing with her baubles not only inspired new designs for her business, it also served as a form of meditation and consolation in her life. Piled on a table and stacked on the floor were open plastic trays glittering with her playthings: Czech crystals, tiny brass bells, metallic amulets and zodiac symbols, millefiori beads, copper and silver crosses, African brass beads. Her beloved semiprecious stones —amber, turquoise, agate, garnet, moonstone, amethyst—as well as sheets of silver and a few precious jewels, were locked in the

safety vault hunkering in the corner. Every time she unlocked
the door to her workroom and saw her loot waiting to be transformed by her skills, she felt like a witch returning to her charms.

If only these sparkling gems and glowing metals really could
work magic! If only she could shape the fates of those she loved
with the same sure results that she could count on in her work.

Her life was in a real jumble. In the past year her father had
died, her mother had sold the family house and taken off for
Europe, her youngest child had fallen desperately—even frighteningly—in love, and her own body seemed to be failing, fading
into bland middle age. Her business was as successful as ever,
but suddenly that seemed the least important aspect of her complicated life.

It was not the complication that bothered her. She'd always
liked complexities and had never let difficulties hold her back.
A talented, artistic, determined woman, she'd intended that her
life be as opulent and intricate as her jewelry, full of love and
sexual pleasure, of children and profound married joy, of chal-
lenges and triumphs at work, of food and friends and books and
music and wine.

And she *had* had years and years of that, all that, success at
work, and a happy family life. Perhaps she expected too much.
Or perhaps she was only experiencing what the magazines called
the "empty nest" syndrome. Chase was twenty, in his second year
at college, and Julia was eighteen, ready for college next year.
Jim joked that they were going through the "empty wallet syndrome," with all the tuition they were paying, but Diane knew
it wasn't financial worry causing his abstracted coldness. Between
them, Jim and Diane had easily been able to afford the boarding
schools the children had attended since ninth grade.

No, it wasn't money at the heart of her brooding. Until now

she'd been able to have at least the illusion that if she worked hard enough, if she did all the right things, she could keep her children safe and happy.

Now that sense of security had evaporated. Her children were changing. Not quite adults, they no longer seemed to think of themselves as children but as superior beings sprung from pure air. Chase and Julia were the heart of her life, while she was to them only a minor planet blipping annoyingly from the fringes of their universe. As it should be, she supposed. Still, she found it hard to realize that what mattered to her was of little importance to her children, and although she'd devoted her life to their health and happiness, she could no longer shape their destinies, and she might not even know what was deepest in their hearts.

Chase especially treated Jim and Diane with a mixture of fond indifference and wariness, as if his parents had grown irrational over the years and were now not quite to be trusted. He'd become arrogant, even disdainful. Two months ago, to celebrate what she considered a crucial breakthrough in the world, Diane ordered a watch from Bloomingdale's. A Russian watch. When it arrived in the mail she stared at it with reverence, cradling it in her hand, stroking the silky black leather wristband, studying the round distinctive analog face encased in shining chrome. The Arabic numerals three, six, and nine were in black, and in place of the twelve was a red star. She strapped it to her wrist, this physical, concrete symbol of the tiny but real steps man had made toward peace in the world. Born in the forties, growing up in the fifties, she had been taught as a child to fear the Russians; now she exulted in the progress the world seemed to have made. She wanted to share this with her children.

She found her son and his friend Sam in the den. The two healthy, lucky, handsome young men sat with their muscular legs wrapped around their chairs as they bent forward over the computer. They were laughing, showing their milk-white, brace-straight teeth. The sight of them filled her with joy.

"Look!" she said exuberantly, holding out her wrist. "My new watch came!"

Chase looked, then grinned. "Cool. High tech. Good, Mom. You bought a watch that *winds*."

Diane was thrown off by his reaction. "I prefer a watch that winds," she protested.

"Yeah, Mom, I can understand that," Chase agreed, grinning. "Those digital watches are really tricky."

Actually, to Diane, they were. She found the new rectangular watch faces ugly, and the flashing digital numbers looked like algebra equations or alarms. She liked to see the hours divided up like pies; she liked looking at a round face to see how big a piece of time was left.

"Good-looking watch, Mrs. Randall," Sam had observed dutifully. "What do those letters mean?"

"I don't know," Diane confessed.

She held out her wrist and the two young men studied the watch face.

B P E M and a backwards *R* were printed underneath the red star.

"I can read a little Russian," Chase informed them. "Ah, yes. It says, 'Made in Chernobyl.' "

Sam snickered.

Diane grabbed her hand back. "That's not funny. You don't understand, Chase—I used to have nightmares about Russia, and now—" But she could see how their eyes glazed over and their faces settled into an attitude of impatient tolerance. "Oh, never mind," she'd said, and left the room, reminding herself that these young men had grown up in a world quite different from hers.

She was afraid Chase's casual arrogance would cause him trouble someday; she could not protect him from that, nor at this point in his life could she hope to change him. In general Chase was a good-natured, healthy young man, happy, kind, and reasonably sensible, and she was grateful to him for his comfortable, contented state. When her children were in pain or sad, she was in agony; that was simply the way motherhood worked.

She worried terribly about her daughter.

Julia, like Diane, was tall, big boned, and slender, with brown hair and blue eyes. Unlike her mother, Julia never wore jewelry of any kind. She'd never even had her ears pierced. She spent her clothing allowance on fabulous undergarments—ribbon-trimmed camisoles, velvet and satin bras—and covered these delicacies with jeans and ragged shirts from secondhand shops. Julia was in her senior year at Gressex, a boarding school in Lincoln, not far from home. Diane had sent both children away at fourteen, partly because she traveled so often—to the Orient to buy gems, all over the States and Europe to jewelry conventions—but mostly for her children's sakes. She wanted them to be independent—and she'd wanted Julia to know that a woman could have children and a flourishing career.

Julia had been happy at Gressex for three years. She was popular, academically successful—a golden girl, really. But suddenly this year, only two months into her first term, her personality seemed to have changed drastically. On the weekends when Diane drove out to take her for a day of shopping and lunch—usually a treat for both of them—Julia had been moody, cantankerous.

Then, just last week, Julia's adviser had called Jim and Diane to tell them that Julia's grades were slipping, and worse, she was cutting classes. Diane had driven out to the school that evening, walked through the dark campus, entered the dorm, climbed the stairs, turned the corner, and knocked on Julia's door.

"Who is it?" Julia's voice was heavy.

"Your mother." Diane peeked inside. Julia was sprawled on her bed. "May I come in?"

"Oh, man," Julia responded, and rolled over to face the wall.

Diane entered, shutting the door tightly behind her. She crossed the small room and sat on Julia's bed, putting her hand lightly on her daughter's shoulder. "Julia. Sweetie. We have to talk."

Julia didn't reply.

"Your counselor called. She said you've been cutting classes."

Again Julia didn't respond but simply lay there, her rigid back eloquent with anger and misery; and in her anxiety, Diane snapped, "Stop it, Julia! Stop acting this way! Turn over. Look at me. Tell me what's going on!"

Julia turned onto her back and looked up at her mother. "I hate my classes."

"Anything else?"

Julia shook her head.

Diane sat a moment, then asked, "Are you taking drugs?"

"Oh, please," Julia replied, exasperation provoking her to roll over and sit up on the side of the bed.

"Well, then, what is it? Are you sick? Are you unhappy here?" Diane's voice rose with her frustration. Julia stared down at her hands. "*Julia*," she pleaded. Reaching out, she took her daughter's soft hands in her own. "I'm so worried," she said softly.

When a tear fell on Diane's skin, she looked in surprise at Julia's face and saw that her daughter was crying.

"What!" she whispered, tortured. "Please tell me! What?"

"Oh, Mom," Julia wailed, and her entire body sagged into Diane's arms. "Oh, Mom. I'm in love."

Oh, yes, she should have known. Over the years, she'd tried to teach her daughter to be independent, self-sufficient, able to change a tire or a fuse, ready to take on any career a man could have—she'd tried to let her daughter see that the world was hers for the taking. But she couldn't protect her from the ravages of love.

"Darling, who is it?"

"Sam."

"Sam!" Diane couldn't have been more surprised. Sam was one of Chase's best friends, and his oldest friend from the neighborhood. The adopted son of two lawyers, Sam was bright, intelligent, kind, and exotically handsome. Girls fell all over him. In August Diane and Jim had rented a house on Martha's Vineyard for a month, and friends of their children had crowded the place. Sam had been there, but she hadn't noticed him with Julia in particular.

"How does Sam feel?"

"He says he loves me."

"He does?"

Julia pulled away, insulted. "Why do you sound so amazed? Is it so impossible that someone might be in love with me?"

"Don't be so prickly. Of course not. It's just so sudden. I mean, *love,* Julia. I didn't even know you were dating."

"We started going out in August. He drives up from Wesleyan on weekends, when he doesn't have too much homework. When he doesn't—then I'm always afraid he's seeing someone else." Tears rolled down her cheeks.

"Oh, honey."

"Mom, I love him so much! I don't want to live without him!"

"Oh, sweetie." Diane hugged her daughter, smoothed her hair.

"Mom. I want to marry Sam."

"Of course you do."

"No. I mean really. Now. I don't want to go to college. I want to marry Sam and live with him."

Diane was shocked and, for a moment, angry.

"Honey, you're too young to get married. Your whole life is in front of you. You can do anything you want, be anything you want!"

"I only want to be with Sam." Julia dissolved into tears. Her slender back shook.

"Oh, Julia, I know, I know."

"No, you don't," Julia wailed. "You don't understand at all."

Diane had rocked Julia in her arms, hoping to soothe her.

"I know how you feel, sweetie. Really I do. I remember falling in love with your father. It was amazing, like being hit by lightning. It was so—intense. I was a little scared. But, honey, we all survive."

"I don't want just to survive!" Julia said impatiently. "I want to be with Sam."

Diane had stayed with Julia until she calmed down. Then, unable to relax, she went to a nearby grocery store and bought apples, raisins, shelled walnuts, and, for comfort, chocolate bars and the Graham crackers Julia had loved as a child. When she returned to the dorm room, Julia was calmly working at her desk, a math book propped open in front of her.

"Thanks, Mom," Julia had said politely, while Diane's heart had ached to give more to her daughter than food.

Well, Diane thought now, who ever has the remedy for love? She crossed her studio and leaned on the windowsill, looking out into the street. Fresh air, a sense of perspective.

She remembered feeling that way about Jim. It hadn't been an entirely pleasant sensation. Desperation had been too much a part of it, and an overpowering craving that was really irrational. Well, all early love was a form of madness. With luck, it cooled into an enduring warmth.

And then?

And then, after twenty-one years of marriage, what did it become? The blaze of Julia's emotions cast a bright light on Diane's own heart. She still loved Jim. But did she still desire him?

When she and Jim met, it had been a *coup de foudre,* a thunderbolt—for them both—not a falling in love but an arrival, a jolting moment of recognition, as if they'd walked through a door into the room of their lives. She'd never doubted that Jim loved her—or that she loved him. Her only worries had been about how this love would affect her life, for she had definite plans. She longed to be bohemian, to live in Paris and Amsterdam, to travel to the Orient, garnering ideas for her art. She'd intended to have many lovers, to be famous for the broken hearts she left behind her in every country through which she passed. She planned to be as different from her mother as she could possibly be.

Oh, her poor mother! Leaning on the windowsill, Diane sent a silent note of gratitude and apology winging out in the air. Now, as Chase and Julia neared adulthood, she began to understand all her parents had done for her, all that she had shunned. Diane's father had served as an officer in the Navy during World War II, then had joined a firm of lawyers in Washington, D.C., where he worked all his life, providing for his wife and four children a comfortable, even luxurious, life. Diane had chafed at their expectations and rules. Obviously bright, artistic, she'd disdained studying and lived in a dreamworld. As she grew into her adolescence, she decided she'd be an artist.

Like her mother, she went away to Boston to college, but not to Radcliffe: to the School of the Museum of Fine Arts in Boston. She had high hopes. But she was drawn to work on a small scale and to detail, and her work was considered "decorative," a dirty word among painters. By her second year it was clear that she wasn't destined to be an artist. But by then she was leading what she thought of as the artistic life, and that had been what she'd really wanted. She and two roommates shared a loft on Brookline Street in Cambridge. Scented with eau de turpentine, hands stained from oils, they attended gallery openings, foreign films, poetry readings. They danced, partied, and eventually fell into what they considered in their youthful pride dramatic liaisons with eccentric, artistic young men. Diane loved her life. A teacher suggested that she enroll in the jewelry-making program; when she did, she discovered that this was where she belonged. Her fourth year in Boston she went to work for a jeweler. In 1966 she began stringing beads at home, making karmic faux-gypsy/Indian/astrological necklaces laden with charms that she took around to stores in Boston where they were quickly grabbed up and sold out. By the time she was twenty-four, she had hired one of her friends to be her bookkeeper and sales rep.

She remembered those as glorious days. She, Karen, and Laurie slept on mattresses covered with batik Indian bedspreads. They wore turtlenecks and swirling gauzy skirts. They sat up all night smoking Camels, drinking red wine, discussing the meaning of life.

One summer night someone on Putnam Avenue threw a party. Diane's date was a guy she'd only just met: Roger, a handsome, messy, messed-up, slightly maniacal artist whose idol was van

Gogh. Together they drank beer and argued politics in the
kitchen. They swayed together sweatily in the living room to
music from a record player. It was a hot, humid night. Roger
stopped drinking beer and changed to the hard stuff, whiskey or
vodka or both; it didn't seem to matter. As the night went on,
Roger grew obnoxious, vulgar, and finally, roughly amorous. Diane pushed away from him, or tried to, but they were pressed
together in the crowded room. Just when she was afraid there
would be some awful scene, Roger careened toward her, nearly
falling, eyes bulging. Shoving people out of his way, he staggered
across the room and out the door that was open to the hall.

Perhaps he'd decided to go home, or pee in the hall; she didn't
care, though she did feel vaguely responsible. Squeezing her way
through the crush of dancers, she followed Roger. She found
him in the hallway, being sick over the bannister, while a tall,
slender young man held his shoulders, preventing him from
falling.

"I have to lie down," Roger groaned, and he did, right on the
floor of the hall.

Diane looked down at her date, then up into the young man's
clear brown eyes. For a moment she couldn't breathe.

"Are you okay?" he asked. He was wearing chinos and a white
T-shirt. His arms were long and slender with a swimmer's sleek
muscles.

"I guess so. I feel a little faint. It's so hot, and he wasn't very
pleasant just now—"

"Would you like to come in and sit down for a minute? Have
a glass of water? My apartment's right here, across the hall."

"Oh. Well. Thank you."

"I'm Jim Randall." He held out his hand.

"Diane White. Thanks." She put her hand in his. Looking into
his dark eyes, she sensed a powerful, yet kind, intelligence. The

long, sleek lines of his face gave him an elegant, even patrician air, which was softened by his surprisingly sweet, boyish smile. They stood there, forgetting to shake, just looking at each other. She blushed with desire. "It's so hot," she said again, embarrassed.

"I'm Carolyn Whitney." The redhead standing just inside Jim's door was not amused by all this.

"Oh. Oh, I don't want to interrupt—"

"It's all right. We were just coming in from a movie," Jim assured Diane.

Walking past the disdainful Carolyn, Diane entered Jim's apartment and sank onto a sofa. Immediately she noticed it was the softest thing she'd sat on in some time. Looking around, she saw a room furnished with a desk and chair, a coffee table and easy chair, books and newspapers, a standing lamp—a grown-up room, orderly and organized.

Carolyn perched on the sofa next to Diane. "They throw great parties across the hall—Jim and I've had some terrific nights there."

So. Carolyn was staking her claim. But when Jim handed Diane a glass of cool water, his fingers lingered on hers for a few significant moments. She sipped the water. "It's the first time I've been here. First time I've been out with Roger, too. I suppose this heat affects you when you're drinking." She wanted desperately to connect with Jim. "I live over on Brookline Street, above Barr's Deli, and it's always hot there, so I ought to be used to this heat." There. Now he knew where to find her, if he wanted to. Every time she looked at Jim, she was stirred by a current of desire—and he surely felt it, too. If only Carolyn weren't here . . .

But, of course in the end, she was the one to go. She drank all the water, then had no choice but to say, "That was great.

Thanks," and rise and walk across the bright airy room toward the hall.

"Will you be able to get home all right?" Jim asked.

Before Diane could answer, Carolyn said firmly, "I'm sure she will. She must have some friends there who can help her."

Diane wanted to say, no, I have no friends, I'm alone in the world. Instead she smiled at Jim and stepped out into the hall.

Roger was asleep on the floor. He looked awful and smelled worse. The door to the party was open, and music and laughter blared out. Without a trace of remorse, she left Roger lying there and went home alone. She could hardly sleep. She was waiting.

She knew Jim would come to her.

And she was right.

Sunday morning she awoke before eight, feeling hot and flustered from her restless night. After a quick shower, she slipped on a loose, swirly, thin cotton sundress tie-dyed into streaks and curls of lavender, violet, and mauve that brought out the blue of her eyes. Her cheeks were becomingly flushed from the summer heat and her own excitement. She pulled her long brown hair back with a barrette, then changed her mind and let it hang free; immediately the humidity lifted it into spirals floating around her head. She added a pair of earrings she'd made herself, a long dangle of blue beads and delicate silver bells that tinkled when she tossed her head, which she did often as she moved her warm mane of hair away from her neck. Studying herself in the bathroom mirror, she smiled, approving.

Coming out of the bathroom, however, she noticed that the room she shared with her roommates—both still sleeping—looked absolutely chaotic. Clothes, books, papers, curlers, lipsticks, and plates were scattered around the room. Her own sheets were twisted into waves and peaks on the ancient Goodwill mattress on the floor. She didn't want Jim to see the mess she lived in, not today.

Shutting the door firmly behind her, she went out to sit on the dusty wooden stairs leading up from the street. It was hot in the enclosed and windowless space, so she turned off the overhead light, leaned against the wall, closed her eyes, and lost herself thinking of the man she'd met the night before.

At exactly ten o'clock she heard the creak of the ground-level door and footsteps mounting the stairs. Her breath caught in her throat. Jim rounded the curve in the stairs and came into view.

"Well, hi," he said, stopping two steps down.

Diane swung her feet around and smiled up at him. "Hi. I hoped you'd come over. I thought I'd wait out here. My roommates are still sleeping."

"Oh. Well, um. Want to get some coffee?"

"Sure." She got up, shaking out her skirt. Standing one step above, she was just at eye level with him. He was very tall. She liked his face very much, even more than she had the night before. He was wearing khaki shorts and a spotless white T-shirt. His forehead gleamed with a sheen of sweat, but he smelled of soap, and when he smiled, his teeth were as white as milk.

For a few long seconds they remained on the stairs, looking at each other. A slow flush reddened Jim's skin from his neck up to his freshly shaven jaw. A responding heat broke across Diane's body. She licked her lower lip, then caught it between her teeth and bit it, to rein in her body's tug. The sexual pull between the two of them was intense, but she wanted more.

Jim drew in a shuddering breath and pulled backward, nearly losing his balance. "Well," he said, "shall we go?"

Diane was so entranced that when he reached up to put his

hand on her back she didn't understand for a moment what he meant, but then he turned slightly, and she saw that he was letting her pass by him, to go down the stairs first, a gentleman's gesture.

They walked to a nearby cafe and sat talking over coffee and fruit pancakes. Jim was finishing his doctorate in molecular genetics at Harvard. His voice deepened when he told Diane that he wanted to go into research, specifically in the area of breast cancer. When he was ten, his mother had died of the disease— as he told Diane this, he looked down at the table. His father had been killed in Germany in World War II. He'd been raised by his proper Bostonian grandparents and, when his grandfather died, by his grandmother and a librarian aunt. Diane described her family, her good, all-American, safe and boring family, with all the charm and wit she could summon. She told him about art school and her increasingly successful jewelry business. They talked through four refills of coffee, until a crowd of people came in for lunch.

Then they walked down to Harvard Square to buy the Sunday papers and headed over to the banks of the Charles River, where they settled on the grass in the shade of a towering oak. The heat of the summer afternoon lay against their skin, and when a delicate breeze came up, stirring the leaves above them into a sultry sway, the small hairs on Diane's arms lifted. Light shimmered off the river. Sailboats glided past on the blue water. Children raced by, whooping with laughter; old people toddled past, talking to their dogs.

They were sitting, both of them cross-legged, slightly angled toward each other, the papers lying opened on the grass in front of them. Their knees and elbows were almost, but not quite, touching.

"I can't seem to concentrate on world news," Jim confessed, grinning.

"I know," Diane agreed. "I think I've read this paragraph about eight times."

They smiled, pleased at their mutual beguilement. They looked into each other's eyes. Jim's eyes were dreamily large and luminous, the intense black pupils pulling her into his gaze.

Jim leaned forward and kissed her. His mouth tasted as fresh as the air after a spring rain. When he put his hand on her cheek to draw her nearer to him, he brushed her earring with his thumb, causing a shivery chime from her silver earring bells. She put her hand on his warm, hard chest. Beneath the soft cotton of his T-shirt, his heart beat firmly.

Carefully bracing himself with one arm, he pulled her to him and lowered her gently to the grass. He pressed his long body against hers and kissed her mouth, cheeks, eyelids, forehead, hair. This was sweetness, youth, summer, heaven, the green grass tickling the bare skin of her leg, a momentary breeze ruffling the light skirt of her dress, Jim's kisses coming harder, lasting longer, the tension between them mounting so that she trembled and was grateful for the solid ground.

"Look, Mommy!" A child's high voice broke out. "Those people are kissing!"

Jim drew back. He sat up, abashed, his face flushed, his dark hair falling over his forehead. "I forgot we weren't alone."

Diane sat up, too, smoothing her hair. Her lips tingled. "I wish we were," she said.

She felt Jim studying her face and waited for him to touch her again. Instead, he jumped to his feet. "Let's see what's on at the movies," he suggested.

"All right," she agreed, disappointment rushing through her.

Jim reached out his hand to help her up. "I really want . . ." His voice broke. He began again. "I really would like to do this right."

She understood. Still, she burned with impatience the rest of that day as they sat side by side, arms touching, watching *The Lion in Winter,* then strolled hand in hand through Paperback Booksmith, discussing their favorite authors. They sat in a booth at the Wursthaus, thighs pressed together, eating dinner. When it grew dark, Diane hoped he'd take her back to his apartment; she'd made it clear they couldn't be alone at her place. But after dinner he walked her back to Brookline Street. At the door he said, soberly, "This is our first date." By then she knew him well enough to understand that he was trying to live up to some private standard of behavior. While part of her, the wicked rebel in her, wanted to torment him into passionate action, the wiser part of her advised her to let him have his way, to let them "do it right."

They met the next night for dinner at The Pewter Pot. Afterwards, as the sky deepened into a twilight shade of blue, Jim asked if she'd like to come back to his apartment. She said she would.

Again Diane was struck by how clean and orderly Jim kept his rooms. Newspapers were folded neatly on the coffee table, papers sat stacked in systematic piles on his desk, and even his books seemed to be arranged according to height. In the sink stood a glass waiting to be washed; she could imagine him drinking orange juice that morning and setting the glass there instead of on the floor, or bathroom sink, or windowsill as she might have done in her careless hurry. It almost broke her heart to see this tidy apartment; she could sense the good little boy Jim had been, at the mercy of proper, fastidious old women.

When he pointed out his bed, which was covered with a patchwork quilt in browns pieced together by his aunt, the desire to muss it all up was overpowering.

Diane asked, "Is your bed comfortable?" She sat on the bed,

then lay back on it, stretching her bare arms above her head. "*Mmmm*," she hummed, closing her eyes.

Fortunately, that was all it took on her part. Secretly, she admitted to herself it was a sort of test. If Jim was so strict with himself as to live by his grandmother's rules in his own home, then he was not the man for her. But it was only a few moments before he joined her, kissing her almost violently, as if he could not help himself. That night she'd pulled her hair back with a barrette, which came loose with their tussling and got trapped under her back. The metal grip of the barrette bit into her shoulder blade as she was pressed into the mattress. Jim kissed her, touched her neck, and, moaning, reached down to force her loose cotton skirt up around her hips. He unzipped his white slacks, yanked them down, pulled down her panties. She kept her hands on his head, feeling his hair grow moist and silky with sweat. He shoved his way into her and they both sighed with infinite relief, as if they'd finally gotten where they'd always needed to be. Only a few seconds later, he came, pulsing inside her while she closed her eyes in concentration, trying to memorize the sensation of their bodies joined this way.

Afterward, when he'd caught his breath, he rolled to one side.

"That wasn't how I meant to do this at all," he confessed, embarrassed.

She ran her fingers along his hairline where his dark hair had become ebony with sweat. She put her fingers on her lips and sucked them. His sweat tasted salty and sweet. "It was perfect," she said.

"Perfect? No, really, look—this is what I meant to do." He pointed and, raising herself on her elbows, Diane looked around the room. On the bedside table was a tall candle, which had never been lighted. Next to it were two fine crystal glasses, his grandmother's Waterford she guessed (and later discovered was right), and an unopened bottle of Dubonnet. "I wanted to make our first time memorable," Jim told her.

"Oh, it was memorable," Diane laughed.

Jim returned her smile. They stretched out together, naked, warm, sticky, yet more comfortable with each other now. Jim studied her body, and Diane ran her hand along the handsome lines of his shoulder, long torso, elegant flanks. Then he bent to her, and she closed her eyes. With his gentle mouth, he began to pleasure her, taking his time, for now he had no need to hurry, until Diane cried out for him to enter her again. This time she did not think: his skin, his hair; she did not think. Her thoughts and feelings blurred into a spectrum of fierce delight, and she sank, shivering, shuddering, completely unaware of where she ended and Jim began. He held her gently for a long time afterward, and she didn't return to her apartment but slept all night through with the man she knew she'd love forever.

Jim was passionate about genetics, and in his careful, scientific way, was a profound optimist. His belief in the orderly progress of human beings toward an enlightened state amazed Diane. After years of artistic boyfriends in savage rebellion, Jim's world shone bright with an optimistic light. He showed her through his labs, white, healthy, organized rooms of rather domestic-looking appliances, where Vivaldi played softly in the background from the classical-music station, and people in white coats stared down into tubes and made notations in workbooks.

Jim lived his private life with a similar tranquillity. True, he never dusted and he threw his dirty laundry on the floor of his closet until enough had accumulated to take to the laundromat, yet he imposed a basic order among the bookcases, kitchen cabinets, and the photographs that hung on the cream-painted walls.

Diane found it all immensely enticing. She loved listening to him talk about his work—he was so idealistic, so sweetly ambitious, believing that he would be part of the network of scientists who would be able to find the causes and cures of the world's most terrible diseases. Her heart broke for him when he spoke of his mother's death. She wrapped herself around him then, longing to protect and console him.

Soon after they became lovers, Diane moved into Jim's apartment, which was so much more romantic than her noisy, cluttered place. She had worried slightly that her creativity and concentration might be lost, absorbed by her passion for Jim; she found instead that she was able to work as never before. Perhaps the serenity nurtured her—or perhaps she was fueled by happiness.

One night at the end of the summer, they lay in each other's arms in the mussed bed. They were still engulfed in a blurry sexual haze so that they seemed to be one creature, beating with one heart.

"I love you, Diane," Jim said softly, his breath stirring her hair.

"I love you," she replied.

"I believe we are meant for each other," he told her.

A small thrill ran down Diane's spine. This man, this expert in chemistry, logic, and reason, believed they were destined to be together. She was filled with a sense of power, and connection, and even a small sense of wonder.

Yet, soon after, when Jim told Diane he wanted to marry her, she was both thrilled and appalled.

"If we get married, you'll want to have children, I suppose." They were in bed, where they often did their serious talking, and Diane was turned to face the wall, glad Jim couldn't see the doubt in her eyes.

"Well, of course I will! Think of what wonderful children we'll have!"

"Jim, my work is important to me. I've just started my business, and I'm doing so well, the designs are coming so easily, and I can't keep up with the orders. I won't ever want to give it up."

"Of course you won't. Why are you worrying about that?"

"I don't know—marriage, a house—children. That's a lot of work, a lot of responsibility."

"I'll help you. You know that, Diane. I'll share it with you completely."

Jim was above all things an honest and moral man. She knew he'd keep his word.

Diane had trusted him, and married him.

It was late. She was tired. Grabbing her briefcase, Diane set the alarm system, locked up her shop, and went down the stairs and across Richdale Avenue to the parking garage where her beloved car waited. It was a vintage 1960 red Thunderbird convertible with a white top and white leather interior. She could have had a Mercedes for the money she'd spent on this restored antique, but this was the car she'd longed for in her youth, and now that she had choices, it was what she chose. Just sitting in the Thunderbird, smelling the rich leather, flipping on the radio, or slipping in an Eric Clapton tape infused her routine, responsible days with a feeling of adventure, of endless possibilities. How she loved this car! It had a personality, but no will of its own.

Why do people have families, she wondered as she sped down Massachusetts Avenue toward Route 2 and Belmont. Our relatives absolutely bring us as much worry and pain as pleasure.

By the time she got home, the sky had clouded over and it

had started to rain. She slipped through the cold garage into the warm house.

The front hall smelled of arum lilies and roast lamb. Dumping her briefcase on a Windsor chair, she passed by the mahogany library table that held the vase of fresh flowers and the silver bowl with today's mail. Picking up the letters, she crossed thick oriental rugs directly for the kitchen. No matter how elegant the rest of her house, the rest of her life, the kitchen was still the heart of the house.

Kaitlin, her housekeeper and cook, had left a welcoming note on the long built-in desk that stretched along the width of the kitchen wall. Next to it sat the new demon in her life, the answering machine, blinking with dictatorial urgency not just one red light that indicated message waiting, but the green light, too, protesting that the tape was full. Diane ignored it.

Sinking into the padded swivel chair, she bent to remove her high heels while at the same time she took up Kaitlin's note.

Mrs. Randall,

The lamb will be ready at eight, but another thirty minutes won't ruin it. Put what you don't eat in the 'fridge and I'll make lamb stew tomorrow night. The vegetables and rice just need heating up in the microwave. Mr. Randall said he'd be home by eight. I set the table in the breakfast room. A Mr. Frost who said he's from the FBI was here at five-thirty, asking to speak with you. He just knocked on the door, without an appointment or anything. I didn't let him in. He said he'd be back.

It was eight o'clock now. Jim wouldn't be home for another thirty minutes at least. More and more, he lived his life at the lab.

She had time for a lovely bath. She'd eat dinner in her robe. Another quirk of Jim's was that he never noticed what she wore.

Diane loved clothes and had many luxurious robes: twice in the past few years, Jim, arriving home late and finding Diane in a robe, had hit his forehead with his hand and exclaimed, "Are we late for a dance? The opera?" Julia and Chase loved their father's fashion incompetence. As they went through their various adolescent phases, Julia with blue hair, Chase with black leather, never once did their father say, "You're not leaving the house looking like that!"

She'd dealt with the FBI before, Diane thought as she climbed the stairs. In the early years, when she'd started Arabesque and was traveling to Eastern Europe and the Orient for gems, the FBI had routinely questioned her. Always before they'd come to her office and shop in Cambridge. She couldn't imagine what they wanted now.

Well, the FBI could wait. She wouldn't let it worry her. She'd bathe, then she'd pour herself a glass of good white wine while she listened to her messages on the answering machine and waited for her husband to come home.

On the second floor she passed by the closed door to her small study. She didn't even want to look in. She had had enough work for the day.

She entered her bedroom as if it were a sanctuary. An enormous room with bookshelves, a fireplace, and window seats, its colors were dark green and rich red, a primitive, pagan combination, like the holly with its glossy leaf and startling berry. She kept incense on her bedside table, candles in heavy silver candlesticks, and the latest hardcover novels. On Jim's table, neatly stacked, were tattered periodicals, research folders, and half a year's worth of *Cell,* the journal that he read cover to cover.

The bathroom was huge and luxurious. She turned on the hot water and dumped the jasmine-scented bath crystals in. Several mirrors reflected her body back to her in all its ample beauty.

Turning, she surveyed herself. As a young woman, she'd hated her broad shoulders, full bosom, and large hands. Gradually she'd come to accept and then to admire her hands for their skillfulness and talent, and over the years she'd come to feel the same way about her body. How easily it had carried two babies and given birth, how heartily it craved and consumed food, touch, sex. Hers was a very successful body, quick to give pleasure, almost never sick. She refused to see ugliness in her widened hips or full thighs, rounded stomach, and long, plump breasts. She was healthy. She was whole.

Tying her wavy brown hair up in a scarf, she slipped into her bath. As the lovely heat soaked into her muscles, she relaxed, and her emotional vigilance relaxed also. She was tired. She did tire more easily and more profoundly these days. Between her large blue eyes two lines had engraved themselves, so that she always seemed to be puzzled or frowning. Once or twice over the summer Julia had said, "You look so sad, Mom. What's wrong?" and Diane had realized that from now on, she would always look slightly worried. Tiny brown moles had popped up here and there on the skin on her neck and under her breasts. She'd put off having a mammogram for a year now, because the damn things were so unpleasant. She couldn't read small print without glasses, and sometimes when she tried to recall someone's name, her mind presented her with a blank. When she wore high heels all day, her legs ached. And it had been a long time since she'd felt a rush of pure animal delight.

Minor complaints, all of them. Diane rose from her bath, toweled dry, and slipped into turquoise silk pajamas and a silk-and-cashmere robe of black and turquoise. Jim might not notice, but it made *her* feel sensually pleased, and more and more these days she had to be content with that.

In the living room, she put a match to the pile of kindling and logs that Kaitlin had laid. She clicked in a gentle Brahms CD, then curled up with a flute of sparkling white wine. The firelight twisted and leaped into amazing shapes. Automatically she reached for the sketch pad and pen she kept near her chair—she had these in every room, near each favorite chair, in spite of Kaitlin's misery over how they spoiled the grace of the rooms—and was just beginning to play with patterns when the doorbell rang.

She went to the front door and looked out through the etched and leaded panels that bordered each side. A strange man stood there.

"Yes?" She opened the door.

"Mrs. Randall? Peter Frost, FBI." The stranger held out an identifying badge.

"It's rather late in the evening. Couldn't you come to my office tomorrow morning? I'll be there all day."

"This isn't about your work."

Peter Frost was protected from the gusting rain by the long porch ceiling. His face and water-spotted trenchcoat were illuminated by the porch light, so that he seemed to be haloed, set off from the dark sheets of rain that fell behind him, occasional drops catching the light and shining like falling coins. Black hair, blue eyes, a Botticelli nobleman in a gray suit and trenchcoat.

"Well. All right. Come in." She took his coat and hung it on the antique coat tree, then led him into the living room.

"Please," she said, gesturing to the sofa across from the one onto which she now sank. "Now. How can I help you?"

"We're trying to locate your mother," Peter Frost said.

"*My mother!*" Diane laughed in surprise.

"We believe your mother has something we need."

"There must be some mistake." Genuinely amused, Diane relaxed. "My mother's in her seventies, Mr. Frost. She was recently widowed. All she did all her life was take care of a home and family."

"Do you know where we can reach her?"

"Yes, of course"—Diane caught herself—"actually, I don't. Not exactly. She's in Europe. Somewhere in Europe. After Daddy died— Look, does this have something to do with my grandfather? Or my uncle? They were military men."

"No. With your mother."

"Mr. Frost. You guys don't want my mother. My mother is a sweet little old white-haired lady. She never had a chance to travel around Europe, and she always wanted to. This summer, when my father died, she sold the big family house and moved to an apartment. She thought this might be the time to travel, and we all—my brothers and my sister and I—encouraged her. We thought it might be good for her."

"Do you have her itinerary?"

"No. She didn't really make one. She wanted to go where the mood took her, and she didn't think she'd have trouble finding hotel rooms since it's off-season. She talked about Paris, London, Rome, Brussels, perhaps Amsterdam, perhaps Berlin—my God! You're not trying to tell me she did something stupid and got herself lost in Eastern Europe!"

"No, no, nothing like that, as far as we know. This has nothing to do with her current travels."

"Well, what exactly does it have to do with?"

"When your father died and your mother broke up the house, did she give you anything?"

"Well, of course. She divided everything among my brothers and sister and myself. Furniture, jewelry, china, silver—"

"Papers?"

"Papers?"

"Old love letters. That sort of thing."

Diane thought. "My parents were married at the beginning of World War Two. I'm sure my father wrote her often, but I don't recall seeing any letters or hearing about any of them. Oh, a few are pasted in the World War Two scrapbook. Bert has that. But love letters—well, I've never seen any. It's possible she has some hidden away somewhere."

"How about diaries? Or mementos?"

"Mother kept diaries about us—her children—during the first few years after our births, but with four of us, she must have run out of time. I know she kept many of the little drawings and valentines we made for her, of course. But she wasn't the sort to bring back souvenirs from vacation spots. Really, what is all this about? I can't imagine what you're getting at. Mother led the most blameless life. She did nothing unusual ever."

"Did she ever speak to you about a man she was involved with before she met your father?"

"Mother knew Daddy from the time she was fourteen! There was never anyone else!"

"She was in college in Boston for two years—"

"Yes. Yes, that's true." Diane paused to think. "I don't know. I don't know what I can tell you. She never told me about any other man, and I'm the oldest. I don't think she would have told Susan. Can't you be more specific?"

Peter Frost shook his glossy head. "I'm not trying to be difficult. There's only so much I can tell you. We're hoping that your mother still has in her possession something that was given to her a long time ago. It's quite small. A piece of jewelry. A locket. We're looking for the piece of paper that was put in the locket."

"And what's on this precious piece of paper?"

"I've told you all I can."

"Oh, for heaven's sake! This is all ridiculous!" Diane rose, paced to the window, and looked out—no sign of Jim. Damn.

She turned back to look across the room at the FBI agent. What could he want with her mother? To her dismay, her eyes filled with tears. She turned back to the window.

The man rose and came to stand behind her. She could see his reflection in the windowpane.

"There's no cause for alarm, you know," he said. "I can tell you that your mother was given something a long time ago, and if we can recover it, it will be helpful, but if we can't—well, nothing terrible is at stake here."

"You don't know my mother," Diane said accusingly, turning to face the man.

He was looking at her gently, kindly. "That's true. I don't know her at all. On the other hand—let me put it this way. You have children. Do you believe they know the true you, the whole you?"

His words hit home.

"I see your point." She walked away from the window, sat down on the sofa, folded her hands. "You are looking for—a locket. Do you know that I am a jewelry designer?"

"We do."

"Yes, of course you do. You think you know everything, don't you, with your computerized files."

"If we knew everything," Peter Frost said, coming back to sit in the chair across from her, still smiling, "I wouldn't have to come here bothering you, would I?"

"Is it possible that somehow your—records—have gotten confused and the locket is something I've made, or shipped to Eastern Europe, or something I've brought back from there as inspiration for new designs?"

"No."

"I've been in this business for almost thirty years—"

"What we are looking for was given to your mother before you were born."

Diane sat in silence for a few moments then, reflecting. Peter Frost didn't push her but waited calmly, watching the fire.

"After my father's death this year, when my mother sold their home in McLean, Susan and I went through the house with her. Arthur helped, too, for a day, but he had to get back up to Vermont, and of course Bert came for the funeral but left the same day. The boys"—Diane caught herself, smiled, gestured vaguely with one hand—"my brothers—well, they're not boys anymore, of course. The *men* didn't want anything from the house. Bert had already taken Daddy's war scrapbook, his medals, and so on. Art wouldn't have touched those things—he thinks that stuff is evil."

"But you and Susan took some things?"

"We did. Lots of stuff, actually, everything we could. Not that any of it is terribly valuable, although some of the paintings and jewelry and silver are. But most of what we took has only senti-mental value. You know"—Diane surprised herself once again by the way tears rushed into her eyes—"dividing up one's childhood house is difficult. I had left that house as soon as I could and re-turned only for brief visits. Well, and then once we had the chil-dren, we started to take them to visit their grandparents and then it was different. The house was absolutely gracious. Peaceful. The atmosphere I'd hated as a daughter I loved as a mother."

She caught herself. Peter Frost was aptly named, she thought, with that luminescent white skin and cool blue eyes, his detached elegance. He made her shiver. "I'm babbling, aren't I? I know I am." She got up, looked at her watch. "My husband's very late, and I haven't eaten dinner yet, and I've had a tiring day. Have you spoken with my sister, Susan?"

"Not yet."

"You should. She has some furniture she had shipped to her house, as do I, and boxes of *stuff*. As do I. And when Mother moved into the condominium, she didn't unpack. She was so eager to travel—she just went! What I'm trying to say is that everything in her new home is still in boxes. If what you're looking for is that important—and I assume it is or you wouldn't be here—I'd be willing to sort through the boxes I had shipped back. They're all up in the attic. You would be welcome to help me. Probably it would be excruciatingly boring for you, other people's memorabilia."

"That's exactly what I'd like to do. Perhaps you'd also be willing to go down to Silver Spring with me to search through your mother's boxes."

"Oh, I don't know about that! Without her knowledge or consent?"

"Of course we'll try to reach her to get her permission. We're doing what we can to reach her. But timing is rather crucial now. This needs to be done as quickly as possible."

Diane glared at Peter Frost. She sank back into her chair and fell forward, burying her face in her hands, elbows on knees. Her hair hung down around her face like a weight.

His voice was soft. "I'm not trying to be difficult. I'm not being purposefully secretive. I'm telling you everything I'm allowed to tell you. And I'm asking you for your help."

"All right," Diane said, lifting her head, taking a deep breath. "Look. Let me think about all this, and call Susan, and talk with my husband. You know I own a business. I'll need to rearrange my schedule. I want to be with you when you go through my mother's things."

"Perhaps you could also call your brothers, and any friends of your mother's, to see if they've heard from her. A postcard, a letter—if we could find her, we could ask her directly about what we're looking for and save everyone time and trouble."

"Yes, all right."

"I'll call you tomorrow morning."

"Fine."

She walked him to the door. He put on his raincoat, then turned to shake her hand.

"Thank you," he said. His hand was warm.

Diane watched him hurry through the rain to his dark car, then went to the kitchen to take the lamb out of the oven. It was nine o'clock. She preferred lamb rare and juicy, not well-done. Jim would eat it; he was not particular about his food—one of the blessings of their married life. She wasn't particular about food, either, except that when she was tired, which was often, she had no appetite for anything healthy but craved sweets.

Now she cut an enormous slice of the tart apple pie Kaitlin had baked that day, added a fat scoop of vanilla ice cream, and microwaved a cup of the rich, dark coffee her housekeeper always brewed fresh just before she left at five o'clock. Perhaps the coffee would speed up her sluggish mind.

Sinking onto one of the chairs ringing the big oak kitchen table, she tried to concentrate on the food. But the coffee tasted bitter, the pie and ice cream sickeningly rich. The tears came.

Hormones. Perhaps. Certainly she had been ambushed by helpless tears more this year than ever before in her life. She had never been like her daughter Julia who easily dissolved into wholehearted sobbing over a broken heart, bad grades on a test, or even a TV commercial for dog food.

But this year . . . this year was taking its toll. First had come the shock of her father's death. She had loved her father but had disapproved of him. He was a male chauvinist of the most dangerous sort: charming, educated, suave, kind. Never demanding or arrogant, still he had ruled his home with an old-fashioned, gentle despotism. In her youth, Diane had rebelled against him, but she also deeply loved him. During the past decades, as she became a mother and he became ill, she had made her peace with him.

And she *had* grieved for him. Greatly. When it was discovered, over six years earlier, that her father had cancer, she had grieved then, alone and with her family. She hated his being ill, dying. It hurt. When it finally came, his death brought more release, relief really, than pain.

And when, last month, she and Susan had helped her mother sort, pack, and discard the collected objects of so many years, so many lives, Diane had grieved again. It was agonizing to take part in the breaking up of the household that had existed, in that gracious house, for almost fifty years. She almost believed she could as easily have watched the house burn to the ground.

Later she realized, all by herself, that she now also had to face the fact that it was possible that her mother could die, too. Would die; her mother was in her seventies. Jean White was in good health but not eternal.

All her life Diane had both scorned and adored her mother. She had adored her for her gentle goodness, her laughter, her graceful diplomacy, but she had hated her utterly for her submission to her father. Even before Diane knew enough to form such emotions into words, certainly before women's liberation came along, Diane had resented the way in which her mother put herself into her father's service. She saw her mother as a tree of flame, gloriously bright, leaping with ideas, desires, laughter, energy. Her father's domination caused her mother to channel herself into a lesser object, a sturdy column of steady light burning throughout their household, but an object that was less, far less, than it could have been. That was why she was angry with her mother, because her mother had chosen to live a limited life. How could anyone with so much settle to live as so little?

Diane took her mother's subordination personally. She had been a haughty little girl with disdain in her eyes. Worse, when she was in her twenties, triumphant with her own early spectacular success as a jewelry designer and businesswoman, she'd written her mother a series of eloquent letters begging her to divorce her father and start her own life—her *real* life, before it was too late.

Those letters had wounded her mother deeply, and enraged her.

"You have no right to judge my life so harshly," Jean Marshall White had written to Diane. "You know so little about my life, only what you saw through your prejudiced, insolent eyes."

Diane remembered clearly out of that whole long letter those particular sentences, because, oddly, they had hurt her. She thought her mother was being cruel to write them. For years after that, she and her mother had hardly spoken, communicating only obliquely through Diane's brothers and sister. Diane had not gone back to McLean for Christmas or Thanksgiving holidays; she did not set eyes on her parents for almost seven years. Not until the birth of her own son was there a truce.

Diane looked like her mother. The colors that looked best on Jean Marshall White looked best on Diane White. They shared the same sense of humor. And because Diane was the first child, Jean had told her daughter tales of her own youth that she didn't have time to share with the other children. The boys never sat still long enough to hear their mother's stories, and by the time Susan came along, Jean had no time for strolls down memory lane.

Diane assumed all her life that she possessed a knowledge of her mother that no one else did. She assumed that she knew the *truth* about her, the dark and brilliant, complex, woven fabric of truth. The truth of her mother's life hung like a tapestry as a backdrop to her own life.

Peter Frost's visit had come like a slash of scissors, slicing a gap in that tapestry, exposing Diane to the presence of a vast, dark unknown. She shivered.

Blowing rain battered the kitchen windows. Leaving her plate on the table, Diane went back into the living room where the fire needed more logs. She stoked it, then put on the most monotonous Bach she could find and settled onto the sofa. Folding her hands saintlike across her breasts, she closed her eyes and forced herself to concentrate on her breathing, counting as she exhaled, inhaled. The warmth of the fire was soothing, its snapping and cracking companionable.

She was relaxed, almost asleep, when Jim came in the front door, bringing with him a gust of cold, wet air.

"Don't get up," he said, setting his briefcase on the coffee table. "I'm sorry I'm so late. Actually, one of the lab technicians— I just couldn't leave. Stay there. I'll fix myself a plate and bring it in here by the fire."

"There's roast lamb," Diane murmured. "But it's cold now."

"That's all right. It's still protein."

He went away. She lay still on the sofa, comforted by the sounds of her husband moving through the kitchen in much the same way she'd been comforted in childhood by the sounds of her mother's steady progress through the house.

Jim returned to the living room and sat in the chair that had been occupied by Peter Frost earlier that evening. Placing his plate on the coffee table, he leaned forward and ate, chewing absentmindedly. Diane knew he meant this as a companionable gesture, just as she knew his thoughts were still in the lab.

She studied him with a critical eye. He was still slender, still handsome, and his hair was graying at the temples, giving him a distinguished look. He went through life peering out at the world through his flattering horn-rims, moving with a deliberate, mild, distracted air, as if he were listening to music of planets that normal people couldn't hear. Tonight that air of preoccupation made him seem aloof, especially compared with Peter Frost's intensity, and Jim's soft brown eyes and thick brown hair seemed a washed-out version of the FBI agent's blue-black hair and vivid eyes.

She'd grown used to this half presence of Jim's. She understood the demons that drove him: he was older, he was mortal, and still he had not found the cure for the disease that very well might have been passed on from his mother's blood, through his, to his children's. He'd always been intent on his work, but after he'd turned forty, he'd become obsessed. He was humorless and distracted. Even his one sport—jogging five miles a day four times a week—was not for pleasure but for the sake of keeping his heart in condition so that he could live longer and see his work come to fruition.

He had loved her so passionately twenty years ago! He'd been the pursuer, carrying her into marriage with the force of his ardor. They'd been sexually explosive, and that fire had flared up again with pleasing consistency during the course of their marriage. Lately, though, for over a year, that part of their life together had been . . . ashes.

Still he cared for her. And she for him.

Quickly, she told him about Peter Frost's visit. He was as amused and mystified as she, but not worried.

"This will probably clear itself up fairly easily," he said. "I can't imagine your mother involved in anything complicated. Call Susan and your brothers tomorrow."

"Oh, God, that reminds me. I haven't even listened to the answering machine."

"Don't. If you listen to it, something's bound to get your adrenaline going and you'll be up all night. Let's go to bed."

They scattered the embers and checked the fire screen, turned off the lights, then went their separate ways, Jim to the den, Diane to their bedroom. His way of unwinding was to watch the eleven-o'clock news. Diane hadn't been able to look at news at night for years; it was always too dreadful, too upsetting—some poor person murdered, some country at war, some town shattered by a natural disaster. In order to live her life she had carefully, with enormous effort, erected a structure of belief in a universal good toward which humankind was working, and every night the news at eleven threatened to destroy that structure in a second. The placid, even pleasant expressions with which newscasters reported, for example, the abduction, rape, and murder of a young girl sent Diane into a weeping rage.

So for the thirty minutes during which Jim watched the news, she lay in bed reading novels.

Tonight, in spite of Peter Frost's peculiar visit, Diane was drowsy by the time Jim crawled into bed next to her. His familiar heat, warmth, scent were reassuring. Often she was bitter about the way they shared the bed these days—like brother and sister, like a man and his pet—but tonight the bland familiarity was comforting. She let herself drift toward sleep.

The phone rang.

Diane had refused to have a phone in the bedroom. But it was almost midnight. This couldn't be a casual call. She could feel Jim's breath catch in surprise.

"Probably a wrong number," he said. "I'll get it." He stalked through the dark out of the room, across the hall, into Diane's study, and picked up the phone. Diane heard him say, "Never mind the answering machine. I'm on."

Then she heard him say, "My God."

"My God," he said again. Then, "All right. We'll call Sam's parents. Thank you. Yes. We'll call you if—yes, of course. Thank you."

Diane pushed herself up on her elbows. Jim was a dark shape in the doorway when he said, "That was the school. They've called several times, but we didn't listen to our messages. Julia's run away with Sam. They're going to get married."

Chapter 2
❦ Jean

Jean was traveling through Europe without reservations.

At first she thought it would be wisest to begin in England, where at least she spoke the language, but very quickly she changed her mind: she wasn't going to let caution rule this trip. For the same reason, she chose to go alone. She wanted to go or stay where she wished, when she wished, at her own whim and no one else's.

For the first time in fifty years, she was living only by her own desires.

Because as a college student she'd planned to live in France when she graduated, France was where she now began. Of course France had changed since 1940, and she had changed, God knew. Still, it was the beginning of making a dream come true.

In early September she flew to Orly, rode a cab into Paris, and took a room at the Georges Cinq. But after only two days, she left. The big hotel was too anonymous, with its clerks and waiters who pegged her so perfectly, so insultingly in advance that as she approached the desk or table, before she opened her mouth, they addressed her in English, making it impossible for her to attempt her rusty French.

She thought the Champs-Elysées was beautiful, but crowded, and she hated the feeling that everything she saw was on sale, as if this part of Paris were the world's largest, if magnificent, department store. She found a small *auberge* on the Left Bank, with a view from her third-floor window of the Jardin du Luxembourg, and settled in.

From the days of young womanhood, she had longed to see the grand old sights: the Louvre, Montmartre, Notre Dame. But she found this arrondissement she'd discovered too enchanting to leave—and why she should rush off every day? Those monuments had waited fifty years for her to see them; they could wait a few days more.

So she wandered around the Sixième, taking a late breakfast of café au lait and chocolate brioches in an outdoor cafe, sitting in the garden watching the pigeons for hours, browsing through used-print and -book shops, picking up well-thumbed British editions of Somerset Maugham or E. M. Forster to read in her room late at night.

She looked wonderful, and she knew it because of the way people smiled at her, stopped to sit next to her on the bench in the park, addressing her in French, expressing surprise when she answered in her faltering, mispronounced, Americanized French. That people would assume she was French was to her the highest compliment. She wore long, comfortable skirts, gorgeous silk blouses, loose jackets with deep pockets, and an assortment of jewelry that looked antique but that she'd bought purposely from a shop in Silver Spring that specialized in new "estate" jewelry. She didn't want to worry about having anything stolen. Her outfit, she thought, gave her a rather intellectual look, but in fact she had decided upon it simply in order to wear her immensely comfortable, sporty-looking leather walking shoes.

At forty, she'd had her long brown hair cut and styled in a belled pageboy, Louise Brooks–style, with bangs to hide the wrinkles on her forehead. Her hair was white now, or rather streaked with gray, white, brown strands, because she'd stopped having it colored when Al died. She dabbed on powder and very light lipstick and went out into the world.

Sitting on a bench in the Luxembourg Gardens in the intense October sunlight, Jean enjoyed the sensation that she could be just anyone. She could have six grown children at home instead of four; she could have no children. She could be divorced many times over or never married. Kansas or California or northern Maine could be her home, where she taught sixth grade or college-level physics or where she ran her own boutique or painted watercolors.

For fifty years she had lived her life by one passionate principle: Let her children grow up unharmed and she would not complain about her lot in life.

Well, it had worked, that superstitious pact with Fate. Her four children were grown up, and she had not complained.

Nor had she tried to change a thing about the way she had lived.

Gracious was the word many people used to describe her, even her children, but Jean knew the word that fit her best was *determined.* It amazed her now that she had the leisure and the distance to look back at herself and see just what a controller she had been. Oh, how she had held on to what she had!

Sitting in the slanting evening sunlight, drinking Pernod at a tiny sidewalk cafe, Jean smiled, remembering how shortly after Diane was born, when the tail-like stub of her umbilical cord fell off one day in her daughter's diaper, she had taken the bit of flesh that had bound her daughter to her and put it in a small white porcelain box trimmed with brass and sculpted with flowers. She'd intended to keep it forever. One day a few months later, however, she'd opened the box to find to her horror that the cord was shriveled and blackened, a dried-out worm of flesh. She had wept. But not for long. Her live baby had cried out, needing her, and Jean had tossed the cord out in the trash, although wrapped in flowered paper, as if it were a present.

Didn't people do strange things? Having children had made her such a coward in life that she drove everyone she loved mad with her constant exhortations to take care. But it was from Jean herself that her constant vigilance over the fates of her children exacted the highest cost.

For thirty years after her first child's birth Jean had not been able to sleep at all on the nights when the children went on school trips in buses or other people's cars or started driving themselves or were even moderately ill or had an especially bad time with a friend, teacher, sport, or class or were waiting to hear if they'd gotten into the college of their choice.

Her insomnia had irritated Al so much that during those times when she couldn't sleep she still pretended to for the first hour they were in bed together. Then when he was oblivious to the world, she slipped from the bed with a burglar's stealth, down the stairs, and into the kitchen. Certain tasks were available to her to perform in those dark hours—nothing pleasurable, for she feared her pleasure would jinx her children. She could not, for example, even knit a sweater or crochet an afghan or embroider sheets or linen guest towels. She could not make jam, because she found the scented alchemy of bubbling fruit too delightful. She could clean the bathrooms, scrub the kitchen floor, wash out the refrigerator, line the kitchen shelves with fresh paper, iron damask tablecloths and napkins—very hard physical labor, indeed—and there had even been times in fine weather when she had swept out the garage and washed its windows by moonlight, in her robe.

Pleasant, her black maid, would always greet Jean when she arrived for work in the mornings with, "Lord Almighty, Miz White. What you worried about now?"

Her life, the lives of members of her family, were exceedingly, even excessively fortunate, she knew. Their grand southern colonial house with its four white pillars, its expanse of shining windows, its sheltering trees, beautiful garden, and, inside, its numerous wonderful rooms was the best any family could ever have had, Jean always had thought. Although she had grown up in a house not unlike this, and not far away, in a similar, safe, wealthy neighborhood, still Jean was often brought to a state of amazed wonder that she was living out her life in this beautiful palladium.

Like the chatelaine of a castle or the verger of a church, she oversaw with scrupulous organization that the chimneys and furnace were cleaned in the fall, the trees pruned in the spring, the gardens planted, weeded, fed, and tended during the warm months, the windows washed, the carpets cleaned, the walls freshly painted every few years, the newest household appliances installed in the most accommodating places and, of course, that the house was kept clean, tidy, and gracious every day. Fresh flowers on the hall and dining-room tables. Indian corn on the front door and pumpkins on the steps in the fall. The blue-and-white striped polished-cotton cushions for the wicker furniture on the sun porch re-covered every year.

Perhaps because of her devotion to the guardianship of her house and the lives of her children, as the years progressed, Jean grew less and less comfortable being away from her home. It was not a matter of neurosis—she was not afraid to go out into the world, not really. It was that as long as she was in her house, she felt she was keeping her children safe. On one level, she knew that made absolutely no sense at all. How could her presence in one structure or another keep Bert or Art from falling off the jungle gym or getting hit with a baseball? Why should her lunching with a friend in a pleasant restaurant cause Diane or Susan to be teased or snubbed at school or to skin their knees at recess? Perhaps the habit had evolved from her desire to be there if she was called: with four children to drive to scouts, skating, birthday parties, riding lessons, dentists, and so on, there had been times when one child needed her and she wasn't available because she was in the car driving another child somewhere. No matter the excuse, her failure to be there made her guilty in both the child's eyes and her own. If car phones had been available when her children were growing up, she probably would have gotten one.

Lord. If beepers had been available back then, Jean would have given a portable machine to each child and worn four color-coded sets at her waist, so that the moment a child needed her, he or she could summon her at once. Or one of those little gadgets advertised on television now for the very old or crippled, something attached to the body that could be pushed with one finger, alerting someone to their peril. Why didn't every mother in America have her children wired in such a way, now that the technology made such things possible?

As the children grew up and left home, the world they went out into seemed so alarming that her need to protect them never completely lessened its hold. Bert, Susan, and Art had all in one way or another been involved in the Vietnam War, while Diane kept making trips to the strangest places: Nepal, Bolivia, even Russia. As her children's lives moved outward, so she allowed hers to as well, but just a little. She ladled soup for the indigent

45

in Washington's inner city, worked tirelessly on fund-raising campaigns, helped with the learning handicapped at the local school, stuffed envelopes, made phone calls, typed letters—her house became a headquarters for charity.

Then, in Vietnam, Art had a nervous breakdown and came home for a while. Jean had to take care of him and to run interference between Art and Al, because Al was angered by his son's reaction to the war. It was during that period when she became a grandmother, suddenly subject to the pleas of her daughters and daughter-in-law to come help with the babies, and she gladly went.

Finally over the past decade she and Al had been alone in the big house, and at last her superstitious obsession for safekeeping faded. Of course all the children and their families came home together for gigantic greeting-card Christmases, and again in separate groups for summer vacations, a week at a time, to have "Grandmother" spoil them all; entire weeks of each year were given over to the pleasure of her family, but that was a different matter. At some point, somewhere along the way, Jean had relinquished her vigilance.

Yet over the past years as her husband's illness had been detected, treated, and finally surrendered to, Jean had wondered if perhaps Al's death was not due to some failure on her part to protect him, for she knew that she had never worried as fiercely about him as she had about the children. Al had died of lung cancer. He had given up smoking in his forties, by his own decision and not because of her request: Should she have nagged him earlier to stop? Certainly she had always seen to it that his meals were healthful and well balanced; other than that, she'd had little to do with the supervision of Al's health. He was fastidious and disciplined about the state of his body, faithfully keeping appointments to have his teeth cleaned and his blood

46

pressure checked. Al had wanted to have a career in the Navy
—Jean had not allowed him to do so—but habits ingrained from
his Navy years stayed with him always. He maintained his body
as if it were a necessary machine.

No, she had not been responsible, through sins of omission
or commission, for Al's death at the age of seventy-four. She had
been a good wife, but she had been a splendid mother. No matter
how tiring, how difficult the tasks required of her as a mother,
she had performed them with a joyful heart, with a completely
natural spontaneity; but the role of wife to Albert White had not
come with such perfect ease; a conscious decision always had to
intervene during the most crucial moments between the knowledge of what she should do as a good wife and the actual per-
formance of the deed. Always, that moment, that pause.

A shallow breath quickly taken.

A moment not of anger or even of regret, but still: *that moment,
that pause.*

Then the act performed.

These thoughts now caused Jean White to rise from her seat
at the charming sidewalk cafe, to rise and walk, move, look,
distract herself. She had never been unfaithful to Albert White,
and as far she knew, he had not been unfaithful to her. An
immense fondness and regard for him had always filled her heart,
formed her actions, for he was a good man, a lovable man. During
his final illness she had devotedly waited with him by his bedside
for hours, holding his hand, above all seeing to it that he would
not feel alone. The last face that Albert White saw before he
died had been his wife's, and the last words he had heard had
been her words: "I love you."

At his funeral, she had grieved; she had wept. Her sorrow was
real, but it was not for herself. What she felt for herself, widowed
wife of beloved husband, was release.

She'd lived a good, even a virtuous life. She had no regrets. But still, it was such a profound pleasure to go off on her own to this magical city, to remember with aching fondness the life she had dreamed of living when she was young.

1939
War Stories

She looked like a woman of glamour and mystery. Doubly screened by a gauze of smoke from her cigarette and the polka-dotted veil of her cocky black hat, Jean Marshall sat with a group of intense, intellectual young men and women around a table at the Algonquin Hotel, drinking a very dry martini, listening to Stanley Friedman and Hal Farmer argue.

Hal kept looking at her. Jean thought he'd definitely try to seduce her tonight. Of course, she'd have to put up a show of resistance—she didn't want to seem easy, but she'd been waiting for this night ever since she'd set eyes on him in Cambridge. Although that wasn't why she'd joined the staff of *War Stories;* and they wouldn't have accepted her if she hadn't been talented and dedicated. She had joined the staff, first, because she believed in peace—believed that her work could help move the world toward peace. Soon she came to realize that the co-editor, Hal Farmer, was the most excitingly brilliant man she'd ever met.

She was determined to have a significant life. When she heard that the editors were going to New York over Christmas vacation to try to raise funds for the journal, she decided to head for New York, too. She lied to her parents about the dates of her Radcliffe vacation.

Tonight, as Hal Farmer sat talking, each word that he fired

into the group—"edition" . . . "issue" . . . "acknowledgment" . . . "errata" . . . heated her blood. Each time he looked at her, her cheeks flushed, her heart flipped.

Everything about the man was exciting, electric, rebellious—from his wiry, fiery red hair to the ink-stained tips of his fingers. Behind round, heavily rimmed glasses his ice-blue eyes flashed. He'd paid little attention to her back in Cambridge; he was usually sequestered in his office, the inner sanctum that she had yet to penetrate. But tonight he'd given her a long look and a slow smile as he purposefully pulled out the chair next to hers and sat down beside her. All evening he'd argued and raged with his normal concentrated zeal, but under the table his thigh pressed steadily against hers. Tonight her real life would begin.

Then she saw a man pushing his way through the crowded hotel lobby. Her heart fell through the floor. She didn't think he'd seen her yet, but he was headed toward her table, and there could be only one reason he was here.

"Jeepers," Jean whispered in despair, and because she couldn't think of anything better to do, she quickly ducked under the table. Squatting on the floor among the trousered and silk-stockinged legs, Jean pulled her elbows to her sides and bent her head so that her hat wouldn't be crushed by the tabletop.

"Hey, kid, what are you doing?" Her friend Myra lifted the tablecloth and peeked down at Jean.

Before Jean could answer, she saw a pair of perfectly polished black shoes plant themselves near the table.

"Jean. Come out from under there at once."

There was no escape. There was not even a graceful way out.

"Jean. Come out at once or I'll come in and get you."

She felt her cheeks flaming with embarrassment as she wriggled back up onto her chair, knocking her hat over one eye in the process. Still she tried to brave it out.

"Bobby! I didn't know you were in New York! What a surprise!"

"Jesus Christ, Jean. Have you lost your mind?" Bobby replied. "Now come on. I'm taking you home."

"Well, of course, dear brother, if that's what you want. I didn't realize, but wouldn't you like to join us for a—" Jean babbled, gathering up her cigarette case and purse, smiling gaily, keeping her voice light, trying to save herself from total humiliation.

"*Now,* Jean."

With a roll of her eyes indicating the affectionate tolerance necessary in dealing with her brother, Jean shrugged her raccoon coat up over her shoulders.

"If you'll all excuse me," she said to the grinning group, "I believe my brother has come to take me home."

"You're damn right I have," Bobby said, taking Jean firmly by the arm. Then, with frightening insight, he fixed his angry glare on Hal Farmer and said, "And for your information, bud, my sister is nineteen years old."

Bobby led Jean away from the stunned group. Before they'd reached the door to the street, an explosion of laughter burst from the table, shelling through Jean's dignity. Tears clouded her eyes and a sob rose in her throat.

"How *dare* you!" she spat at her brother once they were out on the street.

Without answering, he pulled her through the throng of holiday shoppers, along Forty-fourth Street, to the spot where his Teraplane Coupé was double-parked. Then he opened the passenger door and shoved her inside. By the time he'd gone around the car and climbed into the driver's seat, Jean's tears were in full force.

"I've never been so embarrassed in my *life!*" she cried. "That was the most awful thing I've ever experienced. How could you have done that to me!"

"Someday you'll thank me," Bobby said gruffly, pulling out into traffic. Cars and cabs choked the streets, their headlights splintering the December twilight.

"How did you know where to find me? Why did you even come looking?"

"It was Al who got me started—"

"Oh, Al!" Jean snapped impatiently. "It would be Al!"

"You'd written him that Radcliffe's Christmas vacation started the fifteenth of December, but you wrote Mom and Dad that it started the nineteenth. I got worried and called Midge. She told me you'd gone to New York and would be at the Algonquin."

"So much for secrets between friends," Jean sniffed.

"Jean, you're lucky I found you! That crowd is much too fast for you."

"How do you know? You don't know anything about them! You don't know anything about me! You've made a total ass of yourself and of me as well!"

"They're a bunch of pseudointellectual Commies, that's who they are. I know exactly who they are. And that literary review you've got hooked up with will be nothing more than a propaganda rag. Nice work, Jean. Dad and Mom would be proud."

Fresh tears flooded Jean's eyes. "You can be a real jerk when you want to," she said.

They passed through the Holland Tunnel, heading toward New Jersey and the road south. For a few moments, as the lights of the city and its spell were eclipsed, Bobby did not reply. When he did speak again, the anger was gone from his voice.

"I'm not trying to be a jerk, Jeanie. I'm just trying to protect you. Hell, I just finished driving six hours straight and now I've got to turn around and do it again."

"I guess I should be grateful," Jean said, moderating her voice in return, "but honestly, Bobby, I'm not. I'm mad. I'm a big girl now. Why don't you let me make my own mistakes?"

"Jean, I'm five years older than you are. I've been out in the world. I know how things work. I know how men think. I—"

"Bobby, for your information, Hal Farmer wasn't chasing me. I was chasing him."

"Not to marry?" Bobby was shocked enough to take his eyes off the road and look at his sister.

"No, Bobby," Jean said carefully, as if speaking to a dullard. "Absolutely not for marriage. For something else completely . . . frivolous."

Immediately she sensed her brother closing up, like a damned clam. It was as if invisible drawbridges were being drawn; she could almost hear the clank of chains. She had said just a little more than a modest woman should say to a brother. This withdrawing was something she associated only with men, because her father and her brother were such masters of the technique —while her mother would argue, explain, and fight until any issue between them had been settled, or at least exhausted.

"Well, I'm not going to tell any of that to Al," Bobby said. "I'll just say you went to New York for organizational meetings for the literary review."

Jean sighed. Then she turned in her seat and faced Bobby. "Bobby, I know you love me, and you know I love you. As far as that goes, I love Al, in my own very sisterly way. But I'm not in love with Al, and I don't want to marry him, and I'm not going to marry him. Why can't you see that?"

"Albert White is the best man this world has yet to come up with," Bobby said heatedly. "Any girl would be lucky to get him. He's decent, intelligent, wealthy—"

Jean stuck her hands over her ears, just as she had when she was younger and Bobby was bossing her around. The ironic thing was that for years she had had a schoolgirl's crush on Al White. He was as handsome as they came, with blue eyes and thick blond hair and skin that was tanned all the time from rowing or sailing or playing tennis. He'd been in Bobby's class at the Naval Academy and had come home all the time with Bobby, because his own home was so far away, out on the West Coast. Jean had been smitten. In fact, in the early years she'd made a pest of herself, but Al had always been kind. She'd spent hours of her life—days, weeks, months!—daydreaming about him, mooning over him. Then, suddenly, they all got a little older. Jean went off to her freshman year at Radcliffe and returned home grown-up and gorgeous. Al confessed to the astonished Bobby that he loved his sister, and Bobby, in a triumphant act that he assumed would make everyone happy, told Jean.

And immediately, Jean stopped loving Al. She'd said, "That's nice," and shrugged.

What had happened? Where had the feeling gone? Jean was as mystified as anyone else. She'd always been told she was perverse, wanting to do the things that boys did, insisting on having her own way, taking offense when Bobby offered a compliment and saying thank you when he insulted her, confusing everything. But this baffled even Jean. She wasn't proud of herself for her fickleness, and in her secret heart she knew that she had stopped adoring Al White simply because he was too good a man. Goodness did not attract her much these days.

Bobby and Jean rode together in a dark truce for a while, both absorbed in their own thoughts, until Bobby said, "I only meant to do the best for you, and now I've ruined your life."

"Oh, Bobby," Jean said, reaching over to pat his arm, "my life isn't ruined. I still have a place on the review, and Hal will probably be more interested in me now that he knows I'm so young."

Ice coated Bobby's voice when he spoke: "I *meant* I ruined your life when I told you Al was in love with you. It was bad strategy on my part."

" '*Strategy,*' " Jean said scornfully. "God, you are such a martinet! And you know what I think about all that, Bobby! That's one reason I'll never marry Al. I have always said that I'd never, ever marry a career Navy man. And I mean it, Bobby. I do. I will not be a Navy wife. And that's the end of it."

Then both of them were angrily quiet. Brother and sister, they loved each other fiercely. There was only a slight bit of jealousy between them; more than anything, they were protective of each other. Their easy intimacy had faded though, because Jean thought Bobby was boring, and Bobby thought Jean was wild. For, like his father, Bobby had gone to the Naval Academy and had decided to make the Navy his life; while Jean constantly and with increasing fervor shunned the life their parents had given them.

It hadn't been a bad life; in its own way it had been both secure and adventurous. As young children, they had moved a lot, from base to base, as their father was transferred. They'd started new schools almost every year and sometimes entered a school in the middle of the year. They learned to rely on each other more than on the people they met—whom sooner or later they always had to leave—and developed a veneer of sophistication, as well as an honest depth of ease about dealing with the world. It was anything intimate that baffled them; they had never learned how to handle things that approached them closely, and their reaction to anyone who intruded into their small, closed circle was one of alarm.

Finally their father's age and experience had gotten him a desk job in Washington. They'd settled into the fine old house on Bancroft Place that their mother inherited from her parents. For the past five years they'd lived in luxurious stability.

Even so, Jean was determined not to be a Navy wife. She admired her mother; she respected her. She loved both her parents, but she had always, from the moment of her first conscious thought, been ambitious for herself. She wanted everything: fame, fortune, adventure, excitement, independence, spontaneity. She was smart enough to get it. She'd proved that. After two years of straight A's at Radcliffe, she'd gotten bored with college life and increasingly fascinated by a group of serious intellectuals in Cambridge.

They were starting a literary review called *War Stories,* a journal of wide-ranging fiction and nonfiction centering on war: firsthand reminiscences or dramatic fictional re-creations of battles in the World War or the Spanish Civil War, heartbreakers about war brides and war widows, new translations of the *Iliad,* research papers on the Crusades, diaries written during the Civil War, poems about the American Revolution. The catch, the beautiful secret, was that antiwar stories, pacific propaganda, and radical ideals would be threaded into each issue in such a skillful way that readers would, over a period of time, be converted, without their knowledge, to the cause of peace. Hal Farmer and Stanley Friedman, the founders of *War Stories,* craftily plotted exactly how to seduce bankers and businessmen into reading their review.

The girl Jean admired most at Radcliffe, a brilliant senior named Myra Kaplan, had taken her to one of the early organizational meetings. Afterwards she'd introduced Jean to the staff. Jean volunteered to work as a secretary for them as many hours a week as she could for no pay. Much of this fall semester she had been holed up in their basement office off Hancock Street opening mail, typing letters, proofreading essays and short stories, and penciling in her own opinions—for they'd discovered that she was sharp and literate, and soon welcomed her remarks.

Everyone was talking about Hitler and how soon the U.S. would end up in another war in Europe. Jean's secret dream—no, her plan, her goal—was to go to Europe as a reporter for *War Stories,* to send back firsthand accounts from the fields of action. She'd be willing to quit college, risk danger, crawl in the dirt, sleep in Polish barns—her imagination was limitless when it came to her future with this review. She did not want to sleep with Hal Farmer simply because he was attractive but because he knew so much, and she sensed that by being as close to him as she could some of those qualities would rub off on her. And she wanted him to know more about her, to appreciate her—to trust her to turn in reports that would make *War Stories* famous.

This was possible because, unlike her father, Hal Farmer thought women were as intellectually capable as men. In fact, Hal often said he wished men possessed more feminine qualities—insight, intuition, compassion. Hal actually spoke of his own emotions and didn't think of himself as any less a man because of them.

This was heady stuff for Jean. The only other man she'd seen in action, close-up, was her own father, and Hal Farmer was as different from Lawrence Marshall as a man could be. Commander Lawrence Marshall was a man of action. Jean loved her father, she supposed, yet she hated him at the same time. He was proud, taciturn, and abrupt—a man used to commanding; and his interaction with his family was also commanding. He was not unkind, but he was unfair, especially, it seemed, to Jean. Doubly undermined by being the second child, the "baby" of the family, and by being female, Jean was refused privileges that Bobby received early on simply because he was male. As she'd blossomed into young womanhood, Commander Marshall had grown even more stern, more censorious with his daughter; he'd made it quite clear without ever putting it in just so many words that her virtue was his territory, his responsibility, his *possession,* and he would decide when Jean should capitulate. Commander Marshall would indeed give his daughter in marriage when she married, for it was clear in his own mind that she was his to give.

Jean's mother acted as a sort of liaison officer between Jean and her father. And as her father's regulations for her life became more and more stringent, Mrs. Marshall could only plead, "Oh, Jeanie, don't you see it's because he loves you so? He only wants to protect you!"

If this was love, she did not want it. And she did not need protecting. Her teachers had always informed her parents that she was smart, and her parents had always translated this information into a belief that Jean was good, that she worked hard, was reliable, responsible, willing to follow authority, eager to obey. Jean knew it meant that she was intelligent, shrewd, quick, capable. Her mind could take her where she wanted to go.

And, at the moment, where she wanted to go was to bed with Hal Farmer. She was nineteen. It was time to lose her virginity. She didn't want to "save" herself for marriage; she hated the implication that a woman's body was only a safety-deposit box for a dowry, one single jewel, her precious maidenhood. Furthermore, she had no desire to marry. Rather she dreaded it, feared it. Marriage was a prison, a trap; marriage was an ending.

She would write her own rules. She would give her virginity freely, without contract, and to a man she knew she wouldn't marry. She had no illusions that she'd marry Hal Farmer. He was already married.

Riding through the cold, dark night in the warm safety of her brother's car, Jean reflected on all these things. She knew her brother loved her enormously, that he would even die to protect her; but she also knew that if she told him how she felt and what she was planning, he'd be horrified, and he would think that it was his duty to lock her up somehow, to protect her until she'd come to her senses and submitted. The men she loved most in her life—her father, her brother—were also, somehow, her enemies.

"Bobby, what did you tell Mother and Dad? I mean, about me?"

"I told them that I didn't want you riding on the trains. They're so crowded these days I was certain you wouldn't get a seat, and you'd arrive home exhausted. That's no way to start your Christmas holidays. I said I wanted to drive up to get you."

"So you didn't tell them I'd gone to New York."

"No."

Jean grinned in the dark. "Thanks, Bobby. I owe you one."

"Good, because I've got one ready."

"Oh, no," Jean groaned playfully, dramatically putting her face in her hands.

"It's not so bad. Al's going to ask you to go to the Navy Christmas Ball with him. I want you to go. We'll get a table, you and Al and Betty and I."

"That'll be a thrill," Jean said, but under her breath.

She had never liked Betty from the moment the little mouse entered their lives: a sweet young thing filling her life with bridge parties, charities, and tennis games while waiting for Bobby to graduate from the academy so that they could get married. The minute they were engaged, Betty had started to come over every night to chat with Commander and Mrs. Marshall while hand-hemming and embroidering linens for her hope chest. Betty had no opinions of her own; she was too quick to agree with everyone, and she was so relentlessly sweet that she made Jean want to throw up.

But the real reason Jean despised Betty was that, under all that sweetness and light, she was greedy; she'd chosen Bobby out of all the other fine young men because she knew he'd eventually inherit a lot of money when his mother died, and she wanted that money. Betty had never said as much, but her interest in Jean's mother's crystal or china and vacation home in Newport was obvious. Once, while accidentally passing through the house, Jean had overheard a conversation that gave her the willies.

In her breathless, high, helpless mouse voice, Betty had said, "Bobby, honey, you know I'll follow you anywhere, but I do worry about the kind of life we'll have. I wish I could change, but I can't help it—you know I've always been delicate. I'll live with you anywhere in the world, but I know a naval officer's salary doesn't provide for much in the way of things that make life pleasant."

Bobby, always the valiant protector of women, had replied, "Look, Betty, I'm going to come into some money someday, and I bet my parents would be glad to advance me some toward getting a maid for you and a decent place to live wherever I get stationed."

"Ooh, do you really think so, Bobby? Oh, that is just so wonderful! I didn't realize you were so lucky. Oh, sweetie, I'm going to make you the best little home you ever saw . . ."

That conversation and the sight of Betty nearly drooling when her future mother-in-law showed her the family Spode china and Waterford crystal that her son and his wife would be given had turned Jean's stomach. Finally, Jean had spoken to her mother.

"Honey, she just likes nice things," Mrs. Marshall had said of her future daughter-in-law. "Perhaps she does have the instincts of a social climber—that will be helpful for her career as a Navy wife. The social niceties are very important; entertaining can be crucial as a couple makes it through the Navy ranks. Betty has drive, and I'm glad. She'll be a great help to Bobby." Mrs. Marshall had smiled coyly at Jean. "Don't be so hard on the girl. I think you're just jealous because she's taking your brother away from you."

Hopeless, Jean had thought to herself, and hopeless, she thought now as she drove through the dark in her brother's custody toward the imprisoning safety of her parents' home. Jean thought of herself as the most wonderful package, a basket of flowers, a casket of jewels that she was only beginning to discover, and in the midst of her joy of discovery she was forced to deal with the knowledge that her family loved only the vessel. They did not know what her goals, dreams, desires were; they did not want to know.

But they were her family, and it was Christmas, and she would be back in Cambridge in two weeks. She would play the part of the good daughter, good sister, for that brief period, and let anticipation, like a liqueur, warm her blood, fill her head with fantasies that in two weeks she would make real.

White paper snowflakes twirled from strings above the dancers' heads in the ballroom of the Army-Navy Club. It was the annual Navy Christmas Dance. Jean Marshall sat at a crowded table drinking champagne, smoking a long cigarette, looking glamorous, feeling vile. So many things were wrong.

First of all, she looked fabulous, probably more wonderful than she'd ever looked before in her life. Her dark hair had been rolled and piled in sophisticated smooth puffs, held by rhinestone pins—and her dress! This dress! Her father had scowled and bellowed about the price, but her mother said, "Oh, darling, don't you see? It's a once-in-a-lifetime dress. We can afford it—let her enjoy it!" It clung to Jean's slender figure like a second skin, floor-length, long sleeved, high necked—in Cambridge Jean had décolleté dresses that her father had paid for but never seen and never would; he wouldn't let her leave the house in anything low cut. This sleek, clinging gown was all black except for the right arm and the right half of the shirred bodice. Those were a vividly contrasting white. Her fingernails and lips were painted crimson. Her earrings were twisted drops of rhinestones.

She looked wicked. She felt wicked.

She looked *experienced.*

But the look, the glamour, the hairdo, and gown were all wasted, because Hal Farmer wasn't there to see her.

But Hal Farmer would never see her looking like this, she thought with deepening gloom, because Hal Farmer wasn't the type to go to formal dances; in fact, Hal Farmer would be philosophically opposed to exactly the sort of affairs where such a dress was appropriate.

Next to her Betty simpered in an insipidly virginal dress of frothy baby pink; she was trying to look innocent, but Jean thought she just looked like a fool. And the way Betty clung to Bobby as they entered the ballroom, oohing and aahing as if she'd never seen Christmas decorations before, made Jean want to spit. The vast room was overflowing with gorgeous couples dancing, laughing around their tables, and pushing their way to the bar. On the dance floor was a woman she'd been watching for a while, a woman Jean admired. She knew something of her history: a senator's daughter, the woman was now twenty-eight, already married and *divorced*; and as if that weren't scandalous enough in 1939, here she was in public, not merely dancing with but practically crawling all over a remarkably beautiful young man who was still at Annapolis! Everyone was talking about her brazenness, but she was obviously having a terrific time, as was her young beau.

Jean wanted to be like that woman, brave, daring, rule breaking, *shocking.*

And there she sat, with Bobby leaning toward her now and then, saying, "I really don't approve of your smoking in public, and I know Dad wouldn't either." Or Betty, squeaking at the top of her rodent voice, "My, Jean, with your hair up like that no one would guess you're only nineteen!"

Al, at least, was leaving her alone. Jean knew there'd been some discussion about her before they even arrived at the dance; probably Bobby had told Al not to worry if Jean was "moody." Jean was civil to Al, but utterly cool. No sense in leading him on. She'd danced the obligatory dances with him but had been so bored while doing so she thought she'd fall asleep in his arms. Not even the admiring or envious glances of other women studying them cheered her up.

When they all sat around the table, crowded shoulder to shoulder with friends and acquaintances, things got a little more interesting: here, too, everyone was talking about the possibility of war. Hitler. Germany. Russia. War. She wished Hal Farmer could see how the men's eyes became bright and wide when they spoke of war, hear their voices grow louder, deeper, as they talked faster, gesticulated more effusively, puffed out their chests like cocky, strutting roosters. From a purely objective point of view it was fascinating: the most peaceful of men seemed to have something brilliant snap on inside of them at the thought of war, something that illuminated them from within.

Jean didn't try to enter the conversation. In Cambridge she would have been in the middle of the controversy, her voice as loud as any of the others, but here she was first and foremost Bobby Marshall's baby sister, and although the men would have listened to her with courtesy, they would not have *heard* her words. After all, she was only a junior in college, and a girl at that. What did she know?

So she yawned. Probably it wasn't a nice thing to do, but Bobby didn't notice; not even Al, who was supposed to be in love with her, noticed. Everyone was discussing the war.

Everyone but one man, who was looking at *her*. He was standing with the group gathered around their table, a drink in his hand, managing somehow to look both part and not part of the crowd. Tall, beautifully dressed, slightly foreign-looking, he was dark, not her type; she liked blonds. Still, he was handsome. No, not handsome. Al was handsome. This man was—worldly-looking. As he looked at her, his expression was admiring and not fresh, but unnerving. When their gazes met, goose bumps broke out all over her skin. Jean liked that.

The woman with him, who was leaning on him, running her hand along his arm, was stunning. She had hair the color of champagne and a chic creamy-colored gown that almost blended with her skin.

I will look like that someday, Jean vowed. And someday I will have a lover who looks like that man.

The man leaned toward her brother and said something that Jean couldn't pick up. Jean looked away.

"Would you like to dance?"

It was that man.

As he bent over her—rather closer to her than propriety might dictate, but how else could she hear him over the commotion? —she looked into his rum-dark eyes, eyes as dark and intoxicating as the liquor her parents stirred into their eggnog on Christmas Eve, and time stopped. That night and for the rest of her life she would remember that moment as the moment when time stood still.

"I've asked your brother for permission," the man was saying. "My name is Erich Mellor and—"

Now Jean nearly smashed into him, she rose so quickly.

"It's really not necessary to ask my brother's permission simply to dance with me!" she declared. Her face was burning.

"But what if I want to do more than dance one dance with you?" Erich Mellor confided, smiling, looking deep into her eyes. "What if I knew the moment I saw you I wanted to get to know you? In that case, wouldn't it have been prudent of me to gain your brother's trust from the beginning?"

Jean nearly fell back into her chair.

Bowled over, she thought, remembering her friends saying, "He just bowled me over," and now she felt that way, hit by a force she couldn't resist, her breath knocked out of her chest, her legs turned to pudding.

Erich Mellor led her to the dance floor, his hand warm and dry on hers. Jean hoped she appeared aloof as she followed him; she was nearly paralyzed. On the dance floor he took her into his arms but did not hold her too close. He was very smooth, but not bold. The band began an especially hypnotic version of "Blue Moon." The mood of the ballroom mellowed like the prismed ball of light glittering overhead; as the lights blurred into one dreamy blue, so did the sound level of the room subside to a muted hum. Couples around Erich and Jean drew closer to each other, the women sinking their heads onto their partners' shoulders or chests, closing their eyes, surrendering to the music. Jean's hand was on Erich's shoulder, and through the material of his jacket she felt his heat and strength, just as she was vividly aware of the sleek languor of her yielding back against his firm hand. Time moved again, not in its usual efficient clicks but in a drifting flow, like warm wind through grassy fronds, stirring, sensuous, beguiling. Jean's body flushed with a sultry, helpless heat.

With a teasing brush of the whisk against the cymbals, the band slid into "Moonglow."

"I asked them to play this set," Erich informed her.

Jean smiled. The amazing thing was not that she was in this man's arms, gazing into his dark eyes, melting under his touch; the amazing thing was that she felt so completely herself as all this happened. She wasn't anxious about being graceful—she wasn't embarrassed about the frankness of her eyes meeting his. She felt *easy*. It was much like the first time she dove into deep water and felt as she sliced through it and it gathered back around her: Oh, I can do this; this is my element.

When the band finally turned again to swing, Erich did not lead her back to the table where her brother and her date and the others sat, but to the bar for drinks and then out to a quiet spot in an alcove where they sat and talked. He was in banking. That made her laugh in surprise. "You look less like a banker than anyone I've ever met!" she said.

He asked, "What do you think I look like?"

"A prince. No—a baron. From some decadent European country."

He laughed. "Sorry. I'm afraid I'm only a shamelessly dull American banker."

She told him about Radcliffe, how she loved being away from the strictures of her family life, and as the evening went on she spoke about *War Stories* and her ambition to be part of it. He told her that her principles and optimism were admirable. He was old. He was twenty-four.

They danced again, whenever the band played slow songs, each time coming closer to each other. Jean could feel the length of his thigh sliding parallel to, not quite touching, hers. He was several inches taller than she was, so that finally toward the end of the evening when he pressed her against him she rested her head on his shoulder, her forehead brushing his chin. She could feel the rise and fall of his chest as he breathed, and the heat of his skin.

It didn't seem possible that the evening could really end, but after a final round of "Good Night, Ladies," everyone clapped and cheered. People drifted off the dance floor. Erich brought Jean back to the table where Al sat deep in discussion with some other men. At their approach, Bobby looked up. He glared at Jean. Bobby and Al both stood up.

Erich stretched out his hand to Al. "Nice to see you again." He turned to Bobby. "Thanks for letting me dance with your sister. And good luck. I hope you get the submarine post you put in for."

Bobby nodded in reply. Any mention of the Navy improved his spirits.

"Thanks for the dance," Erich said politely to Jean.

With her brother and Al looking on, she could return only a stiff smile.

"May I call you tomorrow?" he asked.

Triumph flushed over her. "Of course."

The ride home was miserable. They had gone as a foursome, and as they waited for the car to be brought around, Bobby, mad at Jean for ignoring Al all evening, paced up and down the sidewalk. Hot breath steamed from his nostrils; he looked like a mad bull. Betty, in an attempt to keep everything friendly, cheeped breathlessly. Once in the car Jean slumped against one door in the backseat, weak with lust. Next to her, Al sat, gamely responding to Betty's nonstop chatter.

Because Betty, Jean, and Bobby lived out in Kalorama, Bobby announced that he'd drop Al off at the hotel first. It was a mercifully brief ride to the Carlton. A pang of regret struck Jean; she hadn't ever wanted to hurt Al. Certainly she hadn't wanted to humiliate him. Now the evening was over and he would get out of the car and she'd never have to deal with him again.

But to her chagrin, as they approached, Bobby slammed on the brakes much harder than necessary, propelling Jean forward into the back of the seat, then cut the motor so roughly that the car coughed and jolted them all once more. Al was leaning forward, already saying, "Well, good night, everyone, and, Bobby, thanks for driving—" Bobby turned around and barked at Jean, "Jesus Christ, Jean! The least you could do is apologize to Al! You acted like an ill-bred half-witted Jezebel tonight. You're only a little fool of a college girl. I'm sorry, Al, but it makes me so mad to see her treat a Navy man that way! Jean, I'm going to have to talk to Dad about this and see that you get a royal comeuppance!"

It wasn't Bobby's anger that infuriated Jean; it was his threat to tell their father, for their father held unlimited power over Jean's life. Immediately she knew that if Bobby had his way, he'd see to it that her father forbade her ever to see Erich Mellor again.

"Goddamn it, Bobby!" she said, truly shocking everyone, including herself, because young women of her set did not swear. As she spoke she opened the door on her side of the car and immediately sank one evening-sandaled foot into a snowdrift. "I am not your *child*! I am not *anyone's* child! I'm a grown woman, and you have no right to speak to me that way."

She hurtled out into the very cold December night. She was shaking so hard with rage that she could hardly get the words out, but she leaned forward to yell into the car, "I used to love you, but the way you treat me, without any tiny *bean* of respect, makes me just hate you. I mean it, Bobby. I hate you. You just leave me alone!"

She slammed the door.

Other cars were crowded around the entrance to the hotel to drop off revelers in fancy dress. People in furs and capes stared at Jean with amusement or disapproval. Only low-class, ordinary women made spectacles of themselves like that, not women like Jean Marshall. It was just a good thing she wasn't drunk, Jean Marshall thought as she stalked away from her brother's car, because the street was so snow-covered and icy and she could hardly stand up as it was.

"Jean! You get back in this car right now!" Bobby yelled at her.

Betty rolled down her window and stuck her head out. In a loud whisper, as if to keep others from hearing, she hissed, "Get back in the car right this minute, Jean! You are humiliating me!"

Jean kept on walking. Thank God her raccoon coat was warm, because it was a desperately cold night and the snow had already penetrated her delicate, black high-heels and silk stockings, turning her feet into two cubes of ice.

"You two go on. I'll see that she gets home safely."

"Al—"

"We'll take a cab."

"That'll cost you a fortune, Al. You let me—"

"Bobby. Please. Go on home."

Even though Al's voice was level and reasonable, it reached Jean's ears. Jean was glad to hear what he said because as she reached the relative shelter of the hotel marquee she realized she didn't have a clue about what to do next and no money in her evening bag except what girls called "mad money," money to call home, and home was the last place she wanted to call right then.

Head high, affecting an expression of utter boredom, Jean swept through the door that the doorman hastened to open and into the warmth of the hotel lobby. She sank onto a banquette, still shivering with anger and cold, and watched with relief as Al White approached.

He sat down next to her and leaned back, then turned his hat in his hands for a few seconds.

"Well, Jean," he said calmly, "why don't you let me get a cab and see you home."

"It will cost the earth."

"I believe I can afford it."

"I don't know why you're being so nice to me."

"Let's just say it's because we're old friends."

What if Erich walked in right now and saw her sitting in a hotel lobby with Al? What would he think? Jean wondered.

"All right," she said. "Thank you."

She waited in the warm lobby while Al went out to have the doorman hail a cab. Soon Al came back in for her and off they went, together again in the backseat of yet another vehicle carrying her irrevocably toward her parents' home.

Chapter 3

Julia

Monday night, while Diane tossed in her bed, worrying about her daughter, while Jean drank café au lait on the other side of the ocean, Julia lay curled up as close as she could get to Sam. They were in the good old Howard Johnson's Motel, where all the rooms looked the same, so that each time they went there, no matter the room number, it seemed like the same room, their own room for making love.

Sam's skin smelled like hot apple cider, Julia thought as she snuggled next to him. Sam was naked, asleep, and Julia was naked, too, curled up against him, her arm flung over his body. Her face was pressed against his back, and with each breath she inhaled his scent. His skin was the color of maple syrup, Julia mused, realizing with that thought how she tended to think of Sam in terms of food. Well, it was true—she was always hungry for him. She wanted to put her mouth, her tongue, on him, anywhere— his eyes like dark chocolate, his hair straight and gleaming black like licorice. Sam was short, fine boned, with milk-white teeth. Because he was a half-black, half-Vietnamese war orphan who'd been adopted by a pair of liberal Bostonian lawyers and raised in a home that was unusually affluent even by American standards, his speech was softly cultured and his bearing was confident. As a child, because of his beauty, he'd often been mistaken for a girl. He didn't mind being part this, part that, but he was completely male and wished that, at least, were clear.

It was clear to Julia. Her Sam was young, passionate, responsive, a man. Sometimes she'd come up behind him, wrap her arms around him, and slide her hands down inside his jeans. His gasp was her victory. She'd caress him very slowly. He'd have to unzip his jeans. She'd stroke him, feeling him stiffen, feeling her power. Sooner or later he'd twist away from her arms, push her onto the floor, yank down her pants, thrust himself into her. Those times he didn't bother about her pleasure. Those times he knew her pleasure came from her power over him. She'd lie with her arms under her head, smiling, his servant, his queen.

She lived for Sam. She lived because of Sam.

Now, she'd gotten what she wanted, to be with Sam.

She didn't understand why she was still so afraid.

Her day had begun at Gressex that morning. She'd gone, with great reluctance, to her scheduled conference with Mrs. Derek, her college counselor.

"Well, Julia!" Mrs. Derek was good-hearted and energetic. Her tiny office was cluttered with stacks of books on colleges, testing procedures, rating forms. She gestured Julia to a chair, shut her office door, settled back in her seat, and took up the clump of papers that represented Julia's academic career. "Isn't it a beautiful fall! Did you have a good summer?"

Julia smiled. Yes, she thought, because Sam and I became lovers.

"Pretty much," she replied. "Although my grandfather died."

"I'm so sorry."

"Well, I got to go down with my mother to help my grandmother pack up her house."

"Ah, yes. This is the grandmother near Washington, D.C., the one you're so close to?"

"Right." Julia flashed on her grandmother, a memory accumulated from all the times she'd visited her. Julia and Jean had had a ritual from Julia's childhood: when Julia awoke early in the morning, she ran to find her grandmother down in the kitchen, waiting for her. Together they prepared a beautiful bed tray with breakfast tea and muffins and jams laid out on Jean's most delicate china. They carried the tray back up to Julia's room, crawled into the high four-poster bed together, and snuggling, they ate breakfast and talked, wriggling their toes against each other's. Grandmother's body was as soft and cozy as pillows.

"And did you tell her you wanted to go to college in the Washington, D.C., area?"

Julia looked at her hands. "No." Defensively, she pointed out, "The time wasn't right. They were packing up the house and thinking about Grandfather. And Grandmother was talking about going to Europe."

"Did you discuss with your parents this idea of yours about going to a cooking school?"

"No."

"Julia. You promised me you'd at least mention it to them over the summer."

"I know. There just wasn't a good time."

There would never be a good time, but how could Julia explain this to optimistic Mrs. Derek? She'd imagined telling her parents a million times, but each time the same tape began to play in her head. "Mom, Dad, I don't want to go to college—I want to go to cooking school." Her father wouldn't care, wouldn't really hear. He'd nod, looking wise and concerned, all the time thinking of test tubes and genes. Her mother would freak out. "You want to *cook!* You can do anything in the world and you want to *cook?* We send you to a private school so you can have every opportunity in the universe and all you want to do is *cook?*" Diane could be terrifying when angered or disappointed.

"Have you considered my suggestion?"

Julia snapped back to the present, to Mrs. Derek's kind and eager face.

"Your strongest subject is foreign language. You've got four years of French under your belt and three of Spanish. If you major in French, you'd be in great shape when you graduate from college. You could go France. You'd be fluent. You could study at Le Cordon Bleu. You'd have a college diploma, so your parents would be happy—and you'd have a marketable skill, one that you love."

Julia could tell that Mrs. Derek had really worked on this, fitting together the jigsaw pieces of Julia's life. She didn't want to disappoint her by confessing that she couldn't stomach the idea of four more years of classwork. "It's a good idea," Julia replied.

"You like it."

"I like it." She wanted to get out of the counselor's office. She was tired of talking.

"So we'll take that as a starting point?"

"Right." She'd agree with anything to get away.

"Right. Good. Now. Did you look at any of the universities in the District of Columbia area?"

God, didn't Mrs. Derek ever let up? She was so pushy. "No. I meant to, but—with my grandfather's death and all . . ."

"You usually spend Thanksgiving in McLean, don't you? If I remember correctly."

God, the woman remembered everything; she should work for the CIA. "Yes."

"If you go down this Thanksgiving, it would be the perfect time to look at the colleges. You have excellent grades, Julia, except in science."

Julia grinned abashedly. Where were her father's precious genes now? She couldn't think scientifically. It was all just mush to her, and she'd gone through torture to pull a C from her required biology courses. She couldn't draw, either, in spite of all the hours spent in her mother's studio trying to copy Diane's swift, clever movements. Chase could do both. He was majoring in chemistry and would probably follow in his father's footsteps if he pulled himself together and stopped being a wiseass goof-off. Julia knew her mother would love her to join her in Arabesque. Her heart burned with guilt at her failure, her treachery. She was no good at art, and worse, she didn't want to be. Her mother's world seemed cold and even clinical, channeled inward and down, focusing on specks. Julia hated jewelry, the vanity, the narcissistic fuss of it all. She preferred the expansive world of cooking, the generosity of food. Her mother meticulously picking away at tiny stones, holding her breath, shoulders tense, as she set a ruby into a gold ring, seemed a selfish sight to Julia. By contrast, working with her grandmother or her Aunt Susan stirring handpicked, homegrown raspberries and sugar into a bubbling jam was a happy magic, an alchemy that moistened the air with delicious fragrance. What they produced, glistening just as prettily as jewels in their quilted glass jars, could be given to friends and family, to brighten a multitude of winter days.

"I've made a list for you." Mrs. Derek broke into Julia's reverie. She handed Julia a sheet. "American University. George Washington University. Georgetown. I want you to read about those in your college books."

"Okay. Thanks." Julia took the paper and rose.

"Hang on—not so fast. We've got to make another appointment, and I want to see your work sheet for your applications. Also, I need your extracurricular activities form updated."

"All right."

"Julia." Mrs. Derek's normally sweet voice turned sharp. "Listen to me. You're not focusing. This is a crucial time in your life. This is it; this is the crunch. You've got to do the best academic work you can this semester. Colleges pay the most attention to the first semester of your senior year. You need to analyze your strengths and weaknesses and goals and put them into a clear presentation for your applications. Your entire future rests on decisions you make now. Gressex has given you an excellent foundation. You have the whole world before you. Stop fading away into those dreamy moods of yours! Julia, you've got so much going for you! Don't let it slip through your fingers!"

"All right, Mrs. Derek. Thank you."

By the time Julia escaped from the office, it had happened to her again: she was trembling, and she couldn't get her breath. Gasping, she raced back to her dorm and the telephone. She'd call Sam. She'd talk to Sam. She always felt better when she was connected to him.

Sam Weyborn had grown up three houses down from the Randalls in a quiet, tree-lined neighborhood within easy commuting distance of Boston. The homes were beautiful and the yards spacious, but children were scarce. Sam was two years older than

Chase but played with him because there were no other boys close by.

During her childhood, Julia had been their shadow—or had tried to be. Two years younger than Chase, four years younger than Sam, she was treated with impatience and scorn by her brother and with amused tolerance by Sam. "Get your own friend!" Chase would yell at Julia when she tried to tag along, but there were no girls within walking distance. If they had a baby-sitter who could drive, she'd sometimes take Julia over to a friend's house, but arrangements were complicated. So many parents had their children's schedules booked up with lessons—music, horseback riding, swimming, tennis, skiing, skating.

The summers were the worst. Each summer the Randalls tried to find a new, fun, baby-sitter for their children, and some years they were luckier than others. Julia hated to whine about having no one to play with, because it upset her mother so much.

"Oh, what can I do?" Diane would agonize, nearly tearing her hair out. Almost frenzied, she'd pull Julia up on her lap. "Look, sweetie, look at this photo album. I was a full-time mother for the first eight years of Chase's life, the first six years of yours. If I don't concentrate on my work now, I'll lose it all! Look, look at this picture. I made you that birthday cake myself! It took me a whole day. No, more than that—two whole days if you count all the time it took to buy the ingredients. I made it from scratch. Isn't it beautiful?"

"It's beautiful, Mama."

"Do you remember it?"

"Yes, Mama. It was chocolate."

"It was strawberry! So it would be pink! Your favorite color. Oh, I went to all that trouble and you don't even remember. Julia, what I'm trying to prove is that I love you, you're my darling girl, but I can't stay home to take care of you all day anymore. See, when women grow up they work just like men, they make things, they have important jobs. Look, tomorrow I'll take you to my studio with me. How about that?"

That was even worse. Julia knew her mother was trying to give her a treat when she brought her to Arabesque, just as her father was whenever he took her in to show her around his lab. Both places were boring, in much the same way. They were full of machinery that smelled like hot metal and tiny bright glass stuff that was breakable and could not be touched. Both her parents retreated into a private world when they worked, leaving Julia with a box of beads to string or a pad and Crayolas. She felt compelled to be still and silent.

At last, when Julia was eight, they came to a brilliant solution. While Chase went off to baseball camp, Julia was sent to stay with her grandparents in McLean, Virginia, for one month, then over to Kansas City to stay with her Aunt Susan's family for another month. That was bliss. Her grandparents doted on her. They took her into the Smithsonian to see the historical costumes and drank lemonade on the Mall; they took her shopping and let her buy her choice of dolls and doll clothes. Here Julia could have her beloved Barbie, who had been banned, with much pontification and drama, from Diane's house. Here Julia could buy Barbie the most glittering, frothy clothes, pretending that the little doll was the princess of a magic kingdom.

This past summer when Diane and Julia flew down to help Jean pack up the house after Grandfather's death, it had of course been Diane who had discovered the hatbox at the back of the guest-bedroom closet.

"What is this?" Diane had asked. She'd pulled the perky doll out upside down, pinching the arched feet between thumb and finger, as far away from her as her arm would extend, as if the doll would bite. Looking at Jean, she'd said, "Mom. Don't tell me."

"I plead guilty," Jean had confessed, sitting on the bed. She took Barbie and smoothed down her skirt. "Such a pretty doll."

"A sexist male fantasy," Diane had complained. "You know how I feel about it! I didn't want Julia growing up thinking this was what real women's bodies look like!"

"Lighten up, Mom," Julia had suggested. "Barbie's not my role model. Do you see me trying to dress like that?"

Diane swept her eyes over her daughter's clothes, which had been selected from the finest thrift shops in Boston. "Point taken," she admitted and had dropped the subject.

Julia had placed Barbie back in the hatbox with all her tiny gaudy clothes and carried it down to the pile of things to be taken to the Salvation Army. Some little girl was in for a treat.

It was also at her grandmother's that Julia had learned to cook. During the hot summer days, her grandparents' big house drowsed in the sun, humming gently from its window air conditioners, its rooms and hallways shadowy from the curtains and shades drawn against the brilliant light. Jean woke early. And no matter at what hour Julia trained herself to stir, by the time she'd dressed and scurried down to the kitchen, her grandmother was already there, drinking coffee and reading the paper. Together they prepared the breakfast tray. Up in Julia's bed, snuggled in pillows, they ate and talked and planned the day's menu, fitting it to the predicted weather and the day's events. After dressing, they'd prepare anything they could for dinner ahead of time so that they wouldn't have to cook in the severely hot afternoons. They shopped, stopping off at specialty stores for the freshest fish, the plumpest vegetables, lettuces glittering with diamonds of water, glistening summer fruits.

There was all the time in the world to cook. It wasn't so much that Jean taught Julia to cook elaborate foods, although there was some of that, but that she taught her to cook everything with care. Jean could make even cinnamon toast look and taste like a delicacy. Julia learned how to make pie crust and pâtés, gellied soups and soufflés, jams and preserves, meringues like snowdrifts. Jean's kitchen was roomy, comfortable, old-fashioned, and full of peonies and irises from her garden. An entire farmyard of cute ducks, dogs, cows, and cats populated the curtains, dish towels, hot pads, and bowls.

The next month, when Julia went out to her aunt's house, she'd show off her newest recipes. Aunt Susan was always glad when Julia came to help cook for her husband and four sons. It amazed Julia that Susan and Diane were from the same family. They were entirely different. Susan and her family lived in a lakefront house outside Kansas City. The entire family was addicted to sports, and Susan was also a nurse, so their house was always a hurricane of people running in and out the door, grabbing bags of chips to eat on the way to some game or meet. Aunt Susan's house was noisy. Compared to Diane's house, it was messy, and in the summer, even dirty, as everyone tracked in mud and dust and tossed down wet swimsuits, ropes, balls, bats, gloves, cleated shoes, sweatshirts, baseball caps, T-shirts. Aunt Susan didn't mind. She was a hearty, easygoing, joyful woman whose part-time job gave her a balanced perspective: compared to what she saw in the hospital, her home was bursting with healthy, beautiful life.

When Susan worked, her arrival home in the late afternoons was a celebration. "God, Julia, that smells good, you are an angel!" she'd exclaim, passing through the kitchen, grabbing a Diet Coke and an apple. "Come in and tell me how your day went."

Julia would trail down the hall to the huge master bedroom

with its windows full of lake and sky. Susan would collapse on the bed, quickly joined by the dog, the cat, and whatever sons happened to be around.

"Mom! Mom!" the boys would clamor. "Look at this!" They'd present her with a garter snake, a skinned knee, a tangled fish line, or a clump of hair matted with bubble gum. Susan would reach out, clever hands soothing, sorting, somehow talking to everyone at the same time. "Ooh!" she'd call out. "Joey, your elbow's in my side!"

Julia couldn't remember ever sprawling like that with her mother. Her parents' bedroom was their inner sanctum, which Chase and Julia could enter, but only after knocking. Her mother's life was more formal, Aunt Susan's more gregarious, and neither one was right or better, Julia told herself. When she grew up, she might want a sanctuary like her mother's—but she'd definitely want to be a mother like Aunt Susan.

This past summer after the funeral, Aunt Susan had stayed on for a couple of days to help Jean, Diane, and Julia sort through the house. Late one night Julia couldn't sleep. Softly she tiptoed down the staircase, trying not to awaken anyone, heading for the den and some comforting late-night television. Hearing laughter but seeing no light, she padded into the living room. Aunt Susan and her mother were on the screened porch, giggling like girls.

"God, I haven't done this in ages!" Diane said, coughing. "Oh, yum. I love nicotine."

"Once every now and then won't kill us," Susan said.

"Once every funeral," Diane pronounced. This struck them both as hilarious. Julia realized that they were tipsy. She turned to leave, then heard her name. Edging into the room, she leaned against an armchair to listen.

"Julia's becoming a beauty."

"You think so? I hope so. I can't judge my children. Especially in the clothes they wear these days."

"God. Think of what you wore at their age."

"Yes, but I wanted to be artistic. Julia just dresses like her friends. She doesn't want to be anything special."

"She's young."

"I know. But still. I wish she had—a dream. A passion."

"Diane, give the girl a break. Her grades are great, and she's in everything—chorus, softball, school clubs—"

"Yes, everything interests her and nothing fascinates her. At her age, I—"

"She's not you, Diane. Hey, you don't expect Chase to follow in your footsteps, do you? I know I don't expect that of my boys."

"Hm. Well, you're right. But they are boys. I mean, it's different when you have a daughter."

"I don't know, Diane. Look at us. I mean, you throw up at the sight of blood and I'm a nurse. You design jewelry and I can't remember to put my earrings on. Mother wasn't a nurse or an artist. For that matter, look at our brothers. Bert's in the Navy and Art's a pothead pacifist."

"I know. I know. I know all that. Still. Honestly, Susie, sometimes Julia just breaks my heart. I've spent my life trying to be a good role model for her, to show her women can do everything men can do. I've sent her to the best schools. She could be a doctor or a lawyer or an artist or a diplomat! And do you know what she likes to do? *Cook!* God, where did I go wrong?"

"You didn't go wrong. She's a wonderful young woman. And you're right—she could be anything she wants to be. Maybe she wants to be a chef."

"Oh, Susie, she's so bright, so capable, so energetic. I don't want her stuck in a restaurant chopping garlic. I want her life to be wonderful. I want her life to be beautiful and blessed. And I'll fight for that."

Julia had tiptoed back upstairs, unable to listen to any more. Lying on her bed in her grandmother's house, she started to wish she were an innocent little girl again, until the hum of the air-conditioning floated her off into the solace of sleep.

Even though she spent most of her childhood summers visiting relatives, Julia still found herself alone a lot, especially after school and on weekends. When she was ten, Sam went away to boarding school, and Chase went away when she was twelve. She had a wonderful room with every kind of artistic toy and intellectual game, but she was lonely. She talked on the phone to her girlfriends. She watched television. Sometimes the housekeeper would drive her to meet friends at the mall. She couldn't wait until she was old enough to go away to boarding school.

She'd applied to, and been admitted to, a number of schools, including the one where Chase went. She chose Gressex not because Sam was there but simply to please her parents. Gressex was the most prestigious, the most difficult. That Sam went there made it seem a friendly place to her, a place where she could be happy.

She'd been at Gressex for three weeks, and she'd made some friends, and she had just been walking across campus with her roommate Sonja one sunny September morning when she and Sam passed each other going to classes.

"Hey, Julia!" Sam had called out.

At the sight of him, her heart leaped.

"Hi, Sam," Julia had called back, tilting her head sideways, smiling, clasping her books to her chest to keep her heart from jumping out.

"You know him?" Sonja asked. "God, he's dreamy."

"He's my brother's best friend. I've known him forever." Fourteen-year-old Julia kept her voice casual as she secretly absorbed the shock of what she was feeling.

She was in love with Sam! Perhaps she had been all her life.

She knew he was going with someone, a turquoise-eyed blonde named Buffy. They'd been going out for months, and everyone knew they were serious. Buffy was as smart as she was beautiful, and like Sam she excelled in science. They were the only two students in the Advanced Placement chemistry and physics tutorials.

Many times that first year at Gressex during her sixth period when she had no classes, Julia would sneak up to the sagging second-floor balcony of the student center. If she pressed her nose against the window, she could just see across the grassy quadrangle into the first floor of the science building where Mr. Weinberg, Sam, and Buffy moved together in such a tight knot that Julia couldn't tell whose body was whose. If the light was right, the sun would glance off a vial, microscope lens, or specimen plate so that teacher and students appeared to be conspirators in a fiery magic. Then Julia would be pierced with envy and desire.

She suffered even more after Sam graduated and went to Wesleyan. She tried going out with other boys, but they weren't the same. They weren't Sam. When she saw Sam over Thanksgiving or Christmas or the summer, the punch in her stomach told her she hadn't stopped loving him, and so she began to dream and plot.

First, she tried to share Sam's interest in science. She took every science course the school required for graduation, but no matter how hard she studied, she couldn't get it. Biology, chemistry, physics, all were labyrinthine, confusing, endless.

When her parents saw her grades, they counseled her to give up on science. "It's not for everyone," her father told her, kindly. "To be honest, Julia, I'm beginning to believe it takes a certain kind of defective mind to really understand the sciences."

"A nitpicking kind of mind," her mother added, throwing a teasing look at her husband. "Julia, what were you loading up on all these sciences for anyway? Honey, look at all you can do. Look at your ease in languages. That's where you should put your time. Why, you could be—an ambassador!"

Julia didn't want to be an ambassador. She was sure her facility with languages wasn't deep. It was only that she'd had a head start from two years with her French *au pair*. That her parents were so damned understanding, trying to encourage her to think well of herself, made her feel even more rotten.

This summer, just before her last year at Gressex, the crunch year, the Randalls rented a large house on Martha's Vineyard for a month. Chase, a sophomore in college, was given the apartment over the garage. He and his friends usually joined the rest of the family for evening meals and often they came over to watch TV or use the VCR, but for the most part they partied and slept above the garage. Julia and her friends were given a wing on the second floor. They swam, tanned themselves on the beach, biked into town, watched videos, painted their nails, analyzed their clothes, all the while waiting for the college guys to amble in. The high-school boys they met on the beach seemed like babies compared to Chase and his friends—but the college girls who showed up for parties were so slick and sophisticated they filled Julia's friends with despair.

But not Julia. Sam had broken up with Jackie, the girl he'd been going with for the past two years, after he had broken up with Buffy. Now it was her turn.

It was easy to find ways to be with Sam. She'd done it for years. She knew the television shows he liked: *Saturday Night Live,* old *Star Trek* reruns. When he came in to watch TV, she would already be there. It was only natural for him to sink down on the sofa next to her.

"Want a chip?" she'd ask, holding out a bag of barbecued potato chips, his favorite kind.

She knew he preferred looking for seashells to swimming, so she'd wander off alone down the beach, and eventually they'd run into each other.

"Look at this," she'd call out. "A perfect pair of angel's wings."

She knew Sam liked to take long, early-morning bike rides. She programmed herself to wake at daybreak. Quietly she'd pull on shorts, a T-shirt, and sneakers and slip downstairs. When Sam approached the bike rack near the back steps she'd be sitting there, sipping a cup of steaming coffee, listening to the birds sing. It was as natural as the rising sun for him to ask her if she wanted to join him. By the middle of the month, they were going off together nearly every morning, exploring different parts of the island. They were relaxed with each other, easy in each other's company, developing their own set of jokes, remembering their shared history. Now, Julia thought, if I can just get him to notice that I'm female.

One Sunday they returned from an early-morning ride, wheeled their bikes up to the stand at the back of the house, and started up the back steps, intending to help themselves to coffee and orange juice. But Sam stopped abruptly. He held his hand palm out, stopping Julia. They froze outside the back door.

"Honestly, Jim, you make me crazy!"

"Diane, I don't see why you're so excited over a little bit of trash."

" 'A little bit of trash.' That is so typical of you. Look. We agreed when we decided to try a summer place that we'd each have a chore. Chase does the grocery shopping, Julia and I keep the house relatively clean and do the cooking, and all you were supposed to do is take the trash to the dump once a week. The children do more than you do!"

"You should have reminded me."

"Why? Why should it be my responsibility to remind you to take the trash to the dump? It's not *your* responsibility to remind me to cook!"

"I've just had other things on my mind."

"That's clear. If I'd known you'd spend half your time driving back up to your lab or reading your damned reports, I wouldn't have bothered to try a family vacation. Jim, this is probably the last time we'll all be together. The children are almost grown up."

"Look. I said I'm sorry. What more can I do?"

"You could take the trash to the dump before our luncheon guests arrive."

"Is the dump open on Sundays?"

Sam and Julia could barely hear Diane's reply: "Is it my responsibility to find that out?" Their voices faded as they went toward the front of the house.

Julia leaned against the shingled wall, hanging her head in embarrassment. Sam stood next to her. Awkwardly, he reached out and took her hand. He stroked it.

"It's okay, Jul. My parents fight like that all the time, too. Just like that."

His touch mesmerized Julia. She couldn't speak. Sam's body

was just inches away. She could smell his sweet-apple fragrance and healthy sweat.

"Jul," he whispered, "don't cry."

He moved even closer, still holding her hand. She felt him looking at her. His look was like heat. She flushed.

When they were kids, they'd tumbled together, arms and legs flailing, as they fell off their sleds into cold, sparkling snow or played tag in high green grass. They'd fed each other Julia's experiments in cooking, Sam's less appetizing experiments in science. They'd shared Play-Doh, bubble gum, popsicles, ice-cream cones. Each had seen the other scolded by an angry parent, and Julia had even witnessed Sam getting a spanking after he'd triumphantly managed to set a bunch of leaves and dry grass on fire using only a mirror and the sun.

Sam had been a bony little boy, slighter and shorter than Chase. He'd been careful. Chase would charge bellowing into a pile of autumn leaves, brandishing a stick, plowing through the middle, scattering twigs and leaves every which way. For his turn Sam would patiently rake the leaves back into a billowing pile, return to the opposite end of the yard, and race like an arrow, silent, gathered, intent on the moment when he swung his arms up in the air, pushed with his feet, and leaped up and forward, into the perfect heart of leaves. He'd sink like a dolphin in water, leaves spilling over him, rustling, and he'd lie there in silence for so long Chase and Julia would never be able to stand it. Afraid he'd suffocated or broken his neck, they'd call out, "Sam? Are you okay?" He'd sit up, leaves in his glossy hair, grinning.

Sam's hand on Julia's was silky, but fine black hair glistened from the backs of his fingers and along his arm. Julia saw a scar near his elbow and remembered a car accident he'd been in two years before when a friend of his had been driving drunk.

"Hey, Jul," Sam said. He lifted her chin with his hand and with his thumb lightly wiped away a tear.

Julia looked up into Sam's dark eyes. He leaned forward and kissed her mouth. Startled, they separated, then kissed again. Then they put their arms around each other and simply stood there, both of them slightly trembling in the steady beam of the morning sun. Unruly rose of Sharon bushes flowered at the corner of the porch, shielding them from the garage windows. Julia felt how new Sam's body was to her, a sleek young man with hard arms and a deep chest. When she rested her head against his shoulder, she sensed his strength.

They kissed again. Sam pressed his tongue between her lips and into her mouth. His tongue was huge; her knees felt weak and she sagged against him, needing him to support her, and he did support her, moving a hand down to press her hips against his. He was shaking.

He pushed Julia away, so that the shingles of the porch warmed her back.

"We can't do this. Chase would kill me," Sam told her.

"Why?"

"Because you're his little sister."

"You can't kiss Chase's little sister?"

"*No one's* supposed to kiss his little sister!" Sam grinned and leaned against the house next to her, still holding her hand.

"Sam." Why was this so hard? She'd dreamed of this moment a million times, but now she could hardly speak. "Forget Chase."

"He's my best friend."

"I love you." There. She'd said it. As she said it, Sam squeezed her hand, hard, in response, and she felt his body jolt a little with the surprise.

"You're just comfortable with me."

"No. I love you. God, Sam, can't you tell?"

He dropped her hand. "We can't do this."

Desperation made her brave. "Sam, Chase would be mad if you just played around with me. It would be different if we were serious about each other. I'm serious about you." She waited, looking right into his eyes.

He shook his head. "I've got to go."

He turned, jumped off the porch, and raced toward the garage. Julia waited on the porch for five minutes, ten, twenty, until she knew he wasn't coming back. She went into the house, into her room, and fell facedown on the bed. Her friends were just getting up for the day.

"We're going to the beach now," Sonja said. "Coming?"

"I just got back from a bike ride. I think I got sunstroke or something. It's hot. I'll come later." Julia kept her head buried in her pillow. She didn't want her friends to see her face.

"All right. See you."

All day Julia lay in a trance. Upon request her obedient mind replayed the moment with Sam over and over again, freeze-framing the kiss, each time sending delicious shots of desire and pleasure through her. She could see Sam bending toward her, his upper lip beaded with sweat, his mouth parted to reveal his almost perfect teeth—he'd had braces but had chipped a front tooth playing ice hockey. When she told him she loved him, he'd squeezed her hand so tightly it had hurt.

That evening Chase and his friends left for a party on the other side of the island, and Sam went off with them. The next day Julia went to the beach with her friends, knowing Sam was there, but he was surrounded by people, and there was no way she could talk to him alone. He didn't look her way all day. Julia felt quietly desperate. Only three nights remained before everyone left the Vineyard to go back to their fall lives, Julia at Gressex, Sam at Wesleyan.

Then her parents announced that they were going off on an overnight sailing trip with friends. They left money for pizza and a list of instructions. The moment their car pulled out of the driveway, Chase was on the phone, organizing an end-of-the-summer party. He and his friends carried most of the furniture and anything valuable into one of the downstairs rooms and locked the door. They filled new plastic trash barrels with ice, beer, and wine. Chase had his portable CD player with him, and he and his friends stacked their CD's, R.E.M., Pearl Jam, Def Leppard, Nirvana, beside it; he put the speakers on top of the antique cupboard in the dining room where they'd be most effective. Julia, Amy, and Sonja spent the day doing their nails and hair. After trying on every outfit they'd brought, and all of one another's clothing, they ended up in shorts and T-shirts, so they wouldn't look as excited about all this as they felt.

Word of the party spread like wildfire. At eight Julia and her friends put out cheese and crackers and emptied chips and nuts into bowls. By ten, most of the food was gone. People they didn't know were searching through the refrigerator, grabbing apples, orange juice, anything they could find. Everyone Chase and Julia knew and about fifty people they didn't know were dancing in the living room or guzzling beer in the kitchen.

It was a hot, humid August night. With the house crammed with people the temperature seemed about two hundred degrees. Julia saw Sam when he helped Chase carry in a keg. "Hey, Julia," he said, nodding, not looking directly at her. Then he hung out with a group of guys laughing in the kitchen. Occasionally a girl would break into the knot to pull Sam out to dance, but sooner or later Julia would see him threading his way through the crowd back to the kitchen. He leaned against the counter, drinking a beer, wiping its icy wetness across his forehead and chest, and his T-shirt became transparent in its wetness, so she could see his dark muscles under the white cloth.

Several guys came up to Julia but she was cold to them all, until about midnight, when a tall blond guy, cute, lumbered up to her. "Wanna dance?"

"Sure." When he took her hand to lead her far into the living room, she pulled back. "Let's stay here. I need to keep an eye on things." What she needed was to be sure Sam could see her dancing. She moved deliberately, suggestively, swaying her hips and letting her head loll so that her long hair fell down her back.

"You're a good dancer," the blond guy said.

"Thanks." She looked over at Sam. He was watching her.

A slow dance came on. The blond-haired boy reached for Julia. She looked for Sam—was he going to stand there and watch this, too? Sam was looking at Chase, and Julia understood. Chase was hugging a redhead, a girl he'd met on the beach when they first arrived. Julia let the blond guy pull her against him. She danced, watching Sam over her partner's shoulder. The boy's every movement annoyed her. He was too tall, too heavy, too thick. As he pushed and pulled against her, he felt like the squirming toddlers she used to have to put up with when baby-sitting.

Chase went out the back door with the girl.

"'Scuse me," Julia said to the blond guy. Forcing herself out of his grip, she made a path through the crowd toward Sam.

Now Sam had his own blonde to contend with, a voluptuous young woman with a deep tan so oiled she looked like a piece of furniture. She had Sam pinned to the stove. With one hand she twirled a hank of blond hair, with the other she gestured as she talked.

". . . but I might take the year off and just do Europe."

"Hello, Sam," Julia said. Without hesitation or embarrassment, she slid between him and the blonde, putting her hands on his shoulders, pressing her body against his. She could feel the tension grip his body.

"Julia."

"Chase left."

"I know." Sam put his hands on Julia's shoulders and lightly pushed her away from him. "Julia—"

"Well, it's been great talking to you," the blonde said, sarcastically, moving back into the crowd.

"What?" Julia asked.

Sam swallowed. "I've been thinking . . . about us. About your family and mine. We can't just— Julia, it's got to be all or nothing."

Julia smiled. She said, "All."

She reached into the pocket of her shorts and brought out the key to the downstairs locked room. It gleamed against the palm of her hand.

For a long moment she was suspended in a capsule of time, a diamond of suspense, which blocked out all sound, so that she could clearly see the bodies of the dancers wavering hotly like a mirage in the far landscape of the dining room, and nearby, Sam's face, his black hair damp on his forehead.

Sam looked odd, almost angry. Then he grabbed Julia's hand. Forcing his way through the crowd, he hurried down the hall, to the room where the door was locked.

Julia opened the door with shaking hands. Once inside she locked it again. They didn't turn on the lights but made their way through the shadowy room by the light from the moon and the stars spilling in from the high, wide windows. The room was piled haphazardly with furniture from the rest of the house, and in one corner several dhurrie rugs had been brought in to protect them from spilled beer and dancing feet. Sam led Julia to the pile of thick carpeting.

Julia lay back and Sam stretched out against her, half on his side, half pressing against her. He kissed her for a long time. She ran her hands over his fine, silky hair, down the back of his neck where the bristles made her fingers tingle, over his shoulders, down the length of his torso.

He was exploring her, too, very gently running his hands over only her shoulders, arms, waist, and hips. She understood his restraint and loved him for it, as she loved him for everything he was, this man who as a little boy had wrestled with her, not hesitating to grab the crayon or Monopoly piece they were fighting over from her hand. Now they were grown-up, and she understood his tenderness. He did not want to hurt or shock her. She took his hand and placed it on her breast. She felt his stomach muscles contract in surprise.

"Julia. Do you know what you're doing?" His voice was tense and husky with desire.

"I want to make love with you, Sam."

He pushed himself up, and she sat up next to him. "Do you have a condom?"

She was shocked. "No." Her voice was small.

"That's just dumb. You shouldn't have sex with anyone without a condom. And you know that." He was staring straight ahead, and it was too dark to see his expression.

"You're not just anyone, Sam. And I don't want to have sex. I want to make love. With you." When he didn't reply, she said, "I've never done this before."

He turned on her then in a fury. "But I have. What do you know about me? I'm a senior in college. How many women do you think I've been with? I could have anything—"

"I trust you, Sam."

"Well, you shouldn't. You shouldn't just trust anybody. You should at least ask questions."

"All right. Do you have herpes?"

"No."

"AIDS?"

"No."

"Are you sure?" she asked, teasingly.

"Yes. I had a test this summer."

She was shocked into silence.

"I'm fine," he added. "I was just concerned because a girl I—went with—for a while last spring was pretty—active. I just wanted to be sure. I haven't been with anyone since then."

She put her hand on his back. "Then it's okay."

Sam cleared his throat. "I care a lot for you, Julia. I wouldn't want you . . . hurt."

Julia held his words in her mind, searching them, inspecting them for meaning. Did "I care a lot for you" mean only that he was fond of her, or did he love her? That was too much to hope for, so perhaps it meant he liked her very much—and then Sam turned and she saw in his face all she'd ever dreamed of. He pulled her T-shirt up over her head, and she slowly shook her long brown hair so it fell down her back. He slid her bra straps down her shoulders, then moved his hands behind her back and unsnapped her bra. It dropped silently to the rug. Sam looked at her breasts in the moonlight.

"God, Julia, you're so beautiful," Sam whispered.

His words made her shiver. He cupped her left breast in his hand so that her nipple pressed against his palm. His hand was warm. She could feel her heart thudding against his wrist.

Mirroring his movement, she put her hand on the left side of his chest so that she felt the marblelike hardness of his nipple.

When he gasped, she understood what friends had told her, that men were sensitive there, too. They sat facing each other, breathing rapidly, not speaking. Sam raised his arms to take off his white T-shirt and Julia saw the tufts of black hair under his arms, the swirl of black hair on his chest and belly. She slid her hand down his hard stomach and inside his jeans, and she had barely touched his pubic hair with her fingertips when almost roughly he pulled her shorts down, taking her underpants with them, and unzipping his jeans, pushed her back on the carpets. He knelt between her legs, supporting himself on his slender, muscular arms. Looking up at him, Julia let her eyes roam over his body from the hollow in his throat to his flat belly, his narrow hips, his upturned, dark, rigid penis. She tilted her pelvis eagerly, but to her surprise Sam slid downward and, running his hands over her body and pressing kisses against her breasts and belly, he nestled his face in her pubic hair. She gasped and grabbed his shoulders and tensed her muscles in surprise. She was embarrassed. She felt invaded, exposed. Looking down, she saw only Sam's shining black hair just above her abdomen, and she was about to speak, to stop him, when she heard him moan.

"Julia," Sam whispered. He put his hands on her hips, his hands warm against her skin, and steadied her as he moved his mouth over her skin with kisses so gentle, tender, and lingering that Julia realized in a rush of joy that Sam did love her, that he loved her *here*.

"Oh, sweet Sam," she replied. And as he brushed his lips over her curly pubic hair, over the hard rise of her pubis, then down into the intimate hot furrow where her thighs joined her crotch, Julia felt his tenderness, and knew she trusted him completely. She breathed in deeply. Closing her eyes, she relaxed and opened herself up to him. In psychology she'd been taught that the self is centered in the forehead exactly between the eyes, but now she knew that was wrong: her true and most intimate self was centered here, in this hot and secret depth between her legs. How could anyone ever, *ever* make love with a stranger, she wondered, and then her thoughts blurred, and she was overcome with sensation.

Sam was kissing her now and repeating her name. Julia felt the hardness of his teeth against her lips. His tongue was like a finger, probing and parting the silky grooves of her skin, pushing a little way into her vagina, pressing against the peak of skin at the top of her vulva. He pinched her nipples, causing lightning bolts of pleasure to pierce deep inside her. A dense cloud of sensation swelled up into her abdomen, then split apart, flooding her. Julia cried out and shuddered helplessly. Immediately, Sam rose up over her and entered her while she was still coming, and there was an almost intolerable moment of pain and rapture and a sense of being forced open past possibility. Then Sam cried out, collapsing against her, burying his moist, musky-smelling face in her hair.

Julia had never felt such pure joy as she did then, all entwined with Sam, engulfed in his heat and smell.

"Oh, Sam," she said, breathless.

Sliding off, he lay next to her, panting, holding her in his arms.

"You like that?" The boyish friend of her childhood was in his tone of voice.

She felt so at home. "I like that. I loved that."

"I love you, Julia," Sam said.

"Sam. I love you, too," she replied. She was tearful with happiness.

He stroked her hair. "Julia," he whispered.

They snuggled against each other. "What?" she answered.

"Just 'Julia,' " he repeated. "Julia."

She smiled in the darkness. Within moments they were both asleep, naked, uncovered, warm, and safe.

In the very early morning they were hungry. Pulling on their clothes, they stumbled upstairs. The house was wrecked. An enormous guy in a football jersey was snoring on the living room floor. Clearing a path through potato-chip bags, empty Styrofoam cups, beer bottles, and dishes full of cigarette butts, they pried a package of bagels from the freezer, nuked them in the micro-wave, and took them back to their locked room to eat with glasses of water.

Julia sank down onto one of the rugs that had been last night's mattress. "We're going to have to clean up before my parents get back."

"I wonder if Chase has seen the damage." Sam sat next to her, close enough to touch.

"You sure do think about my brother a lot." She smiled.

"We've been best friends for a long time."

"Are you going to worry about what he'll think about—us?"

Sam thought. "Yeah, sure." He chewed in silence. "I'm con-cerned about what everyone's going to think. Chase. Your par-ents. Mine."

Julia's heart became a separate creature, a tiny animal waiting breathlessly to hear whether it would be allowed to live or die.

"They might think it's cute that we're going out, or they might think it's strange."

Her heart relaxed slightly. "So we're going out," she said.

Sam looked at her. Gently he removed a bagel crumb from her lip. "More than that, I'd say."

"Oh, Sam, I love you."

"I love you, Julia."

"You do?"

Sam laughed and pulled Julia to him. They fell back together on the rugs. "I think I've been in love with you for a long time."

"I know what you mean."

"I've been thinking about it a lot this last week. How I've always had fun being around you. How I've always been glad when you came over with Chase. Even when we were little kids, I liked it when I touched you. Remember the game we had, touching tongues in the pool when I was trying to teach you to swim underwater with your eyes open? I think even then I was probably in love with you."

Julia lay dazed at Sam's words, happy.

"We've always had a good time together," Sam continued. "And I always thought you were good-looking. But recently . . ." He squeezed her hand.

Julia rolled next to Sam and twined her arms and legs all around his. With her ear next to his chest, she could hear his steadily beating heart.

After a while she said, "What are you going to do after you graduate?"

Sam kissed the top of her head. "My parents want me to go to medical school. I've got the hours in chemistry. But I want to go into research. I don't want to be a doctor—I don't like the blood, the disorder. I'd be much better in a lab. But I don't know if I can stand to disappoint them. They've done so much for me."

"They wouldn't want you to do something you'd hate."

"I don't know. I mean, I don't think they believe I'd really hate it. I've tried to talk to them about it. 'Just give it a try.' That's what they say, no matter how I approach it. 'Don't say no till you try.' The thing is, I know they'd pay my tuition for medical school, but anything else—I don't think I'd even feel right taking their money for anything else. I owe them so much already."

Julia flashed on Hal and P. J. Weyborn, their discreetly wealthy, determinedly generous lives. The walls, mantels, and side tables of their home held a multitude of photos of Sam: as a grinning baby, a toothy toddler, on his first tricycle, on his first two-wheeler, on ice skates, on a sled, on skis, in a swimming pool, on a pony, on a horse, on a Sunfish, in a scull, in the car they gave him for high-school graduation. They had given him every-thing they could and taken pride in the life they provided. And they'd taken pride in Sam.

"I know how you feel," Julia said. "Sometimes I wish my par-ents would just move to Mars for a few years. Or I wish I could turn them off for a while—you know, disconnect them and put them away in the closet just till I get steady on my own two feet. They're always knocking me off balance."

"Listen," Sam said, raising himself up on one elbow. "Sounds like people are waking up. We'd better get out there and help clean up."

"What will we say if Chase asks us where we were?" Julia asked.

"We'll just say we were together," Sam told her. He put his hand on her wrist. "And later, when I'm alone with him, I'll tell him the rest."

Cleaning up the house had been a fevered, concentrated activity. Everyone was grumpy, hung over, tired. The last two nights at the Vineyard were low-key. People packed up their gear, or collapsed in front of the television. Even Julia needed sleep; she and Sam satisfied themselves with hungry kisses on the back porch before going their separate ways to bed.

Back home, the rush of getting ready to return to school kept them busy during the day. They found ways to be together most of the evenings. They found ways to make love, in Sam's room when his parents were out for the evening, or in Sam's car. Every moment they spent with each other bound them more closely together.

Julia didn't know if Sam had told Chase about them until the day Chase left for college. He clomped up to Julia's room to give her one of his awkward good-bye hugs. His back was much thicker than Sam's, his shoulders broader. They hadn't been close recently, but as Julia felt her brother's warm solidity, she felt a surge of affection for him. She hoped he would find someone he loved as much as she loved Sam.

As if reading her mind, Chase stepped back. He blurted out: "It's cool about you and Sam. But be careful." His face flamed and he quickly turned, left the room, and galloped down the stairs.

Julia knew Chase meant contraception. She wanted to get some birth-control pills but hadn't had time. Sam was good about using condoms. She wanted to tell her parents, especially her mother, about Sam, but Jim and Diane were suddenly engrossed in their work again, and all at once the summer was over, Sam had driven away to Wesleyan, and Julia was back at Gressex for her last year.

As she walked through the campus to her classes, she realized that Gressex had, overnight it seemed, become a monstrous enemy to her—an institution with a hundred doors slamming into place, imprisoning her with examinations, regulations, study sheets, black ink, white paper, straight lines. Her friends talked about nothing but the agony of choosing the right college. In addition to her schoolwork, application forms piled up on Julia's desk instructing her to write essays about "my most important quality," or "the most significant moment in my life," or "how I envision the future of the world." The documents seemed to give off an angry static that radiated through her room, giving her headaches.

Sam drove up every weekend in September. He wrote her love letters that made her melt. He called her almost every night, when he could get through on the single phone in the dorm. He was as intensely in love with her as she was with him; Julia knew that. Yet they both knew that as the semester continued, with its required papers and tests, their time to be together would be eaten away to nothing.

What she had done was drastic. She knew that. But she wasn't sorry she'd done it. Her actions had gotten them here, in the Howard Johnson Motel, in bed, wrapped around each other.

She didn't want to go to sleep. On the other side of sleep was waking up, and facing the consequences. Sam wanted her to call her parents to let them know where she was. The thought made her wince. They'd be so gruesome, so tyrannical.

She was not going to go back to Gressex, no matter what. She was going to marry Sam if she could persuade him, and she thought she could. She'd persuaded him along this far. He had taken her away from Gressex. He was in her arms, spent and sleeping, and she held on to him for dear life. The bandages on her wrists itched. Otherwise she was fine.

Chapter 4
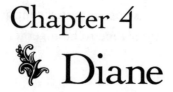
Diane

After the headmaster's call late Monday night, Diane couldn't sleep. She tossed in her bed, worrying about Julia, while by her side Jim slumbered deeply.

When the alarm went off at six-thirty, Diane was already dressed. When Jim came downstairs, showered and shaved and ready for the day, she handed him a cup of coffee and a cinnamon roll wrapped in a napkin. He looked surprised.

"We've got an appointment with Mr. Holmes," she reminded him.

"Oh, right," he said, looking at his watch.

"I'll drive. You can have your breakfast on the way."

"Good. Thanks."

They settled into his Volvo—her convertible made Jim nervous. As they negotiated the early-morning traffic, then sped along on Route 2, Jim listened to the news on the radio. How could he? Diane wondered. How could he think about the rest of the world? All she could think about was Julia.

They parked in the circular drive in front of the administration building at Gressex and walked through the echoing old halls to Mr. Holmes's office, which very much resembled a smoking room in a British men's club. Diane was surprised to see Sonja Stevens sitting primly on a leather sofa.

Mr. Holmes greeted them politely and shook their hands, but his expression was guarded. Indicating chairs near his desk, the headmaster said, "Please sit down. I have some more news for you. Or, rather, Sonja does. Sonja?"

Sonja perched on the edge of the sofa, leaning forward toward Diane as she spoke. "Julia's okay, Mrs. Randall. She really is. I just thought someone should know." She swallowed. "Julia . . . slit her wrists with scissors yesterday." Diane gasped and Sonja put out her hand. "No, really, she's all right. It's harder than you think, to slit your wrists. It really does hurt. She just sort of stabbed the point of the scissors in . . . she only made little cuts . . . she was doing it because Sam was there and she wanted him to take her away and marry her."

"She was composed enough to wrap her wrists and pack a duffel bag," Mr. Holmes added, his voice cold. "She was not in true psychological distress. She knew what she was doing."

"What did Sam say?" Diane asked, her voice shaky.

"I don't remember what he said exactly," Sonja replied. "I mean, he didn't want to take her with him, but that was the only thing he could do to get her to stop cutting herself." She turned to the headmaster and her face went scarlet, but she spoke, "She *was* in distress, Mr. Holmes. She was crying. She wasn't faking. She was very upset."

"Nevertheless, this is not the kind of behavior we can tolerate in a school like Gressex. We're deeply sorry for Julia, Mr. and Mrs. Randall, but you can understand, I'm sure, that the only option open to us is to expel her."

"You're kidding!" Diane exclaimed, so surprised she almost laughed.

"Is that really necessary?" Jim asked. "I would think that—"

"If you'll read Section Fourteen of the school handbook—" Mr. Holmes began, but Diane stood up, blood rushing to her face, anger shooting through her body, and announced, "Do you think we care if she's expelled or not? Do you think we even want her to return to this place—a place she hated so much she cut her wrists in order to get away? You'll be lucky if you don't have a lawsuit against you and your school, Mr. Holmes!"

"I'm sorry you feel that way," the headmaster said, his tone becoming syrupy. "I'm afraid I have no recourse but—"

"Sonja," Diane said, interrupting the man, crossing the room to take the girl's hands in her own, "tell me. Please. Anything else you can tell me about Julia."

Sonja looked wildly from Diane to the headmaster, then back to Diane. "I think she's really all right, Mrs. Randall. The cuts were just slits, really, and we bandaged them and she didn't need to go to the hospital or a doctor or anything. She looked happy when she went off with Sam. She was smiling." Tears filled the young woman's eyes. "I didn't know whether or not to tell you. I didn't want to worry you, but then this morning I talked to some friends and we agreed you should know."

"I'm glad you told me. Thank you, very much."

"Do you think they went back to Middletown?" Jim asked.

"I'm sure they did. Sam has classes, and you know Sam. And he really does love Julia. He'll take care of her."

"Thank you for saying that," Diane said. She hugged Sonja for a long moment, tears welling up and spilling down her cheeks.

"If you'd like, I'll discuss this matter with the disciplinary committee," Mr. Holmes told them.

"Don't bother!" Diane nearly spat the words out.

"Come on, Diane." Jim rose to put a restraining hand on her arm. "There's nothing more we can do here. Sonja, will you call us if you hear anything?"

"Of course."

"We called Mr. and Mrs. Weyborn this morning," the headmaster told them. "They assured us they would try to reach Sam, and they'll let us know as soon as they talk to him."

Jim and Diane spoke the necessary, empty words of polite parting, then walked back through the building and out into the sunlight in silence. They settled into the car, Jim behind the wheel now.

"It's nine-thirteen," he said, looking at his watch. "Let's say nine-fifteen. It took us forty-five minutes to get here from the house but that was in morning rush-hour traffic. I'll drop you at home and be able to get to the lab by ten if I hurry."

"Jim. How can we just go to work? We should do something."

"The only thing we can do is wait. Let's be logical. We know she's with Sam. We know Sam's levelheaded. He'll get in touch with us when the time is right. Or he'll call us if something is terribly wrong. The Weyborns are trying to reach him at Wesleyan. They've got several calls in. We're doing all we can."

"But she tried to slit her wrists!"

"Sonja said the cuts weren't deep. She didn't have to go to the emergency room. The bleeding stopped before she left. Come on—think about it. Think about Julia. She's dramatic."

"This is more than dramatic! This is—stupid! Self-destructive. It's crazy."

"Teenagers do stupid things. And Julia wasn't trying to destroy herself. She was manipulating Sam."

"If she succeeds in dying it won't matter what her motivation is, will it?" Diane dug in her purse for a handkerchief. She was weeping from fear and helplessness. "I'm going to drive down to Middletown and find her."

Jim turned and placed a sympathetic hand on Diane's shoulder. "I know." He patted her consolingly. "I know you want to rush down and rescue her. But, Diane, you can't."

"Why not?"

"Honey, Julia's not a child anymore. She's eighteen. She wants to get married." After a moment's silence he said carefully, "She's in love."

"Yes, with *Sam*!" Diane cried.

"What could you possibly have against Sam? He's a good guy. He's smart, reliable, we've known him forever—"

"Oh, I like Sam, but he's so predictable. He's so on track, right through college, into grad school. He'll have Julia working as a waitress to support him. She'll never get to travel, have a career, experience life; she'll never reach a fraction of her potential!"

"Her potential for what? What's important, Diane? Maybe this way Julia will be happy."

"Oh, yes, you would settle for 'happiness' for your daughter," Diane said scornfully, her tears drying up, her face flushing as her fear fueled her anger. "Let her be barefoot and pregnant in the kitchen, cooking food for the man all her life. You wouldn't let Chase get married now, become a waiter, and stay in a house dusting and baking pies. Would you? Would you?" Before Jim could answer, she continued. "No, of course not. *Chase* is brilliant. You certainly want your son to reach his full potential, and you can't deny it. But you don't want the same thing for your daughter."

Quietly, Jim said, "I want the same thing for both my children.

Happiness. It just happens that Julia's the one who wants to get married now, not Chase."

"I know," Diane agreed bleakly, her anger subsiding. Sighing, she leaned back against the headrest.

Jim started the car and drove out of the school grounds. They rode in silence for a while. Diane stared out the window at the mellow fields and forests that bordered Route 2. She was always surprised to come across this rural beauty so near Cambridge and Boston, and she was surprised now that she could appreciate it while filled with worry for her daughter. Several maples still flamed with color. Farm stands at the side of the road caught Diane's eye. Long tables set out under the autumn sun held buckets of glowing golden chrysanthemums; straw baskets were piled with rosy apples, pyramids of green and orange and striped and spotted gourds.

Her stomach growled. She'd had only a quick cup of coffee early that morning. What kind of mother am I? she wondered, not for the first time. My daughter's slashed her wrists and run away from school, and I'm admiring the landscape and longing for a glass of apple cider.

Perhaps she hadn't been a good mother. Just as she hadn't been a good daughter. She was too selfish. Indeed, even now, autumnal brass shapes bloomed in her mind; if she had her pad and pencil with her now, she'd be sketching. That was her gift, and her shame.

"That headmaster is a pompous jerk," Jim was saying. "All he cares about is expelling Julia and erasing her existence from Gressex before she can leave any kind of blot on its record."

"Um," Diane replied absently. The headmaster didn't interest her. He'd been supercilious, couching his self-interest in convoluted expressions of concern for Julia's welfare. Now that Julia had run away from Gressex Academy, he wished to wash his hands of her—fast.

"I don't give a damn if she's expelled," Diane said. "I don't even want her at that place if there's so little attention paid to the kids that they can go around attempting suicide. I want to find her, and bring her home, and talk some sense into her."

They pulled into their driveway, and Jim put the car in park but did not turn off the engine. "Look," he said, facing Diane, speaking with forced patience, "there's nothing you can do now. You know Sam's sensible. He's bound to call you as soon as he can. He won't do anything stupid. Nothing will be gained by your flying down to Middletown and knocking on doors in a panic."

Diane's shoulders sagged. "You're right. I know you're right."

"I've got to go. Call me if you hear anything."

"I will."

Leaving the car, she slammed the door, frustrated with Jim and his cool logic. Then a thought hit her, and she hurried into the house and back to the kitchen. A light was blinking on the answering machine. Trembling, she hit the wrong button. It took several minutes to find the message: Peter Frost wanted her to call as soon as possible. Peter Frost. Since the phone call from Gressex the night before, she'd almost forgotten about him. She dialed the number he'd left and spoke with him briefly, arranging for him to arrive after lunch to start looking through her mother's things in the attic. Well, she thought as she went up to change into jeans and a sweatshirt, at least the search would be a distraction.

While she waited for the FBI agent to arrive, she called both her brothers and her sister to see if they'd heard from their mother. No one had, but when Diane heard Susan's warm voice, she told her about Julia, her voice breaking as she spoke.

"Oh, honey, I'm so sorry. You must have been out of your mind with worry last night. But Julia will be all right."

"I hope so." Diane sighed.

"I know she will," Susan said, "I just know it," and even though that wasn't logical either, still Diane felt calmer when she hung up the phone.

"Hello," Peter Frost said pleasantly as he came in the front door that afternoon.

"I see you didn't take my advice," Diane remarked. Wear old washable clothes, she'd warned him earlier, the attic's filthy. But here he was in a three-piece suit. His short black hair was shining, as perfect as a helmet.

"This is all I brought with me from Virginia," he told her. "I left my jeans at home."

The idea of Peter Frost in jeans and a T-shirt was oddly exciting. He really is a gorgeous man, Diane thought as she took his trench coat and hung it in the closet. Undoubtedly the FBI used that. "Well, Peter," she could just hear them say, "we've got another invasion-of-privacy job. It's a woman this time, so we'll send you. Shine up those pearly whites and get to work." She smiled in spite of herself.

"Is your answering machine on?" he asked.

"Yes."

"Good. I'm expecting some calls."

"So am I. Well, not expecting them, but hoping for some." She paused, then blurted out: "My daughter's run away from boarding school."

"How old is she?"

"Eighteen."

Peter smiled—a wry, sideways smile that brought a dimple to

his left cheek. Suddenly he seemed human. "I have a son who's twenty. The year he was eighteen was the longest year of my life."

"Is he okay now?"

"Yes." He smiled again. "But I'm exhausted."

"Your wife must be, too."

"I wouldn't know. My wife and I've been divorced for a few years. We seldom talk."

"Oh. I'm sorry."

"I'm not."

The blue in his eyes seemed to darken, contradicting his words, and for a moment Diane stood looking up at the man, curious about what emotions he might be hiding. Then she shook her head and turned to mount the stairs.

"I hate letting go of control of my children," she confessed over her shoulder. "I hate giving them the responsibility for their own lives."

"I know what you mean," he replied.

Yes, she thought, thinking of the air of tacit but powerful authority with which Peter Frost moved, I'll bet he does know what I mean.

Still she felt oddly vulnerable as she led the stranger through the long second-floor hallway, past bedrooms and baths, to the attic door at the end of the hall. She hadn't shut the bedroom door this morning and Kaitlin hadn't been up here yet, and as they passed, the open door exposed a tousled bed and a floor littered with Jim's pajamas, jockey shorts, and socks. Trust Jim. He could locate a polyneucleotide chain in DNA but he couldn't find the clothes hamper in his own bathroom.

"You have a lovely home," Peter said. "And a great backyard." He was looking out the window at the end of the hall, and Diane smiled, surprised and pleased by his sensitivity, by the way he purposely directed his gaze outward.

"Thank you." With her hand on the doorknob, she admitted, "It's hard to let a stranger into our home."

"I'm sure it is. I'm sorry to trouble you. I'm trying to get clearance to tell you more—when you understand, I know you'll feel better about this."

"Well"—she shrugged and opened the door—"it's up these stairs."

The attic was one open room but so divided by bookcases, piles of cardboard boxes, and clutter that it seemed to be broken up into shadowy chambers. She sensed Peter Frost standing quietly behind her.

The kitchen was the heart of her house; the attic was the memory. It slumbered in the slanted light, full of dreams of the days when the children were babies and Diane wore a size ten. She led him past boxes of fine, soft newborn clothes and blankets that she was saving for her grandchildren, past quilted garment bags of dresses that she kept only because she couldn't bear to see them go, past open trunks jumbled full of Christmas wrapping paper, pastel woven Easter baskets, and orange plastic pumpkins in which the children had collected their Halloween loot. This Halloween Diane had not carved jack-o'-lanterns or roasted the pumpkin seeds for them all to munch on as they listened to their old, scratched record of "The Legend of Sleepy Hollow." Without young children, a year could slip by, unmarked in its seasons.

"Good God! What's all that?"

She followed Peter Frost's gaze and laughed. "Treasure," she told him. Near the boxes of children's costumes, feathered Indian headbands, spangled tutus, capes and crowns and swords and shields were several boxes overflowing with jewels and gold. Even in the dim light, the treasure gleamed and beckoned. "Costume jewelry. Imperfect bits and pieces. I used to buy bags of this stuff at cut-rate prices, toss in anything broken or left over from my own work, and make pirate's loot for Chase and Julia. We'd have treasure hunts on rainy days. I suppose I should donate all this to some day-care center."

Diane moved past him and knelt before a chest. She put both hands into it and lifted up two scoops of glittering gemstones. Emeralds, rubies, diamonds, rings and chains and coins rained back down into the chests with tempting dainty clinks. False jewels, each one was like a memory of the days when her children were blessedly young, innocent, safe, when Chase and Julia were rich within the realm of her love.

Now she knew those days were treasures. *Then* she'd thought the noise and mess and unpredictability of each day would drive her mad.

She rose. "Attics are like private museums, aren't they?" And it's *my* life on display, she thought silently.

"I miss having an attic," Peter said. "My ex-wife has the house and all the photo albums, the memorabilia of my past."

Diane looked at him and thought his eyes were sad. She felt drawn to him, wanting to touch him gently, in consolation, but instead she turned away.

Still, she appreciated his kindness in offering up bits of his life; it made it easier for her to open hers to him. She brushed her hands together as if removing dust and said briskly, "Well, you're lucky, in a way. Most of this stuff is useless, I suppose. Taking up space." She held up a bit of white sheet wrapped around a Styrofoam ball and trimmed in orange. "Casper, for example. Our wounded Halloween ghost. We used to hang him from the hall chandelier every Halloween, but gradually he became rather—seedy. I guess I thought I'd fix him up sooner or later, but now my children are too old to get excited about Halloween." She looked around her. "I really should clean this place out. Throw stuff away."

"No," he said, "Keep it. Someday you might enjoy remembering times past."

Diane stared at Peter, surprised and touched. He returned her gaze. After an intensely intimate moment, she had to force herself to drop her eyes. Turning away from him, she moved down through the crooked aisle to the spot where her mother's boxes stood.

"Nothing's marked or sorted. Susan and Mother and I just sort of tossed stuff into whatever box was handy. Mother was a pack rat, and I am, too, I'm afraid. My God, I didn't realize I'd brought back so much junk."

An odd thing had happened in her parents' house in July: Diane and Susan had reverted to a childish sibling rivalry. They'd cloaked it within adult gestures of generosity and goodwill, but it had been there. Their mother had always loved Susan the best of the girls, and Diane didn't blame her. Susan had been the good girl. Well, all the children had been good, freed by Diane's rebellious black-sheepdom.

Until she was in her forties, Diane had been bitterly stung by the multitude of pictures of Susan's life that her mother displayed in her house: Susan graduating from college, Susan in a fabulous lace wedding gown, Susan and her mother smiling through tears in the hospital when Susan's first son had been born with both Susan's husband and her mother in attendance. God, Mother, it's as if I didn't even exist for you! Diane had thought. She'd been miserable, ill with envy.

But as her own children began to enter adolescence, Diane

remembered her youth. Her mother had no pictures of her progress through life because Diane hadn't had any taken. Diane
hadn't gone to her own graduation or been married in a church
in a gorgeous gown. Jim would have gone along with anything,
but she'd insisted on a small private wedding without the fairy-
tale trimmings. She'd disdained the ceremonies and rituals of her
parents' lives. Their home, filled with its predictable, ordinary
things, had smothered her.

Yet this past summer when her mother dispensed with the
collected objects of her life, Diane had grabbed all she could.
Not the china or crystal or silver or antiques; she had enough of
that stuff. Susan, who served her family on brightly colored,
expensive plastic plates—because her four boys were such
klutzes—had been thrilled to inherit some of her mother's beautiful things.

Diane had chosen to take entire unsorted contents of desks,
and boxes of clothes from her mother's attic. She'd blithely insisted she really wanted her mother's very old dresses, hats,
scarves.

"They're so terribly out of style, and you couldn't possibly fit
into them," Susan had said.

"Oh, they're not for me," Diane replied. "They're for Julia.
Girls love old clothes. Besides, you know me. I get ideas for my
jewelry from all sorts of things."

"Darling," her mother'd said, "are you sure you want to take
all that old junk? I don't even remember what's in half of those
boxes."

"It'll be fun sorting through them, Mother," Diane had insisted.
She'd been pleasant, but adamant.

"I think some of my old diaries are in there."

"Mom!" Susan exclaimed greedily. "I didn't know you ever
kept diaries!"

"When you children were very young I did. I don't know where I found the time. They aren't very interesting. I can't imagine why I bothered."

Diane had rummaged through the cartons as soon as she'd gotten back to her house with them and had found the diaries. Her mother was right. They weren't very interesting.

" '. . . Diane smiled at me this morning. The doctors say a baby one week old can't see and differentiate and smile, that it's only gas, but I know they're wrong. I saw her lying awake in her crib and I said, 'Hello, my sweetie pie,' and she smiled at me.' "

" '. . . The morning sickness is so bad that today I just lay on the kitchen floor while Diane toddled back and forth, taking every single pot and pan from the cupboards and arranging them to her satisfaction under the kitchen table. Yesterday she took all the shoes out of the shoe bag in the closet and put them in the bottom drawers of my dresser. They're still there. Our house is beginning to look rather bizarre.' "

" '. . . The baby doll we gave Diane when we brought Bert home from the hospital is abandoned under a chair. I've tried to encourage Diane to feed and dress her baby when I do, but she shows no interest. Fortunately she does love to color, and we keep her supplied with huge pads of blank paper and fat crayons. Diane says the baby is noisy. Well, she's right, he is. I think he must have what they call colic. He cries every evening from five until eight, three hours straight of crying, and nothing soothes him. Mother says to dip a pacifier in sugar and scotch, but I wouldn't dream of it. I just rock him and rock him and now and then Al takes a turn so I can read to Diane or take a bath.' "

The diaries went on for years, trailing off just after Art was born. Diane found them oddly impersonal. Her mother had recorded the minutiae of their lives without including any sense of how she felt about it all. Had her mother ever wept with exhaustion or regretted the changes in her body, the thickening of her hips? Did she feel passionate love for her husband? She must have—look at all the times she got pregnant! Had she never desired a dress with a plunging neckline or had a secret crush on a movie star or longed to travel to China?

Perhaps not. Perhaps her mother had been the sort of woman Susan was—unselfish, devoted to . . . *completed by* her family.

Diane had been a terrible daughter, and a terrible sister. She had loved her children and put their needs first, but she had never been completed only by her family. Always there were other things she enjoyed all by herself—friends, travel, work, books, a sense of adventure.

Of course everyone felt private, slightly guilty pleasures, like the tang of lust she felt now for Peter Frost.

Looking around the attic, she said, "I suppose I brought at least twenty boxes back from my mother's." Running her hand over some quilted blue dress bags, she said, "These are filled with dresses she wore as a young woman, and some old grungy furs. Some have beads I thought I might cut off for jewelry . . . and I thought my daughter might like to have the rest someday."

Her daughter.

Where was Julia now? Was she safe?

In July Julia had gone down with Diane to help pack up the house, but the old odds and ends had bored her and she'd offered to help by cooking lunch and dinner for everyone. They'd been a real mutual-admiration society, Jean and Julia—Jean praising Julia's pastas and pies and Julia babbling on about Jean's wonderful bright big old kitchen with its wooden table and thick English-pottery mixing bowls. When her daughter, her mother, and her sister grew engrossed in an enthusiastic conversation about various chocolate-cake recipes, Diane had felt oddly slighted.

Now she wondered: Had she been too introspective this summer, mourning her father, remembering her own youth? Had Julia been dropping hints about her emotional stability that Diane just hadn't been observant enough to notice? No. It had been a happy time.

Diane knew she couldn't be happy again until she knew Julia was safe.

She moved to the largest pile of boxes. "Her diaries are in here—all about her babies. Photograph albums, too. I know, because when I brought them home I looked through them. But over here, these boxes—well, they're filled with God knows what."

She and Peter Frost knelt beside the tall pile of boxes. A shiver passed over her. She was seldom this close to such an attractive, unknown man. Jim's hands were slender with long, tapered fingers. Peter Frost's hands were broad, massive, thick, and tufts of dark hair crept under his white shirt cuffs and down past his wrists. She imagined that his naked body would be almost shaggy. She found herself imagining that his lovemaking would not be gentle and civilized but demanding and greedy.

His hand accidentally touched hers as they pulled open the folded lids of the first box. Diane drew her hand back.

"How do you want to do this?" she asked. She felt herself flush. "I mean, would it be faster if we each took a box? There are so many."

"I'd rather take my time and be thorough," he told her.

I'll bet you would, Diane thought, surprising herself. She rose. "There's an empty box over there. We can use it to put stuff in so we don't end up with a pile on the floor."

"Fine." He crossed the wide attic and got the dusty cardboard box.

It was a cool October day. The rain had stopped, but clouds

still dimmed the sky, parting as the wind moved them to let sudden shafts of sunlight pierce through the gabled windows. In spite of the electric lights, the air in the attic was a shadowy blue. Peter Frost's breath sounded intimately close and loud.

The boxes revealed a jumble of letters, photos, knickknacks, jewelry, postcards, chipped souvenirs, scarves, diplomas, medals. Peter Frost insisted that they open every envelope and shake it to see if a locket was inside.

One box, which had to date back to around 1968, contained jubilant letters and postcards from Diane as she toured Europe from Yugoslavia to the Netherlands, a brilliant red peasant babuska still folded and creased, not Jean White's style at all, and a heavy, gaudy necklace made from links of brass and a mélange of glittering beads—Diane's first wildly successful jewelry design, beautifully intricate in an Eastern Orthodox way. Nestled with those items were photographs and letters from Susan, a Navy nurse stationed in Soc Trang; letters and photographs of Bert on a destroyer in the Pacific; and incomprehensible scribbles meant to be letters from Art, sent from Vietnam along with an ornate hookah pipe about which Jean White probably hadn't a clue.

Diane removed and inspected each item before dispatching it to the pile of examined objects. She worked in silence, but she was filled with emotion. How her mother had loved all her children! How democratic and nonjudgmental she'd been, treasuring each relic of their very different lives. How generous her love had been.

After two hours, Diane rose from the box and stretched.

"My back's breaking," she said. "Can we take a break and go down and have some coffee? And I need to check my answering machine."

Peter Frost looked at the jumble around him.

"All right."

They clattered together down the stairs, past the bedroom where Kaitlin was running the vacuum, to the kitchen. The day was still so dim and dreary she flicked on all the lights.

The answering machine was blinking: message waiting. She flicked the button to rewind, then to play.

"Hi, Diane." Susan's warm voice filled the room. "Just calling to see if you've heard from Julia. Call me when you get a chance. Everything's going to be just fine, you know. Love ya!"

Her sister's affection and concern brought tears to her eyes, and Diane turned away quickly from Peter before he could see.

"I'm going to heat a muffin. Want one? They're good—honey and date." Her words sounded oddly flirtatious to her ears and she blushed, glad to be busy with the coffee.

"That would be nice."

Peter Frost's presence filled the kitchen. As she moved around setting out place mats and knives and the butter dish, she was aware of his eyes on her, and she was glad to have something to keep her busy. Finally there was nothing to do but wait for the coffee to drip through the filter and the muffins to heat. She leaned against the counter, folding her arms over her chest. He was standing near the microwave. On purpose?

Looking up at him, she said, "I *hate* just waiting like this. I feel so helpless."

"Do you have any idea where your daughter is?" he asked.

"I think so. She went off with her boyfriend, a nice young man—my son's best friend, actually. So I don't think she's in any danger, but still . . ."

"Still, you need to know. I guess it's the first time she's done something like this."

"Yes." A thought hit her, and she shook her head slowly. "You must run into this sort of thing often in your work."

"Sometimes."

"Do you like your work?" she asked, genuinely curious.

"Very much."

"Why?"

"It's important. It's necessary. It's exciting, sometimes."

"Dangerous?"

He smiled. "I don't do much that's dangerous anymore."

Suddenly, she wanted to hear about the dangerous things he had done. She imagined him moving stealthily through the dark, carrying secrets.

He stepped close to her and reached out his arm. Diane froze. He picked up the sugar bowl from where it sat just inches from her elbow.

"May I?"

The microwave pinged. Diane put the muffins on a plate, poured mugs of coffee, and gratefully sank into a chair across the table from him. She watched as he stirred sugar into his mug.

"And I like to travel," he added. He smiled. "I get to meet interesting people."

She smiled at the implied compliment. "I travel a lot in my work, too," she told him. "I love new sights, new experiences. New tastes." Why, she wondered, did every single thing suddenly seem sexual?

"You don't seem like the traveling type," he remarked.

"Why not?" she asked, insulted.

In answer, he gestured around the kitchen. She saw her life reflected here through his eyes: the pegboard on the wall cluttered with cartoons, letters, invitations, appointment cards; the counters decorated with clever ceramic canisters and a multitude of domestic appliances; the sparkling white curtains and thick dish towels; the bowl filled with fresh fruit in the middle of the table.

"It's all camouflage," she told him, pleased with her answer and thrilled with the understanding smile that he flashed her. Again a flame of desire sparked through her.

The phone rang.

Julia! Diane hurried to answer it.

"It's for you," she said, disappointment creasing her face. She handed the phone to Peter Frost and waited just a few feet away from him, listening as he spoke.

"We have some information about your mother," he told her when he put the receiver back. "She checked in to the Georges Cinq about a week ago but checked out after a few days. No forwarding address. But at least we know where she started from."

"But not where she is now," Diane said. Something crumbled inside her, and she began to cry. She put her hands over her face.

"I'm sure we'll find her," Peter Frost assured her. "She's not in danger, you know."

"I know, but it's all too much! My mother and my daughter both missing—" She couldn't speak for her tears.

"Perhaps they like to travel. Like you."

She raised her head to glare at him. "They aren't like me at all! Not either one of them! They're both babies!"

"They'll be all right. I'm sure they'll be all right," he said. They were standing face-to-face, and he reached out to pat her shoulder reassuringly. His hand was large, warm, and steady, and all at once Diane was vividly aware of her breasts beneath the cotton of her sweatshirt. His hand remained an extra, significant, few seconds. He was so very much *there* with her at this moment that Diane felt the strangest desire simply to bend her head and rub her cheek along his hand, to touch him, skin to skin.

Instead, "I'm okay now. Thanks," she said, looking up at him. He returned her look evenly, and for a moment they were joined on a knife edge of understanding. "We should head back up," Diane said, grateful that her voice worked.

"Yes, we should."

Back in the attic they worked quickly in silence. Lust had joined them like a third person, reclining on a nearby box, perfuming the air, grinning wickedly. She'd never had an affair, had never even been really tempted, although she had enjoyed the occasional attentions of interested men. She'd been glad to know she was attractive; and if now and then her body surprised her by being interested in return, that had been pleasant, too, providing her with a little lift like any special physical treat—a massage, a new dress.

What she felt now was different, and troubling. When Peter took off his suit jacket and turned to drape it over a box, she could not keep herself from studying his body, which under his shirt was well-defined and muscular. He must have to keep himself in good shape, she mused. As he unbuttoned and rolled up his sleeves, he smiled at her as if he knew her thoughts, and several times that afternoon when she handed him a box or took an item from him, his hand brushed hers, causing a spark of desire to leap within her.

There were so many boxes. Diane worked steadily, glad to use the flashes of adrenaline that her anxiety about Julia and lust for Peter Frost sent rocketing through her.

One carton held a number of promising small containers that upon inspection divulged hundreds of recipes on note cards, miscellaneous old sterling flatware loosely tied up with ribbons, three brass napkin rings, cracked goblets, decorative tea tins, pretty bits of broken porcelain, tubes of glue, jars of silver polish. The most fascinating find of the day for Diane was an ancient trunk that opened to reveal mementos from Jean's college days. Train tickets, playbills, folders with class notes and schedules, phone numbers, addresses, photographs, pens and pencils and erasers and boxes of carbon paper, textbooks and writing tablets had been tossed in carelessly, a jumble. Several copies of the same journal were piled in the bottom of the trunk; Diane lifted them out and read the black letters on the maroon cover: *War Stories*. Opening one to the table of contents, she saw her mother's maiden name listed next to an article entitled "A War Widow's Tale." Vaguely she remembered her mother talking about this, long ago, but she'd never read it, and so she kept one issue out to look at when she found time.

By the end of the afternoon, they had gone through most of the boxes without any luck. Diane was both relieved and disappointed when Peter Frost rose, rolled down his shirtsleeves, and picked up his jacket.

"I guess we'd better stop for the day."

"Yes," she agreed. It was almost dark outside, and the attic shadows were thick in spite of the electric lights.

"I'll be back tomorrow morning. We should be able to finish this in an hour or two."

"Fine. I'll wait for you." Her words sounded coquettish when she meant them only as a matter of fact. She felt her face flush and quickly pushed past him and down the stairs. Hurrying into the kitchen, she checked the machine again: no messages.

"I can understand what a difficult time this must be for you," Peter said, coming up behind her. His voice was deep and resonant; she could feel it in her chest. "I really do appreciate all your time and trouble."

She turned. He was standing very close to her. "Thank you," she replied.

"You've worked hard. Let me buy you a drink. Or dinner." The tone of his voice made the invitation sound only kind, not seductive, but she shook her head.

"I need to stay here. In case Julia calls. But thank you." Then, boldly, she added, "Perhaps another time."

He smiled at her—not his wry, sideways smile but a gentle smile that brought a glow to his eyes. "Good."

Diane couldn't bring herself to move for one long moment, and then she roused herself and said, "I'll get your coat."

She brushed past him, her body inches away from his as she slipped through the kitchen doorway into the hall. He followed her and took his trench coat from her, then left, with a nod of good-bye.

She walked through her house, gathering her thoughts. It was after five. Kaitlin was gone. Jim was not yet home. A quiche that Kaitlin had made sat on the counter ready to be heated. This entire day had passed without a word from Julia. The big house felt cold and empty now, and Diane was overcome with sensations that felt like the common flu. She was tired and light-headed. Well, she had a right to be after a sleepless night and this long day of waiting and worrying.

She dialed the Weyborns' number and got their answering machine. "Hi, it's Diane. I'm just calling to ask if you've heard from Sam," she said into the electronic silence. She knew the Weyborns would call her the moment they heard anything; still she felt better after trying to reach them. She didn't know Sam's number at Wesleyan, or she would have tried him, too. She couldn't think of anything else to do but wait.

She climbed the stairs, went into her bedroom, and for the first time in years, she crawled into bed with her clothes on.

The night before she'd hardly slept. Now she closed her eyes, hoping at least to rest. But it was like trying to relax inside a bomb shelter; her nerves were jangled with anxiety. Jim, she was sure, was plodding away methodically at work, his hands calm, his mind clear. No wonder he loved chemistry: DNA, nature, had not bound him with unremitting ferocity to his children. Jim's life proceeded along a straight, true line, while hers had been a tangle of love and ambition, work and motherhood.

When Chase was born, she and Jim had intended to deliver the baby together in a Lamaze childbirth. Diane followed through, panting and blowing and cursing and weeping. Jim fainted in the delivery room when his son's bloody head crowned in Diane's swollen vagina. She had her sister, Susan, fly up to help her through Julia's birth.

In the very early days of their family's life, Diane had thought it only natural that she would be more closely connected to her son than Jim was; Chase had been in her body, she had nursed him, there was an instinctive logic involved. But after six months, then a year, and after Julia's birth, Diane realized that she was connected to her children in a way Jim would never be. It was an invisible, unbreakable bond that was more than chemistry— it was like radar, or the eerie communications of whales. She could put a closed door or half of Cambridge between herself and her children and still her senses remained alert, everything pricked up, her body nervous to the very bones, until she was back again, holding her babies safely in her arms. Nature had not deigned to burden Jim with a similar obsession. He could read while Chase cried in the other room. He could relax and talk with friends while Julia toddled around in a wet diaper on a hot day. And he responded strangely to their many childhood illnesses, in an old-fashioned stiff-upper-lip way that he must have learned from his aunts. It was not that he didn't want to comfort his children when they had colds or chicken pox or tummy aches; it was that he *couldn't*. He seemed almost to resent the children for being sick.

Friends told her not to worry—men were baffled by infants, but as the children grew older, fathers got more involved, more interested. Yet Diane realized something else was at work here, something personal. Orderly, logical Jim was incapable of dealing with the general mess and noise of children. She thrived on it, the tugs and tears and babble and urgent needs. Jim retreated. He'd loved children as a concept, but he found the reality irritating and even frightening, far past the control of his most meticulous arrangements.

Somehow during her pregnancies and the early years of her children's lives, Diane had managed to keep Arabesque afloat—barely. At night when the babies slept she experimented in the basement with bead designs, then took patterns and the materials to the women who strung the necklaces and bracelets for her in their homes. She was happy in a way she'd never known before; and if she was tired, it was in a dazed, blissful way—much like the moments just after making love, when all senses were satisfied. Walking the floor with her babies at night, she hummed ancient lullabies; the tunes and her exhaustion worked like hallucinogens, so that new designs floated up around her in the darkened room. She realized she was immensely proud of herself for the most natural deeds: keeping her son and daughter safe and healthy, nursing them through colds, teaching them to brush their teeth, soothing them when they were unhappy.

Jim spent more and more time at his lab. When Diane told him he had to help out more because she wanted to start a new line of jewelry, he told her he couldn't. He was at a crucial point in his work. He didn't want to chance losing his grant. He suggested that they hire a housekeeper/baby-sitter, and so Diane did. She put an ad in the *Boston Globe,* interviewed fourteen applicants, chose one, wrote out a list of duties, and trained her. But she felt betrayed. Before they were married, Jim had yearned for children and he'd assured her he'd share equally in their care. Now, when she reminded him of his early promises, he snapped, "I *will* help! In just a few more weeks!"

As the children grew from infants into toddlers, Diane realized that as far as Jim was concerned, his work would be continually at a crucial stage. Her exhaustion was tempered by contentment that sometimes deepened into a feeling of smug superiority. If nature had caused her to undergo the difficulties of pregnancy and the pain of childbirth, it had also rewarded her with a hormonal pleasure from which Jim was excluded. Her children's existences satisfied her profoundly; they were her treasures, her pride, her joy. Nature had not provided Jim with equal rewards, and she understood clearly why he searched for fulfillment in his work.

Still, she grew increasingly frustrated by his reluctance to enter into the scramble of their daily life. She tried reason; she tried cunning. Nature had brought her into contact with her children with inescapable violence. She would draw her husband into family life with relentless, gentle requests. When they ate dinner together, she asked him for help with just one task: bathing one child, or helping Chase scrape gum off his shoe. Usually Jim responded with absentminded acquiescence. Then he either did the deed incompletely or forgot all about it. She felt overwhelmed, and finally angry. For the first time since the children were born, her own work was tugging at her now like yet another child.

A design had been haunting Diane, floating ghostlike at the back of her mind. One afternoon, when Chase was in preschool and Julia was napping, she sat down with pen and paper and sketched it out: a necklace of metal links leading to an octagon, cast in brass, with beads and tiny bells hung on colored silk cords from eight corners. She designed coordinating accessories: earrings, bracelets, belts. She carved the wax model and took it to Providence to have a mold made and the pieces cast, and on a hunch, she dipped into her savings and paid to have a gold-plated, sterling-silver version cast as well. She took the jewelry to Bonwit Teller herself because she had a friend from art school who worked there, and they took her entire lot on consignment. They sold out within a week.

She began to work furiously, designing a line of jewelry that she seemed to have been dreaming of all her life. But the basement wasn't large enough, bright enough, safe enough—or private enough. She couldn't concentrate even when the housekeeper was watching the children. A thump, a cry, and her mind flashed away from her work to worry whether a child had been hurt, whether she should rush upstairs to hug and console.

So she'd rented a small space on the second floor of a building near Porter Square in Cambridge. The front room was for the office manager she hired and their files of invoices and orders. Behind was Diane's studio, a large open space with a wooden floor and a lovely big sink, a wall of windows, a skylight. Now she could have her workbench, acid bath, acetylene and propane torches, drill press, polishers, and the hand tools that could have hurt a child badly in the blink of an eye. Here, she designed and experimented, coming up with elaborate, exotic jewelry, pieces like mazes, knots, labyrinths studded with dark, unusual gems and stones: agates, cat's eye, topaz, peridot, jade.

At Christmas she gave her mother one of the most expensive, most ornate necklaces.

"How amazing," Jean said when she called on Christmas morning after opening her present. "Do you know what your jewelry is like? It's as if you had lifted up the designs from our Bokhara and made them three-dimensional."

Diane was stunned. Her mother was right—that design had been waiting for her in her memory since she was a child.

When Jean and Al White were married, they'd received, among a score of silver trays and electric toasters, a gorgeous Turkish rug, obviously old, but still vivid with color, deep red, dark blues, black. The card, addressed to them both, said merely, "Congratulations on your marriage." It hadn't been signed. They asked their friends and finally assumed that some friend of Jean's father, who was in the Navy and had at one time traveled a great deal, had sent it. In fact, both Jean's and Al's parents had many friends in all corners of the world. They would find out sooner or later who had given it to them, they thought. Then they were married, and although they never forgot the mystery, they never had time to solve it, either.

Now Diane said to her mother, "I guess that's been hiding away in my brain all these years."

"I've been studying Bokharas, by the way," Jean continued. "I even had an expert out to the house to look at ours. He said we shouldn't be using it on the floor; we should hang it on a wall, or even give it to a museum. It's that valuable."

Diane laughed. "I'd hate to think of all the baby goo I put there."

"Mr. Yarinen says our rug is probably one of the famous 'red rugs' made by the Turkoman nomads in Russia. It's about a hundred and fifty years old. Amazing how the color has lasted, isn't it? And, Diane, the central medallion of your necklace, the octagon-shaped piece?—that's repeated over and over again in our carpet. It's called a 'gul'; it means flower or rose in Persian."

"Aren't you a veritable font of information," Diane teased. Privately she was thrilled to be having this conversation with her mother about something other than children or holidays or family birthdays. Her mother cared about her work, had *noticed.*

"Well, you know I've always been so curious. And with you children grown, I've got a little more time on my hands."

"I wish *I* had some free time," Diane said with a sigh.

"Oh, darling, I admire you so. You do so much."

Warmed by her mother's words, Diane confided, "I only wish I could get Jim to help me just a little bit more."

"Your father was never much help with you children, either," Jean said.

Diane tossed her head. The comparison rubbed her the wrong way. She and Jim were of a different generation. "Oh, it's not so bad, really. We're muddling through."

Then Julia came down with a hideous cold, the sort of gobby, globbing cold that plugged up her small respiratory tract like glue.

Her breath came with difficulty, each intake accompanied by a ragged, wet pop. Diane had given their baby-sitter the day off, because she wanted to stay home to nurse Julia. So she was alone in the house when the phone call came from Chase's preschool: during a game of tag, Chase had fallen against the side of the brick building, slicing his forehead open. He would need stitches. And he had passed out. Perhaps he had a concussion.

Jim was in Washington at a DNA conference that day.

Frantically, Diane dialed the houses of various baby-sitters, but no one was home, and so she had bundled Julia up and stuffed her in her car seat and driven to the hospital where Mrs. Eames, Chase's teacher, had taken Chase. There, during the course of the long afternoon, she waited at Chase's side, rocking a miserably uncomfortable Julia in her arms. Chase had quickly regained consciousness, but the doctor wanted to keep him in the hospital overnight for observation: the cut required eight stitches, and the swollen area was enormous. The doctor was reassuring, though—this was really just a typical child's accident. Nothing out of the ordinary.

Young and exhausted, the doctor suddenly noticed Julia. He nearly snatched the little girl from Diane's arms and, after a rapid scrutiny, said sharply, "You shouldn't bring a child this ill out into this kind of weather!"

Diane held her tongue, she didn't want to anger this doctor who held her son's life in his weary, trembling hands. And she was glad she was, for once in her life, femininely submissive; for the doctor insisted on taking Julia's temperature, listening to her chest, and then, in an even greater fury, prescribing antibiotics. Coldly, he insisted that Diane take her little girl home and keep her in a room with a consistently warm temperature and a vaporizer. A kind nurse—a *saintly* nurse—held Julia, who was screaming and twisting with fury at the intrusiveness of these strangers—while Diane made the necessary phone calls. Sheila, a good friend of hers, agreed to come in to spend the night with Chase in the hospital. Her own husband was home and could take care of their children.

So Diane carried her daughter, who with her teary anger seemed to have grown heavier and more awkward in her arms, down through the antiseptic halls of the hospital, down the elevator, down to the hospital pharmacy. While waiting for the antibiotic prescription to be filled by a stern older woman, sitting on a bit of hard, scooped-out plastic masquerading as a chair, Diane's eyes fell on the gift section of the pharmacy: hopeless stuffed animals, dusty games, and heart-and-flower-decorated plaques printed with mawkish, cloying sentiments.

One Pepto-Bismol-pink heart read:

God couldn't be everywhere
So he invented mothers.

Until that moment, Diane had been in control. Now something snapped.

"How dare they!" Diane said. It was as if she had been slapped in the face. "How dare you sell such stuff! No one has the right to charge mothers with such responsibility!"

"Excuse me?" the bun-haired pharmacist asked.

"What about competent physicians? *I* don't know how to make my son well; I can only hope that prepubescent doctor can! For that matter, what about *you*? I don't know the first thing about pills. I have to trust that you know what you're doing, that you've got the sense to put the right medicine in that bottle for my baby, that you've measured it correctly and not accidentally added strychnine or digitalis!" In her extremity, Diane had risen, clutching the startled Julia to her breast as she shouted at the pharmacist.

"My diploma is hanging right there on the wall for you to see!" the pharmacist shot back, but she made the mistake of glancing down at the bottle of syrupy medicine in her hand as if in doubt.

"They should print a sign saying that God couldn't be everywhere so He invented antibiotics! And physicians! And reliable pharmacists! Right? Right!"

"Madam," the pharmacist said, drawing herself up stiffly, "if you're going to raise your voice, I'll have to ask you to leave."

But Diane was explosive.

"What if I were a single mother!" she cried. "What if I were poor! What if I had *five* children! I couldn't do it alone. I can't do it alone now. And I will not accept total, sole responsibility. What are you being paid for? Simply to pour fluid from one bottle to another? No! You are being paid for doing it with intelligence and discrimination and caution!"

The pharmacist glared, then relented. After a long moment of silence, she said, "Assuming that your doctor and the company didn't make a mistake, I'm sure this medicine will help your child."

Diane went limp with exhaustion. She'd made a scene and, in doing so, had not helped her children at all. She had only helped herself, and yet the pharmacist's admission brought her no comfort, and not the slightest sense of safety. When she spoke, her voice was meek.

"Do you have a plastic spoon? If I could give her the first dose right now—so that it starts working as soon as possible—we have a long drive home—it would be a relief—"

By the time she got home, Julia had fallen into an invalid's deep sleep, her cheeks flushed with fever. Diane set up the vaporizer and tucked the covers around her little girl. Then she sat on the bed awhile, watching her daughter sleep. She loved this child so much she thought her heart would break with it.

"The sign should say, 'Mothers couldn't be everywhere, so they invented God,' " she whispered.

Finally she left her daughter's side. After a quick, immensely comforting hot shower, she pulled on her warmest flannel nightgown and her favorite quilted robe—clean, but permanently stained with cherry cough syrup and baby food. She was beginning to feel like that robe, marked by motherhood. Collapsing into a chair, she dialed the hotel where Jim was staying in Washington. When he answered, she burst into tears.

"What's wrong?" Jim asked.

"Oh, it's been such a terrible day . . ."

"Are the children all right?" His voice sounded aggressive, even hostile. Only later, when she replayed the conversation in her mind, would she realize it was laced with fear.

"Well, yes and no. Chase fell against a brick building when he was playing at preschool. He's got a cut on his forehead, and possibly a concussion, and Julia has an awful cold."

"What do the doctors say?"

"Chase is in the hospital." She sniffled. "They're keeping him there for observation. They say it's just a typical childhood accident. He didn't vomit or show any signs of concussion, but they want to be sure . . . Sheila offered to stay with him tonight. Oh, God, Jim, it took eight stitches to sew up his forehead."

"Well, if he's at the hospital, he's in good hands. What about Julia?"

"I have antibiotics for her. And I put a dehumidifier in her room. Oh, Jim, I'm exhausted. Won't you please come home?"

"Why?" Jim seemed honestly baffled. "It sounds as though you've got everything under control."

"Chase is in the hospital."

"That's obviously the best place for him."

"He's a little boy in a hospital. He needs a parent with him."

"You just said Sheila was with him."

"Sheila's not his parent!"

"Diane, calm down. I can't stop work every time one of the children is sick. That's unrealistic."

"*I* stopped work."

"It's not the same. You've got your office manager to cover for you."

"You have employees to cover for you."

"I need to be here. This is an important conference."

"So was the one last month. And the month before that."

"Diane, listen. You're just tired. The baby-sitter will be back tomorrow and—"

"Jim, I'm frightened. And I'm so tired."

"Then go to bed. I'll be home in two days."

"You were the one who wanted to get married; *you* were the one who wanted children, but I'm the one who's doing all the work."

"Diane, this is ridiculous. It's late."

"Jim. If you don't come home and share all this with me, help me through it, I'll never forgive you."

"Diane, I'm tired. You're tired. Let's go to sleep. You'll feel better in the morning."

Diane hung up the phone without saying good-bye. As she wept, she listened for a ring, for Jim to call her back, to apologize, to soothe her, to calm her. But the phone was silent.

She carried the weight of that crisis in her heart like a stone, a heavy dense mass of stone that she polished with her anger each time Jim refused to help. Sometimes she considered divorcing him but decided against that: she loved him, after all, and she knew that in his own reserved way he loved her and his children. Then one day, years later, she understood something about the man she had loved for long.

All during his childhood, spirited, energetic Chase managed to keep himself covered with scrapes and bruises. When he was nine, he and Sam built a tree house in the Randalls' backyard. One bright summer evening, fooling around, Chase fell out of the tree house. He landed on his arm, which snapped. Diane rushed him to the hospital. After the X rays, the doctors informed Diane that Chase would have to be kept in the hospital overnight. It was a compound fracture, which required anesthesia that they couldn't administer because Chase had just eaten dinner. In the morning, they would set the arm and put it in a cast. After the painkillers took effect, Chase relished the experience, loving the attention, thrilled that he'd get to have a cast. Since Diane had grown up with two brothers, this all seemed just another part of childhood, and she brought seven-year-old Julia to the hospital with her and pointed out the nurses' uniforms, their mysterious instruments and charts. Sam and his parents arrived with a package of comic books and word puzzles. The whole episode turned into an adventure, for all of them.

Jim arrived separately. He'd gone back to his lab to work after dinner, but when Diane called him from the hospital, he drove over immediately.

"Hi, there, sport." Jim's words as he entered Chase's hospital room seemed normal enough, but he spoke stiffly. He carried himself oddly, leaning backward and looking around apprehensively.

This was the first time she'd been in a hospital with Jim since the birth of her babies; and now, freed of the immediacies of those events, she realized that her husband was almost paralyzed with fear.

"Hi, Dad. Guess what! I get to have a cast. And they're going to knock me out. Sodium Pentothal. The truth serum!"

Jim went pale. He turned on Diane. "Is that absolutely necessary?"

"The doctors X-rayed his arm—"

"Who's the doctor? Does he know what he's doing?"

Jim was sweating. Diane wanted to get him out of there before he frightened his son.

"Jim. Let's go down to the nurses' station and they can explain it to you."

To her relief, Jim instantly agreed. It was eight o'clock and the doctor had gone home, but a nurse carefully outlined for him what was really a routine procedure. When she was finished, she said gently, "There's no need to be alarmed. He'll be fine."

"I'm not alarmed!" Jim barked, digging his chin into his chest.

"Well, that's good," the nurse replied, smiling. As she walked away, she raised an eyebrow at Diane.

Through the night Diane was aware of Jim's restlessness. He

tossed and turned; twice he got up and pattered downstairs, roaming their house in the dark. He wouldn't talk to her about it, but she realized that he was afraid—afraid of hospitals, doctors, injuries, illnesses. He had been just Chase's age when his mother had been diagnosed with breast cancer, and only a year older when his mother died. How had she not realized this before?

Diane understood at last that Jim saw all chaos as threatening. If he couldn't bring order to any kind of confusion, he would retreat. She sympathized with him and felt a wave of affection for him that surprised her. But she was determined to pull him into the lively complexities of their family life in spite of himself. She tugged; he retreated. She cried and lectured; he responded with silence. The more heated she got, the colder he became.

In 1980, Jim was asked to head a well-funded lab connected with Harvard that was engaged in genetic research on breast cancer. This was the work he'd been aiming for all his life. He settled into it with obsessive devotion. He was home less and less, working at the lab into the night.

The children were ten and eight. They could tie their own shoelaces, fix their own sandwiches, be reasoned with. Even better, they were wonderful fun. Diane loved going to movies with them, playing board games together at the dining-room table on rainy Sundays, sharing jokes and gossip. Her energy and ambition for her work returned.

One May afternoon she sat in her studio sketching a design for her fall collection, a necklace of stamped brass pieces: pumpkins, leaves, and squirrels.

"Lisa," she called through her open office door, "come look at this. What do you think?"

Her office manager entered the studio. Holding the pad in her hand, she scrutinized Diane's painstakingly detailed work: "It's cute," Lisa said.

" 'Cute.' Yes. Great. Pumpkins and squirrels. Too young for my clientele." Diane ripped the page from the pad, crumpled it fiercely in her hand, then tossed it across the room.

"Well, the leaves are pretty."

"*Mmm.* I don't want 'pretty.' " With her pencil, Diane sharpened the points and angles of the leaves she'd drawn. "I want unusual. Eye-catching."

"You'll come up with something," Lisa assured her. "You always do."

Diane dropped her pencil and walked over to look out her window. "I hope so. I've certainly got my energy back. But my mind keeps running in circles."

"You need a vacation."

"I'll be going to the Vineyard for two weeks in August."

"With your family."

Diane turned to stare at Lisa. "You know, you're right. With my family. No wonder my ideas are juvenile—I'm always with my children!"

"Perhaps you should go somewhere by yourself. Someplace you've never been before. Someplace wild!"

"I went to the international jewelry convention last year."

"That's hardly wild. That's one night in New York. You go there all the time."

"Well, where should I go?"

"God, anywhere!"

Diane rubbed her neck. "I don't know, Lisa. It's so hard to leave the children."

"Well, if you don't go now, when will you?"

"You really think I need a trip, don't you?" Diane asked.

Lisa smiled. "I really do."

"Well, I'll think about it. I know you're right. A change would do me good." Pulling open the window, she leaned on the sill and let the cool spring air sweep in, making her shiver. "I'm going to somewhere exciting!"

And she had, for a while.

She'd paid for it dearly.

Was she still paying for it now?

Chapter 5
 Jean

Jean decided she could quite easily become addicted to the life of a traveler. It was not what she saw outside the walls of her hotel room that pleased her as much as how she felt inside those walls.

She felt so free. She was free. It was not her responsibility to see that the sheets were changed, the bed made, the small sink scrubbed, the carpet swept, the trash emptied, the windows washed, the insurance on this building paid on time, the roof repaired, the gutters cleaned out, the walls freshly painted.

This was also different from her life in the condominium. There, too, someone else took care of the basic building necessities. The difference was that residence in a condominium implied permanence of a very limited nature: a giving up, a settling down, a closing in, a narrowing of life to small rooms and small routines performed within them. Life in a hotel, on the

other hand, implied movement, change, fresh starts, new discoveries, infinite possibilities.

On any morning Jean might awaken and decide to lie in bed
reading a Maigret mystery or to dress quickly and spend the
whole day at the Louvre. She could leave for Versailles for a day
or two, keeping this room, or depart for good for Rome, because
the weekly rates were so low that it wouldn't trouble her to lose
the money. She was becoming very fond of her little hotel room
in Paris, however, and found herself simply curling up in various
corners to watch the way the sun entered at different hours of
the day. The afternoon light against the white plaster walls was
as brilliant as snow. The wooden legs of the upholstered armchair
near the window were scratched and gouged, but the headboard
of her bed was a thick, scrolled dark walnut. Nothing in the room
quite matched. The fake oriental carpet was mostly wine-colored,
the skirt around the little sink a garish pink, the cushions of the
armchair a splotchy blue and green, and her duvet a deep rose;
yet she wouldn't change a thing. It was her room.

Here in her charming, shabby hotel room she pondered the
nature of belonging. In all the spacious houses she'd lived in for
forty years and left this summer, she'd never had one room that
suited her so well.

This summer, when she and her children packed up the house,
she'd sensed how her touches were everywhere, but no one room
was only hers.

Al had had a private room, his study. When she and her children went through Al's study, it had taken days, because they
had spent so much time exclaiming over discoveries. Her husband had had a secret life. Everyone has a secret life, but Al had
a room for his. They found nothing shocking or obscene—no
old *Playboy* magazines hidden beneath his atlas, no love letters

in his files. Of course Al had known he was dying, and probably had been wise enough to discard anything repellent or offensive—if he'd had anything like that; as probably, because of the sort of man he was, he hadn't.

Still, he surprised his family. They knew that he had had an enduring, even obsessive, love for the United States Navy, and the walls of his study were hung with beautifully matted photographs and drawings of various battleships and submarines; the shelves of his study were stacked with giant, glossy coffee-table-type books on the history of the Navy, which his wife and children had given him over the years for Christmas and birthday presents.

What they didn't know and were amazed to discover was that he had kept, hidden in a locked filing cabinet, a multitude of newspaper clippings and magazine articles about the Navy. The label cards on the wooden doors of the file read "Insurance and Will" or "Warranties and Service Information," but all that pedestrian household stuff was crammed together at the bottom of the filing cabinet under a section headed "House." The rest of the chin-high cabinet held an orderly array of files, arranged chronologically, month by month, year by year, the file folders headed "June 1981," or "December 1989." Inside each folder was an article about the Navy and at the top of each article, in Al's clear, determined handwriting, the name and date of the publication: *"The Nation,* June 1986"; *"U.S. News and World Report,* August 1986"; *"Life,* September 1987." The files seemed to have begun in 1981, the year Al retired from his law firm, although they found in a large box in the bottom of his study closet a mass of uncatalogued clippings dating from the fifties.

"Oh, Mom! Poor Dad!" Susan had cried out. She, like all the children, knew that her father had wanted to be a career man in the Navy but had relented in the face of Jean's pleas for a more normal life. He had resigned his commission after World War II, finished law school, and joined a firm near Washington.

"What if your father had had a passion for Antarctica or Borneo?" Jean had responded. "Would you have wanted to spend your life there? We were all much better off with his having the Navy as his hobby rather than his life!"

This summer, packing up the house, and for the fifty years beforehand, Jean had been adamant in her righteousness, but now in her rented room in Paris she gave herself the freedom to reconsider, at least to imagine how it might have been. If Al had stayed in the Navy, there would have been no spacious sheltering colonial to provide stability and refuge; instead, there would have been a series of houses of varying sizes throughout the world, wherever Al was sent. The family would not have accumulated so many possessions; they would not have had one house standing as a museum of their lives. If Al had stayed in the Navy, he would have been a happier man, there was no doubt about that. And Jean would not have had to work so hard to please him, to make up to him for what he had sacrificed for her. Their marriage would have been completely different.

Jean had not insisted that Al resign from the Navy because she wanted a grand white house and a sheltered, stable life. She hadn't insisted because she didn't want to spend her life paying court to the wives of her husband's superiors, as her own mother had done. She had insisted that he resign because she knew that the life of a military man could be dangerous, and she wanted him to live.

No, she was not sorry for the life she had imposed upon Al.

In any case, his life had not been totally within her control or even within her knowledge. In the bottom drawer of his desk, under some L.L. Bean catalogues, was a miscellaneous collection of photographs and descriptions of pipes. Al had obviously begun this collection when he learned he had lung cancer and was forced to give up smoking. It was this hidden cache that made Jean weep. The physical pleasures of the last few years of Al's life had, because of his illness, grown more and more restricted. The image of her husband sitting alone in his study at night, secretly running his fingers over the cold and printed lines of a meerschaum, imagining the sweet taste of tobacco and the tug of his lips at the heated stem, seemed infinitely sad. He had never, to her knowledge, smoked a pipe; but this, at least, was not her fault. When he gave up cigarettes, he did not try cigars or pipes or chewing gum. But the well-thumbed pipe catalogues were proof that he had spent hours dreaming of smoking just as a woman might look through fashion magazines, fantasizing about romance.

Other secrets surfaced when Jean and her children dug deep to the bottom of Al's desk drawer. Al had been a handsome and dignified man, distinguished even, and much admired. Anything he considered a weakness in himself he kept as well hidden as he could, and so Diane had been astonished at the number of medications he kept locked in his middle desk drawer. Salves for hemorrhoids and arthritis, thick, milky potions and chalky pills for indigestion and constipation, blood-pressure pills and antihistamines. Pain pills. Jean knew about most of these medicines and had always guessed he kept them hidden in his study because they were not in the medicine cabinet in their bathroom—too available to the eyes of a cleaning woman, a houseguest, or a curious grandchild.

By contrast, Jean's life in that house had been spread out on display for everyone to see. Her medicines were in her bathroom cabinet, her skin cream on the bathroom counter, her diet drinks on the kitchen shelves, her checkbook, personal correspondence, and embossed stationery in the unlocked desk in the den. Her life had always been an open book for her family to read at their own whim. When the children were little, it had been only common sense that she establish her desk in the room where they played, because then she could pay bills while still keeping a watchful eye on them. Never in the fifty years of her marriage did she receive one letter she would not have shown to her husband or most innocent child. Eventually, after they moved into the big white colonial, she had a room of her own, but it was a sewing room, and there could hardly be anything secret in the smocked dresses she made for her daughters, the Halloween costumes she created for her sons, or the embroidered flannel skirt she decorated for the Christmas tree. She never shut the door from the hallway into her sewing room. Perhaps there had been days when she had rested there, putting her feet up on an ottoman as she bent over her mending, but everyone in the family always had instant access to her and to that room. No one would ever have thought to knock before going in; yet they always knocked before entering Al's study and waited for him to give permission: "Come in."

All her life she made lists organizing her time; these lists were public property, held by a magnet to the refrigerator door or left on her desk in the den. Her children had given her memo pads adorned with humorous quotes on which to write her lists. Why, then, was Jean moved to tears when she discovered in her husband's study a list locked in the middle drawer of his desk? The list read:

Clean out fishing tackle box, label lures, send to Susan's boys
Remind Art—*tactfully*—he still owes it to his family to get some health insurance
Golf clubs—? Salvation Army? All those damned joke golf gifts
Write Jean a letter

Call Corkins for a tune-up for the Volvo

Château Frontenac in July—visit Diane & Co. and Art & brood
on the way up?

Al had died before July, before getting the Volvo tuned or sorting
out his tackle box or taking Jean on a romantic trip to Quebec
or writing her a letter of good-bye. It was possible he had called
or written Art about health insurance; Jean decided not to in-
quire; Art was a grown man now, living with a woman who had
had two children by him even though they weren't married, living
in upstate Maine pretending to be a farmer, for heaven's sake.
Joy, the woman Art had lived with for the past eight years,
claimed she was a spiritual healer and a good witch; and although
Joy hadn't managed yet to find an herb that would reduce her
rather remarkable excesses of cellulite, it was still a good bet that
she'd vow she would, with her own spells, keep Art so healthy
that he'd never need health insurance.

The golf clubs, expensive ones in a leather bag, had been in
the garage. Jean had donated them to a neighborhood school
fund-raiser. The abundant collection of misshapen, cartoonish,
rather hideous golf figurines—the mug shaped like a golf ball,
printed with the words "Golf is a beautiful walk spoiled by a
small white ball," the suede bag holding golf tees with Al's name
printed on them, the golf club cleaner in solid beechwood, the
several golfing caps, the golfing videos—all these Jean quickly
swept from the shelf in Al's study and into a plastic trash bag
that she carried out to the curb herself. In their foolish abundance
they had seemed like an insult to her husband. That such a
powerful man had come to this, to receiving from his four children and eleven grandchildren such pathetically stupid gifts! Oh,
well, any man was hard to shop for, but these things showed a

lack of imagination, a lack of genuine interest in him. She'd been silently angry for days at each one of her children.

Susan and Diane, who were there at that time, had thought Jean's dark mood resulted from embarrassment at her own stupidity: Jean knew the combination to the small safe in Al's study but could not remember it, or rather could not remember it correctly. On a sunny summer morning, not yet too humid, she and her daughters had gathered in the study after a pleasant, hearty breakfast. Jean had knelt on the floor and worked the combination lock through the three clicks she knew as well as she knew her own name. The lock had not opened.

"I must have done it too quickly," she said and turned the knob again, more deliberately.

Again it did not open. "This lock is getting to be like me, old and cranky and difficult!" She laughed.

For quite a few minutes she continued to try it, still not losing her temper, and when Diane in frustration said, "Mom, let me!" she pleasantly moved aside and told her daughter the numbers. The lock didn't open for Diane, either.

"Oh, Mom, you must have the numbers jumbled in your mind!" Diane said, not hiding her impatience.

Jean did not miss the look that passed between her daughters. Of course she was as exasperated with her memory as they were.

"Look," she told them, "obviously I'm remembering it incorrectly. Let's go do something else. Let's go sort through your father's clothes in the bedroom closet. You know how it is—the harder you try to remember something, the more it hides. If I think of something else for a while, no doubt the right combination will pop into my mind."

The girls agreed, and they spent the rest of the afternoon upstairs, accomplishing so much that they decided to treat themselves to dinner out and a movie. Jean was tired. She did not like to let her daughters know how tired she got these days; she didn't want to worry them. They were used to her as a sort of windup toy of a grandmother now, whirring about with cookies and milk and hand-knit blankets for their children, always cheery and smiling. While she couldn't quite achieve that, now—and they wouldn't expect it of her after the death of her husband— still she did not want them to know the extent of her exhaustion.

So she was grateful for the cover of darkness in the movie theater. She closed her eyes and entered a state that was not quite sleep, and after a while she realized why she had gotten Al's safe combination wrong. She had been working the combination to a similar small safe that had been in a similar spot in her own father's study so many years, so many decades, before.

1939
War Stories

Jean Marshall's family was among the group of old, monied, aristocratic families known in Washington in the thirties as the Cliff Dwellers. But certainly they did not dwell in cliffs. Their houses were beautiful, and luxuriously comfortable. Jean's room was a girl's dream of a room, in polka-dotted dimity and rose-papered walls. Her family ate dinner every night in the dining room, seated at a long linen-covered table, using silver and china, though not the good china; the food they ate was cooked by the black cook and brought to the table by their father's "man." The Marshalls had only two servants: Agate, a calm black woman who came by bus every day except Sunday to cook and keep the kitchen clean, do the washing and ironing, and help Mrs. Marshall with the heavy housework—and Stafford. Stafford lived in an apartment over the garage. He was their butler, chauffeur, gardener, and handyman. Wherever Commander Marshall had been stationed, he had arranged for help in his house—paid for by his wife's inheritance, if necessary. Jean and Bobby had grown up with Agate and Stafford and felt comfortable with having help in their house.

In fact, Jean and Bobby were accustomed to having all sorts of people going in and out of their home. Their mother was the head of various charitable organizations, which necessitated committee meetings and teas and wreath-making parties. Both parents were serious bridge players and held bridge evenings at home at least once a week. In addition, the Marshalls had a seemingly endless stream of old friends they had met while Commander Marshall was on tour in the Navy, and Navy friends and civilians they had known in Malta or California or Guam came to visit for as much as a week at a time. Often these people were accompanied by their children, in which case Jean was politely pressed into baby-sitting or, worse, entreated to entertain some hapless adolescent.

Bobby and Jean were also used to their father's receiving more businesslike visitors at any and all hours of the day or night. Often these men were the same ones their parents met socially for golf or a dance, but when they showed up, without their wives, these men had a gray cast about them that spoke of business. Then Stafford, if he happened to answer the door, or Mrs. Marshall, or Jean or Bobby, would automatically interrupt Commander Marshall at whatever it was he was doing, and the two men would go into his study and shut the door.

It was no secret from anyone in the house that Commander Marshall was involved in naval intelligence work, or that when the gray men came to be closeted with him in his study they were discussing issues of importance. In fact if Jean had been told that her father secretly ruled the world, she wouldn't have been much surprised because her mother was forever impressing on her the significance of her father's work, making her practically tiptoe and bow whenever he entered a room.

In return, Commander Marshall treated Jean as if she didn't have a brain in her head. Perhaps she deserved some of that, for her grades in math and science were not sterling, although she still managed to get into Radcliffe. Commander Marshall was not unkind, but he was nearly medieval in his thinking; he believed there was a hierarchy beginning with the Lord and filtering down quite a long way before coming to any female.

Probably because of that, it never occurred to him that his own daughter would or could betray him, and so it was very soon after they'd moved into Bancroft Place, when Jean was only about twelve, that he asked her to memorize the combination to the small safe in his study.

There were two shelves in his safe. The lower one held a locked strongbox containing Commander Marshall's will and other legal papers. The top shelf was a repository for the odd bits of paper on which he scribbled his thoughts. He often brought his work home to do, finding that in an atmosphere of peace and relaxation problems that had tortured him at his office on Constitution Avenue suddenly presented him with answers. He was not an absentminded man, but he was a very busy one, and so Jean grew quite used to picking up the phone to hear him say, "Jean? Go into my study, dear, open the safe, take out the top sheet of paper, and read it to me, will you? That's a good girl." She never tried to make sense out of what she read to her father, never tried to memorize it, for it was always gibberish: a group of numbers and letters, or four names with odd symbols next to them. Once she had asked her father what a certain message meant and he had answered sternly, "Nothing for young girls to bother their pretty heads about."

Commander Marshall also told his wife the combination to his safe, and she was the one he first asked to get the information he'd forgotten. He'd ask Jean only if his wife was not at home. He did not tell Stafford or Agate the combination, and he made a point of not telling his son because he did not want Bobby ever to be in the position of having to compromise his principles. He knew his son was going into the Navy.

He was fond and proud of his daughter, but not much more fond or proud than he would have been of a clever dog who had been trained to fetch. His highest hope for her was that she marry a Navy man and bring him an interesting son-in-law. Jean would inherit much of her mother's money, and it was a tradition that Navy men marry wealthy young women; just so had Commander Marshall found and courted and married his wife.

Jean's life and her brother's had always been circumscribed by their father's laws, and that cold December night Jean was filled with dread as she rode home from the Carlton Hotel. Bobby would believe it was his duty to inform their father immediately about her behavior at the Army-Navy Christmas Ball, how she'd ignored a Navy man, and flirted with a stranger. Al knew his best friend's family, and for a while the air inside the cab was chilly as Al and Jean were borne closer and closer to her parents' home. Jean pulled her fur coat around her and bent over to shake the snow off the hem of her long evening gown. Her feet were frozen. Outside the windows, the snow drifted down in feathery silence.

"Perfect weather for the holidays, ain't it?" the cabdriver remarked cheerfully.

"It is," Al replied politely, and then it was quiet in the cab until they pulled into the drive.

"Would you like me to come in with you?" Al asked. "Bobby can drive me back."

Jean considered. "That would be great, Al. Thanks. Dad will have to be polite, and he's always glad to see you. It will at least postpone if not prevent the slaughter."

Al paid the cabdriver, put his hand under Jean's elbow, and helped her through the snow. Agate was at the front door. While she took their coats she looked down at the floor, a sure sign she knew that trouble was brewing.

The family was gathered in the living room around a silver coffee service. Bobby had reached home before Jean, and when she entered the room, his chin jutted out defensively. That alerted her. Bobby had told.

"Who's this strange fellow you spent the entire evening with!" Commander Marshall demanded almost the moment the young people were settled in the living room, with Mrs. Marshall scurrying around giving everyone coffee.

"God, Bobby, you really are a pathetic old tattletale," Jean said, glaring at her brother. "It's too bad your own love life is so boring that you have so much energy and attention to give to mine."

"Young lady, it's no good looking at your brother. I want to know about this man, and I want to know about him *now*. I won't have a daughter of mine making a spectacle of herself in public. If you can't give me a proper account of yourself and your actions tonight, you're confined to the house for the rest of the holidays, and I'll have to reconsider whether or not I'll let you return to Cambridge. It seems a lot of radical ideas have been put in your foolish little head. I knew sending you away to a northern college was a mistake."

At this, even Bobby looked appropriately horrified. He had only meant to protect his sister, not to end her college career. Mrs. Marshall kept pouring coffee, handing out napkins, little spoons, offering sugar. Jean did not look to her mother for help;

she knew Mrs. Marshall wouldn't have dreamed of interfering. This was the way of Jean's mother's world; this was the way her own father had treated her, threatening her so many years ago with cutting her out of her inheritance unless she married the right man.

"Daddy, that's not fair! For God's sake! Dancing with Erich has no relation whatsoever to Radcliffe!" Jean felt her face redden with the childish pressure of tears.

"Don't use that tone of voice with me, young lady, and don't take the Lord's name in vain! Who is this man you spent the evening with? How did you meet him? Who introduced you? Does he know anyone?"

By "anyone," Commander Marshall meant only and specifically anyone within the elite group of the Navy and Washington and Cliff Dweller spheres. In fact, Jean wasn't sure Erich Mellor did know any of those people. She waited for Bobby to come to her rescue—after all, Erich had been talking to him—and when her brother didn't speak, she said, "Bobby knows him."

"No, I don't. I chatted with him, but I don't know him."

According to her parents' rules, girls of Jean's age and class were supposed to be introduced to the right people by the right people, and dancing all evening with a man who knew "no one" amounted to wantonness deserving of the worst possible punishment. For a long moment, the room was silent.

"His name is Erich Mellor," Jean began bravely. "He's a banker, with the Washington branch of the Upton and Steward Bank. His family lives in New York."

"New York," Commander Marshall said gruffly. New York, as far as he was concerned, was a city full of Yankees, Jews, and liberals. "What kind of a name is Mellor, anyway? Sounds German."

The silence in the room deepened ominously.

"Sir, I believe Erich Mellor was at the dance as the guest of his cousin Jimmy Heflin, who was two years ahead of Bobby and me at the academy," Al said. Immediately he was rewarded with a look from Jean of such fond gratitude he could almost interpret it as love. He deserved it. He had just altered the truth by elevating Erich Mellor's relationship with Jimmy Heflin from that of friend to cousin. And after all, Al knew Heflin had brought Mellor to the dance, and no one had told him the two men *weren't* cousins, so he hadn't exactly lied to Commander Marshall.

"*Humph.* I suppose he's all right, then. Still, Jean, I thought you'd been raised with better manners than you've exhibited tonight." Commander Marshall paused to gather his thoughts. He couldn't scold his daughter for ignoring Al all evening with Al sitting in the living room, yet he couldn't let Jean's actions go unpunished. "Go to your room. Now."

Jean felt the pressure of indignity push tears behind her eyes and pull down the corners of her mouth, but she rose and politely said good night to Al, then swept from the room without another word to her brother, father, or her hopelessly ineffectual mother.

Once released from the overwarm living room, however, up in the privacy of her bedroom, she felt free and glad. She hated sitting with her parents and Bobby and Al, everyone so stiff and formal. She was mad enough at Bobby to spit, and she hated her father and pitied her mother. She wanted to get away from them all, but she couldn't, not now, not tonight. So she hurried through her bedtime ablutions and crawled into bed, gratefully forsaking all considerations of her family and surrendering completely to thoughts of Erich Mellor.

She remembered the warm, firm pressure of his hand on her back as they danced, how his touch had been guiding but not commanding, and how, over the course of the evening he had gradually, subtly, brought her closer to him, so that finally she had rested her head on his shoulder. At first she'd been embarrassed by the unavoidable knowledge of her breasts pressing against his chest, but before long she'd relaxed and let herself enjoy the full physical geometry of her female shape against his male body.

Jean forced herself to remember how she felt about Hal Farmer. Erich was every bit as intelligent and fascinating as Hal but much more mysterious, and much smoother. Whatever Hal Farmer had called up in her seemed frivolous, light, in comparison to the torrent of emotions Erich Mellor caused.

She wanted to go to bed with Erich Mellor.

Sunday morning Jean went to St. John's with her parents. In her secret heart she had grown impatient with religion, finding it all too hypocritical to bear, but she had to ingratiate herself with her father and win back his favor if she was going to get his permission to see Erich Mellor again.

Her parents were pleased by her docile presence in church and later with her running stream of chatter about her friends and courses at Radcliffe as they sat around the dining-room table for their formal Sunday dinner. She spoke of tea parties and cotillions, the socially acceptable activities.

Jean could see the tension drain from her parents' faces as she blathered on and on. She caught the message her mother flashed her father with her eyes as she asked him if he wanted some more mashed potatoes and gravy: "See, dear, it's all right; Jean's learned her lesson." Could it really be this easy to fool her parents?

Bobby was spending the day with Betty and her family. After the huge Sunday meal, Commander Marshall retired to his study, closing the door in order to work—or to nap on the leather sofa. Mrs. Marshall sat in the living room listening to a program of classical music on their Philco radio as she wrapped some last-minute Christmas presents. Finally, Jean was free to escape with her best friend from high school, Midge Carlisle.

Midge honked the horn of her shining gray Nash sedan and Jean yelled good-bye to her parents, then raced out the door and jumped into the car.

"Oooh, I'm so glad you're here!" Midge squealed, hugging Jean. Her bouncy blond curls were tied back with a red-and-green plaid ribbon.

"I'm so glad to get out of there!" Jean laughed. "And I've got so much to tell you!"

"Shall we go to Bailey's for ice cream?"

"All right, as long as there's no one there we know."

"Well, well, well." Midge rolled her eyes playfully. "What's up?"

"I've just got so much to tell you, and I don't want anyone to hear."

"You've met someone."

"Right."

"Oh, I'm so jealous!" Midge nearly steered the car into a snow-drift in her excitement.

"Well, there must be hundreds of good-looking men at George Washington!"

"Yeah, but the only ones who've asked me out are boring. I want someone *thrilling*."

"So do I," Jean agreed. "And I think I've met him."

"Oh, you've got to tell me everything!"

"Well—" Jean began, and she launched into a detailed description of the night before. They talked about Erich and the dance all through their sundaes and then through coffee, and before they knew it, it was time for them to go back to Jean's house for the Marshalls' annual Christmas party.

It was only two days before Christmas. Mrs. Marshall, with Agate and Stafford's help, had completed decorating the house, and when Midge drove Jean back home late that Sunday afternoon, they saw the plummy Scotch pine towering in the living room, its lights glittering through the mullioned windows. Tonight the carolers would come, and friends and acquaintances of the Marshalls, and they all would be invited in for eggnog and fruitcake and Christmas cookies as they warmed up by the fire. Mrs. Marshall had always set much emotional weight on the holidays. She liked having the entire family gathered around, and Agate and Stafford there, too, discreetly refilling the crystal eggnog bowl and passing around the cookies and cakes. The more friends who arrived for this ceremony, the happier she was, the more content and optimistic about her own particular slice of the world.

Midge had been part of this evening ever since she and Jean had become best friends six years before. She parked her car in front of the house and the young women hurried through the cold night and into the Marshalls' house. They were giddy from ice cream and gossip. They couldn't stop giggling as they took off their raccoon coats, handed them to Stafford, and went into the living room.

"We're not late, are we, Commander Marshall?" Midge asked, all simper and charm. She kissed Mrs. Marshall on the cheek. Her father was an architect, and a Cliff Dweller, so Midge was one of them.

"We can't be late. Bobby isn't back with Betty yet," Jean said, automatically defensive, her voice already edgy with the exasperation she felt every time she was near her parents. She was so tired of having continually to appease and apologize.

Then she saw Erich Mellor sitting on the living-room sofa. Her mouth fell open in surprise, and she stood just staring at the man.

Erich rose, moved toward Jean, and offered his hand.

"Hello, Jean," he said.

Numbly, she shook his hand, but she was still too shocked to speak.

"This young man called me earlier today," Commander Marshall said, noting his daughter's discomfiture with amusement. "Called to ask if he could come by and introduce himself. Turns out we have a few friends in common."

"Oh," Jean said. "Well . . ."

"Hi! I'm Midge Carlisle, Jean's best friend." Midge shook hands with Erich, nudging Jean slightly with her hip as she did.

Jean sank into a hard wing chair at the side of the coffee table. She smoothed her skirt over her trembling knees.

"We've been *so* sinful," Midge gushed. She knew the Marshalls liked an accounting of their daughter's activities. "We ate so much ice cream we'll never fit into our clothes. Ice cream in the winter. *Brr.* I'd love some coffee."

As she chattered, Midge settled herself on the sofa next to Erich. Jean's mother poured coffee for Midge and Jean, then handed Erich a cup. Jean was surprised at how docile he looked, trapped on chintz between females, the dainty cup and saucer in his hands.

"We've found something out about your new friend!" Mrs. Marshall announced.

"Oh?" The one syllable was all Jean could manage.

"It just so happens that Erich is a bridge buff!" Her mother beamed, truly pleased, for she loved nothing more than a good game of bridge. "I think we've got time for a round or two before the guests arrive!"

So it was arranged. The card table was unfolded in the living room, the waxy flower-backed cards in their elaborate holder brought out with the score pads and the stubby pencil, and they sat down to play. Erich teamed up with Commander Marshall, Jean with her mother. Midge flitted around the table, looking at their hands. She'd always thought bridge was boring.

Jean wasn't crazy about the game herself, but it was a sure way to win over her parents, so she played her hand with the best humor and concentration she could summon while seated so close to Erich. Her hand, arm, elbow were only inches away from his. Now and then she was sure the touch of his knee against hers was deliberate. She wished he wouldn't do that; she was afraid her face flushed scarlet each time she felt the gentle, urgent pressure.

The sound of his voice aroused her deeply. Yet his words were commonplace, so dishearteningly normal. As they played—Commander Marshall won the bid of four hearts; and Erich laid out his cards on the table—Erich handed out bits of information about his life.

"Where are you living?" Commander Marshall asked after covering Jean's jack of spades with his king.

"I have an apartment in the Wardman Park Hotel," Erich said. "Several of us New Yorkers call it home. I'm with the bank, Brigham Phelps is with an architecture firm, and two others are with the government."

"We're seeing so many changes in Washington these days, so many new people," Jean's mother said plaintively.

"It's only just beginning," Commander Marshall said. "These New Dealers FDR's bringing in, not to mention all the internationals coming and going with all this fuss Hitler's stirring up in Europe."

"I'd be down here anyway," Erich told them. "Upton and Steward have had a Washington branch since before the turn of the century."

"Do you like it here?" Mrs. Marshall's voice was coyly suggestive: he should answer yes.

"Actually, I find it a bit boring compared to New York," Erich said. Mrs. Marshall's lips went rigid in disapproval—she hated to have anyone hint that her town was not the ultimate place for life to be lived. But Jean's heart beat a little faster with relief and excitement: at least Erich wasn't going to be a yes-man, ingratiating himself with her parents. And she would have been disappointed if he hadn't liked New York more than Washington.

When Bobby and Betty arrived, the bridge game broke up. Agate and Stafford brought in the crystal bowl and cups for eggnog, while Mrs. Marshall supervised Jean, Midge, and Betty as they scurried through the kitchen and dining room setting out sandwiches and cookies. Erich went back into the living room to talk with the men. Jean could tell that Bobby was abrupt with Erich; he didn't like this intruder involved with his sister. Then Al arrived. The guests came in groups, filling the house with rushes of fresh air and laughter. The carolers swept in, sang exuberantly, drank eggnog, greedily devoured the Christmas goodies, and left. Jean didn't have a moment to talk with Erich, or even to stand near him.

Still, when the evening was finally over, Erich had invited her to the movies with him the next night, and had her parents' permission to take her.

They went to Loew's Palace Theater to see a Betty Hutton movie, which might have been projected upside down and backwards for all Jean knew. As the shadowy images moved on the screen, similar ghostly shapes flickered within her. After carefully helping her remove her coat and align it along the back of her seat, Erich did not let his hand linger against her back. He did not try to hold her hand during the long movie or even to rest his arm alongside hers. She was aware of his steady, gentle breathing; the calm rise and fall of his chest pulled her vision sideways. Every time she dared to glance at his profile, she saw a man engrossed in a movie, almost unaware that he had a companion. His long legs stretched down into the darkness parallel to hers but never touching. Yet he seemed to be purposefully infusing the air with his own special odor, an incense of attraction.

After the movie Erich took her for a drink at the Metropolitan Club. It was the first time she'd been there without a member of her family, and as she sat sipping her martini at the small table Jean felt exquisitely sophisticated. She'd gotten drunk enough times by now at Radcliffe, and earlier, when she and Midge had experimented with liquor with ghastly results, to know that she could handle one drink, and perhaps two, without losing her dignity. But the combination of Erich's proximity and gin was a heady mixture. There was so much she wanted to know about him, yet she found herself babbling on and on about herself. It was nerves. And excitement. And anticipation mingled with terror because the moment of losing her virginity seemed to her now to be very close.

"What are they saying up in Boston about this war in Europe?" Erich asked.

"I can't speak for Boston, or even for Radcliffe, but I can tell you what I'm doing about it. I hate war, hate the very idea of war. I'm volunteering for a review called *War Stories;* its debut issue will come out this spring. April, we hope." As she described the review, she watched carefully for his response. Her brother,

her father, Al, would have exploded by now at what they would see as harebrained, treacherous idiocy, but Erich was listening with what appeared to be detached interest.

Finally he said, "You're very brave to become involved with such a publication."

"Well, thank you. I would like to think I am brave."

"If it's any help, I agree with your goals. I hate the idea of war. And in my own way, I'm working toward peace."

"You are? How? What—?"

Erich looked at his watch. "It's complicated. And it's gotten late. Let me tell you about it another time. I'd better get you home, or your father will worry."

This time it seemed to her that when Erich helped her into her raccoon coat his hands lingered on her shoulders in a firm, deliberate caress. His body stayed behind hers a significant few seconds too long, and a significant few inches too close for courtesy. Her face flushed. During the ride home, they spoke of casual, common, everyday things: he was leaving the next day to spend some time in New York with his family. He would be back around the twenty-ninth. Would she spend New Year's Eve with him?

Jean was glad for the chaos of Christmas. The family rituals, the visitors, the presents, the festive meals, all helped make the time pass toward the day of Erich's return. Al had gone back to California to spend Christmas with his family, so Jean was relieved of the burden of dealing with him. She knew she was fond of Al, but every word she spoke and gesture she made toward him was weighted by her fear that she was giving him hope.

In this house, so sturdy, safe, and warm, provided by her father, kept cozy by her mother, with her smiling family milling around her like animals in a child's picture book of a perfectly happy home, Jean knew she was a furtive, deceptive, desperate creature. She was a fox in a bunny's costume. Her mother pampered her; her father responded to her good-girl behavior with suspicious approval.

On Christmas morning, they gave her a car.

Jean stood out in the driveway surrounded by her family, weeping. They had hastily pulled coats over their nightgowns and robes in order to hurry outside to inspect the shining dark blue DeSoto sedan, then Jean slid inside, onto its rather scratchy gray seat, and put her hands on the wheel. She was overwhelmed with emotions: gratitude, guilt, and glee: this would be her getaway car.

On New Year's Eve there were parties all over Washington. Commander and Mrs. Marshall were invited to one set, Bobby and Betty to another, and Erich was taking Jean to yet another: a small private dinner at the home of Mr. and Mrs. Upton, then to various celebrations at ballrooms and clubs all over town. It was possible, Jean told her parents and brother, that they'd run into each other sometime during the evening.

Secretly she hoped she wouldn't encounter any of her family. But during the dinner party at the Uptons' palatial home she thought her family might as well have been there, too. It was a terribly formal function. Erich was seated at the other end of the table. Jean was placed between two older men, one avuncular and jovial, the other ancient and slightly deaf, his cupped hand and inclined head requiring that she repeatedly shout his way. From time to time she looked down the long table to see Erich also deferring to his companions, two older women; once or twice he met her eyes and smiled, but generally the meal was much more work than fun.

Afterwards, the banking crowd went off in their separate cars to the New Year's Eve ball at the Raleigh Hotel. For the first hour Jean and Erich were caught up and swept along in the festivities. Jean grew discouraged—all her beauty, all her *readiness* was going to waste! Midge Carlisle's parents were at the ball with another crowd, and they came across the long room to meet Erich and chat with Jean. Jean had always liked them; but she was especially glad to see them now, because she knew they could verify to her parents exactly where she'd been—in the Raleigh Hotel doing the fox-trot with some fuddy-duddies.

Still, as midnight drew near, anticipation flushed through her. When at last Erich asked her to dance, he drew her far into the middle of the crowd so that they were hidden from those he knew.

"Having a good time?" Erich asked, smiling down at her.

"Oh . . ." Jean said, caught. She wanted to be *herself* with this man, but she didn't want to insult the people he worked with. "Well, everyone is very nice—"

"Oh, Jean," Erich said with a laugh. "I know they're boring, darling, but this has to be done. It's part of the job. You're good to put up with them. I'm grateful. They think you're enchanting, by the way."

He had called her "darling." For a few moments that was all she could think of, that and the pressure of his hand on her back, the warmth of their hands together, their bodies moving together as they danced. She had to look down, away, in order to hide her eyes.

He was leading her farther away from the group, out of the center of the dance floor. When the music ended, as others clapped, he pulled her gently along to the doorway. They escaped from the noisy ballroom into a long corridor, and in silence he led her down the hall, around the corner, to another doorway. He took a key from his pocket and opened the door.

Inside was a very small, plush living room, opening onto a bedroom. He had brought her to a suite, Jean realized. He had a key to a private suite. Her heart drove blood thudding into her ears so quickly she thought she would faint.

Erich didn't stop to notice her reaction but quickly crossed the room and shoved open a window. A blast of cold winter air whisked into the room, bringing with it sounds of merriment from the street and strains of the music from the ballroom down the hall.

"Here," he said, beckoning.

She noticed then that on the table by the window was a silver bucket with a champagne bottle in it, and two glasses.

"I thought that after we paid our dues to the good folk out there we should have a private New Year's celebration ourselves. Don't look so alarmed. I have no intention of tossing you over my shoulder and carrying you into the bedroom to ravish you. I wanted a private living room for the two of us, and all they could give me was this suite. Here. Have a glass of champagne."

"Thank you." Jean took the glass of champagne. She sipped, and the bubbles tingled in her nose. She looked up through her eyelashes at Erich. He was studying her.

She studied him back. He wasn't anywhere nearly as handsome as Al; he wasn't even as handsome as Bobby. His nose was crooked. He didn't have that shining quality her brother and Al had; he didn't seem so new. Bluish stains spread under his very dark eyes. Perhaps he was tired. He'd only just gotten back from New York.

"What do you think?" he asked.

"I think you're older than you say you are."

He smiled. "Perhaps I am, in many ways. But I promise you, I'm twenty-four."

He let the silence last. Jean took a deep breath and bravely said, "What do *you* think?"

"I think," he said, "that it's midnight."

He leaned forward and kissed her lightly on the lips. When he pulled back after only a few seconds, she was disappointed. That wasn't much of a kiss! But he was only setting his glass on the table, then taking hers from her to put on the table, so that he could take her properly into his arms.

During the next hour they gradually moved from the table to the sofa where they sat and finally lay in each other's arms. She had never been so thoroughly kissed. She was glad she'd put perfume on her throat, behind her ears, at her elbows and wrists, for he kissed her there, returning to her mouth often, then kissing her closed eyes, her cheeks, her hair. They didn't speak. She could not keep from murmuring, and sometimes, in spite of herself, she moaned. Without any hesitation he put his hand on her breast; through the layers of their clothing she felt his body pressing against hers. Terrified by her audacity, she put her hands under his tux jacket in order to touch his body directly through the one soft layer of shirt. The smooth wide muscles of his back sank into the hard bony furrow of backbone which she traced with her fingers from his neck to the waistline of his trousers. She wanted to move her hands on down and to press his hips harder against hers, but she wasn't that brave.

His hands and lips were in her hair, on her throat, on her mouth, on the naked skin swelling from the bodice of her evening gown. His hands were on her breasts, on her waist, but he did not move his hands lower. The long, entreating movements of his legs were muffled by all the material of her full skirt; still, she could feel Erich's lower body between her legs.

And then she felt the thrust of his hardness against her. Through layers of soft clothing came an insistent, gentle battering. She tightened her arms around his back and twisted her head to one side, hiding her face against the sofa seat, concentrating on this new sensation. Erich's body arched and shoved, and Jean's body replied, searching to keep the connection. Her underpants were wet, and their struggles made the silk of her slip slide against her inner thighs and against her crotch, causing small exquisite thrills, along with the deeper, blunter pleasure of Erich's hardness pushing against her flesh.

Erich supported his weight on one arm as he burrowed his face into her neck, kissing and biting lightly. She wanted to force him into her, and she ground against him with such strength it almost seemed she would in spite of all their clothing.

"Oh," she cried. "Oh, Erich. Please."

He let all his weight fall upon her. He took her face in his two hands and turned her mouth to meet his. His mouth crushed hers. His body crushed hers.

Suddenly he pulled away from her. With a series of awkward, almost desperate movements, he pushed himself up and away until he ended up sitting at the far end of the sofa. A lock of dark hair had fallen down over his forehead, and he pushed it back. His chest was heaving. Jean, embarrassed and baffled, sat up, pulled herself together, and rearranged her disheveled clothing.

"I'm sorry," Erich said.

" 'Sorry'!" Jean repeated, shocked. It was the last thing she'd expected him to say.

"That was ungentlemanly of me. To force myself on you."

"It wasn't—you weren't—" She did not know how to respond. Certainly Al had never moved in on her with such ferocity, but she had never wanted him to. Al's kisses, caresses, what few there had been, had been gentle—*considerate.*

"We should rejoin the others," Erich said, rising. "They'll be wondering where we've gone. There's a—powder room— through that door if you'd like to freshen up."

Jean collected her purse and went into the privacy of the hotel bathroom. Her face in the mirror dazzled her. She was radiant, flushed, glowing, beautiful. How could he resist her! What an odd man he was, what a mixture of impulse and restraint!

By the time she came out of the bathroom, he had smoothed and straightened his clothing, and together in silence they left the hotel suite and walked down the hall to the ballroom door. The pulse of music struck Jean's senses like a blow: so much noise and movement, laughter, light—an entire world was going on. They slipped back into place among the dancers. Erich held Jean just a slight bit away from him, so that their legs and chests did not touch. A glaze had come over Erich's face, and his eyes were distant. It was almost as if he were angry with her— but why?

They rejoined the banking crowd gathered around the tables. Many people had gone home. Jean looked at her watch and was startled to see that it was almost two o'clock. They had been together on the sofa for almost two hours! It had flashed by like an instant.

"I should take you home now," Erich said, coming around the table to stand next to her. "We don't want your parents to worry."

"They may not be home yet from their own parties!" Jean protested.

But Erich did not relent. He stood, smiling a somehow official smile, while she gathered up her purse and said polite good nights to the people around her. At the coat check he helped her into her fur with only the briefest of touches. He was silent as they walked through the lobby of the hotel and waited for the man to bring the car around.

Chapter 6
🌿 Julia

Light began to seep through the opening in the motel-room curtains about six Tuesday morning. Between half-closed eyes Julia watched the glow slide and brighten. She'd slept a little, mostly tossed and turned. Beside her, Sam still slept the sleep of the blessed, completely relaxed.

Julia remembered a conversation she'd overheard once between her mother and Sam's.

"Sam is a remarkable boy," Diane had observed. "He's so calm, so happy."

"He always was that way," P.J. had replied. "He was given to us when he was only a few months old, but even then he was happy. A serene baby, if you can imagine such a thing. It always seemed to us that Sam was glad just to be here on this earth."

Julia had wondered then, and still she wondered, how it might feel to be glad just to be here on this earth. At some moments in her life, she'd been happy, or high, triumphant, or giddy, but she'd never felt serenely happy just to be alive. As she grew older she found the business of living more and more frightening. She was just terrified of being here on this earth.

She'd started this year, her senior year at Gressex, feeling as if she were on ice skates, headed on a downhill slope of glass. Time was pulling her along. She had no control over her life. Over the past year she'd looked at colleges with her mother or father or Chase, and now she had to start the backbreaking task of filling out college applications. She had a full schedule of courses. She had her assigned dorm room and her old boarding-school friends. Everything was familiar and routine—yet it all felt like a prison. Everyone expected her to plod along with the herd into college and through another four years of books, term papers, boring lectures, and grades—a life cut up and sliced off into black-and-white columns. Just thinking about it made her whole body feel weighed down, as if all the rules she was forced to live by were piled upon her.

The only time she wasn't anxious was when she was with Sam. Every weekend after they became lovers, he drove up from Wesleyan—a short trip, just over an hour—to visit her. They'd go to a motel room, the same motel they were lying in now. They'd make love, go out to dinner or a movie, then return to make love again. Sam was so calm. Julia felt reassured by his presence. She didn't tell him that she was having anxiety attacks until last weekend. When she did tell him, she meant it as a compliment; she was trying to please him.

It hadn't worked out that way.

Last Sunday afternoon they'd gone over to walk around Walden Pond. The day was brilliant with sunshine, and the trees encircling the pond were shivering and dipping in the breeze, flashing out oranges, crimsons, and golds. The side of the pond nearest the road was crowded with tourists and families with children playing on the shore, so Sam took Julia's hand and they followed the path through the grass and low brush until they came to a solitary spot far over on the opposite shore. They settled shoulder to shoulder, almost hidden by the tall grass, with their feet dangling over the bank just inches above the dark blue water.

"I love being with you, Sam," Julia said, sighing.

"I love being with you."

"Sometimes when I'm not with you, I can't breathe."

Sam was quiet, thinking. Then he asked, "What do you mean, you can't breathe?"

She could feel the tension in his body. "Don't worry, Sam. It's nothing. Sometimes I just can't breathe, that's all. Like a weight's been placed on my chest. And my stomach. I can't inhale—like this." Julia pulled up her navy T-shirt to show how her diaphragm rose and fell as she took several long, deep breaths.

"When does this happen? At night? Or in a particular class?"

"Anytime. No one special time. I can just be walking along talking to people. Or in the shower. Sometimes when I first wake up in the morning."

"What do you do?"

"Well, to start with, I'm just aware of it. It's like I realize, ohmygod, I can't get my breath. Sometimes it just goes away. Sometimes I have to curl up in a ball and cover my ears and eyes." She was embarrassed. "And sort of sing to myself."

"Jesus, Julia, that sounds like a panic attack."

His alarm frightened her. She didn't want to scare him off. "What do I have to be panicked about?" she asked teasingly, flirting, trying to lower the tension level.

"I don't know, Julia. I can't imagine. You know I love you.

You're beautiful and intelligent and popular and clever. You've got lots of friends."

"I wish I hadn't mentioned it. God, Sam, if you saw the rest of the girls in my dorm you'd know how sane I am. Everyone else is purging and starving or doing drugs or freaking out about college."

"What are you thinking about college these days?"

"Oh, I just hate it," Julia groaned and, pulling up a blade of grass, began to shred the stem.

"Hate what?" Sam asked. Gently he put his hand on her back.

"All this college-application shit. All the competition! Sam, I'm not even sure I want to go to college. Four more years of books and exams? I don't know if I can handle it."

"Sure you can."

"All right, I can. But do I want to? I don't think I do. I'm tired of this kind of life. I hate it."

"What do you want to do?"

"Guess." Julia tossed the grass into the water.

"Travel. Wander through Europe."

"Nope." She put her hand on Sam's thigh.

"Work. Start piling up money."

"Wrong again." She nuzzled against his neck.

"Teach retarded children, feed the starving masses! Come on, Julia, I can't read your mind." Tired of the game, Sam pushed up from the ground in one lithe movement. "I'm hungry. Let's go get something to eat."

"Okay. Help me up." Julia held out her hand, and Sam pulled her to her feet, kissed her absentmindedly, then led her back to the path. She let the subject of her future drop; her mother, her Aunt Susan, her friends had all told her that men were dense. She'd just have to approach him another time, in another way. Or perhaps she should get pregnant.

As they crawled into the old brown Volvo Sam's parents had given him, he said suddenly, "But you can't ignore this breathing business, Julia. I think you should see a doctor about it."

"All right," Julia agreed. "I will." But she was lying. She knew she didn't need a doctor. She only needed Sam.

All last week she'd fretted about that conversation at Walden Pond. She was afraid she'd scared Sam off with her fears, or bored him. When he called on Friday to say he couldn't come see her this weekend, she hadn't been surprised. He said he had to study for an exam, but she feared the worst, that Sam had stopped loving her, that she had driven him away.

She'd tried to enjoy just hanging out with her friends, and she'd gotten through Saturday well enough. But on Saturday night she wasn't able to sleep, and by Sunday morning she was exhausted and hyped up, frantic to the point of weeping. She found a half-full bottle of Tylenol in Sonja's things and took them all, then escaped into a blissful sleep that lasted all Sunday afternoon and night.

But Monday her fears were still there, and then she had her counseling session with Mrs. Derek and felt her hopelessness return. No matter what she told anyone, the adults in her life would pat her on the head and expect her to stay in line.

She had to do something drastic.

She called Sam at lunchtime Monday. Luckily, he was in his dorm.

"I have to see you," she told him. "You *have* to come up here today."

After a long pause, he replied in a tight, troubled voice, "All right. I'll leave right away."

"Sam—" she pleaded, but he'd hung up the phone on her. Hugging herself, she bent over, trying to get her breath. What if he was really mad at her? What if he broke up with her because he couldn't stand the way she was acting?

During the painfully long hour and a half of waiting, Julia paced her room between her unmade bed and her desk piled with textbooks and papers. Muttering to herself, she rehearsed various speeches, trying to find the perfect words to convince him to take her back with him, to live with her, to marry her.

But when Sam actually walked into the room, his beautiful face strained with confusion and alarm, all reason fled.

"What's going on?" he asked immediately, not even hugging or kissing her first.

He was wearing old jeans, a plaid flannel shirt, and work boots, and he looked so handsome, so sexual, so desirable that even as he stood in her room he seemed unattainable. Julia felt wild with need.

"Oh, Sam!" Her voice was barely above a whisper.

Sam crossed the room and took her in his arms. "Calm down, Julia. It's all right."

Together they sat down on her bed. After a few moments Julia caught her breath.

"Sam, I need to get out of here. I hate it here. I want to be with you."

"Come on, Julia. Get real. That's just not possible right now." Sam suddenly stood up and stalked across the room.

Julia blinked. Was he going to leave already? "Sam. You don't understand. I—"

"Julia, I can't believe you got me up here to talk about this. I thought you were in trouble or something."

"I am in trouble, Sam. What do I have to do to prove it to you?"

"Julia, look—"

She heard exasperation tinge his voice as he stood far across the room from her, near the door. "No, you look!" she cried and grabbed a pair of nail scissors lying on the desk. She pressed the tip into her wrist. "I'm tired of hinting, Sam. I'm tired of waiting. If you don't take me away from here right now, I'll kill myself."

"Oh, Julia, don't be so stupid!" Sam exploded.

So Julia dug the scissors quickly into one wrist and then the other. They watched as the fine lines of blood widened, then streaked down Julia's arms. So bright, so fluid, so red.

"Go, then," Julia ordered. "Just go. If I can't be with you, I don't want to live. Go on! Go!"

"Julia, Julia, what are you doing?" he cried, rattled, scared. He rushed across the room to get her, but she raced away from him and out the other door into the large girls' bathroom. Drops of her blood dripped brilliantly on the white floor tiles.

She fended him off with outstretched hands, blood running down her arms.

"All right, Julia." Sam surrendered. "All right! I'll take you with me."

"Oh, God!" Sonja entered the bathroom.

"It's all right," Julia said. "Sam's going to take me with him." Then she fainted.

When she came to she found herself on the bathroom floor, her head cradled in Sam's arms.

"You're okay, Julia," Sam whispered. He was smoothing her hair away from her face.

"I need to be with you, Sam."

"I know. I'll take you with me."

"You promise?"

"Promise."

He helped Julia stand. After a momentary dizziness, she was

steady. Sonja found some Scotch tape with which she bound bits of paper towels around Julia's wrists. Then while Julia threw clothes into a duffel bag, Sonja and Sam wiped up the bathroom floor.

"Okay, let's go," Julia said.

"You're going to be in big trouble," Sonja warned Julia.

"I don't care."

"What am I going to tell the dorm parents? The headmaster?"

Julia smiled. "Tell them I've run away to marry Sam."

"Oh, God, Julia. That will make them crazy," Sam protested, but Julia was running down the stairs.

She reached his car before he did. She threw herself into the front seat and locked the door.

Sam tossed her duffel bag into the backseat, then sat down behind the steering wheel.

"I would really like to take you to a hospital," he said. "To check your wrists."

"They're fine, Sam. Really. Let's go to Howard Johnson's."

"Will you talk to me there? I mean talk sensibly?"

"Yes. I promise. Just get me away from here."

Checking into Howard Johnson's was like returning to their own home. "All right," Sam said, shutting the door. "What's this all about?"

Julia sat against the headboard of one of the double beds. She was fully clothed, but chilled even so. She yanked the covers up to her chin.

"I just couldn't be there anymore," she said. "I had an appointment with Mrs. Derek this morning. This getting into college business. It's such a crock. I couldn't stand it anymore."

"Why do you say that?" Sam sat on the end of the bed, not quite in reach.

"Okay, maybe it's great for some people. You got through it. But I'm tired of it. I'm tired of the tests, the pressure, the expectations—"

"So you don't want to go to college?"

"Not at all. I'm sick of teachers. I'm sick of rules."

"So what do you want to do?"

"Really? I'd like to work in a restaurant." Julia waited for his reaction, and when he only looked at her calmly, she continued. "I'd like to work in a restaurant and marry you and put you through school and live with you."

Sam got up. He walked across the room. He pulled the drapery cord so that the curtains opened to let in a hazy light. He pulled the cord and the curtains shut.

"It's not so impossible," Julia said. "You're twenty-two. I'm eighteen. Those are reasonable ages to get married."

"Your parents would kill you."

"My parents are going to kill me anyway for what I just did."

"Gressex will probably expel you."

"I don't care! I hate it there. I want to be with you, Sam."

Sam walked over to Julia's bed. He sat down close to her and took her hands in his. His face was earnest. "I just don't know what to say, Julia."

"We're right for each other. I know it. I've always known it."

Sam didn't reply.

"You know it, too, Sam," Julia said. She leaned over and grabbed his face with both her hands. She turned his face toward hers and, looking in his eyes, she saw what she needed to see. He did love her.

But Sam pulled away. "Just because we're right for each other doesn't mean we should get married."

Julia put her hand lightly on his arm. "Will you at least think about it?"

Sam slid his arm up and turned it so that his palm touched hers, and he closed his hand upwards, lacing his fingers through hers. His touch was warm and steady. "Yeah, okay," Sam said softly.

" 'Yeah, okay,' " she echoed solemnly. They sat together for a while, silent, intensely in love, until Julia broke the mood. "Oh, Sam, I love you!" She laughed, throwing herself at him, smothering him with kisses. Then she stood up, briskly straightening her clothes. "I'm starving!" she declared.

They went out for a pizza, which they brought back to the room and ate in bed as they watched *Wayne's World* on the pay TV. Julia felt her anxiety level drop and float away. But when the movie was finished, Sam looked at her and said, "I wonder if the school has called your parents."

"Probably. I don't care." Julia went into the bathroom to wash the pizza sauce off her hands. The paper towels on her wrists had dried to a crusty red. She decided not to mess with them tonight. She threw herself back onto the mussed bed.

"Julia. Your parents will be worried."

"They'll know I'm with you."

Sam sat on the bed again. Once more they went over it all, Julia's desire, her need, Sam's hesitancy, his common sense.

Finally Julia said, "Okay. Just do this. Take me with you to Middletown. I'll find an apartment. I'll find a job. I need to be near you."

"Your parents—"

"This is my life."

"They'll never forgive me."

"Would you stop thinking about my parents!" Half angry, half laughing, Julia pushed Sam, toppling him over backwards on the bed.

He wrestled her around until she was under him. Holding her arms down but carefully avoiding her wrists, he studied her, seriously. "You are the strongest-willed person I've ever met."

"Well, I know what I want," Julia replied, looking steadily into his eyes.

Sam kissed her forehead, then slid down until he was lying alongside her. "And I know what I want," he whispered. He gathered her against him, kissing her face slowly and holding her very close, pressing her against him, smoothing her hair.

"What do you want, Sam?"

They were wrapped around each other, legs entwined. "I want you to be safe," Sam said. "I want you to be happy."

Julia held her breath, closed her eyes, and made a wish, and Sam continued, as if in answer to her wish, "I want you to be with me. We'll work this out."

They made love then, with a sudden shyness sprung from this new, unspoken commitment. At first Sam was very gentle, watching Julia as he undressed and caressed and kissed her, and she let him see her need. He entered her, and she clutched him to her with her arms and legs and clung to him with all her might. They never stopped looking into each other's eyes. Tenderness, mingled with lust, made Sam's face seem somehow naked, and vulnerable. Her own eyes filled with tears; she knew her face was glowing and flushed. The sweet tension between them grew so intense it became almost unbearable, and finally Sam groaned and, abandoning his gentleness, thrust himself into Julia so forcefully that she bit her lip in pain. He drove himself against her with an urgent, possessive passion that rocked her through.

When it was over and she could speak, trembling and weeping

and laughing, she said, "You see, Sam? You see? You can't ever leave me."

"I know. I see. I'll never leave you, Julia. I promise," Sam whispered in return. "Oh, God, I never want to be without you."

Almost at once they fell asleep, sated, exhausted, and—at last—calm.

Yet when Sam woke up Tuesday morning, he looked at Julia in consternation. "Oh, God. I can't believe we're here."

"Well, let's leave," Julia teased, then sobered: "Take me to Middletown."

"Will you call your parents?"

"Okay. Once we get there."

Sam just looked at her. He went into the bathroom. When he came out, he was dressed.

"All right," he said. "Dad always says to sleep on a problem, and I did. Listen to me, Julia. I'll take you to Middletown with me, and we can even consider living together for a while. On one condition. Don't you ever pull that wrist-slashing business on me again. Understand? That's not fair. It scared me. You do that ever again, I don't care if we're married, I'll leave you for good."

Julia's voice was meek. "I'm sorry, Sam." Her heart was flipping around in her chest with hope. "I'll never do that again. I promise. I was just—trying to make my point."

"Well, you made it," Sam said flatly. "All right. Let's go."

They listened to soft rock on the radio during the ride. When they approached the outskirts of the college town, Julia said, "Let's just try it. I'll get a place. I'll get a job. You can come be with me when you're not in class. We'll have fun."

"It would be nice to be with you every day," Sam conceded.

Julia bit back a triumphant smile.

Once in town, they went directly to a drugstore down the hill from the college. There was a board where cards advertising jobs and rooms were posted.

They copied down four addresses, then set out in the car. All the places were within walking distance of Wesleyan. None was in an especially attractive neighborhood. But at the third one, Julia cried out, "Stop! This one looks good!"

Sam rolled his eyes. Like the first two, the apartment house was an old Victorian frame building that had seen better days. It needed paint, a new roof; it needed everything. But yellow and orange chrysanthemums had been carefully nurtured in front of the house, and in the backyard was a long clothesline hung with fresh laundry flapping gaily in the sun.

Dutifully, Sam parked the car and went up to the door with Julia, who quickly checked to be sure her wrists were covered by her shirtsleeves. Her knock was answered by a grandmotherly woman of gigantic proportions who introduced herself as Edith Overtoom. She led Julia and Sam through the hallway to a bedroom at the back of the house, providing a running commentary as they went.

"It's a nice bedroom. Large and sunny. And it's on the first floor. I know I should move my bedroom down to the first floor and let you youngsters climb the stairs, but habits are hard to break. You'll have your own bathroom. Across the hall."

The air of the room was slightly fusty. The bed was lumpy and the furniture was chipped, but the sheets were clean. And the bed was a double bed.

"Would I be able to use your clothesline?" Julia asked.

Mrs. Overtoom barked out a laugh of surprise. "Well, I don't know why not. No one's ever asked about that before. Usually they prefer to do their laundry at the laundromat down the street. You can have kitchen privileges, providing you clean up after yourself and don't get into my food."

"Great. I'd like to take it."

"You up at the college?"

"Sam is. We're going to get married pretty soon. I'm going to get a job and save money."

"Well, I'll need two weeks' rent in advance. No loud music after midnight. You have to wash your own linen and keep your bedroom and bathroom clean. Do you smoke?"

"No."

"Good. No parties. But your fiancé can come and go as he likes. I'm a very modern landlady!"

"That's great!" Julia exclaimed. "Sam!" She flashed him a genuine smile. "Welcome to my new home!"

She had plenty of money from her clothing allowance and summer baby-sitting jobs. She paid Mrs. Overtoom, feeling enormously grown-up as she took the handwritten receipt. Sam waited while she unpacked her duffel bag, then they went together up to the campus for lunch. Friends of Sam's drifted up to talk. Sam went off to class, leaving Julia to hunt for a job. Instead, she found herself wandering around the beautiful college grounds. She couldn't believe she wasn't at Gressex. She searched her soul for a bit of remorse, and found none. Even if Sam didn't marry her, even if he came to despise her, she still had no regrets. She was free.

In the early evening she met Sam and walked back down to her room, stopping on the way at Marino's to pick up a six-pack of Diet Cokes, some sandwiches, and a tin of Band-Aids. Back in the room, Sam helped Julia take off the brown, blood-stained pieces of paper towel. He smoothed the bandages over her cuts, which were small, but ugly and jagged, crusted red-black, as if irritated. Then Sam did his homework on the floor while Julia lay on the double bed looking at the want ads in the local newspaper.

At ten o'clock, Sam said, "All right!" and slammed his book shut. "I've kept my end of the bargain, Julia. Now you keep yours. Call your parents and tell them where you are."

"Okay." Julia sighed.

Together they went out of her room, down the hall, and into the living room where Mrs. Overtoom, whom Sam had already secretly nicknamed Mrs. Overload, sat watching television.

"Would it be all right to use your telephone?" Julia asked.

"Local?"

"Long distance. But I'll make it collect."

"All right. It's in the kitchen. You can use it for local calls as long as you don't tie up the phone, but no long-distance calls charged to this number."

"No, of course not. I won't be on long."

Together Julia and Sam went back into the kitchen. He sat on the table while she stood next to the wall phone. Her mother answered and said she'd accept the collect call.

"Julia! Darling! Where are you? Are you okay?"

"I'm fine, Mother. I'm in Middletown with Sam. I'm sorry about worrying you and Dad, but I just couldn't stay at school any longer."

"But Sonja said you—" Diane's voice broke.

"I'm fine, Mother!" Julia was instantly impatient. "I was just— Look. I'll explain it all to you some other time. I just wanted to let you know where I am."

"I'm so glad you're all right, darling. What are your plans?"

"Mom, I'm going to get a job. I don't want to go to school. I want to stay here and work and see Sam."

"Oh, Julia—"

"Look, Mom, I don't want to argue. Listen. I'll call you again in a few days. I'll talk to you longer then."

She slammed the receiver back into place, cutting off their connection.

"Julia," Sam said, "that wasn't very nice."

"Oh, I hate talking to her. She always expects so much of me."

"Like what? What did she say?"

"Oh, she wanted to know what my *plans* are. She probably thinks I should have every day of my month scheduled in a Filofax the way she does. She just doesn't understand me, Sam. Please, don't push me. I've done what you asked. I told her where I am and that I'm safe and with you. Now she won't worry. I'll call her back in a few days."

"I'd better call my parents, too," Sam said.

Her throat constricted with fear. What if the Weyborns convinced Sam—*ordered* him—to take her back? She crept back down the hall to her room and collapsed on her bed. Her hands on her throat were ice cold. She held the Band-Aids on her wrists to her nose, finding comfort in the sharp antiseptic smell that they gave off. She tried to inhale it. She closed her eyes and focused only on the scent.

"Julia? What are you doing?"

Sam came in the room and shut the door behind him. Turning, Julia waited for him to say he was leaving her now, his parents had insisted, he had to go back to his dorm room. . . .

"Julia."

Sam sat down on the bed next to her and pulled her to him. When her head touched his chest, her breath returned in an explosion. She gasped and shuddered. He kept his arms around her. Warmth returned.

"Oh, Sam," she whispered. "Sam."

They fell down together on the bed and held each other. Sam pulled a blanket up over them. Exhausted, they fell asleep.

In the morning Julia and Sam awakened very early. They made quick, silent love in the bumpy double bed before he pulled on his clothes and hurried up the hill. Julia dug around in the plastic bags she'd brought in, found a Diet Coke, and crawled back into bed to drink it as she contemplated the day ahead. She leaned back against the wall—the bed had no headboard—reliving the moments she'd spent that morning with Sam, hearing again the words of love he'd spoken, and then, with a spurt of energy, she jumped from the bed to begin her day.

First she had to wash some clothes, mostly underwear and socks. She'd been away from Gressex only two days, but she hadn't brought many clothes with her, and she'd always been fastidious about what touched her skin. Although she bought her clothes at thrift shops, she washed them constantly. In the large bathroom down the hall she'd found a plastic container of Ivory Liquid and set about soaking and scrubbing her clothes by hand in the small sink. White cotton socks, expensive, lacy underwear, white cotton shirts. She wore kind of a uniform of white cotton turtlenecks and white cotton oversized men's shirts that went over blue jeans.

It was the most wonderful experience, hanging her sweet-smelling clothes on the clothesline with knobbed wooden pins exactly like the ones her grandmother used. It was a cold day, but sunny, and Julia felt cheerful. She would not have taken a spoonful of sugar for her coffee without first asking the landlady, but as she slipped into her bedroom and pulled the door shut behind her, she held a wooden clothespin tightly in her hand. She intended to go out searching for a job, but the rumpled bed beckoned to her. She kicked off her loafers, crawled back into bed fully dressed, and lay looking at the clothespin as if it could stake down one more clear thing in the whirlwind of her life.

Julia didn't quite sleep, but she felt herself entering that relaxed state where the mind drifts free. The wooden clothespin in her hand blurred until she was in her grandmother's backyard in MacLean, and it was this past July, when she had gone down with her mother to help her grandmother move out of the wonderful house.

Aunt Susan had come for the funeral, then flown home to organize her family, and was due back in two days to stay for a while to help. It was morning, and Julia was walking through the house munching Cheerios dry from the box as she stood studying each wall and corner of the rooms, trying to memorize every inch of this house she was losing forever. She'd wandered out onto the screened-in porch, which was lushly covered with climbing roses, ivy, and morning glories, and purely by accident she'd overheard her grandmother and her mother arguing.

Diane was talking in a brittle, cheerful manner. "You know, Mother, in your condo you won't be able to hang your laundry out on a line."

Julia was shocked by the gloating, even vicious, pleasure in her mother's voice. She sank down onto a flower-cushioned wicker chair to eavesdrop.

"I know," Jean said, wistfully. "I've thought of that. It's always been one of my greatest pleasures in life, hanging out the wash."

"Oh, for heaven's sakes, Mother. You talk like some dotty old

187

peasant caught in a time warp. Everyone's been using dryers for years and years."

"Well, I'm not 'everyone.' The smell of the sun and wind on my sheets at night is one of the things I've always treasured. Your father liked it, too."

"I'm sure he did. And I'm sure he liked knowing that you were using up hours of your days lugging this heavy basket outside, bending and stooping like a washerwoman, when other women were free to use dryers, and could save time and *do something* with their lives!"

Julia's stomach clenched at the bitterness in Diane's tone and was surprised at the mildness of her grandmother's reply.

"Darling, I did do something with my life. You and I have always had our disagreements about that. It makes me so sad when you continually blame your father. I had a dryer. And I had help with the housework. It was *my* choice to hang out the laundry. I've always considered it a sort of ritual, Diane. You can laugh at me. But I always felt, each time I pinned clothes on the line, that I was invoking a kind of blessing, as if benevolent spirits were being blown into the fabrics that touched my family."

"Oh, God, Mother, sometimes you sound as superstitious as a pagan. Benevolent spirits! The stuff from the dryer was always soft, and whatever I took down from the clothesline was always scratchy and stiff!"

"Well, Diane, you now have your own home and your own dryer. I've never tried to convince you to hang your clothes on the line. Have I? Have I? So won't you please let me do my clothes my way. I don't see why you're getting so worked up about it."

"Oh, you're just determined to be old-fashioned, aren't you?" Diane concluded.

The distress in her mother's voice made Julia rise from the wicker chair and peer out through the thick lacing of vines. Diane was striding toward the house, swiping angrily at tears that were flowing down her face. Jean continued to hang up her wash, carefully shaking out a blouse, pinning it by its tail, uncoiling a sleeve so that it hung free.

It was getting hot. The air was heavy, and now so quiet that Julia could hear the hum of bees on the other side of the screen. She lay back in the wicker chair and closed her eyes. Her mother was such a nag. She was always trying to get people to do things her way. Julia had been puzzled all her life by the way her mother kept trying to change her father, when it was obvious he was always going to stay the same.

Julia lay in the mussed and bumpy bed in the rented room in Middletown, Connecticut. It was October but she was suspended between sleeping and waking, staring at the wooden clothespin that had brought back a day from summer.

Now it brought back more.

Julia's memory had switched channels and she was no longer at her grandmother's but in her own home, a little girl mystified by her parents' endless, teeth-clenchingly civilized battles.

Every night their mother gave them a bath, looked over their homework, and read them a bedtime story before tucking them in and kissing them good night. The nights she was out of town on business always held a tang of loneliness for Julia. Worse than that were the nights their mother tried to persuade their father to join in their routine. Often Julia and Chase would crouch at the top of the stairs holding their breath, listening to their parents' whispered arguments.

"Jim, it's almost nine. You promised me you'd put the kids to bed tonight."

"I can't, Diane. I'm busy. I need to finish reading this article. Can't you take care of it?"

"Of course I *can*. But I was hoping—"

"Look, I'm involved in something important here! I wish you wouldn't keep interrupting me!"

Other disagreements arose with an almost ritualistic frequency over everyday breakfast madness.

"Oh, no!" Julia would cry. "Mommy, I spilled my Cheerios!"

"That's okay, sweetie. Ask Daddy to sweep it up."

"Daddy—"

"Better ask your mother to do it, sport. I don't know where she keeps the broom."

"Mommy—" Anxiously Julia would look from one parent to the other.

Her mother would speak over her shoulder as she hurriedly spread peanut butter and jelly on bread. "Jim, the broom's in the broom closet. Over by the basement door. Or I'll sweep it up and you finish making their lunches."

"I don't know how to make their lunches. Anyway, I've got to go—"

"Jim, I can't do everything by myself."

"Diane, would you stop nagging me!"

The door would slam as their father left for work.

•   •   •

Another time:

Chase's seven-year-old voice, plaintive: "Mommy, there's sticky stuff on my shoe."

"Ask your daddy to clean it off, darling. Daddy forgot to clean the kitchen floor after dinner last night; that's why there's sticky stuff on the floor and on your shoe."

"Okay, sport, I'll clean off your shoe. Let me see it. Yuck. Diane, how can I get this off? I don't think it'll come off with just soap and a paper towel." Her father sounded genuinely baffled.

"I'm sure you'll come up with something," her mother answered, speaking in the no-nonsense, sensible voice that always warned Julia not to mess around.

But her father didn't seem to hear the warning. "Yeah, but I don't know what this stuff on the shoe is. *Hmm.* Do we have any cleanser?"

"Probably."

"Where is it?"

Her mother's voice was becoming tight with irritation, and a corresponding tightness clutched Julia's chest. "I assume it's under the sink."

"Or do you think cleanser would just stick to this stuff? It's so gluey."

Diane turned to Julia and said, sweetly, "Honey, you're not eating your carrots. Here. Let Mommy cut them for you."

At the sound of Diane's normal tone, Jim seemed to relax. "Look, son," he said, "let's deal with your shoe after dinner. My food's getting cold."

Diane's voice suddenly became shrill. "Jim. Chase will finish eating before you do. He always does. If he runs through the house with that on his shoe—"

"Okay. Chase. Tell you what. Take your shoe off. I'll clean it up after dinner."

"Jim. You told me you're going back to the lab after dinner."

"So?"

"So please clean his shoe off now. He'll need it for school tomorrow. If you don't do it now, you'll forget about it."

"Then I'll clean it off when I come home tonight."

"No, you won't! Jesus Christ, Jim, why do you make me go through this every time? You never do *anything* when you come home from the lab—"

"Mommy, I'll clean my shoe off! Look. I'm getting it off."

"Oh, Chase . . . here." Their mother's voice seemed to collapse. Quietly she said, "Let Mommy have it. It's okay, honey. You sit with Daddy and eat your dinner."

Julia sat at the table, staring at her plate, while their mother stood at the sink, scrubbing Chase's shoe.

Another time. The worst time. The time that stuck her raw, wounded stomach with savage stabbing pins:

"Julia? Julia, sweetie? Listen, it's Daddy. Baby, we're going to go to the hospital now so they can make you feel better. Remember what Dr. Walker said? That you might need to go? Well, he just called, and we're going."

"I want Mommy."

"I know you do, sweetheart, and we're trying to reach her. We're calling her on the telephone, and she'll come home as soon as she can. Here, honey, let Daddy put this blanket around you. I'm going to carry you down to the car. Mr. Donalin's driving us. Won't that be nice, in his big red car?"

"I'm eight years old. I don't want you to carry me. I'm a big girl."

"Oh, come on and be my baby just one more time. Let Daddy carry you. We'll get Teddy and you can hold him."

"I don't want the blanket, it's too hot! It's too hot when you hold me, Daddy. Your skin is too hot. It's hurting me! I want Mommy!"

The blur of white rooms, people dressed in what looked like white sheets, hands in rubber gloves, whispers everywhere, light that was so bright it burned her eyes. The voices.

"We're testing for spinal meningitis."

Her father's face flinching, his eyes so full of pain Julia cried to see them. Julia didn't understand the words, but she could clearly sense his terror. Who could take care of her? Who could fend off this white room, this heat, these strangers?

"I want Mommy!"

"Mommy will come. Mommy will come."

But Mommy did not come.

In her bed in her rented room, Julia crammed her face into her pillow and sobbed. The wooden clothespin, forgotten, rolled off the bed and fell with a barely audible click onto the floor.

When Sam woke Julia, it was early afternoon.

"Lazybones," he said. "There I was, slaving away over a hot calculus book and you were sleeping."

Julia had trouble opening her eyes. She felt warm and drowsy. Through her eyelashes she saw Sam, beautiful Sam, and smelled his apple-cider smell, cold now, fresh, from the outside air. She reached her arms up and pulled him down against her.

"*Mmmmm,*" she breathed, hugging him tightly.

But underneath, she felt his tenseness, resisting her.

"Let's run away, Sam," she said urgently. Sitting up, she grabbed him by the shoulders. "Let's run away and get married! Today!"

Sam pulled back. "Julia. It's right in the middle of the semester. I can't run away. My parents have paid a year's tuition."

"Oh, they have all the money in the world. Why worry about that? You can go to college anywhere! We just need a little time, another place, far away—"

"Julia, stop it. I've brought you here. Let's just take it easy."

"Your parents don't want you to be with me."

"That's not true, Julia. They're concerned about you. Don't be so paranoid."

"What did they say last night?"

"They asked me to bring you home this weekend. Just so we can all talk. Julia, they want to help you. We all just want to help you."

"*Help* me."

Julia searched Sam's face. This was not how she'd imagined it would ever be.

"Look. I've got homework. And we need to eat." Sam's voice was edged with impatience.

Sam sat, all sensible and civilized from having walked into his classes, all friendly with teachers and parents, on the side of this rented bed, staring at Julia.

Julia sat looking at him. She could feel her body shrinking inside the white cotton shirt, shrinking just slightly, as if her body were water becoming ice. She knew she was aggravating Sam, but she couldn't help herself. What it came down to was: He didn't really want to marry her. She wasn't safe.

"Let me wash my face, then I'll walk up to the dining hall with you," she said. She could actually see the tension leave Sam's body because she was acting normal again. She went into the bathroom and closed the door behind her, and as she washed her face she studied the little room and envisioned a scene: She'd be in the bathtub, with a kitchen knife, with warm water running.

Chapter 7
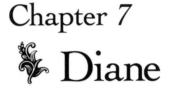# Diane

On Tuesday night, just after ten o'clock, Diane stood in her kitchen staring at the phone buzzing in her hand. Julia had just hung up on her—but at least she had called. Weak with relief, Diane sank into a chair and buried her head in her hands. Julia had been impatient, but her voice had sounded strong and steady. She was all right.

After her heart stopped racing, Diane took a deep breath and dialed Jim's lab. Twelve rings and no answer; he must be on his way home. Such a reasonable, optimistic man, Diane thought. He hadn't spent the whole evening lolling around like a fevered invalid, indulging in memories and doubt. He'd gone on as he always did, in orderly steps, trusting that all would work out for the best. She envied him his serenity.

She'd only just pulled herself out of bed, away from her memories, which lingered with her still as she moved around the kitchen brewing a pot of decaf. Now, relaxing in the knowledge that her daughter was safe, Diane sank into a chair and sat staring out the window and saw, instead of the dark night, the one time she'd tried to live only for herself, the one time Jim had lost his composure.

It was 1980. Jim was happily ensconced in his new lab, Chase and Julia were ten and eight, engrossed in their school and friends, and Diane was wild to get back into her work. All summer as she chauffeured her children to the beach or took them shopping for school clothes, she remembered her springtime conversation with Lisa. She needed to take a vacation just for herself. Where should she go? What should she do?

At the end of September that year, she managed to get down to New York for the International Jewelry Convention, where the hustle and chatter and glitter of the other jewelers and their displays usually revitalized her. This year she found herself drawn to a Finnish jewelry designer, Tarja Wiio, whose work Diane had admired for a long time. Even though Tarja herself seemed formidably cold, she asked her to join her for dinner that night.

They skipped the banquet held in the ballroom of the hotel and took the elevator to the restaurant on the top floor, where the lights were low, the prices high, and the food sumptuous. After ordering champagne and salmon and duck with cherries, Diane leaned back in her chair and smiled.

"God, it feels so good to know I get to eat an entire meal without interruptions!"

"Oh?" Tarja looked puzzled. In many ways the Finnish woman resembled Diane—both of them were tall and large boned. But Tarja's hair was white-blond, cut helmet–style, and her posture was almost military. "Who interrupts you?"

"Why, the children. The telephone. Or one child gets home

late from ballet, and the other has to leave for a scout meeting. That sort of thing."

"I see. I have no children, fortunately."

"Are you married?"

"Oh, no." The Finn seemed slightly offended by the thought.

"Do you live alone?"

"Yes."

Tarja didn't elaborate, and Diane didn't want to seem intrusive. She changed the subject. "I like your new designs, Tarja. They are strong, powerful. Almost shocking—but I mean that as a compliment."

"I understand. Thank you." Tarja speared a flaky piece of salmon with her fork. "I liked the design you did about five years ago. The handsome pins that looked like military medals."

Trust Tarja to speak honestly, rather than praising her current, tired, redundant line, simply to be polite, Diane thought. She smiled. "Thank you. I was proud of those pins. I'd like to get back to that kind of work. I have a feeling that women's jewelry is about to change. With more women working at executive levels, they'll want *serious* jewelry."

"Go on . . ." Tarja urged, smiling slightly.

"I'd like to develop a new fine-jewelry line for Arabesque. I've been thinking about it for months. Using gold, silver, precious and semiprecious stones set in opulent, ornate, but very formal designs. Heavy. Weighty." Pulling a pen and pad out of her purse, Diane quickly sketched two examples. "Like this. And this."

Tarja studied them, then nodded. "Yes. I see."

"But they're not quite right, are they?" Diane stuffed the pad and pen back in her purse. "I'm so frustrated! I can't quite *see* what I want. My mind's crowded with images of Darth Vader and Strawberry Shortcake and Winnie-the-Pooh! Whenever I have a quiet moment in my studio, I find myself drawing cartoon shapes—daisies, balloons, building blocks."

"You need a vacation."

"You're right. I do." Diane took a swallow of champagne. "I need to get as far away as possible from my ordinary life."

"Why don't you come to Helsinki?" Tarja suggested. "I could show you my studio, my city, and then we could fly together to Leningrad and see the Hermitage."

"Oh, I couldn't!" Diane declared, discovering that she was surprised and even slightly—and depressingly—frightened by such an extravagant thought.

"Why not?" Tarja demanded.

"Well—it would be so expensive. The airfare. Hotels."

"You could stay with me, of course. I have plenty of room."

Diane stared at Tarja. "How long does it take to fly to Helsinki?"

"Fifteen hours, more or less. Are you afraid of flying?"

"Oh, no. It's not that. But I'd have to be away from the children for so long—"

"That would be good for you," Tarja declared. "Were you not only now just saying so?"

"Yes, yes . . . I think I'd better order some coffee," Diane told her. It was so appealing, the thought of experiencing two truly foreign countries, especially Russia, with its history of excess and opulence, its wealth of artwork.

"Your children are old, are they not?"

"Eight and ten."

"And healthy?" Tarja's voice was stern.

"Yes. Yes, they are healthy."

"And they have a father."

"Yes, and we've got a housekeeper, now, too." Diane hesitated, then was surprised to hear herself saying, "Yes, Tarja. I think you're right. I think I should go." It will be good for Jim to have to truly be in charge for a while, without relying on me, she thought. And it will be good for my children to know I have a life, and that they can survive without me.

Tarja seemed to read her thoughts. "It will be good for you," she declared.

Before she left, Diane sat Chase and Julia down in front of a globe of the world and pointed out exactly where she was going. She pulled out volumes of the encyclopedia and had them read aloud to her about Finland and Russia. Finland lived in an uneasy alliance with its vast neighbor. It was an odd country, struggling for its own singular identity. Diane felt a kinship with it. She felt like a country struggling to be free but attached by irrevocable geography to a magnificent, obstinate territory: motherhood. Jim traveled away from his children often, without worrying about their safety, without feeling a tug, a pain, or any agonizing guilt. Diane wanted the same for herself.

The weather, so golden in Massachusetts, was bronze in Helsinki. Light glanced off the modern glass-and-stone buildings in brilliant chips, and the air was crisp and metallic, as if extracted from coins.

Tarja met Diane at the airport, put her up in her chic apartment in residential Tapiola, and spent two days showing her the city. The second day she took Diane to her studio, which was located in the heart of Helsinki in a brazen chrome-and-glass arrow of a structure that shot its way skyward between two neoclassical brick edifices. Tarja's shop was remarkable. Her jewelry was displayed not under a glass counter, but instead in small silk- or velvet-lined vaults built at eye level into a dark blue wall, brightly lighted, protected by locked glass doors. Most of the jewelry was one of a kind, made from silver or gold, some set with precious stones. It could not be called pretty. It was powerful, unsettling, some of it ugly. The heavy, twisted, peaked, and pitted pieces seemed like bits of landscape wrested from the surface of the moon. Diane imagined their cold weight against her hand.

"Extraordinary. Fantastic."

"Let me show you my workroom."

Tarja led Diane through a narrow hallway to a windowless room at the back of the building. Immediately Diane was accosted by the familiar, not-unpleasant odor of melted metals, wax, and plaster, of crucibles cooling from the small furnaces. Safety goggles and face shields lay on plain wooden workbenches near Plexiglas collection boxes for precious-metal filings. Drills, magnifiers, electronic scales, propane and acetylene torches, polishing lathes, all stood gleaming. In one corner was a security vault for the priceless sheets and crumbs and ingots of gold and silver.

"This is my idea of heaven," Diane said wistfully. "God, I envy you, Tarja. You're serious about your work."

Tarja shrugged. "I am an artist." She didn't seem surprised or complimented. "And I have no children who require my time and energy."

The next morning Tarja ushered Diane into her small mini and drove north, up to her summer cabin on a lake near Lappo. The day was brilliant with sunshine. Almost immediately the road was surrounded by battalions of forests with pines trees so massive that they looked like statues of trees, their trunks hewn from iron.

About an hour from the city they turned off the much-traveled major road onto a smaller, quiet one, and from that onto a lonely, winding narrow path. The forest opened up around them. Cylinders of light shimmered down through the evergreens, exposing sunny open spaces lush with wild-berry bushes, underbrush, fallen deciduous leaves, moss-coated rocks. In the midst of all this stood Tarja's cabin, unpainted pine, satiny as skin, with bright circles of colored glass hanging in the windows. It looked as at home in the middle of the forest as if it had sprung up from the roots of the surrounding trees.

"Oh, it's wonderful!" Diane exclaimed, jumping out of the car.

Tarja smiled. The two women crossed back and forth over the crunchy carpet of autumn leaves, carrying their luggage and groceries into the cabin.

"Put your things in the bedroom. I'll sleep in the living room. I insist," Tarja directed.

While Tarja turned on the heat and electricity, Diane looked around the cabin. There were just two rooms: a long rectangle serving as living room, kitchen, and dining area, and a bedroom; a tiny hallway led to a bathroom and sauna. It was all stark, plain pine, slick glass, polished ceramic. The lines were squared and angular, the colors of the curtains, bedspreads, towels, even the cushions on the benches bright, blank reds and blues and yellows.

"Now, come with me," Tarja said when she'd finished her chores. She led Diane outside through a spacious woods of birches and pines that spread around the cabin. Very quickly they came to the shore of an enormous, jewel-blue lake. The sun was deceivingly bright; it made the air look warm. Diane had taken off her coat and gloves in the house. Standing in only her wool slacks and sweater, she shivered.

"Are you hungry? While the sauna heats up, we'll take a quick dip, then have a sauna, then I promise you your food will taste like heaven."

"What do you mean, take a quick dip, Tarja? That water must be freezing."

"It's not *freezing*! Do you see any ice?"

"Well, Tarja, I know that. I can see that. What I mean is, that water must be very, very cold."

"Of course it is. It will be a shock. Then the heat of the sauna will be shocking, too. But it is good for you. We Finns do this all the time. I do it every weekend that I can, every month of the year, except perhaps in February. That's why I am so slender, and why my skin is so good, and why I look so young. It improves the circulation. It is restorative. You'll see."

"Well, go ahead since you're used to it, but I can't possibly— I'd have a heart attack and die. I'm really not the outdoor type, anyway."

But Tarja was already striding back toward her cabin, so Diane slowly followed her strange friend along the narrow leaf-strewn path through the woods, considering. A few years ago she would have eagerly relished such a new, invigorating experience. Wasn't this exactly the sort of thing she'd come for—to experience the new and foreign?

Certainly she was seeing a new side of Tarja—not just her naked body as, back inside the cabin, the Finnish woman una-bashedly stripped off her clothes—but a bolder, brassier facet of Tarja's personality. Here in her own country Tarja was still not cheerful, but she was self-assured, even bossy. She did not exude happiness so much as triumph, and Diane watched her with a growing mixture of admiration, amusement, and fondness.

Oh, well, in Rome do as the Romans do, Diane admonished herself, and how bad could it be, for Tarja was undressing with an extraordinary eagerness. Tarja's body, exposed to the brilliant sunlight, was as geometric as the jewelry she designed—so thin that her hipbones protruded, making, with the swollen mound rising at her crotch beneath a concave stomach, a triangle. Her small, tight breasts were mere doorknobs. Tarja was long, straight, narrow, and her skin was so pale that it seemed like translucent silver leaf stretched over her luminescent white bones. In this place you believe in fairy tales, Diane thought, watching Tarja race naked out the door and along the forest path, her flashing body as natural, as elemental, as if she were a fish-woman risen from the lake.

In contrast, Diane recognized the languid weight of her own body as she peeled off her wool slacks and sweater. Even though she was standing in a patch of sunshine, her skin pimpled and constricted as it was exposed to the chill air.

"Come on!" Tarja yelled.

"I'm coming!" she yelled back, then dashed out the door. Immediately she was shocked by herself, as painfully embarrassed by her nakedness in the outdoors in the daylight as if she were in a spotlight onstage with an audience of hundreds.

She ran with her arms crossed over her chest, partly from shyness, partly to support her heavy breasts, which bobbled as she ran. Sticks and brittle leaves snapped beneath the delicate skin of her feet like tiny explosions of cap guns, powdering her soles with their dust. Her own movements as she ran along made the sunlight flicker unsettlingly against her eyes, and the air became eerily more substantial—as if she were passing through not shade and brightness but through matter, now sharp, now soft.

Ahead of her Tarja screamed piercingly as she hit the water. At the shoreline Diane hesitated, watching as the other woman leaped and frolicked.

"Don't stop now!" Diane urged herself. Then she jumped.

The water was so cold she felt as if her skin were sizzling against her bones. Already, from the run and the chill of the northern air, her heart was thudding, but when she plunged into the water's icy depths, it was instantly transformed into a jack-hammering machine, automatically functioning like a steel motor within her appalled, assaulted flesh. The cold of the lake water drove her breath from her lungs. Her body was a scream of pain. She sank, feetfirst, through the blurry cold, each organ, muscle, bone, and nerve flinching fiercely. Gleaming water closed over her head. This was like childbirth in its extremity. Everything human in her was helpless.

Not of her own volition, she suddenly surfaced. Almost without consciousness she gasped and sputtered, thrashing her arms against the freezing, burning blue. As she pulled the frigid air into her tortured lungs, her body became a statue: marble solid, still. Her limbs, her torso, her heart, and veins were made of rock. And this hardening was bliss.

She let herself sink down once more.

"Come out now!" Tarja was yelling. "You must—" Then she splashed out from the shore and grabbed Diane's upper arm and pulled her. Diane didn't help; she couldn't. Tarja hauled her upward until Diane lay curled on the grass, gasping for air. This air, warmer than the water, hit her once again like a slap, as if the universe had convulsed against her. Diane's ears were ringing; her sight was blurred.

"Wow. You are in terrible shape," Tarja scolded. "Come on." She pulled Diane up against her and they stumbled toward the cabin. Diane could not feel her feet or legs or any part of her body. Her consciousness had shrunk to a nugget within a fiery field of red. If Tarja had not pulled her along, she would simply have toppled over woodenly and died. But by the time they reached the cabin, her fingers and feet were tingling, and the warm air inside was balm to her lungs.

Tarja pulled Diane to the back of the cabin, opened the heavy wooden sauna door, and brought her into the tiny room of intensely dry heat. At once Diane's skin dried so fast she felt as if it were cracking like the skin on plump, ripe grapes. Her heart, which had been laboring mechanically inside her, swelled with an animal flexibility until it bulged against her chest.

"I'm going to die," Diane gasped.

"No, you won't. Just lie down. Catch your breath."

Tarja arranged Diane's weak body on a narrow, flat plank. It was so fiercely hot it seemed airless. Diane fought off a wave of claustrophobia.

"Wake up!"

She was not aware that she had passed out.

"Wake up, Diane. Sit up."

She felt Tarja's hands pulling at her until she was sitting, leaning against the sauna wall. Strange pricklings at her hairline told her that she was sweating. Odd, every bit as odd as childbirth, how her body continued to slug along on course, to live, to function, without her permission or even her desire.

She felt like someone who has traveled very far.

"Here," Tarja said, handing her a small glass of very rich, dark beer. "Drink this."

Diane obeyed. The beer was delicious. Her breath came back to her, her senses returned, and she was at last completely relaxed.

Later she showered and dressed, then sat feasting on herring with sour cream, onions, and dill, poached salmon with a creamy mustard sauce, new potatoes, moist radishes gritty with salt, and dense sweet dark bread that she slathered with butter. Far beyond the confines of the forest the sun was setting, sinking the sheltered cabin into a cozy gloom. Diane and Tarja did not talk except to say, "Do you want more of this?" and "Yes, please"; they sat quietly watching the darkness come. Later they did the dishes in a companionable silence, then listened to an opera on Tarja's portable stereo before going to bed.

Her sleep was thick, creamy, dreamless. It was as if her bones had melted into milk. When she awoke, Diane lay very still beneath the Marimekko duvet, looking at the sunlight on the papery skin of the silver birches outside the window. Her pleasure was complete.

Here in Finland Diane recognized the depth of the infidelity of which she was capable: not of experiencing ecstasy with another man but of finding it on her own, by herself. It was as if in the Finnish lake she'd set herself free, singed the claims of her children and her husband from her skin, from her heart. She wasn't ashamed. She wasn't sorry. She was triumphant. She was herself again, Diane, alone.

She was ready to go to Russia.

Tarja was a naturally quiet woman, not given to small talk. During the drive back to Helsinki, to the airport, and during the flight to Leningrad, Diane leaned her head against the cold windows and let her thoughts drift free. It was the first time in years that she'd had so much uninterrupted time.

Perhaps it was being so far north that made her think of the winter before, when Chase had entered a figure-skating competition. Diane went to the town rink with some other mothers to watch the competition and the award ceremony. She noticed how she and her friends talked and laughed with a shrill vivacity they hadn't exhibited since they were adolescents. When Chase skated out on the ice, a tiny brave figure alone in the bright lights, Diane's heart caved in with love and terror. If he fell, if he embarrassed himself, she would die right there in the bleachers. He didn't fall, and she didn't die, but she knew her heart had been scarred, as if burned by the intensity of her apprehension.

When, the previous spring, a popular second-grade girl named

Melony didn't invite Julia to her birthday party, Julia's distress had inflamed Diane like a fever. She'd held her daughter, soothed her, reasoned with her; she'd taken her out for a hot-fudge sundae and a Disney movie, and all the time her heart was black with hate.

It wasn't only sorrow and fear that mauled her heart; it was hope, and sometimes happiness so powerful it hurt. Diane knew what was important to her children, and it wasn't that they have a mother who made pretty jewelry; it was a mother who made brownies and brought them to school for their birthdays. Diane made those brownies. She dyed eggs at Easter and hid them, along with straw baskets, balls and bats, water pistols. She made Christmas cookies with them and labored over homemade Halloween costumes. She volunteered to ride in buses when their classes went on field trips to the Museum of Science or Old Sturbridge Village. All the commotion of those trips, the giggles and shouts and popped bubble gum, the little girl sick in the aisle, the little boy who caught his finger in the metal seat frame—those marked her heart, too. Being around little children was like living inside a hailstorm.

Now that her children were older, she still didn't know, she thought no one knew, where the child ended and the mother began. Of course there had been times when she and Jim were first in love when she'd felt this same union with him; looking into his eyes as they lay in each other's arms, she had thought: I am you, we are each other, we are one. That melting rapture returned between them occasionally, reminding her that when the children were off on their own, they would still have each other. But when would that be? Would a cord snap between them? Would she feel it break, hear the twang? When would she know that her actions didn't influence her children's lives? For even as she drove across the Finnish countryside and flew deep into the Soviet Union, she felt delinquent, guilty, as if she were stealing something—her mind, her emotions, her body—that really still belonged to her children.

Tarja and Diane arrived in Leningrad at night, in time to be driven to the Astoria Hotel where Tarja had made reservations. Diane was exhilarated at being in Russia but exhausted by the traveling, and by her thoughts. She sank into a deep sleep on her rather lumpy bed.

The next morning, after a breakfast of black bread and tea, they were met by their Intourist guide, a pleasant young woman who introduced herself as Khristina Ahkmatova. She led them to her gray Volga and pointed out landmarks of the city as she drove toward the Hermitage.

"On your right you will see St. Issac's Cathedral. St. Issac was the patron saint of Peter the Great. Across the square you will see Mariinsky Palace, home of City Soviet, what you would call our town hall." The woman handled her car deftly and spoke English well. "Now you see before you the famous Bronze Horseman, that statue of Peter the Great given to him by Catherine the Second. The rearing horse symbolizes Russia, trampling the serpent that symbolizes the forces opposed to his reforms."

"It's beautiful," Diane said. Neither of the other women replied, so she sat in silence looking at the city, which gleamed even on this dreary day.

They drove into Dvortsovaya Ploshchad. Diane had read that the Winter Palace was four blocks long and contained more than a thousand halls and rooms, but actually to be one tiny figure in the midst of such enormity was overwhelming. Like a child, she pressed her nose right against the car window for the best view. The buildings surrounded a parade ground wide enough to hold an army of thousands. In its center rose the Alexander Column, as phallic as the Washington Monument, if more slender, with an angel on top. The massive complex of buildings was both sedate and grandiose; the sheer size was a statement that over-powered the severe and rather monotonous classical facade.

The line of people waiting to tour the Hermitage was equally overwhelming. Diane and Tarja stood patiently behind their guide in a line that looked endless but moved fairly quickly. Diane could catch snippets of French and German and what she thought was Finnish, but most of the people spoke in Russian and looked Russian.

"We have over two and one half million objects on display in over fourteen miles of halls and galleries." Without preamble, Khristina Ahkamatova began to lecture. "The museum is so vast and the displays so glorious that visitors have been known to faint."

Diane understood. During the long day as they walked through the Hermitage, so much exuberant beauty dumbfounded her. She gaped at samovars thick with gold and silver, encrusted with jewels, at the vast bronze-and-gold throne room where a twenty-seven-square-meter map of Russia sparkled with semiprecious stones, the cities and rivers marked by emeralds and rubies, at ornate mirrors, crystal chandeliers, painted ceilings, marble statues, gilt-trimmed malachite pillars. Turning, looking down, catching her breath, over and over again her eyes caught on the head scarves of the Russian women, who dressed somberly for the most part but covered their heads in material brilliant with color, swirling with intricate designs. A sense of recognition swept over her. A wonderful intoxication, a kind of lust, an excitement that always invaded her blood, making her restless, sleepless, irritable, moody—and that always preceded a period of real creative accomplishment—was beginning to assail her. She was both sorry and glad when it was time to go back to the hotel. She was exhausted. But they would return the next day.

In the hotel dining room, over a first course of caviar and *starka,* Diane said, "This is exactly what I needed, Tarja. I'm this close to coming up with my new designs. This close." She held up her thumb and forefinger, indicating the fraction of space between her mind and its breakthrough.

The next morning the two women rose early. When they went down to the lobby to meet their guide, the desk clerk called Diane over.

"Mrs. Randall? We have something for you. It just arrived."

He handed her an envelope. She ripped it open and read:

JULIA IN HOSPITAL.

MENINGITIS.

COME HOME.

JIM.

"Oh, God!" Diane moaned. Her body rocked backward as if from a blow. "Tarja. My daughter's sick. I must go home at once." Turning back to the desk clerk, she said, "I need to leave at once."

"Oh, no," he assured her. "You cannot leave for four days. You see what your ticket and your visa says."

"I know, I know, but my daughter is sick. Here, look at the telegram."

"I'm sorry. I cannot help you." The man turned away.

"Diane," Tarja said, "calm down. You must be calm. This is going to be difficult. They do not like spontaneity or change. I'll make some phone calls. I'll see what I can do."

"Thank you, Tarja. I'll get the Service Bureau to book a long-distance call to the States for me."

The next few hours passed with a vivid intensity, each minute clicking by with the sharpness of a knife blade slicing its mark into Diane's heart. Various Russian officials listened and mumbled and nodded at Diane, then informed her that changes could not be made; she would have to wait until the time her visa stated to leave. When Diane insisted that they make the necessary changes, or put her in touch with someone who could, the clerks would nod and disappear, eventually returning with another functionary. While she waited, she tried to reassure herself: Jim would be with Julia, and Jean would fly up; Julia loved her grandmother, and Susan would fly in, too. The telephone operator could not get a line through to Boston. Officials came and went, sometimes listening sympathetically, sometimes speaking with Tarja in barking syllables, always referring the problem to someone else. Khristina Ahkmatova arrived to take them to the museum. When they explained Diane's problem and asked for help, she said merely, "I'm sorry. I am not qualified for that. I am only your guide. I am sorry." Eventually she went away.

Tarja advised Diane to wait at the desk. She went to their rooms and packed both bags, just in case.

Diane sat by the desk and waited. She thought of Julia, and she cried. She'd refused to believe in some abstract system of justice that delivered punishment to mothers who went off on their own to indulge in completely selfish experiences. Jim certainly didn't narrow his life by such superstitions. But sitting there as heavy hours went by, she felt guilt grow until it overshadowed her. Of course. Motherhood was a universal thing, an organic, mysterious, jealous power. Diane had spurned motherhood, choosing to indulge in a few moments of pure,

free, individual ecstasy—and now she was paying the price.

Tarja said, "Come eat lunch."

"I can't eat. I'm not hungry. How can I eat when my daughter is deathly ill? I'm so far away. What is it with these people? Why can't they help?"

"Probably they're checking on you. Their system doesn't allow for easy changes. You must be patient."

"Perhaps I should take a taxi to the airport and see if I can get on a plane, any plane anywhere."

"That wouldn't work. Their system doesn't allow for that, either."

" 'Their system . . . their system.' "

"Yes, it is convoluted. Everything must be checked and double-checked, and no one wants to take responsibility for an unofficial act. But you knew this before you came, Diane. I wrote you that it might be cumbersome."

"Yes. I know. I never dreamed this would happen."

So Diane waited, sitting in the lobby of the Hotel Astoria, blind to the beauty around her, focused on thinking only of her daughter.

At about three o'clock in the afternoon, she was approached by a tall, slender, dark-haired, dark-eyed man in his early sixties. Unlike the hotel officials, he was expensively dressed in a well-tailored suit of dark gray wool. He looked Russian, but his English was perfect.

"Hello, Diane Randall," he said. "My name is Erich Malenkov. I understand you have a problem."

She leaped from her chair. "My daughter— This came this morning." She held out the telegram. "I must leave at once."

"Yes." Maddeningly, he sat down in a chair and gestured her to hers. "Could I see your passport and your hotel identity card?"

She handed them to him in silence. He studied them carefully. "What is your husband's name?"

"Oh, really. Is this necessary? Time is passing by—"

"Diane." Tarja spoke her name, only that, as a warning.

"If you will help me, I will help you." Erich Malenkov's smooth tone did not change.

Diane sighed. "Jim Randall."

"Your parents' names?"

"Al White. Jean White."

"Your mother's maiden name?"

"Marshall."

"Do you have brothers or sisters?"

"Two brothers, one sister. And two children, ten and eight, and the eight-year-old is sick—" She found herself pleading, "She has meningitis. Please, can we cut through this red tape—"

"Yes," Erich Malenkov said, surprising her. He stood. "We can go now. Your bag is ready?"

"Well, yes—" Diane was confused.

"I'll drive you both to the airport myself. We have reservations for you on a plane to Helsinki that leaves in three hours, and on to Boston via London from there. Perhaps in Helsinki you'll be able to get a phone line to Boston more easily."

He led Diane and Tarja to his car—a long, shining black sedan.

The scenery of the city, the river Neva, wound past her car window. She'd traveled so far to see this, to be here, and now every cell in her body ached to be gone from this place, to be back home.

Leaving his car with a porter, Erich Malenkov escorted Diane and Tarja through the airport, down a corridor, to the waiting room of a plane boarding for Helsinki. When he held out her ticket to her, Diane nearly ripped it from his hand.

"Thank you," she said. "Thank you so very much. I can never thank you enough."

He nodded. "I am glad to help."

On the plane, seated between Tarja and an enormous Russian whose shoulders shoved into her seat, Diane fastened her seat belt with shaking hands. She leaned back into her seat, closed her eyes, and prayed silently, as the plane shuddered, roared, and lifted off into the cloud-flecked sky.

Not quite twenty-four hours later, she landed at Logan. She'd put a call through to Jim from Helsinki and again from London, and as she went down the narrow ramp from the plane, she saw that Jim was waiting for her at the gate. He looked as tired as she felt, and as frightened.

Brushing past an embracing couple in front of her, she reached Jim. "How is she?"

"Better. Not out of danger, but better."

Diane put her hand on his arm in a gesture that was both beseeching and steadying. Jim didn't move to hug or kiss her but took her heavy carry-on bag from her hand and turned away. "The luggage ramp's this way."

As they waited for her suitcase to come off the conveyer, then hurried to Brigham and Women's Hospital, Jim described Julia's illness and its symptoms in painful detail. Diane knew he was not trying to torture her, and yet he seemed angry with her, as if her having left had somehow sparked this terrible infection. For it was an infection of the spinal cord, a complication of the common cold that Julia had been recovering from—or so Diane had thought—when she left for Finland. Julia had complained of chills and a headache, and a rising fever made her increasingly apathetic and miserable. Jim had thought it was simply the flu. But when he took her to see their pediatrician, Dr. Walker had discovered that Julia's neck was so stiff she could not bend it forward. Immediately he'd put her in the hospital and run blood tests. When the tests came back, the doctor's suspicions were confirmed—the meningitis was curable but required constant vigilance. She'd be in the hospital at least two weeks.

After what seemed an eternity, they arrived at the hospital, parked in the enormous echoing underground lot, and raced through the wings and down the long hall to Julia's room. And there she was, lying in bed, pale and unmoving, her eyes shining with that false brightness that results from fever and dehydration. Diane could see that in only six days Julia had lost weight. Her cheeks were sunken. IV tubes ran from a nearby stand down into her arm.

"Oh, baby," Diane cried, rushing to her daughter.

"Mommy," Julia said. "I'm scared."

Diane bent over her daughter, putting her cool cheek against Julia's warm face, kissing her hair. She put her own fears aside. "You don't have to be. Daddy says you're fine, and the medicine is helping you. You'll be better soon."

"And you're here now."

"Yes. I'm here now." Diane sat on the bed and held both of her daughter's hands. "Oh, honey, you'll be all right, I promise."

And she was. For the next eight days Diane sat by her daughter's side in the hospital, reading aloud her favorite books, singing to her while she dozed, laughing at idiotic children's TV shows with her, and then finally when Julia felt well enough to be restless the last few days, cutting out paper dolls and teaching her to embroider. When memories of her splendid dive into the crystalline Finnish waters flashed uninvited to her mind, Diane shoved them away with the same flush of guilt with which an adulterous married woman puts away thoughts of her lover. Not here, not now, it wasn't appropriate, it wasn't safe.

The next spring Diane came out with her line of fine jewelry: brooches, earrings, necklaces cast in silver with a fused gold overlay, shaped in scrolling Byzantine forms that were almost letters, or lilies, or lions rampant, intertwined, each with a semi-precious stone centered in the middle. She'd invested heavily in national advertising; the company had come up with a picture of a sleek dark-haired executive woman wearing a navy blue suit, a white silk blouse, and an Arabesque brooch at her neck, as she talked to a boardroom of men. The line sold out.

She'd never tried to go back to Russia again. She'd never wanted to tempt Fate, or whatever force it was that ruled the lives of mothers.

Ten years later, Diane sat alone in her kitchen, waiting to hear her husband's step at the door, eager to tell him that they'd weathered another crisis: Julia was safe.

Chapter 8

 Jean

That the Jardin du Luxembourg was frequented by an older crowd than the Tuileries should come as no surprise, Jean decided, yet as much as she loved the Left Bank, she missed the sight of mothers pushing baby carriages or chasing after their toddlers. Jean had been surprised all her life at the pleasure it gave her to see babies. This especially baffled her when her own children were teenagers, caught in the metamorphosis from children into adults that was often violent, always shocking. As her four children reached their later teenage years and cut the connection to their mother in variously cruel ways, Jean had been bitter. Why had no one told her what lay in store for her? Why had no one warned her? Why hadn't any other women—not just her mother or her mother's friends, but women on the street, charitable strangers—approached her to pass on the word? "Don't have children. It's too hard. It's too painful. Yes, they love you when they're small. They love you until they are about twelve, perhaps fourteen. But then they change, and they criticize you, disdain you, even truly hate you, and they hold you accountable for everything that is wrong in their lives. And then they leave you."

Well, she had not told her own children that. She had not warned Diane or Susan or Bert or Art. Of course by the time they were old enough to have children, they routinely disregarded all her advice anyway, so if she had told them it wouldn't have helped.

But the odd thing was that during those painful years when Diane, her oldest, became critical of her mother, then rebellious, then downright hateful, and Bert, just two years younger, went through a wild spell, Jean still found that the sight of other women's babies brought her heart solace and balm.

Why? It was not because of some vague, altruistic hope that some mother somewhere would get it right. It reminded Jean that whatever she had now, once she had had a life redolent with sweet and overwhelming love.

When her children were younger, they had asked her: "Mom, which one of us do you love best?"

"I love you all the same," she'd always answered, but while that reply was not a lie it was also not the truth. Of course she did not love her children all the same, except that she would have thrown herself in front of a bus to save any one of them. But they were so different, one from another, and her relationship with each of them was unique.

The first child and the last had been the most difficult: Diane because she'd been strong willed, Art because he'd been what she termed "sensitive," and what her husband considered weak. The two middle children, Bert and Susan, had been easier, more like their father, levelheaded and practical.

Jean loved them as much as she loved her other two but felt

they were, at heart, more like Al. It was the troublesome two, Diane and Art, who reminded her of herself as a young woman.

1940
War Stories

When Erich took Jean home early on New Year's morning, he kissed her slowly and sweetly at the door, but he didn't make a date to see her again.

Jean thought she understood. Alone in her room that night, she couldn't sleep. She tossed in her bed, crushing her body against her pillow. She replayed every second, every breath and touch of New Year's Eve in the hotel room with Erich. He had wanted her. Of that she had no doubt. But he thought she was a good girl—well, she was a good girl, a classy girl—and being the sort of man he was, he would not take advantage of her. No matter how strong the desire, honorable men did not take women of her set to bed. Last year her best friend, Midge, had gone through a similar ordeal with a junior professor at George Washington. He'd been too poor to marry her, so in spite of their mutual attraction, he'd stopped seeing her. Damn these honorable men! Jean thought.

During a painfully long New Year's Day Jean docilely attended a brunch, a tea, and a cocktail party with her parents. This pleased them, and she hoped it would take her mind off Erich, but it did not. Whenever she found the chance, she slipped away from the parties, found a phone in a quiet spot, and called home—only to hear from Agate or Stafford that no, Miz Jean, Mr. Mellor had not called.

As they finally returned home that evening, her mother was babbling gaily about the latest gossip, her father was already thinking of work waiting in his study, and Jean felt that she had nothing ahead of her but her lonely bed and, at best, a book. She'd been wrong. The magic had been all in her mind. Erich hadn't called.

The phone rang just as she and her parents went into the house and were taking off their coats.

"It's for you, Miz Jean," Agate announced.

"Jean," Erich said, "sorry to call so late. Do you like to ice-skate? They've just flooded the swimming pool at the hotel, and everyone's out having a great time skating by moonlight. I thought I'd bring you over and we could skate and have a late dinner."

She would have gone swimming with him on this frosty night if he'd suggested it.

Dutifully, she replied, "Let me ask my parents."

"Oh, dear, it's so late," her mother fretted, but her father, after hearing what the call was about, headed on back to his study, a sign that he was leaving the decision to his wife.

"Mother, I'm on vacation! Everyone's there now! Please?"

"Well . . ." Her mother yielded.

"Thanks, Mom!" Jean grabbed her mother and kissed her on the cheek before she could change her mind. "Give me time to put on some slacks and find my skates!" she told Erich. Then she flew up the stairs to get ready.

Erich arrived in an argyle sweater and a red wool muffler that set off his dark good looks. He escorted her to his car, then slid into his side, giving her a smile as sweet as a kiss. Jean was so purely happy to be with him that she chattered foolishly about every little thing they'd done that day. At least, she thought, now he knows I wasn't sitting home waiting for him to call.

The grounds of the Wardman Park Hotel had become a winter wonderland. Snow iced the trees and sparkled in fantastic drifts along the walking paths. The air around the skating rink tasted like champagne. It was cold and glittery and dazzlingly bright. Skaters sailed along to the waltzes piped from the hotel. Couples sat on benches lacing up their skates or moved arm in arm over the ice with laughter trailing after them like their brightly knit scarves. Here and there lovers hid to kiss behind the shadowy protection of a tree, or hurried into the hotel for a hot rum toddy.

They sat side by side on a bench putting on their skates.

"Ready?" Erich asked.

"Ready," Jean answered, smiling.

He put his arm around her and took her other hand in a skater's embrace with a firmness that told her he wanted her next to him. They glided out onto the ice together.

Erich was an accomplished skater, strong, graceful, and quick. Yet at first Jean held herself stiffly, her mind full of warnings: she mustn't trip, mustn't clasp his hand too tightly, mustn't breathe so rapidly, mustn't embarrass herself. She concentrated on matching her stride to his and following his lead. Simply being so close to him, tucked up against him, made her heart pound. She knew he could feel the trembling lift and fall of her ribcage beneath his large, steady hand.

After a few turns around the rink, she began to enjoy herself. The stretch and sweep of her legs was pleasing. The night air was chilly against her face, but her body against Erich's made a pocket of heat. Surrendering to the rhythm of the lilting "Skater's Waltz," she warmed and loosened and at last relaxed completely into his hold. Overhead the stars and lamplights seemed to dip in time to the music. The tempo quickened. Erich's hand tightened on her waist, and they sailed together, faster and faster, skimming the surface of the sparkling ice.

After a while Erich brought them to a stop at the dark end of the rink so they could catch their breath.

"You're a wonderful skater," he told her.

"So are you." She was on fire from the movement and a building elation: here she was, where she'd always longed to be, at the sweet white-hot heart of life. She knew her cheeks were rosy. Snatching off her red beret, letting her curly brown hair tumble down her back, she lifted her face to the sky and laughed with pure joy. "I'm so happy!"

Erich smiled down at her, then pulled her to him and kissed her mouth. She rose onto the toes of her skates, wrapped her arms around his neck, and kissed him back.

It was a long time before they spoke, and by then their breathing was ragged with desire.

"I promised you dinner," Erich whispered against her ear. "Shall we go eat?"

"No." She nuzzled against his neck.

"Do you want to skate some more?"

"No." His hands held her tightly against him at the hips. Shamelessly she rubbed against him.

"Do you want to go home?" His voice deepened.

"I want you to take me upstairs."

Reaching up behind his neck, he took her wrists in his hands and broke their embrace, bringing her arms down and holding her away from him. He looked at her seriously, considering. Jean's set weren't supposed to be wild; they were supposed to be good. But he could see she cared nothing about any of that. She lifted her chin and lowered her eyelids in a seductive taunt.

"All right," he said.

He led her across the ice to a bench where they sat side by side, unlacing their skates. Her ankles burned and threatened to collapse when she stood up. They walked into the hotel, through the lobby, to the elevators. Here Erich didn't speak or hold her hand. At the fifth floor, he led her off and down a long corridor. He unlocked the door and ushered her into a room, turning on the lights.

Jean blinked, stunned by the sudden quiet. The room was pleasant enough, even luxurious, but impersonal. She saw no framed photographs, no papers piled on the desk, only sitting-room furniture and, through an open door, the bedroom.

"Do you live here?" Suddenly she was nervous.

"Yes. Just temporarily."

"It's—nice." She couldn't meet his eyes.

"We don't have to—do this, you know." His voice was kind.

She flushed, embarrassed, but looking up at him gave her courage. She gazed upon his face, and said, "I want to. Oh, I want to."

He put his hands on her shoulders and kissed her gently. She responded to him with a violent surge of desire, awkwardly wrapping herself around him so passionately he almost lost his balance.

Erich put his hands on her face and forced her to look at him. "Wait, Jean. Listen to me. You've got to know something." He took a breath. "I can't marry you. I can't even propose to you in the hopes that we can marry later. A war is on the way. We may not like it, but it's coming. I have no security to offer you, no future."

"I don't want security. I don't want the future. I want us now. Together, now."

"Jean—"

"I'm sure. Don't you believe me?" She broke free of his grasp, twisted away, took a step backward. Holding his eyes with hers, she began to pull off her clothes, dropping her red sweater to the floor, bending to step out of her gray slacks. She reached behind her back to unfasten her bra with fingers that trembled so much she could scarcely work the hooks. Her chest rose and fell so rapidly she was afraid he could see her impetuous heart drumming under her skin. She pulled her bra down, off one arm, off the other, and let it fall to the floor.

"You're so beautiful," he said.

She was shivering with fear and desire. Putting her hands on her waist, she began to roll down her panties, but this was too hard. She turned her back to him, crossing her arms protectively over her bare breasts. She was afraid she was going to cry. Instantly Erich was behind her, wrapping his arms over hers, kissing the top of her head, forcing her to turn to him, kissing her mouth, caressing her shoulders with his large warm hands, moving her arms down to her sides, bending to kiss her cheek, her neck, her collarbone, bending to kiss her breasts. The fabric of his clothing was rough against her bare skin. She cried out and arched backward. He steadied her with his hands.

"You're beautiful," he said again. Sliding one arm behind her knees, he picked her up and carried her into the bedroom. As he laid her on the bed, his belt buckle scraped her side, a tiny irritation. She remained as he placed her, on her back, hands crossed over her chest, and watched while he took off his clothes. When he pulled his argyle sweater up over his head, his thick black hair crackled with electricity and stood up like a rooster's comb. This made her laugh, and Erich smiled at her pleasure. It seemed as though he took forever to unbutton his white cotton shirt. He pulled it up out of his pants and off, dropping it on a chair. His chest was matted with dark curls of hair. His torso was long, lean, the muscles of his arms and abdomen prominent.

He undid his belt. Unzipped his trousers. Let them fall to the floor, revealing rumpled white boxer shorts straining to contain his penis, now huge beneath the fabric. It made her slightly frightened. As if he understood this, he didn't take off his shorts but came to the bed and lay down next to her. Lying on his back, he pulled her on top of him, bringing her down so that he could kiss her mouth. Between the silk of her underpants and the cotton of his she felt the shape and push of his penis.

He kissed her mouth for a long, long time, while his hands stroked her back, her thighs, her ticklish waist, both soothing and exciting her. Finally he gently pushed her back up until she was sitting. He lay for a long moment gazing up at her breasts. The lightness of his touch as he brought his fingers down her throat and over the slope of her breasts made an invisible necklace of desire bead her skin.

Erich rolled over, so that Jean was beneath him and, still kissing her, he very slowly pushed her legs apart. When his hand slid up her thigh, against her crotch, she felt her heat flood and gather. Her hands were all over him, she couldn't touch him enough, his smooth back, curved arms, his chest where the black hair was damp with sweat. At last he slid his hand down inside her panties and between her legs. As she relaxed and opened up to him, a languorous warmth uncurled inside her. He moved his fingers against her skin. She moaned. He pushed up, kneeling, and took off her underpants, then his. She didn't look down, she couldn't, she closed her eyes, she felt him lower himself over her, she felt him part her with his hand, and then felt a firm bluntness shove its way inside her, push further, force its way deeper, harder, so that she moved her legs wider apart. She stopped shaking. Her blood slowed. She strained against him. A rose of heat budded in her pelvis, then suddenly unfolded in fiery petals of pleasure.

He waited until she opened her eyes to speak. "You can't have any idea how lovely you are," he said.

"I'm so happy," she replied. "I've never been so happy in my life."

"This doesn't hurt—?"

"Oh, no."

Then he raised himself up on his powerful arms, so that ropes of muscle twisted beneath his skin. His breath ragged, he thrust against her, seeming to lose all his self-consciousness and cautious control. Jean watched him, shaken and amazed by the intensity of his passion. Experimentally she moved her hips and tightened the muscles between her thighs. In answer, Erich moaned; it pleased her, excited her, and she moved again. He shut his eyes. He seemed to be falling into her, and she was overcome with a hot exultation. Then Erich shuddered, his jaw clenched, and all his skin, chest and arms and the back of his powerful thighs, broke out in goose bumps. He fell against her and buried his face in her neck. Jean sighed with triumph and content. Touching her tongue to her lover's shoulder, she tasted his sweat. She licked, then fastened her teeth softly against his skin, an instinctive, animal's act of possession.

They lay together in silence. He grew heavier as his chest rose and fell with his slowing breath. He lifted himself off and lay next to her, one arm around her, his mouth against her hair. They drifted toward sleep.

Erich broke the spell. "I don't want to move, but I should take you home. I don't want to upset your parents."

"Everything upsets my parents," Jean groaned.

He chuckled. "When do you go back to school?"

"In two days."

He ran his hand over the curve of her hip. "I'll come up to Boston when I can. And I often go to New York on business. Could you get away and meet me there sometime?"

"I'll find a way." Curling her fingers into the thick black hair on his chest, she smiled, pleased with herself.

"Do you ever come home during the term?"

"Sometimes. If there's a long weekend. I haven't come home very often. There's never been any reason before. But now—" Reality was returning, flooding over her like a rush of cold air.

"Won't your parents be suspicious if you start making trips home?"

She shook her head. "They're all in such a state now over this war business, they probably won't even notice me. That's all anyone in my house talks about. Father's more preoccupied than I've ever seen him. Bobby's applied for submarine training and he's like a bull in a cage, waiting for his orders. Al—you know Al White, Bobby's best friend—already has his orders. He's being shipped to join the command group of a battleship. What about you? Will you enlist?"

Erich turned to punch a pillow up under his head. "I don't know. I don't approve of war, but I might have no choice."

Jean nestled against him, burrowing her head into his shoulder. She murmured against his skin. He couldn't hear the words, but she needed to say them. "I couldn't stand to lose you. I love you," she whispered.

"We should go," Erich told her. "It's late."

The next day she told her parents she was meeting Betty for lunch and an afternoon of shopping. Betty promised to cover for her, then Jean brazenly drove to the hotel, where she went to bed with Erich. Then, terribly pleased with herself, she drove home and got ready for a "date" with Erich.

She was sitting in the living room waiting for Erich to pick her up for dinner, spending a few diplomatic good-girl moments with her parents, when Bobby and Al came in.

Al's face lit up when he saw her. "Jean. I'm glad you're here."

He sat down next to her on the sofa. "I've come to say good-bye. I'm going back to Norfolk tomorrow."

She was wearing a boxy black wool suit that she knew her parents would find reassuringly prim. Beneath it her body was still tingling from an afternoon in Erich's arms, and Jean felt brimming with good luck, spilling over with goodwill.

"Oh, Al, take care. Will you?" She saw the hope kindle in his eyes at her words. He *was* a lovely man, handsome, kind, intelligent, good, and in the glow of her happiness she found she was truly fond of Al.

"It's nothing to be concerned about, not yet. I'll just be in training," Al told her.

"Oh, good. You mean so much to me, Al," Jean said softly, and she meant it. She touched his hand lightly.

Across the room, her father cleared his throat.

"Look, Jean, Al and I are going to pick up Betty and go out to dinner. Why not join us?" her brother suggested.

Jean saw the lights of Erich's car flash in the driveway. "Oh, I'd love to, Bobby, but I've already made plans and I can't get out of them." She rose and moved toward the door. "I'm sorry. A bunch of us are going out for a meal"—she lied—"and we don't want to be late, so I'd better hurry. 'Bye!" She was out the door before anyone could speak, skimming down the snow-edged sidewalk to Erich's car. She jumped in before he could turn off the engine, and the moment they were around the corner, she slid across the seat and put her hand on his thigh.

On the third of January, after Bobby had helped her pack her car, Jean said good-bye to her family and drove off, waving gaily, headed back to Boston and a new semester of college.

She made one stop on the way, at Erich's hotel. They had agreed that there wouldn't be enough time for them to make love if Jean was to drive during the few remaining hours of daylight. But when they embraced, intending only to kiss good-bye, lust leaped like lightning between them. Erich pulled her on top of him as he sat on the sofa, he undid his trousers, she kicked off her shoes, yanked off her stockings, hitched up her skirt, and straddled him, feeling his hardness beneath her. She stared into his eyes as they moved together, shuddering with desire, consuming him with her eyes, her mouth, her hands, her tongue, her sex.

When they'd finished, she slumped against him, her head on his shoulder.

"I love you, Erich." There, she'd said it.

She felt the sharp intake of his breath at her words. After a while, he spoke. "I love you."

January 15, 1940

Darling Erich,

I love you and miss you more than words can say. I think of you constantly. I can't wait to be with you again.

Yet the hours are flying by. Erich, I'm so happy! I returned to Cambridge to discover that Hal Farmer and Stanley Friedman have moved up the publication date of the first issue of War Stories *to the first of February. And everyone's so frantic that they even assigned an article to me! Oh, Erich, I was nervous, but the story turned out to be so marvelous I couldn't help but do a good job. I interviewed Penelope Farley, an Englishwoman in her sixties who has been living in Boston since the end of the Great War. Mrs. Farley lost her husband, her two sons, and a brother in that war, and her home in London was destroyed in a bombing. Hal and Stanley said my essay was brilliant, and it will be the* second *piece in the review. They didn't cut a word. I'm so pleased. Erich, I might actually do some good, have an impact. I mean that with this article, I might tip the balance in a few people's minds away from war.*

I'm so happy these days. I'm doing so much, working on War Stories, *attending classes, and somehow even keeping my grades up.*

And always, always, every second of the day, I'm thinking of you. That's why I'm happy.

Please call me, darling. Please come up or let me meet you in New York. I need to be with you.

All my love,
Jean

January 30, 1940

My darling,

It's three o'clock in the morning, and I can't sleep. I want to be with you. But since I can't have that, I can at least remember our time together last week in New York. It was more wonderful than I ever imagined anything could be. Not just the lovemaking—you know I loved that—but every minute of our time together was perfect. I loved walking through Central Park with you, I loved having coffee and talking at the Algonquin, sitting together all warm and cozy while the snow swirled down outside. I'm glad you feel as I do, that war is wrong and we must work for peace. It means so much to me that you believe what I do and think it matters. *My brother and my father are convinced of my insignificance just because I'm a female. Now, because of you, I feel absolutely smug about being a woman.*

I can't wait to see you again.

All my love,
Jean

On February 1 the first issue of *War Stories* was published. On February 4, Jean's father called her and ordered her to come home at once. Although her father had refused to discuss the subject over the telephone, she knew why he was angry. He'd take this personally, of course; he'd consider *War Stories* subversive. He'd lecture her, reprimand her, and dole out some kind of punishment. She would have to listen, head bowed in penitence.

Then she'd tell her parents she was going to visit Betty. Instead, she'd surprise Erich at his rooms in the Wardman Park Hotel. Perhaps she'd even figure out a way to spend the night with him before driving back to school.

Jean drove straight from Boston to Washington in one day, stopping only for gas and coffee. It was almost ten o'clock at night when she finally arrived. As she pulled into the driveway, she saw her mother watching at the window. She grabbed up her overnight bag and, holding her chin high, strode to her front door.

Her mother came hurrying down the hallway to let Jean in.

"Darling, how was your trip? Are you hungry? I've made you a plate of sandwiches and some hot chocolate. Here, let Agate take your bag up to your room. Father's waiting for you."

He really must be on a tear, Jean thought, because her mother was nearly twitching with nerves. Jean tossed her coat on the coatrack and went into the living room.

"Shut the door," her father ordered. He was standing in front of the cold fireplace, and he gestured for her to sit in a chair facing him. "I believe you owe me an apology, young lady," he announced.

"I don't think I do," Jean retorted, and the battle began.

The first hour or so went fairly much as she had expected. Her father's anger was even worse than she'd thought it would be. He delivered several low blows about how she'd hurt and shamed her brother, who might be killed in the coming war.

"You are an ungrateful little fool!" Commander Marshall railed. "I've given you everything, and you repay me by insulting my work and my beliefs, by trying to undermine all I've fought for all my life!"

"Father, please understand that that article has nothing to do with you. I didn't write it to hurt you. I wrote it because I believe it."

"What are you, a communist?"

"No—but I'm an American who doesn't believe in war."

"And you don't think that reflects on the father whose life work has been to defend his country through war? No—don't bother to answer me. We've spent an hour in here and gotten nowhere. You're the most pigheaded, stupid child I've ever heard of. You make me ashamed of you, Jean. Do you hear me? I'm ashamed of you."

"I'm sorry, Father, but I have to stand up for what I think is right."

"Well, you're not going to stand up for it anymore supported by my money. I'm withdrawing you from Radcliffe."

"What? Father, you can't!"

"Of course I can. Who pays your tuition? You don't. Your goddamned anarchist friends don't. I do, or I did. I won't anymore. Unless you offer me an apology and a promise not to have anything more to do with that rag."

"You are behaving like a tyrant."

"It's my right. It's my money sending you to that damned liberal college. I knew it was wrong. From the start, I knew it was wrong."

"The tuition's already paid up for this semester."

"Fine. Go on back. But we're cutting off your allowance. See if those intellectuals will buy your clothes or gasoline or movie tickets or dinner at a restaurant. See if you can find someone to pay your tuition the next year and the next, because I'm not going to do it."

"I don't believe this!"

"Believe it, Jean. You've gone too far. I've had it. And I'm keeping the DeSoto."

"What? It was a Christmas present!"

"It was a gift. To my daughter. You're not acting the way my daughter should act. You have no legal right to it. It's registered in my name, not yours. So if you think you're going to drive back to your college and your rebellious ways on my nickel, you're wrong. You can walk back if you want to. I'm not giving you money for a train ticket. I'm not giving you the money for a cup of coffee."

Jean was stunned into complete silence.

"I've said all I have to say to you, Jean. You go on to bed now and sleep on what I've told you. If you're ready to apologize to me tomorrow, I'll be willing to accept your apology. If not, you know what the consequences are."

Commander Marshall stalked across the room and opened the door to the hall.

"You make me sick to my stomach," Jean said clearly.

Her father's back stiffened, but he did not turn around. He went out of the room, down the hall, and soon she heard him open and close the door to his study.

Her mother came skulking into the room then, wringing her hands like a whipped servant.

"Jean," she began piteously, then stopped, helpless.

"Poor mother," Jean said. She rose, walked past her, and went upstairs to her room.

That night Jean sat up in her bed struggling with her emotions and envisioning schemes for revenge that she knew she could never carry out. She longed to call Erich. She ached to see him—there she was in Washington, where he lay sleeping only a few blocks away, and he didn't even know it! But she was too full of anger and bitterness to speak to him now. And she would not throw herself on him like some helpless maiden seeking a knight to rescue her. She had to think all this through and come to some solution herself.

She would not apologize to her father.

Would she give up college and all that it provided simply for her beliefs?

Yes. Yes, gladly.

Of course, she thought, as the sun began to rise, it did make a difference that if she didn't return to Radcliffe she could stay here in Washington, and then she could see Erich every day. But her decision wasn't based only on her desires. For once, her principles and passions were on the same side.

Perhaps *War Stories* would like a Washington correspondent! This was the town where it was all happening. Even she had heard about the chaotic comings and goings of diplomats from the various embassies. At her mother's weekly bridge parties, congressmen's wives gossiped about the Rumanian ambassador's wife taking a job as a saleswoman in a local department store and tsk-tsked because a German diplomat's wife wouldn't attend a party if a certain Italian envoy's wife was also invited. Half the people Jean had gone to high school with had parents or relatives working in Washington.

She knew plenty of people she could interview. She could get some kind of docile secretarial job, move into a boardinghouse, and write articles at night! That would show her father that she wasn't a little girl to be ordered around anymore. Besides, most of her college courses had bored her—writing for *War Stories* was exactly what she wanted to do.

Her head was buzzing. She stretched out on the bed and fell into a deep, brief, refreshing sleep, waking two hours later to the sounds of her mother and Agate bustling around in the other bedrooms. She arose, bathed, and put on clean clothes, her best tweed suit and her cocky little felt hat.

Her mother heard her clicking on her high heels down the stairs and into the kitchen and came scurrying along behind. It was after nine o'clock; her father would already have left. Jean poured herself a cup of coffee and ate some toast with jam.

"Darling, what are you doing?" Mrs. Marshall said.

"I'm eating breakfast, Mother. Then I'm going out. Don't worry, I won't use Father's new DeSoto. I'll take the trolley."

"Oh, darling, really, I'm sure—"

"Mother. Let it alone."

"Where are you going?"

"Out."

She didn't mean to take her anger out on her mother, yet why shouldn't she? What had her mother done to defend her against her father? Jean gulped her coffee, grabbed her coat from the hall closet, and went out the door.

Jean headed for Pennsylvania Avenue. She knew exactly for whom she wanted to work. For months she'd heard her father complain about Harry Woodring, formerly governor of Kansas, now secretary of war, and a fierce isolationist. He was completely opposed to going to war in aid of the British and French. If she worked for him, she'd infuriate her father and be able to collect information for *War Stories* at the same time. With Washington awakening to the possibility of war, more office workers were urgently needed, and almost anyone who could type was hired. By mid-afternoon, Jean had a job. It wasn't, unfortunately, quite what she'd envisioned. She had been sent from office to office in the War Building, and finally over to the creaking old Munitions Building on Constitution Avenue. A harried supervisor named Polly Anderson had interviewed her for five clipped minutes before giving her a job in the secretarial pool.

"I was hoping for something a little more—advanced," Jean had said. "I've written articles for—"

"Do you have a college degree?"

"No, but I—"

"You have a high-school diploma and you can type, right? This is the job that matches your skills. If you don't want it, go somewhere else. You'll probably find what you want. Everyone needs help these days. I don't have any more time. Good-bye."

"No—wait. I want the job."

"Good. You start tomorrow."

She had a celebratory lunch in Scholl's Cafeteria, reading ads for rooms in the *Times-Herald.* Georgetown was her best bet. It was an area in transition. Many of its once-elegant homes had been turned into rooming houses, and Jean looked at three before settling on one on M Street. It was an ugly little closet of a room, but the bathroom down the hall was clean and modern, and the landlady was timid.

"Do you allow men upstairs in the evening?" Jean asked.

"Oh, my dear, I never thought . . . no one has ever asked. Well, I suppose I do . . ." Mrs. Connors blathered, looking at Jean's raccoon coat and leather purse and gloves.

"Great," Jean said. "I'll take it. I'll move in tomorrow."

Riding the trolley back to her house, Jean calculated sums in her head. Her salary at the Munitions Building would bring her one hundred twenty dollars a month. The room would cost sixty. That didn't leave much for food and clothing, especially since silk stockings cost three dollars a pair, but she thought she could count on her mother to keep her stocked with a few basic necessities. She might not be able to afford bread, but her mother would certainly bring her cake. Jean smiled.

It was quiet in her house. Her mother always took a nap in the early afternoon. Jean called Midge's dorm and left a message for her friend to call her right away at home. Wouldn't she be surprised! Then she put on some old slacks and loafers, went down to the basement to scrounge around for Bobby's old summer-camp trunk, and dragged it up to her room. She began to pack. Midge called, shrieked with gleeful astonishment at Jean's news, and promised to cut classes the next day to drive Jean and her things over to Mrs. Connors's.

It was almost time for her father to arrive home from work. Jean could hear her mother in the living room now, readying the cocktail glasses. Stafford came in through the back door, his arms laden with logs for the fire. Jean ate some of Agate's homemade oatmeal cookies and drank a glass of milk standing up. Then she pulled on her snow boots, fur coat, and gloves and slipped out through the back door.

She walked to the nearest drugstore, slid into the phone booth, closed the door, and dialed Erich's number.

Those few weeks in February would always last in her memory as the happiest days of her life. She loved her work, seated at a creaking desk typing endless forms on an ancient typewriter. Polly Anderson ran her office like a sorority house, and the air was full of laughter and chatter and the smell of perfume and nail polish. No one seemed to have a clue about what was going on, but everyone bustled with purpose and energy. A feeling of optimistic anticipation filled the air. Army officers and civilian executives came and went, flirting with the office girls.

Her relationship with her parents had settled into an uneasy truce. Her father seldom spoke to her, but her mother was genuinely happy to have Jean living in Washington instead of so far away. She told Jean to come for Sunday dinner—or any other time she wanted to. "Your father will come around in time, dear," she said. "He's really glad you're working for the government, you know." Jean visited home often, partly to please her mother, but also to pick up any tidbits of Washington gossip.

She spent most of her nights with Erich.

He was out of town a lot these days, traveling to New York on business. Companies were gearing up and modernizing their factories for faster production; that meant money loaned right and left.

When Erich was out of town, she relished her time alone in her ugly little room. So far there was only one other boarder at Mrs. Connors's, so Jean could be selfish with the bathroom. She spent luxurious hours washing her hair, soaking in bubble baths, hand-laundering her underwear, blouses, and dresses. She'd started keeping an elaborate diary, and the nights she was by herself she wrote in it for hours. Hal Farmer had liked her suggestion about being their Washington correspondent, but he advised her to take her time about it. Keep track of everything, he'd told her when he'd called her one night from Boston. Write down detailed descriptions of every diplomat and congressman and general who walks through the office. Note how often certain people show up. If you have dinner at home, listen for any news your father might drop. Send me a weekly letter briefing me on whatever you've learned, and I'll let you know if we've got anything we can shape into an article. Sometimes Jean's hand cramped from all the writing she did in her large, locked diary. So far she was disappointed; she hadn't come across anything very exciting. But she would. She knew she would.

When Erich was in town, she didn't have time to write. It wasn't just that they spent hours and hours making love in his room or hers, but that before those sweet nighttimes, they met at restaurants for dinner. Neither one of them was interested in cooking, and there were plenty of inexpensive cafeterias where they could sit at a table for hours, talking to each other. They made each other laugh recounting the stories they'd heard. An American woman sat outside the Senate chambers every day wearing full mourning garb—black dress, hat, and veil—hoping her presence would move the congressmen to avoid war. A fat, monocled German tried to crash various embassy parties, each time dressed in the costume of a different country. An aristocratic matriarch from Georgia rented a mansion and moved into it, announcing her plans to give a party a week until she found husbands for her five daughters among the diplomats and commissioned officers flooding the city.

They speculated on what Hitler would do. They wondered aloud about the part the Soviet Union would play in all this— relations with Russia were shaky at best. The current ambassador from Russia, Constantine Oumansky, kept the town buzzing with tales of the offensively anti-American tirades he launched at any public gathering, including high-level diplomatic dinner parties. Already the Russians had invaded Finland, but Jean couldn't get excited about Finland; she couldn't imagine it the way she could England and France.

The core of her discussions with Erich centered on what they could do as individuals to keep peace. They had joined a new group called the American Peace Mobilization, but so far all they'd done was sign petitions. Jean wanted to do more. She burned to make a difference.

These were passionate, vivid, glorious days and nights for Jean. Her ideological fervor was pale compared to her lust for Erich.

She could not believe what they did to each other in bed. No one, not even experienced Midge, had told her that such things could happen between a man and a woman. She was shameless. There was nothing Erich didn't do to her. There was nothing Jean wouldn't do for him.

One night toward the end of February sleet fell, making the roads dangerously slippery. Erich had been in New York for three days and was due home that evening. Jean waited in her rented room heating up canned soup, afraid the weather would keep him away. She was longing for him.

To her relief, he arrived at nine. He tossed his soaking coat over a chair, his suitcase on the bed, crossed the room, and held Jean to him. They kissed, but Jean sensed an urgency in his embrace that had nothing to do with love. She pulled away.

"What's wrong, Erich?" she asked, searching his face.

His smile was forced. "Nothing, Jean. I'm just tired from the trip. Let me catch my breath and have a drink and I'll be back to normal."

Jean poured him a scotch and water, just the way he liked it, and fixed a weak drink for herself. Erich collapsed in the armchair. She handed him his glass, then sat on the arm of the chair and massaged his shoulders. Dark circles stained the skin beneath his eyes. He leaned his head back against the chair and stared at the ceiling.

Rising, she leaned over him to undo his tie. Often when she did this, the closeness of her body caused him to pull her down on top of him, and they'd begin to make love. But tonight he only sat motionless, preoccupied.

Jean pulled the rickety wooden kitchen chair across from him and sat down. She took a hearty swig of her drink.

"Erich," she said. "Talk to me. Please."

He looked at her then with an expression in his dark eyes that she'd never seen before. It was as if he were judging her, weighing her. Then he sighed deeply, set his drink on the table, and leaned forward, elbows on his knees, hands clasped under his chin.

"Anything I say to you now must not be repeated out of this room. Even if what I say angers you, even if you leave me, you must promise me you won't tell anyone else what I'm about to say."

"Erich! For heaven's sake! I love you! I'd never repeat a conversation if you asked me not to!"

"I'm asking you to swear to that."

Jean grinned, from embarrassment and surprise.

"All right, Erich. I promise. I swear on the Bible—I swear on my life—that whatever we say tonight will never go past this room."

He continued to study her face in silence. Then, abruptly, he rose and paced across the room in his stockinged feet, turning to look at her before pacing its length one more time.

"You know how I feel about you, Jean," he said, when he was standing as far away from her as he could in the small room. "I can't promise marriage, or security, but I love you. I guess you know that. I know you love me. But what I'm about to ask of you could very well cause you to walk out now and away from me for good."

"Don't be ridiculous—" she began, but Erich cut her off.

"What I've got to ask is offensive, I know that. It's just damned difficult to say what I've got to say."

"I won't be offended," Jean said softly. "Nothing you say could offend me."

Erich came back and sank down into his chair. "All right, Jean. I've joined a group of businessmen who are fighting for peace.

Half the time when I've been in New York I've been meeting with them. I can't tell you who they are. I can't give you any names. But you'd be surprised and probably thrilled to know how many of our top people want to keep America out of this European war.

"One of the leaders of this group, and I can't divulge a single thing about him, except that he owns a large company that produces something the military's going to need if we do enter this war, this man—this man needs some information that your father has."

He paused. Jean's heart skipped a beat, but she remained silent, waiting.

"As you know, your father's an expert cryptographer for naval intelligence. The Navy's gotten hold of a coded message between Berlin and a German officer on the Western Front. If your father can break that code, the Navy will have access to invaluable information. We want that code. We've got a man who could break it faster than anyone in the military, and if we can get to the information before the Navy does, we'll be able to forge an antiwar plan to take to the President.

"I know your father often takes his work home. You've told me, and so have some other sources. It's more than likely that he's taken this code home to work on in the peace and quiet of his study at night. The War Building's a three-ring circus these days. I'm sure he can't concentrate there.

"I want you to look in his study, on his desk, see if you can find anything that looks like this code. Get it, bring it to me, let me have it for a few hours, then you can put it back." He looked at Jean. "Can you do that?"

Jean hesitated. "I don't know . . . You know how I feel about my father, but . . ."

Erich rose in one brusque, almost angry move and walked

toward the window. "I understand. I never should have asked you, Jean. Forget it."

But she jumped up and caught his arm in her hands and turned him to face her. "No, wait. I do want to help you. Look—couldn't I copy the message for you?"

"No. We've got to have the original. It could be in invisible ink or ink that shows up only in certain lights, and the code might be difficult to duplicate. Never mind. I'm sorry I asked you." Shaking his head, looking tired and distracted and worried, he gently pushed her away from him and returned to sink into his chair. He leaned his head back and ran his hand over his eyes as if they hurt.

Jean bit her lip, then made up her mind. "Erich." She crossed the room and knelt in front of him, taking his hands in hers. "Please. I do want to do this. I will do it. Tell me when."

Erich opened his eyes and studied her face for a long moment. "Jeanie, I don't want you to do anything you object to."

"No. I really want to do it."

"We need it as soon as possible."

"All right." Her knees hurt, and she stood up and paced the small room, restlessly. "I feel so—excited. So important!"

"You are important. You could be crucial."

Erich's words were like a match to dry timber. "I'll go on Sunday. Mother's always begging me to come for Sunday dinner. Probably she can't bear to be alone with Betty now that Bobby's off in submarine officer training. Father usually takes a nap after dinner. That will be the perfect time for me to slip into his study."

"It may not be left out in the open," Erich said. "He might have it hidden in books, or beneath files of routine paperwork. It's not the sort of thing he'd leave exposed, not with all the people who come and go in your house. You'll have to be imaginative. I suspect you'll have to spend some time searching."

Jean smiled, a slow, smug, Cheshire Cat smile. She crossed the room and slowly slid onto Erich's lap. Wrapping her arms around his neck, she said, "If it's that important, I know exactly where it will be. In his safe. And I know the combination."

"You do?" Erich's eyes widened. "Good girl!"

"What's my reward for all this?" Jean asked, softly squirming against him.

For just a split second, she felt him resisting, holding himself tense. "This isn't a joke, Jean. It's serious."

"I understand that. But this is serious, too," she replied and bent to kiss him.

Their lips touched, his breath hot and sweet against hers, and Jean slid her hand up his thigh and twisted on his lap so she could press all her body against his, but Erich put his hands on her arms and gave her one small shake, like a parent trying to shake sense into a child. When he spoke, his voice was husky with emotion. "Wait, Jean." He gently pushed her from his lap and, rising, crossed the room and stood looking out the window, his back to her. He stood there a few minutes, as if in deep thought, as if conversing with himself, and then seemed to come to a decision. He shook his head several times and said in a low voice, "No. This is the only way. It has to be done this way."

"Erich?" Jean stood waiting by the chair. "Is something wrong?"

Now he left the window, came up to her and, cupping her face in both his hands, tilted her head so that she was looking up at him. His dark eyes were luminous with emotion and with what even might have been the beginning of tears.

"Dear Jean—my sweet, beloved Jean," he whispered, the very tone of his voice a caress, "I love you so. I would rather die than endanger you or cause you any kind of suffering."

Jean stared at him, puzzled, then replied, "Don't worry about this code business, Erich. I know I can do it. I'm not afraid."

"You're wonderful," he told her.

"So are you," she said, smiling, glad to see the worry leave his face.

"I do love you, Jean, with all my heart," Erich said.

"I love you," she told him.

Later they lay naked together in her narrow bed.

"Is there anything more you can tell me?" Jean murmured. "I mean, my father's desk and study is always the most amazing hodgepodge. I'll have *piles* of papers to sort through, not to mention whatever he's got squirreled away in his safe."

Erich shifted so that he lay facing her. He drew his fingers through her hair as he spoke. "We don't have much to go on. It could be in German, or English, or Swahili for all we know. It could look like a mathematical formula. But it will be brief. On a strip of paper, one that's been folded or curled. One thing we do know is that it was sent by carrier pigeon."

"Carrier pigeon!" Jean burst out laughing. "You must be kidding. Germany's got submarines, fighter planes, and torpedoes, and you're telling me plans for using them are transported by a bunch of birds?"

"We can keep better track of machines than we can of birds," Erich said. "It might be antiquated, but it works. Or it did until your father's people intercepted one of the messages."

"All right, then, what I'm looking for is a curled or folded strip of paper with a message on it."

"Right. It could read like a love note or a cake recipe or a crib sheet off the bottom of a college student's shoe. But it will be brief. That's the clue."

"You can wait until Sunday, can't you? Otherwise they might

get suspicious. I haven't spent much time there, as you know. But Erich, what if Father goes into his study after his nap to work on the code later that evening?"

"I'll contact some of the others. They'll see to it that your father is summoned out to an emergency meeting that will keep him up so late on Sunday night that he won't have time to think of the code. You can go back on Monday morning on the pretext that you left something you need, and put the code back in his study."

Jean mused aloud. "We have Sunday dinner about one, after Mother and Father return from church. Then Father takes his nap about two or three and Mother listens to the radio and knits. But she often dozes in her chair. I ought to be able to slip into the study without anyone noticing. As soon as I find the code, I'll kiss Mother good-bye, trot out the door, and down to the trolley stop."

"I'll be waiting for you in the car at the trolley stop. That will save time."

"Swell. And I'll leave my umbrella at the house. No, that's too lame. Oh, I'll think of something. Erich, I'm so glad to be part of all this!"

I should have been an actress, Jean thought smugly as she sat at dinner with her family on Sunday. As she was growing up, she'd automatically fallen into role-playing: the Good Young Woman. Today she was outdoing herself. Today she was the Loving Daughter, more saccharine even than gooey Betty, who sat across from her twittering on about the colors for her wedding. Bobby was coming home in March, and they would be married then. Jean was to be one of Betty's bridesmaids.

At the head of the table her father sat eating in silence. He was preoccupied. An unexpected pang of sympathy pierced Jean's heart as she studied her father. He looked older. He'd gained a lot of weight over the past three months, more weight surely than was good for him, and fat pouches of skin swelled under his eyes. He didn't look healthy. He didn't have the same kind of eager energy that so many of the military men she saw in the Munitions Building had these days. He looked worn down.

If her father was aware of her scrutiny or her concern, he didn't show it. He was absorbed in his own thoughts. But more than that, he seemed to have unofficially cut Jean out of his life. He was furious that she was seeing Erich when she should have married Al, a Navy man and the man he had chosen for his daughter. He was embarrassed that his daughter was working instead of going to college, in spite of the fact that he was responsible for withdrawing her from school. As a final insult, Jean was working for the Army instead of the Navy. He knew where she worked, but he didn't ask her about her job. He didn't ask her anything or speak to her unless she addressed him directly.

If it hadn't been for Betty, blissfully chirping on about her wedding, the dinner would have been gloomy indeed. But they got through it in a civilized manner, at last Betty went home, and Jean's father went upstairs for a nap.

As they had for years of Sundays, Jean and her mother cleared the dining-room table and did the dishes—it was Agate's and Stafford's day off. Jean was glad to have something to do. She was so nervous, she was nearly jumping up and down. Sitting calmly through dinner had been a trial for her, and several times she'd gushed about the forthcoming wedding in squeals that matched Betty's. The rush of hot water and the hard work of scrubbing the roasting pan calmed her. Whenever she thought about what she was about to do, her hands shook.

The dishes done, her mother went into the living room, turned on the radio, and soon was dozing off by the fire.

Jean hurriedly tiptoed upstairs. The door to her parents' bedroom was shut. She assumed her father was asleep. She scurried back downstairs and into his study, leaving the door ajar so she could hear any noises. She'd decided that if her father caught her in his study, she'd say they needed a copy of her birth certificate for her file at work.

With only a glance at his paper-stacked desk, she crossed directly to the safe hidden behind a vast map of the world on the far wall. Cautiously, she lifted the heavy wooden-framed map off the wall and set it on the floor. She knew the combination as well as her own name and worked it in seconds. There. The door to the safe clicked open.

The safe was crammed full. Jean had never seen it this way. Her father kept personal papers and the velvet box holding her mother's diamond-and-pearl heirloom necklace on the bottom shelf of the safe. Official work was usually on the top shelf, but now both shelves were crowded. Jean grabbed the sheaf of papers from the top shelf and quickly flipped through them. What a mess! It seemed hopeless. There was just too much stuff here to sort through. No wonder her father looked so tired. Her energy evaporated, and a dreary feeling of hopelessness took its place.

But too much was at stake. If she was going to do this, she'd do it right. She lifted out the pile of papers and put them on the floor behind a big red leather chair. If her mother walked past on her way to the kitchen and happened to glance in, she'd see nothing out of place.

Rapidly Jean began to scan the papers, one by one, picking up each one and placing it facedown to the right of the original pile.

When she was done, everything would be in its original order. Most of the papers were on stationery with Navy insignia. A few had the President's seal. Many were memos, scribbled in her father's handwriting. Nothing looked like what Jean was searching for. Nothing seemed coded or brief enough.

She rose and carefully replaced that pile of papers. Gently pulling out the pile from the bottom shelf, she sank once again to the floor behind the chair. These, too, were military business—memos, requisitions, orders, briefings. Only the papers that had columns of statistics looked even slightly like the sort of thing Erich wanted.

Leaving the stack of papers on the floor, Jean rose and rummaged through the rest of the safe. She opened the jewelry box—nothing there but jewelry. She took out the accordion file folder that held family papers and, on the spur of the moment, extracted her birth certificate. Why not take it now? She checked through every alphabetized partition in the file and found nothing unusual. Finally she took everything out of the bottom of the safe and looked. Nothing. She stuffed the papers back in.

What now? She was bitterly disappointed. If she had to sort through the papers on her father's desk, she'd be there for hours and probably wouldn't get through it all. If the code was as important as Erich had said it was, certainly her father would keep it in the safe. Or—he wouldn't bring it home at all.

She'd go through the papers on the shelves one more time.

Slowly, patiently, she removed the bundle and went through the papers one by one. She took the time to study every sheet. Nearly in tears, she rose to replace the documents.

Over an hour had gone by. The sun had shifted. Now a gleam of light reached into the safe, hitting something dark at the back. It was black and thin and flattened against the safe wall so that it looked like part of the wall.

Jean reached in and pulled it out. It was only a wallet. A common black leather man's wallet.

She opened it. Inside was a strip of paper, thick, cheap, creased paper. Something was written on it—something she couldn't understand, for it seemed to be a combination of a mathematical formula and a language that she didn't know but thought was Russian. Not German, but Russian! This had to be it. In her elation, she almost kissed it. Instead, with trembling hands, Jean slid the paper into the wallet and the wallet into the pocket of her dress. She replaced the pile of papers exactly as they had been and shut the safe door, twirling the knob. She replaced the map on the wall. She tiptoed out of the library and down the hall. The house was still quiet. Her mother was snoring gently to a Viennese waltz. Jean slipped into her coat and quietly crept out the front door, pulling it closed behind her without a sound. She hurried down the street toward Erich and his car.

In her fantasies, she'd imagined that Erich would greet her with an embrace, but when she slid into the front seat next to him, he said only,

"Did you find it?"

"I think so. I'm as sure as I can be. Want to see it?" She held out her hand. She'd removed it from the wallet and refolded it according to its crease lines. Now it lay in the middle of her palm, a slender strip the size of a cigarette paper. She unfolded it to show the odd line of letters, numbers, and signs. "I can't make any sense of it, but it was in this leather wallet at the back of the safe. I brought that, too, but it's empty. It took forever. Still, I thought—"

"You did the right thing." Erich slipped the paper and wallet into the pocket of his jacket. "Let's go. We don't have any time to waste." Erich started the engine and began to drive. His face was impassive. "I'll drop you at your boardinghouse, then go on to meet the others. We'll probably be all night working on this. I'll pick you up around seven tomorrow morning. That will give me time to drive you to your house. You can replace the wallet, then I'll drive you in to work. Or will your father be at the house then?"

"I'm not sure. I haven't spent the night there for weeks. He usually doesn't leave the house before eight."

"All right, I'll pick you up at eight. You'll just have to be late for work."

"That's all right. I've never been late before, and Polly Anderson won't mind. Do you think I got it?"

"I won't know until the others see it. It fits the description. It's small enough to be carried by pigeon; it's been creased and weathered. And it certainly looks like a code. We'll just have to see if it's the code we're looking for."

"If it isn't, I can always go back and look again."

"I hope you won't have to do that," Erich said. "We don't have a lot of time."

Jean studied Erich's face as he drove in silence. In the vivid afternoon light he looked older, tired. She longed to scoot across the seat and caress his hair, massage his neck and shoulders, ease away some of the tension.

He brought his car to a halt in front of her boardinghouse but didn't turn off the engine. Turning toward her, he stretched his arm along the back of the seat. He stroked her hair and drew his hand gently down the curve of her cheek.

"I can't come in, Jean. I wish I could. But I've got to get back with this."

"I know. Oh, Erich, I hope this is what they need!"

But Erich didn't return her excitement. Instead, he sat looking at her in silence. He seemed to be memorizing her face.

"I do love you, Jean. Never forget that."

She put her hands on his face. The bristles along his jawline scratched the tender skin of her palms.

"I love you."

Leaning forward, he kissed her tenderly, then hugged her against him with a barely restrained urgency. She buried her face against his shoulder.

After a long time, gently, he pushed her away.

"I'd better go."

"All right." She gathered up her coat and purse. With one hand on the door handle she said, "I'll see you tomorrow at eight in the morning."

"Right," Erich agreed. How sad he looked, how grave. She stood on the curb watching until his dark car rounded a corner and disappeared.

All that afternoon and evening she hand-hemmed and em-broidered a set of heavy percale bedsheets and pillowcases, a wedding present for Betty and Bobby. As she worked, she imag-ined telling Myra and Hal Farmer and Stanley Friedman what she'd done. Would they ever be impressed! She wished she could go out for a long, gossipy dinner with Midge. How Midge's eyes would widen if Jean told her. But she'd promised Erich she wouldn't tell, and she wouldn't. Ever.

At eight o'clock the next morning she was standing just inside the front door, watching out the side window for Erich's car to pull up.

By eight-fifteen, she went outside and waited at the curb, as if that would make him arrive sooner.

By eight forty-five, she was worried. She shook her wrist and put her watch to her ear: she could hear it ticking. Perhaps her watch was fast. Click-clacking up the front walk, she hurried back inside the house to check the clock on the mantel in Mrs. Connors's living room. Eight forty-six.

She drew her raccoon coat around her shoulders as she went back out into the weak winter sunshine. She shivered. Something was wrong. If Erich knew his code breakers needed more time, why hadn't he called her? He *would* have called her. So he had to be on his way. He'd been delayed somehow.

She paced up and down the sidewalk. She counted the cars that passed by, superstitiously deciding that Erich's car would be number thirteen. Number thirteen came and went. She decided that if she didn't look up and down the street for five full minutes, he would show up. Religiously staring at the sidewalk, she continued to pace. After five minutes, Erich still hadn't arrived.

She saw Mrs. Connors looking out of the upstairs bedroom window. Jean waved cheerily at her landlady, pretending to be at ease. Mrs. Connors returned a timid, limp wave and let the curtain drop back into place.

It was nine o'clock. She should be at work by now. If Erich did come by and found her gone, he'd know where she was. He could come into her office if necessary. Or call her there. He'd given her no instructions for this sort of complication. She could only do what she thought best and trust him to find her.

When she finally arrived at the office, an hour late, Polly Anderson took one look at her and suggested she go back home. But the thought of lying in her tiny room alone with her worries was hardly appealing. She was fine, she insisted; she wanted to work. Polly gave her the easiest project that day, a repetitive pile of requisition forms to be typed. Jean worked through her lunch hour to make up for the lost hour that morning.

The day drifted by like smoke at a party. The babble of her fellow secretaries, the uniformed and bemedaled men who came and went, all blurred around her. She concentrated on typing as if her life depended on it. Still her forebodings gathered into one shrill and ceaseless voice, like that of a witchy teacher she'd had in elementary school. Where was Erich? Why hadn't he called? What was wrong? Could he have gotten *caught?* Caught by whom? He loved her; he would not willingly put her through this torture. Perhaps he'd had a car accident and was now lying injured in some hospital. That was possible, even likely; it was about the only way she could explain his absence. Or what if someone had killed him!

She had to stop imagining things. She had to relax and trust Erich. She forced herself to think of him as a lover, to remember the sweetness of his mouth on hers, the endearments he'd whispered to her. Erich. He was her one true love. She had to be patient, which was never easy for her, and he'd come to her as soon as he could and explain everything.

There were no messages waiting for her at Mrs. Connors's when she returned home that evening.

Jean stripped off her clothes and wrapped up in her warm winter robe. As she heated some soup on her hot plate, she realized she hadn't had anything but coffee since breakfast. She wasn't hungry even now. Anxiety filled her. She sipped some soup, unaware of its heat or saltiness, grateful for its warmth. She curled up in her bed, pulling the covers up to her ears for the comfort. She waited for the phone to ring.

At some point when the windows filled with darkness, she fell asleep. In the middle of the night she awakened in a sweat, heart thudding, a nightmare curling around her head. What had happened? Nothing. The house was quiet. Gradually she calmed herself, closed her eyes, and waited for the dawn.

The next morning she called Polly to say she couldn't come in that day; she was sick. She dressed carefully, taking the time to curl her hair and put on powder and lipstick.

She hurried to the trolley and rode through the morning sunshine, not down to Constitution Avenue but up to the Wardman Park Hotel. Chin up, she strode through the lobby to the elevator as if she belonged there. At his floor she hurried to knock on his door.

No answer.

She went back down to the lobby and approached the main desk.

"I'd like to leave a message for Mr. Erich Mellor," she said.

The man flipped through his books. "I'm sorry, miss. We have no Erich Mellor listed."

Jean let out a sigh of impatience. "He's not in the hotel. He has an apartment here."

Smiling pleasantly, the man went through his records slowly, carefully. Jean knew when he looked up at her that he was sure of his information, and sorry for her.

"We have no record of a Mr. Erich Mellor at all. Sorry, miss."

"Thank you," she said, her voice scratchy.

She was so very tired, she took a taxi that was waiting by the hotel back to Georgetown. Drained, she went up the stairs to her tiny room. It was a sunny day, but she was cold. She stripped off her clothes and let them fall on the floor. She pulled on her nightgown and crawled into bed. She was still too shocked, too disbelieving, too baffled, even to cry.

All afternoon she fell in and out of a restless doze. When the sky turned dark in her small square of window, she rose, found the bottle of scotch she kept for Erich, and poured some into a water glass. It tasted medicinal and harsh, but she forced it down. Sitting in a chair in her robe, looking out at the black sky, Jean sipped the scotch, and finally it loosened the knot of misery inside her and she began to cry. Erich had left her. She had betrayed her father, and her country, and the man she loved beyond reason had betrayed her and disappeared from her life. She had to hide her face in a pillow to smother the noise of her sobbing.

At some point during the night she fell asleep. Because she was young and healthy and of an optimistic nature, and because the day was clear and bright, she felt less gloomy when she woke up. As she lay on her back for a few moments, soaking her puffy tear-swollen eyes with a cold, damp washcloth, she counseled herself to have faith and patience. She wore her snazziest outfit to work, exhorting herself to enjoy the budding cherry trees just ready to burst into bloom, the cheerful chatter of the other secretaries in the office, and the sweet hot coffee and iced cinnamon rolls Polly Anderson set on her desk when she entered. She felt her energy reviving, and suddenly she had a brilliant idea. As soon as her coffee break came, she hurried down to the public phone by the ladies' washroom, called the telephone operator, and was connected with the switchboard of The Upton and Steward Bank.

"I'd like to speak with Mr. Erich Mellor, please."

Even if he'd been moved to another city, they'd have a forwarding address for him.

"I don't find a Mr. Erich Mellor in my directory," the operator said. "Do you know what department he's in?"

"He was . . . well . . . I *know* he worked there. He was an executive. He worked with the branch in New York, too." Jean's head filled with exploding lights. She couldn't think straight.

"I'll check again," the operator said pleasantly. After an eternity, she said, "Sorry. We have no Erich Mellor listed."

"Thank you."

Jean hung up the phone and leaned against the wall. She had never called Erich at work; she'd never even asked for his number. He'd always called her. It was possible that the operator was mistaken. But given his disappearance, it was more possible that he'd never worked at the bank, or that he'd worked there under a different last name, one she didn't know.

She'd been in love with someone who didn't even exist.

The knowledge descended on her, a heavy iron weight crushing her heart.

She went back to her desk and sat down to work.

Over the next few days Jean's hope changed to despair, and she forced herself to face the truth. She would never see Erich again. He had used her. Why? For what purpose? Had she endangered her father in some way? What would her father do when he couldn't produce the paper she'd stolen? Her father had never trusted Erich. Bitterly she acknowledged to herself that he had been right, after all. What she thought had been love, profound, eternal, had been only an illusion.

She had been a fool.

Sorrow and self-loathing numbed her.

In March, two weeks after she had seen Erich Mellor for the last time, Bobby returned to Washington for his wedding to Betty. Al also had leave, to serve as Bobby's best man. Their first night back, the Marshalls invited "the young people"—Betty and Bobby and Jean and Al—to dinner, and Jean was honestly glad to go, glad to get away from her lonely apartment and bitter thoughts. She was unusually quiet all through the evening, watching her father, relieved to see he showed no particular signs of vexation. In fact, he seemed reinvigorated, and he, Bobby, and Al talked enthusiastically about Roosevelt, Hitler, and the coming vote to renew the draft and the many steps that would have to be taken to rebuild the United States military forces. Germany had been at war with Great Britain and France since September, and Commander Marshall, Bobby, and Al agreed that now it was only a matter of time until the United States entered.

These men could die, Jean realized as she sat in the luxurious safety of her family home. These good men could die. She wondered what Erich had really wanted the code for, what nationality he was, what political affiliation he held. How horrible it would be if she had somehow given Erich information that would hurt the U.S. military—and her brother and father and Al! She shivered with remorse and with fury at her own stupid gullibility.

"Are you all right, dear?" her mother asked.

"I'm fine, Mom. Just tired."

"Are you working too hard?"

"No. I'm fine, really." Even her mother's solicitude, which Jean usually found overprotective and intrusive, tonight seemed terribly kind, and she wanted to put her head in her mother's lap and be soothed as she had as a child. Jean studied her mother's carefully coiffed white hair and slender, upright figure. Mrs. Marshall paid attention to the details of life, and because of her things went smoothly: the leg of lamb served tonight was perfectly cooked, not too well-done, and the dining room gleamed with polished silver, hand-shined mirrors, and mellow candlelight. "I really admire you, Mother," Jean said quietly, so that she wouldn't interrupt the men. "You make everything so beautiful."

Her mother looked startled, then blushed pink with pleasure.

"Why, thank you, darling. I didn't realize you noticed, and I can't think of anyone whose opinion means more to me than yours!"

After dinner the group rose and went into the living room, but quickly Bobby and Betty excused themselves to go off to talk about the wedding, and Al asked Jean if she'd care to go out for a drink with him. Jean said she would. Al looked slightly different to her after his three months in Norfolk. He had a weathered look about him, and an air of authority, and Jean realized that he was in charge of people and secrets and plans about which she knew nothing. In spite of her low spirits, the mysteriousness of it all excited her.

Al told her a little about the submarine training he was involved in, including some dangerous survival maneuvers. Jean listened with genuine interest. In turn, Al asked her about her job and how she liked it, and then, casually, he said, "Where's Erich Mellor these days? Didn't your parents let you invite him?"

"I'm not seeing him anymore," Jean answered truthfully. "I don't even know if he's still in Washington."

"My God, that's good news for me, Jean!" Al said, smiling. "I thought you were going to marry that guy."

"Oh, no," Jean replied.

Al pulled the car over to the side of the road. He switched off the ignition and turned to face Jean. He was such a handsome man, so pure and shining; he was a man who deserved happiness.

"Jean. You know I love you."

She had desired him when she was younger. She had yearned for him then. She had always been fond of him. She could imagine living a good life with him. If she could not have what she wanted, she was certain that she could make him happy, and that knowledge reassured her of her own worth in the world. And she was superstitious enough to believe that perhaps if she was very good for a long time, she could make up for any harm she'd done when she took that slip of paper from her father's safe.

Still, because she did really care for Al, she wanted to be forthright, and so she said softly, looking out into the dark night, "I don't deserve your love, Al. I'm not what you think I am. I've done some . . . silly things in my life."

He put his hand over hers and leaned forward. "What silly things?"

"Well, I belong to a pacifist group in Cambridge. I write for a journal called *War Stories*."

"I know all about that. Bobby told me. That's no sin, Jean. I can understand it. I wish the world could have peace, myself."

Jean turned to look directly at Al. "And I thought I was in love with Erich."

Al smiled. "I know. I can understand that, too. I've thought I was in love with other women, too."

"You did?" For some reason this was amazing to Jean, and a flame of desire and jealousy shot up inside her. "When?" she demanded.

"Oh, it doesn't really matter. It was nothing—nothing compared to what I feel for you. We're right for each other, Jean. I know we are."

She studied his handsome face, seeing him for the first time as a man of experience and at the same time seeing in him the deeply satisfying comfort of his trustworthiness. He would never betray her. He kissed her then, chastely, and she returned his kiss, and was pleased to discover how eagerly her body responded to his, how a happy heat bloomed and flowered within her as she wrapped her arms around him and breathed in his breath and felt his cheek brush hers. She cast all her other secrets on the winds of fate. She could not bring herself to tell him she'd taken something from her father's safe. She could not disillusion him that much. She wasn't that brave.

Al pulled away from her, caught his breath, and smoothed her hair, then ran his hand along her face and traced the curve of her lips with his fingers. He reached down and took both her hands in his. "I wanted—I hoped for a more appropriate time, a more romantic moment, but I've got to go back to Norfolk in two weeks. Jean, will you marry me?" When she hesitated, he said urgently, "Please. Say yes."

"Yes," she said.

The passion with which he moved across the car, and gathered her to him, and kissed her, surprised her. Mild-mannered, equable Al White devouring her so ferociously with his hands and mouth shocked and even frightened her. She hadn't imagined that love with Al would be so physical. She found herself pushed up into the corner of the car, her head pressed against the window, her raccoon coat pulled halfway off, her skirt pulled up almost to the top of her thighs.

"Please," she gasped. "Not like this."

Immediately Al withdrew his hands and returned to his side of the car. In silence they straightened their clothing. "I'm sorry," he said softly. "I—I've been waiting for so long, Jean."

"There's my apartment—" she offered shyly, but Al shook his head. "No. We'll wait until our wedding night."

"All right." Jean smiled in the dark at such a sweet thought.

Al turned on the engine and flicked the heater to high. "If we get our blood tests tomorrow, we can be married before I go back to Norfolk. We might even manage to have a double wedding with Bobby and Betty."

Jean smiled. "Betty would kill us. No. Let's just get married quietly, by a justice of the peace."

"Won't you mind not having a big formal wedding?"
"Of course not. I just want to be your wife."
"Mrs. Albert White."
"Mrs. Albert White."

That evening, when they told Commander and Mrs. Marshall they were getting married, while Mrs. Marshall wept with joy, while Commander Marshall went down to the cellar to find a bottle of celebratory champagne, while the four of them sat drinking, discussing their plans, Jean sat in a daze. What was she doing? It was, suddenly, as if Erich Mellor had been just a dream. Was it possible that she could be happy and safe, while at the same time secretly atoning for having betrayed her father?

Commander Marshall did not seem to have realized yet that something was missing. Jean knew her father well, how he moved through the house like a thundercloud when he was upset, how her mother bustled even more rapidly in her housekeeping when she knew something was bothering her husband. He seemed relaxed. So perhaps the slip of paper had not been important. When she thought of how vital it could have been, she felt nearly ill. If this was life's way of letting her balance out the scale, she was lucky.

She and Al took their blood tests and applied for their licenses. Her parents had suggested, and Al had thought it only wise, that Jean give up her room at the boardinghouse and move back in with her parents again, into her old room, until Al came home from the Navy. It made good wifely sense to do so; Jean would keep her job but instead of spending her money on rent, she'd save it for some nice piece of furniture for the house she and Al would eventually buy. Al was eager for her to be safely ensconsed with her parents. Jean's father was delighted by his daughter's snap back to sanity and treated her accordingly. He gave her back her car. It was tacitly understood that she wouldn't continue to write for *War Stories,* not with a husband in the Navy.

Two days before they were married, Al and Jean drove to Georgetown to gather up her things. It was early March, and sunny, but unseasonably cold and windy, as if winter were struggling against spring to keep its hold on the weather. Jean grabbed her raccoon coat from the closet and tied a silk scarf around her head.

At M Street, she explained her happy news to Mrs. Connors and insisted she keep the full month's rent.

"You are a dear girl, and I wish both of you a life of happiness," the landlady said, sniffling sentimentally into her hankie. "Oh, by the way, dolly, there's some mail here for you. Now where did I put it?"

Jean's heart lifted and flipped like a kite in the March wind.

"Al . . . darling . . . perhaps you could bring in the packing boxes from the car," she suggested as winsomely as she could. She didn't think she wanted him to see her mail.

Mrs. Connors handed her a small package tied with brown paper and string without a return address. While Al went out to the car for the empty boxes, Jean hurried to the second-floor bathroom. Blessedly, the door had a lock on it.

Savagely ripping off the paper, breaking a fingernail in her haste, Jean uncovered a small black velvet jeweler's box.

She opened the box. It made a tiny click. Nestled on violet silk was a small gold heart-shaped locket on a gold chain. Inscribed on the back of the locket were the words:

FAMILY SECRETS

For Jean,
With Love
E.M.

Inside a small white envelope was a card. It read: "I'm returning to you what isn't mine."

She was stunned with his arrogance, with the insult—returning her heart to her because he no longer wanted it.

She tossed the paper and box and locket in the trash. Damn him! And thank heavens for Al and his reliable, decent love.

She had her hand on the knob of the bathroom door when something—a wave of memory, of pleasure, of sweet regret—swept over her. She went back, bent over the wastebasket, and lifted out the shining gold heart. It was over, but she was not sorry it had been. Running her fingers over the cool gold, she slid her thumbnail into the tiny space between the two halves, intending to open the heart, to see what Erich had put in it, if anything.

"Jean?" Al knocked on the door. "Are you all right?"

A shiver of guilt ran through her. "Fine! I'm coming!" she called back.

She dropped the locket in the left pocket of her raccoon coat, unlocked the door, and went out to join the man who would be her husband. Together they carried her belongings from the one room in her life where she'd been neither child nor wife, but for a brief while lover, and writer, and revolutionary.

Jean and Al were married by a justice of the peace, with Bobby and Betty and Commander and Mrs. Marshall and a red-nosed, weeping Midge in attendance. For their wedding night, they drove out into the countryside of Virginia, to an inn that once had been a stopover for horse-drawn coaches and hadn't changed much since those days. Their bedroom had a fireplace where a log fire roared, throwing shadows across the four-poster bed and its hand-sewn quilt.

Al waited politely while Jean undressed; she took off her robe, draped it over the chair, and slipped into bed, still wearing her sheer, white, lace-trimmed nightgown. Al came out of the bathroom in his plaid dressing gown, lit the two candles waiting in their brass candlesticks, then slid into bed next to her.

"My darling," he said, turning to her, and Jean reached up her arms and embraced him.

What she experienced that night with Al was not the same sort of oceanic, fainting, nearly unbearable bliss she had been brought to by Erich. Instead she felt . . . warmed. From the tips of her toes to her fingertips she felt relaxed and enriched and rosy, as if a blush of health had risen up from her blood. For the next few nights, until Al had to leave to go back to Norfolk, they stayed at the Carlton Hotel, and Jean was secretly amused and flattered by the attentions Al gave to preparations for their love-making. He kept candles to light every night—not on the bedside table but across the room on the chest of drawers so that the light they shed was soft and flattering. Close at hand, on a nearby chair, or the footboard of the bed, he draped, in advance, a towel. If these considerations seemed a bit conscientious, Jean gradually learned during her married life that they were also just terribly nice. She was grateful to whatever manual he'd read or woman who'd taught him, for Al thought that it was a man's duty to pamper a woman during lovemaking. Often he liked to give her a back rub before or after, and he always took his time, concentrating on bringing Jean pleasure. On their wedding night he did not remove her gown but merely raised it up to her waist, and it wasn't until later that she realized *he* never would remove her gown. She took it off and was delighted to see that this was enormously exciting to Al. He always believed that having access to her body was a privilege not to be taken lightly.

On her wedding night, and every night thereafter, Jean was glad she had married Al. He made her happy, he kept her safe, he cared for her deeply, and she sensed that they were right together. She had no regrets.

Not until many days later, after the wedding and the wedding night, after the emotional good-byes when Bobby and Al left for their bases, not until she was alone, a married woman, in her childhood room, did she remember the locket. When she looked for it, it had disappeared from her coat pocket. She sat on the end of her bed, mentally retracing her steps. She remembered opening the package in Mrs. Connors's bathroom, and feeling guilty and disloyal to Al at the sight of the golden locket. She remembered tossing it into the wastebasket, and she remembered taking it out, putting it in her coat pocket, and then rushing out to join Al in packing up her things. Had she somehow slipped it into the box of jewelry and accessories she kept in that little bedroom? Had it fallen into one of the suitcases she'd packed? It occurred to her now that perhaps the locket held the slip of paper she'd taken from her father—or perhaps that was only wishful thinking, and she chided herself for wanting to believe that Erich had returned it to her.

"Jean, dear!"

Jean jumped at the sound of her mother's voice. Even thinking of the locket made her feel that she was being unfaithful to Al.

"Darling, another wedding present has arrived. Come open it."

"All right, Mother. I'll be right down." She'd have to search for the locket another time. Now she clattered down the stairs to the dining room.

Her parents' dining room had become a repository for the gifts she received: silver, linens, ice buckets, cheese plates and, from her parents' many friends stationed overseas, hand-painted tea sets, wool blankets, carved wooden candlesticks.

Now a long, heavy package wrapped in canvas and tied with rope had arrived, addressed to Mr. and Mrs. Albert White. Jean unwrapped it to find an oriental rug, predominately red, intricately woven, fringed, obviously valuable. Enclosed was a card with the printed words: "Congratulations on your marriage," but there was no signature.

That evening Jean sat with her parents as they tried to decide which of their friends had sent the gift. Someone stationed in the Orient, or in the far-eastern Mediterranean . . . Odd, they couldn't think who it could be. This was embarrassing. It would be rude not to acknowledge such a magnificent wedding present. Yet they could only wait for someone to ask if the gift had been received.

Every night Betty drove over to the Whites' to spend the evenings embroidering bed sheets and pillowcases and hand towels with Jean and her mother. Betty was miffed at the sight of the rug—she hadn't received anything nearly so valuable, and Bobby was older than Jean.

Within a month it was obvious that Jean was pregnant, and Betty was miffed at that, too. She stabbed her needles into her embroidery frame as if the printed pattern were Jean's flesh. Clearly it wasn't fair that Jean should get pregnant first. Jean lay on the sofa, a cool cloth over her eyes, listening to the radio, ignoring Betty's glares.

"Clever Al," Jean's mother said about the baby, as if Al had done it by himself. "Won't he be over the moon about this!"

So the days went by. Jean's thoughts turned with hope and love to the baby growing inside her—really a remarkable thing, she thought, really a miracle. The months went by, and she almost never thought of Erich Mellor. All that had been a sort of lark, the kind of thing you do when you are young. She forgot about the locket completely. Then Diane was born, and her real life began.

Chapter 9
 Julia

Late Wednesday afternoon Julia splashed cold water on her face, then studied herself in the splotchy mirror in Mrs. Overtoom's bathroom. Her eyelids were swollen from sleeping all afternoon, and her eyes were red from crying. Sitting on the side of the bathtub, she forced herself to breathe deeply. She really had to get herself under control.

Little laughing yellow ducks with red umbrellas and black galoshes danced around the room on the sun-faded wallpaper. The window curtains were white cotton edged with a fringe of white balls; through them Julia saw the backyard, where her clean clothes stirred slightly in the breeze. Smiling wryly, she told herself she'd accomplished *something* today. She'd take the laundry in when they got back from eating dinner. Her clothes would smell of fresh air and sunshine.

A bottle of lavender toilet water stood on the small white wicker stand in the corner of the bathroom. Julia sniffed it and dabbed some on her wrists and on the back of her neck, deeply inhaling the comforting, familiar old scent.

"Julia? Are you okay?" Sam's voice came from the other side of the door.

Julia stood up, pulled the door open, and smiled at him. "I'm great. Just had to smell this." Playfully, she reached out and touched the tip of Sam's nose. "That's what my grandmother's house smells like."

"Nice," Sam said. He grabbed her hand. "Come on. I'm starving."

Side by side she and Sam walked up toward the campus. It had grown colder during the day. Autumn leaves carpeted the streets and sidewalks and drifted down around them as they climbed the hill. In one yard three small children rolled in a pile of leaves, shrieking with glee.

"More! More!" they yelled. The mother, watching as she leaned on her rake, smiled and began to rebuild the pile.

Without speaking, Sam and Julia stopped to watch the children. As the mother gathered the leaves, two little boys with curly brown hair chased each other around the yard while the third child, a toddling girl whose hair glowed bright red, bent over to inspect something moving among the flowers.

"Ready!" the mother called.

She was a good mother, Julia thought. She probably had gingerbread and apple cider waiting in the house.

What would a child of hers and Sam's look like?

She leaned against Sam's body, squeezing his hand, washed over with fond desire, but to her surprise, Sam abruptly moved away, releasing her hand. He strode, almost ran, up the hill.

"Hey, wait a minute," she called.

Sam kept on going. He held his back stiffly, hands jammed into his jeans pockets.

"What's wrong?" Julia asked, running to catch up with him. "Sam?" She linked her hand through his arm and searched his face.

"Nothing. I've got a lab tonight. I don't have much time to eat."

Julia walked in silence next to Sam for a while, trying to figure out what had triggered this sudden coldness.

The children playing on the lawn . . .

"Life was easier when we were kids, wasn't it?" she asked. When he didn't reply, she thought of something else that the sight of children might have sparked. "I'm not pregnant, Sam."

But Sam only looked at her, his black eyes impenetrable.

"What's wrong?" she whispered, almost begging.

A shade of sadness moved in Sam's eyes. "Look. We'll talk about it later, okay?"

"Okay," she agreed, for they'd arrived at the campus, and as they cut across the grassy yard they were surrounded by people. When they entered the warm building, the bright fluorescent lights hit them and chatter and laughter surrounded them. They joined the line in the dining hall, chose trays of food, and found a table.

"Do you like your lab teacher?" she asked, trying to steer the conversation to something neutral.

Sam shrugged. "He's okay."

"What will you do tonight?"

"Study the mutative traits of genetically altered worms," Sam said in a monotone, not looking at her.

"Oh. Fun, huh."

Sam shrugged in reply.

Her food was tasteless. She couldn't swallow. An icy weight lay against her abdomen. She was unable to eat. If this kept up, the ice would soon press against her lungs, cutting off her breath.

"Sam. Please tell me."

"Tell you what?"

"Why you suddenly shut me out down there. By the yard with the children."

"It was nothing, Julia. Drop it."

The icy weight slid through her. She had to move; she had to go outside. "Fine. I'm going back to my room. I'll see you later." She rose.

Sam looked irritated. "I'm going to sleep in the dorm tonight. I've got an early class tomorrow. It'll just be easier."

"Suit yourself," Julia responded. Shoving the chair back against the table, she walked off and out of the dining hall.

It was like diving into a pool of cold, black water. While they'd been eating, night had fallen. It took her a few moments to orient herself and find the right way back to Mrs. Overtoom's.

"Hello! It's just me!" Julia called as she entered the boarding-house. The aroma of onions and cabbage filled the air.

"Hello, dear. Can't chat. My show's on." Mrs. Overtoom was ensconced in the living room in front of the television set.

Julia walked down the long hall, through the kitchen, and out the back door. She took her clean clothes, stiff with cold, down from the line. For a long moment she stood in the dark backyard, burying her face in the bunches of cotton, breathing in the freshness of a day out in the sun.

In her room, she folded her clothes carefully and put them away in the drawer. She made the bed and tidied up. She didn't want to watch television, and she didn't want to read. She wanted to go back up the hill, to search for Sam, to find out whether or not he was angry with her. She shouldn't have run away from the dining hall. What was the matter with her? She couldn't do anything right. Everything was confusing. Kicking off her shoes, she crawled back into bed and immediately fell into a deep sleep.

When she awoke, she could tell by the heavy silence in the house that it was late. Sitting up, she rubbed her hands over her face. Her eyelids were still swollen and tender from crying earlier in the day.

She reached over, flicked on the lamp on the bedside table, and looked at her watch.

It was eleven-fifteen.

It was eleven-fifteen and Sam hadn't come. He'd said he had chem lab, but no class lasted till eleven-fifteen. Then she remembered he'd said he was going to spend the night in his dorm. He didn't want to be there with her.

She crawled out of bed and walked around the room, restless. All that she longed for—to be married to Sam, to make their life together rich and pleasurable and their own—was at odds with what everyone expected of her. She'd tried to get what she wanted, and she'd failed. And she'd probably made everyone she cared for hate her.

On the dresser her hairbrush, lipsticks, and pens spilled out of her purse. She ran her hands over them. Mostly plastic, they clicked slickly against one another.

She went to the door, leaned against it, listened. The house was so quiet. Opening the door a crack, she listened more carefully: no canned laughter or rumble of television. Mrs. Overtoom must be in bed. Julia imagined her landlady's slumber would be billowy and sweet. She smiled at the thought and slipped out into the hall.

She was still fully dressed in turtleneck, jeans, and white socks, but she'd taken her shoes off when she got in bed and now in her socks she made no noise as she slipped down the dark hallway toward the kitchen. She felt like a black spirit moving in its element.

She didn't want to turn on any lights. If Mrs. Overtoom was not a heavy sleeper, perhaps even a click would awaken her. Julia moved through the kitchen like a blind person, feeling the wall, the chill enamel of the sink, the blank, flat face of the refrigerator. The October night was thickly dark.

Her hands closed on what she wanted: a long meat knife stuck in a wooden block.

As quietly as she could, she pulled the knife out.

The overhead kitchen light flashed on, its brilliance as loud as a noise.

"*Aaaaah!*" Julia screamed, shocked by the sudden light.

"*Aaaaah!*" Mrs. Overtoom screamed, her eyes wide with terror at the sight of Julia with the long knife in her hand.

Mrs. Overtoom's gray hair was wrapped around little pink rubber curlers only partly hidden by a frilly flowered cap meant to hold them in place. Her enormous body was draped in a white flannel nightgown covered with pink roses; a pink ribbon tied the neck of the gown together under her chins. She looked like a big, happy pig in a bonnet.

"Child," she said, "you gave me the fright of my life. What are you doing?"

"I'm sorry I woke you, Mrs. Overtoom," Julia said. She looked at the knife in her hand and thought fast. "I needed to cut the tag off a new nightgown, and I didn't have any scissors."

"Really? Or were you planning to give yourself a little abortion in my bathtub?"

The horror of Mrs. Overtoom's words made Julia flinch. "Oh, no! Oh, Mrs. Overtoom, *no.* I'd never do that. I'd never kill my own baby."

"Ah, then perhaps you were going to hurt yourself?"

Julia opened her mouth to object, but looking down at the hand holding the knife, she saw the telltale Band-Aids on her wrists protruding from her sleeve. She didn't speak.

"Sit down, child, and let's have some cocoa," Mrs. Overtoom said. Without waiting for an answer, she swayed across the kitchen, a symphony of pink-flowered flannel, to the stove. "There," she said to Julia, indicating a chair.

First Julia put the knife back in the block. She'd get it to use later, but if she sat at the table with the great big thing in her hand she'd look like some kind of maniac from a Stephen King movie, and she didn't want to give Mrs. Overtoom a heart attack. The kitchen table was covered with a yellow tablecloth with a vase of plastic flowers in the middle of it. The salt-and-pepper shakers were a Pilgrim man and an Indian maid.

"Cute, aren't they?" Mrs. Overtoom said, noticing Julia's gaze. "I'm just going to heat up a little snack for us. It's been hours since I had dinner, and I won't be able to sleep on an empty stomach. Look in the cupboard behind you. I've got an entire collection."

Julia moved her chair around so that she could open the cupboard door. Lined up in pairs, a little midget colony, were salt-and-pepper shakers for every possible occasion. Matching Santa Claus heads with ivy wreaths around their hats; smiling white-sheeted ghosts for Halloween; ducks and bunnies for Easter; green leprechauns for St. Patrick's Day; fat Kewpie dolls with white banners blaring "Happy New Year"; and a really pretty pair of porcelain hearts and flowers for Valentine's Day. Crowded against those were ceramic shakers in the shape of penguins, puppies, kittens, bluebirds, tugboats, rosy-cheeked peasants, Cinderella and Prince Charming, the Eiffel Tower, and more.

"I have more in the dining room," Mrs. Overtoom said. "The

really valuable ones. You'd be surprised how many I've got. I don't even know myself. I started collecting them a long time ago, and my friends and children have always known what to bring me as a souvenir of their trips. My collection was written up and photographed in *Yankee* magazine!"

As she talked, she set a plate of buttery scrambled eggs, crisp bacon, and blueberry muffins in front of Julia. She set her own place, then gave them each a glass of orange juice and a mug of steaming hot cocoa.

"What do you like to collect?" she asked, grunting slightly as she lowered her bulk onto her chair.

"I used to collect dolls," Julia said shyly. God, how embarrassing, how dorky. She'd die if anyone knew about this conversation.

"What kind? Madame Alexander? Barbie?"

"Barbies at my grandmother's. And of course baby dolls when I was little."

"Did you have ones that wet their pants?"

"Yes. And I had one that cried until you stuck a pacifier in its mouth."

"Well, that will prepare you for real life. Here's some butter for your muffin. Please use the salt and pepper—I didn't put any on the eggs."

They ate in a companionable silence for a few moments.

Mrs. Overtoom smacked her lips and leaned back in her chair. "Well, Julia," she went on, without any indication that she was changing the subject, "what's going on? Are you pregnant?"

Julia sighed. The warm food was comforting. She could feel the tension melt from her body.

"No. I'm not pregnant. I wish I were. I want to get married and have lots of children."

"But . . ." Mrs. Overtoom gently prompted.

"But Sam doesn't want to. At least not without telling our parents."

"And your parents wouldn't approve."

"My parents would kill me."

"Why?"

"Oh, because . . . my mother is such a superwoman and she expects me to be that way, too."

"What does your mother do?"

"She's Arabesque." Julia waited for the awe to appear in Mrs. Overtoom's eyes. "Arabesque! Oh, I know you know about them— Wait." She got up, tore into the living room, snatched up a glossy fashion magazine lying open on the sofa, and brought it back in. Flipping to the page with a brilliant ad on it, she pointed. "That Arabesque."

"You mean your mother works for them?"

"I mean she *is* them. She owns the company. She started it. She designs the jewelry. She travels all over the world."

"You must be very proud of her."

"I hate her." She let the magazine flap closed on the table and slumped back into her chair. She bent over her plate, hiding her face.

"That's too bad," Mrs. Overtoom said softly.

Julia raised her eyes enough to see how the landlady was reacting. Mrs. Overtoom was putting jam on toast. Julia continued. "She runs the house like a general giving orders to a corporal— my father. She never cooks. She's always had a housekeeper to do that stuff. She travels constantly. And she wants me to be just like her, to do something original and fabulous. She's always saying, 'Oh, Julia, darling, you're so smart and clever, you can be anything in life!' Like she's expecting me to be the first woman President or something. I mean, she's really expecting me to do something like that. She's always praising herself for making it possible for females of my generation to *be something,* but the things I want to be—a wife and mother—aren't enough for her."

"Have you told her how you feel?"

"I don't have to. I know how she thinks. She acts as if my Aunt Susan is a kind of happy peasant because she has four boys and does everything in the house and only works—she's a nurse—when the hospital needs her. Mom won't even go visit Aunt Susan. She says all those dogs give her a rash and she feels claustrophobic on the sailboats. She wouldn't even let us have a dog. Or a cat. Too much work, too much hair."

"And you want a life like your Aunt Susan's."

"Yes. Or like my grandmother's. My grandmother makes things. *Real* things. Homemade bread. Apple pie." Julia felt her body relax as she spoke about her grandmother. "My grandmother's house feels like a home. She had four children, and she loved them, and she did stuff like was the pack leader for her sons' cub-scout troop, and she always has time to sit and listen to you, and she hangs her laundry out to dry in the sun instead of tossing it into the dryer. You can always find her to talk to. Half the time if you try to talk to my mother, she'll be hiding away in her office on the second floor, or on the phone to her business manager."

"And where's your father if you want to talk to him?"

"Well, he's at work, of course! His work is really important. He's a molecular geneticist. He's trying to locate the gene that carries breast cancer."

"My."

"You would think my mother who is not totally moronic would realize that compared to what my father does, her 'work' is insignificant. But no, she has to act as if they're of equal value, and

Dad's supposed to spend the same amount of time at home as she does. She has nagged about that every single minute of her life!"

"She sounds like a very unpleasant person."

Julia was surprised. Mrs. Overtoom's words hit her like a slap. "Oh, well, not really. You wouldn't think so. I mean, she's not unpleasant except to me. And she doesn't mean to be unpleasant. It's just that she wants me to be like her, and I don't want to be."

"So what were you going to do with the knife?"

Startled, Julia grinned spontaneously, goofily, the inappropriate way you sometimes do when you hear someone's died. "Well. I guess I was going to slit my wrists." She flashed a quick look at the landlady. "In the bathtub where it'd be easy to clean up." When Mrs. Overtoom didn't respond, she said, "Sorry."

"Maybe we should call the Samaritans," Mrs. Overtoom said after a while.

"Oh, I'm not religious," Julia said. "I mean, I believe in something, but I'm not sure what. I'm sort of in between gods."

"No, no, the Samaritans are those people who specialize in suicide. I mean in preventing it. They'd know what to say. I don't know what to say. I'm not even sure I understand why you want to die." The landlady looked at Julia, shaking her head. "I've had a lot of losses and a lot of pain in my life, and I've still never wanted to die. And if I were young and beautiful like you . . ."

Julia looked at Mrs. Overtoom in all her old pink fatness. A little tuft of gray hairs was growing out of the woman's chin. Julia glanced away, hoping Mrs. Overtoom hadn't noticed her staring. A great wash of contrition swept over her.

"I won't kill myself tonight, Mrs. Overtoom. And if I do, I won't do it here at your house. I promise."

"Well, that's a relief." The landlady rose, pushing herself up with both hands. She carried her plate and cup to the sink. "It's after midnight. Will you be able to sleep?"

Julia brought her plate and cup over. "Yes. I'm sure I will. Would you like me to wash these before I go to bed?"

"No, no, dear. That's all right. I'll wash up in the morning."

"Thanks for the food. It was delicious."

"You're welcome, I'm sure."

For a moment Julia felt like hugging the old woman. For a moment it seemed as if she'd known her forever, that they were friends or, more than friends, relatives. But Mrs. Overtoom turned away and lumbered over to the wall. She put her hand on the light switch, ready to turn it off. She was waiting for Julia, so Julia smiled and went down the hall to her room.

This time she undressed completely before getting into bed. The room was cool and the air against her bare skin was refreshing, almost like a touch. She slid under the sheets and pulled up the covers. She was so tired of thinking. Her stomach felt soothingly warm and full. She closed her eyes and fell asleep.

She'd only been asleep for a few minutes when a noise awoke her. Drowsy, she didn't open her eyes but merely listened. Someone had come into the room. She heard the sound of clothes falling on the floor, then the bed sagged under new weight, and Sam lay next to her, pressing his body against hers, wrapping his arms around her.

"You awake?" he asked.

She hadn't realized how cold she was until his arms were around her, his warmth covering her like a quilt.

"*Mmm,*" she said, snuggling against him.

"I tried to sleep in my dorm room, but I couldn't," Sam whispered against her hair. "I pulled on my clothes and ran all the way here."

"I'm glad." She hugged him tightly.

They held each other for a few moments. Sam kissed her forehead, her hair. "I wasn't being fair," he confessed. "I did close up this evening. When we saw the children. I need to tell you something."

Julia's breath caught in her throat as she waited for his next words. When they came, she was surprised.

"I always envied you and Chase."

"You did?" Twisting against him, she looked up at his face. It was too dark to make out his expression, but she didn't want to turn on the light and interrupt the mood.

"You always had each other to play with."

"To fight with is more like it."

"Maybe. But you fought in your own shorthand, over things I didn't know about." Sam punched his pillow, stuffed it behind his back, and sat up in bed, leaning against the headboard. "When the three of us played together, I was always the one who had to go home alone, or who was left alone. I'd watch out the window. You and Chase would argue while you walked home, or you'd run after each other. You had all sorts of plots to make the baby-sitters let you have your way. The two of you would gang up against your parents. You'd warn each other. 'Watch out. Mom's in a bad mood.' I love my parents, and I know I ought to be grateful to them for adopting me, and I am grateful. But I wish more than anything in the world I'd had a brother or a sister."

"Oh, Sam," Julia cried. "I never realized."

"I never want to say anything about it to Mom and Dad. I owe them so much. But, Julia, all my life, I've promised myself I'd have a lot of children. Not just one. Even more than two. I used to daydream about it. I want to have two of my own, and adopt two." Sam paused, then continued, his words coming out in a rush, "And that wouldn't be fair to you."

"Why not?" Julia sat up facing Sam, her legs tucked against his chest. She pulled a blanket up over her shoulders for warmth.

"Because that's not all. The other part is, I don't want my kids raised by baby-sitters. I'm really serious about that."

"That's what I want, too, Sam."

"You do?" He sounded genuinely surprised.

"I want to stay home with my children. I've always wanted that. Remember when I was in the hospital with spinal meningitis?" Even now her heart thudded at the memory. "I swore I'd never let a child of mine go through something like that without me."

"Your dad was there."

"That wasn't the same. Maybe for some people it is, but it wasn't for me. I was eight years old. My mother was like a goddess to me. I felt safe when I was with her." Julia shivered and changed positions so that she could cuddle against Sam, burrowing her head against his chest. The strong beat of his heart against her ear steadied her. "No, never," she declared. "I'll never go away from my children until they're old."

"What about your restaurant?"

"What restaurant?"

"You've always said you were going to have your own restaurant. Remember how you used to fix up a restaurant in your garage and serve fancy meals to me and Chase?"

"Graham Cracker à la mode," Julia smiled, remembering.

"You made really good Triscuit-and-melted-cheese pizzas."

Julia laughed, then grew sober. "My mother hated it when I served you and Chase. 'Don't wait on them! Let them wait on themselves. You haven't been put on earth to serve males.' Oh, God. She got so mad."

"My mom, too. She'll be furious if you marry me and stay home with the children."

"Our mothers are a lot alike. They're both ambitious. They're both successful—"

"See?" Sam interrupted her, squeezing her shoulder as he made his point. "Just the way you said that—'they're both successful.' Will you think you're not successful if you don't have a career? If you're just my wife, if you just raise our kids?"

"Of course I won't. I mean, I won't just raise kids and die like a bug or some kind of lower form of life. I can always start a restaurant or something when I'm older." She drew her fingers along Sam's arm, thinking. After a while, she said, "I want a lot of children, too, Sam. And I want to stay home with them." She took a deep breath. "I just don't want to have them yet."

"God, I don't either!" Sam nearly leaped from the bed. "I didn't mean that I wanted children now. That's why I got so upset this afternoon. Seeing those children. Julia, I want to be with you, and I want to have children with you, but not yet."

"So we won't have children right away. We can just be together. I can work. I can save money for us, for the future."

"Next year I'll start grad school. I hope I get into Johns Hopkins. Or Stanford."

"I could go with you."

Sam pulled Julia against him in a one-armed hug. "I like the thought of living with you instead of in some boring dorm, eating cafeteria mush and sleeping by myself."

"It would be fun to live somewhere else, someplace really different. I've never been to California. Or to Maryland, for that matter. My parents have taken me to Europe, but I've never seen the rest of the United States."

"You could go with me when I look at the schools and interview."

"If you go to Stanford, we could take trips to Mexico. Tequila, señor."

"Your parents will be pissed."

"Mom will be. Dad will be oblivious as usual. But I can't live my life to please my mother."

Julia could sense Sam's mind working; she would have bet anything he was considering his debt to his own parents. "Sam," she said softly, "we should go to sleep. You've got a class at eight."

"Yeah. You're right." Sam stretched, then scooted down into the bed, pulling Julia with him.

She fussed with the covers, arranging them around Sam's shoulders, then snuggled close to him. Her breath came easily now, and she felt all warm and drowsy. "We can talk tomorrow," she told him. "We've got all the time in the world."

"I know." Sam wrapped his arms around her. "I love you, Julia."

"I love you." Closing her eyes, Julia relaxed, safe in Sam's arms.

She was just beginning to doze when Sam spoke. "Julia."

"*Mmm?*" She pressed her hips and legs against his.

"Will you marry me?"

Her eyes flew wide open.

"Oh, Sam. Yes."

Gently Sam turned Julia to face him. Leaning above her on one elbow, he lay his hand against the length of her cheek and drew his thumb lightly over her lips, as if memorizing her by touch. She raised her arms and wrapped them around his shoulders. She could see his eyes shining in the dark. Sam bent and pressed his lips against hers in a kiss as solemn as a vow. They embraced, still kissing, and tears of happiness welled up in Julia's eyes and spilled over, tracing a path to her hair. Still they kissed, and Sam slowly brought his whole body down over Julia's. For a long, intense, sweet while they remained that way, the steady incandescence of their love seeming to fuse them together, so that they were like two sides of a locket closing, clicking into place so completely that no seam could be seen.

Finally, both of them sighing deeply, they moved apart.

"God, I'm happy, Sam," Julia whispered, settling against him.

"I am, too," Sam replied.

Julia felt infinitely snug and complete, with her legs curving against Sam's, his chest warm against her back, his breath stirring her hair, her hand clasped around his wrist with its steady, reliable pulse.

Chapter 10
❧ Diane

Why, Diane wondered, as she sat alone in her dark kitchen, waiting for her husband, why was she thinking about Finland and Russia? Why tonight after so many years? Because Peter Frost was calling up within her a desire for the exotic?

Because in those countries she had been a woman alone, for a while, free to experience the world without translating and taming it for her children.

She was still in touch with Tarja. Every year around Christmas they exchanged long letters and met occasionally at jewelry conferences and conventions. Tarja had never married. She had a dog now, a luscious white Samoyed named Kiki, who went with her from her apartment to her studio to her summer place, riding with intelligent calm in the passenger seat of her car, never needing a leash, barking only at strangers and never at Tarja's friends. When Diane showed Tarja pictures of her children, Tarja reciprocated with photos of her beautiful dog; it never seemed to occur to her that this might be humorous, or that she was less fortunate than Diane.

Well, she chided herself, enough nostalgia. She got up, flicked on the lights, and searched through the refrigerator for something to serve Jim. She found a curry that Kaitlin had made from last night's lamb and was setting it on the counter when she heard the front door slam.

"Jim?" She rushed into the hall. "Good news! Julia called."

"That's great," Jim replied, tossing his coat over a chair. Halfheartedly he pecked a kiss onto Diane's forehead.

"Are you all right?" Diane asked.

"Fine. Just tired." Jim slumped into a chair. "Tell me about Julia."

Diane studied her husband. He looked so very weary. Sometimes after a long day he was stooped and pale with fatigue and her heart would cramp within her at the thought of how he drove himself. "I'll heat up the curry. Want some coffee while you wait?"

"I'd prefer some wine."

Diane poured it and set it in front of him. "Julia's fine, her usual feisty self. She's with Sam, she plans to get a job, she doesn't want to go to school, and she'll call us in a few days."

"I told you she'd be okay."

"I know, but oh, Jim, I've been sick with worry." Suddenly tears flooded her eyes. "I've been feeling like such a failure."

"Why?" Jim seemed genuinely puzzled.

"Because she tried to slit her wrists. Because she wants to get married instead of going to college."

"Are you a success at your business because of something your mother did?" Jim asked. "Are you happily married because of your mother?"

Diane blew her nose on her napkin and glared at Jim. She couldn't decide whether he was wise or merely irritating. She rose and put the casserole in the microwave.

"Have you talked to the Weyborns?" Jim asked.

"No. Good idea. I'll call them right now."

Sam's mother, P.J., answered the phone on the first ring. When Diane told her about Julia's call, P.J. said, "I know. Sam just called here. Until now I've held my tongue, but I'm so angry at both those kids I could spit."

"It's funny, in a way," Diane said. "Remember all the times we worried about Chase and Sam growing up together? We were afraid they'd egg each other on to do something really dumb, drunk driving or going crazy at a college party. Instead, it's Julia and Sam."

"Well, you know, Diane, I love Julia, and I'd be thrilled to have her for a daughter-in-law. Just not yet. Although the kids have some scheme about her working in a restaurant and supporting Sam while he's in graduate school, so it sounds as though they're trying to be realistic. But I think it would be wise for Julia to get some training first. Maybe there's a culinary institute in Hartford."

"What are you talking about, P.J.? 'Working in a restaurant'?"

"Didn't Julia mention it?"

"No." Diane was cut to the quick with jealousy. P.J. knew more than she did about her own daughter's plans!

"Sam mentioned it. He didn't go into detail, but it doesn't surprise me. You know how Julia's always loved cooking. I'm sure they'll tell us more about it this weekend. Sam said he'd bring Julia home then. Not to stay. Just for a visit, so we can see that she's okay."

"As soon as I see she's okay, I'm going to kill her," Diane said.

P.J. laughed. "It could be worse, Diane. Think of all our friends who have children with drug problems, or anorexia, the girls who've already had abortions."

"You're being wonderful about this, P.J. I wouldn't blame you if you never wanted to see Julia again."

"Why, I love Julia, Diane. She's a treasure!"

Emotion tightened Diane's throat so that she could hardly speak. She handed the phone to Jim and sank into a chair, put her head in her hands, and wept.

Jim said good-bye to P.J. "Here, Diane. Take a sip of wine," he suggested.

"All right." She took the glass from him and drank, then wiped her eyes with the back of her hand and took a shuddering breath. "Jim, did you know that Julia wants to cook? I mean professionally?"

"No."

"I didn't, either. She told Sam, and Sam told P.J. Why do you suppose she didn't tell us?"

"Probably because she thinks we might frown on such an ordinary job."

"You're right. I do frown on it. Why should she be a cook when she could be a lawyer or a doctor?"

"Because she wants to?"

Diane glared at her husband, infuriated by his cool detachment.

"You look tired. Let's go to bed," Jim said.

"Okay. I think I'll take a hot bath first, to relax."

"Good. I'll watch the news."

They went their separate ways, but when at last Diane crawled

290

into bed with Jim, he surprised her by snuggling up next to her and wrapping an arm around her waist.

"It's really all right," Jim said softly. "Julia's with Sam. She's alive. We can all go on from here."

Diane flexed her legs against her husband's and burrowed into her pillow. She knew Jim was soothing himself as well as her. She floated down into a warm sleep, where Jim's familiar body was also Peter Frost's, and in the way of dreams, that made sense.

Late Wednesday morning Diane opened the front door to the FBI agent's knock.

"Come in," she said, smiling.

"How are you?" he asked as he entered.

"Great!"

"You look it," he observed, and her smile widened. She was only wearing jeans and a blue denim work shirt, but she knew what he meant.

"My daughter called last night. She's in Middletown with her boyfriend, Sam. I'm so glad she's safe I can't even be furious at her, but I'm sure that will come in time."

"She's okay?"

"She's fine. She's coming home this weekend. I'm looking forward to a good long talk."

"I'm glad you heard from her," Peter said.

Looking in his eyes, she saw that his concern was genuine. "Thank you. I was so afraid . . . Now I feel as if the world is brand-new."

"I know. When my son . . . had some trouble . . . it was the worst thing in the world. I would have given everything I owned, and my arms and legs, to keep him safe."

Diane stared at Peter, drawn to him by his passion. "What happened?"

"It's complicated. But I'd like to tell you someday, when we have more time."

"I'd like to hear about it," she replied honestly.

They looked at each other, savoring the moment of frank mutual interest, then Peter cleared his throat and said, "Well, I suppose we should get started."

Once again they climbed the stairs and walked through the long hallway to the attic stairs. They only had a few boxes left.

The weather was brilliantly sunny, filling even the dusty attic with copper light. As they bent over a box together, Diane thought: in this light he'll see every wrinkle I've got and the ones I'm just starting to get. The way her veins stood out on her hands as she pulled on the cardboard lid embarrassed her. Her body was separating into pieces on its way toward breaking back down into basic molecules.

But Peter Frost wasn't looking at her hands. He was intent on his search, going through each item as slowly and carefully as he had the day before. In response to the heat in the attic today, he'd taken off his suit jacket and rolled up the long sleeves on his white shirt. She wanted to run her fingertips over the swirls of dark hair on his thick forearms.

They worked together into the early afternoon, still without finding what he was looking for.

"My mother was never this disorganized," Diane said apologetically. From the final box they took old bank statements, canceled checks, needlepoint patterns, old Christmas cards from friends, a few paperback mysteries, a church directory, wrapping paper, a box of paper clips, a sheaf of recipes torn from magazines and stapled together. "I think I must have gone crazy this summer. I just went around the house and the attic dumping things into boxes."

He held up the final item from the bottom of the box: a gold beaded handbag that had to date from her mother's college days.

He opened the bag and searched through it, finding one hairpin and a penny. He turned the lining inside out. With infinite care and gentleness, he began to tear the creamy lining away from the purse. The sound of old silk ripping mesmerized Diane.

Nothing was hidden under the lining. He tossed the bag on the top of the pile.

"That's it," he said. "Damn."

He rose and stretched. She saw the dark patches under his arms where the day's heat had caused sweat to stain. She saw his body pressing against the cloth that covered it. Jim was more slender. He looked elegant in his clothing, like the most purebred of British aristocrats. Peter Frost's body was bulky. Stretching, his calf and arm muscles pushed at the fabric of his clothes. He rolled down his shirtsleeves.

"Wait," Diane said. "There are still some dresses and old fur coats."

She crossed the room and unzipped a blue quilted bag. A potpourri of perfume, mothballs, and age drifted out into the air. Here was the romance of her mother's life: the evening gowns and party dresses, the red silk cape, and a mink jacket. Diane took her father's tux out and handed it to the agent.

"I doubt if what you're looking for is in here, but . . ."

He searched it carefully. Diane removed the gowns one by one and slid her hands over their shining surfaces. These were from the later years of her mother's life, she could tell by the size. She moved on to the next garment bag. More beautiful, outdated gowns. A marvelously sophisticated thing in slender black with a white sleeve and bodice. A full-skirted scarlet gown that must have looked ravishing on the dance floor. If these clothes could talk! They would certainly tell of a Jean Marshall Diane had never met.

"I doubt if we'll find anything in all this," Peter Frost said. He seemed dispirited. "Gowns don't usually have pockets."

"But coats do," Diane said. She wanted so desperately to please him, to make him smile at her.

She pulled out an old raccoon coat. "What a great style!" she said, and slipped into it, admiring the wide boxy shoulders. But the skin of the coat was so dry that whole sections of it had come away from the lining. It really looked pretty ratty. She slipped her hands into the pockets. Nothing . . . except . . .

In the left pocket there was a hole.

She took the coat off, put it on a hanger, hung the hanger on a hook on the wall, and began to pat the hem. Like a blind person, she tilted her head away so that her hands could do the searching. The lining was still tightly attached to the fur. Toward the front of the coat she felt a lump.

"Peter."

He stood next to her. She took his hand and put it on the lump.

"Could be a compact or a lipstick," he said, but Diane could see the hope in his eyes.

She stood back to let him part the lining from the fur. For a few seconds it held, so that Diane thought she should get a pair of scissors, then with a tearing sound it gave. The lining came away from the fur in a jagged strip. Something gold fell to the floor, so light its landing scarcely made a sound.

He swooped to pick it up. He held it out, flat in the palm of his hand, for the light to illuminate it, for Diane to see it as clearly as he did.

On a delicate gold chain was a small heart-shaped locket. The front was decorated in elaborate scrollwork. The back was engraved:

For Jean,
With Love
E.M.

"I think we've found it." Peter's voice was low.

"E.M.?" Diane asked, testing the initials. "Who's E.M.?"

Instead of answering, Peter turned the locket this way and that, scrutinizing it, digging at the seam that ran around the side in an attempt to open it.

"Usually lockets that open have little catches at the top," Diane said.

Peter was too intent to reply. Watching him, Diane smiled: his hands were so huge and clumsy around the fragile locket.

"Here," she suggested. "Let me."

Reluctantly he handed it to her. The locket was suspended from the gold chain by a tiny loop of gold at the top. Gently she twisted the loop sideways. At first it resisted. Then, like a shy oyster, the locket popped open, its front and back parting only a fraction.

Peter took it from her and bent the two sides apart. The insides of both halves were rimmed with a tiny edge of gold to hold in pictures. One half was empty. The other half held a strip of paper.

Carefully, he removed the paper from its hollow. He unfolded it to reveal a dark black line of letters, numbers, and symbols much like a geometric equation or a pharmaceutical prescription.

"This is it," he said, excitement creeping into his voice.

Diane moved closer for a better look. He turned his hand

toward her so that she could see it more clearly, but she couldn't make any sense of it. "What exactly is it?"

"An encoded formula." He slid the paper back into the locket. "I'll need to take this with me. I'll give you a receipt for it. Now I've got to make a phone call."

Grabbing up his jacket and pulling it on as he walked, he crossed the attic and hurried down the stairs, leaving Diane alone in silence. She felt oddly slighted, as if she'd begun an adventure with this man, and now he was leaving her behind.

And who was E.M.?

Turning off the lights, she left the attic and went down the stairs and through her house to the kitchen.

Peter was seated at the desk, phone jammed against his ear, talking intently. A note from Kaitlin was propped up on the bowl of apples in the middle of the table telling Diane that she'd gone out for groceries. Diane made coffee, moving quietly, hoping she could overhear Peter's conversation without disturbing him.

At last he hung up. Turning to Diane, he smiled. "We're set."

"Well, good. I guess," she replied.

"Now that we know the paper's in our hands, I can tell you what this is all about. And I need you to sign some things."

"All right. Would you like some coffee?"

"Sure." He went into the front hall and returned with his briefcase. Seating himself at the kitchen table, he flipped through a sheaf of papers and documents.

Diane remembered how he liked his coffee and placed the sugar bowl on the table with a pitcher of cream and a plate of Kaitlin's sugar cookies. When she sat down across from him, her knee touched his. Blood rushed to her face. She readjusted her chair.

Peter sipped his coffee, then leaned back in his chair. "Back in the late 1930s, two men, Patrick Brown, a professor of biochemistry at Georgetown University, and Yuri Oshevnev at the University of Moscow, met at various times at scientific conferences in Europe and began a collaboration in their work toward developing nuclear energy through the fusion of atoms. They communicated through code."

Diane's thoughts jumped ahead. "So that strip of paper is a coded message from an American to a Russian?"

"Right. They sent their correspondence to a contact in Berlin, who then sent it on to Moscow or Washington. By 1940, as we approached the world war, everyone was suspicious of everyone else. One of Brown's coded messages—this one—was intercepted by the U.S. military and taken to your grandfather, who was in charge of naval intelligence. He in turn brought it home, as he often did with his decoding work, and locked it in his safe. Apparently he decoded enough of it to realize it had to do with scientific research instead of with weaponry or war plans. At any rate, he never missed it after your mother took it from the safe."

"My mother did what?"

"When your mother was in college, she was involved with a group of intellectuals centered in Cambridge who were working for the cause of peace."

"My mother!"

"Yes. When she was in Washington, she met a man named Erich Mellor—"

"E.M.—" she murmured.

"—who convinced her that he needed a certain coded message that would help prevent war. Erich Mellor had been educated in the U.S., and his English was perfect, but in fact he was Russian. He wanted to get some information about the U.S. Navy, which was in disastrous shape at that time. He asked your mother to bring him a cryptogram from her father's safe, and she did. But that message—this piece of paper in my hand—wasn't what Erich

Mellor wanted or needed. So he returned it to her, in a locket. He assumed she'd find it and put it back in the safe so that her father would never know it had been missing. Instead—well, it must have fallen down into the lining of the coat."

Diane looked out the window and, instead of the autumn light, saw her mother as a young woman in a fur coat with boxy shoulders, her mother as a young woman who had broken into her father's safe to steal a coded message from the United States Navy.

"She must have been in love with Erich Mellor," she said softly.

"Perhaps."

Her mother, in a fur coat, in love with a Russian. "And he was just using her."

"Not necessarily." Peter leaned forward. "After all, he did care enough to send the locket to her—"

"May I see it?"

She held out her hand, and Peter gave it to her. She stared down at it, holding it only by the corners, not daring to touch the cryptic black letters printed on the page.

"This is a formula related to nuclear fusion?" she asked.

"We think it is."

It was so light it was almost weightless, yet like a jewel, terribly valuable. She handed it back to Peter.

"In the early forties," Peter told her, "scientists discovered how to create nuclear energy by fission, splitting atoms. But they're still working on fusion. This could be a crucial part of the puzzle."

"What about the two scientists?"

"Because of the war, Brown and Oshevnev died without ever sharing their research with the scientific community. It took until now, when things loosened up between us and the Soviets, for researchers to recognize how valuable their work was and start a search for their formula."

"So now what happens?"

"I'll give this to my superiors, who will hand it along the line to the proper authorities. Russia and the U.S. used to cooperate. It looks as if they might do so again."

"Wow. I'm having trouble taking all this in."

"I'm sure you are." He placed a complicated document in front of her, and said, "This is merely a release form. I need your signature."

Diane scanned the form and signed. He gathered up the papers and put them in his briefcase. Then he took a card from his wallet and wrote something on it. "This is my home phone. In case you have questions, or ever want to reach me—about anything."

He was going to leave now, Diane realized, surprised at the disappointment she felt, and at the sudden urgency within her to make him stay. She took the card from him.

"I'd better go," he said, rising.

"Yes." What could she say, what could she do to keep him with her? "I'll walk you to the door."

In silence they went into the front hall, which was warm and bright with late-afternoon sunshine. She took his coat from the hall closet and reluctantly turned to hand it to him, when he surprised her by putting his hands on her shoulders and holding her still as he looked into her eyes.

"I have to go. But I'd like to see you again. I know you're married. I don't want to insult you, but I can't help feeling there's something special between us."

"I know what you mean," she replied, and she tilted her head back so that it was easy, exactly right, for him to step toward her and bend his head down and kiss her mouth. His hands moved down her shoulders to pull her tightly against him, and she let his coat drop to the floor so she could bring her hands up to touch his black hair. It had been a long, long time since she'd been kissed as Peter was kissing her, a ravenous, greedy, improper kiss that brought her body straining against his. Without taking his mouth from hers, he moved her back until she was pressed against the wall and then he brought his hands around and very slowly drew them down from her shoulders over her collarbone until they rested on the swell of her breasts. She felt the curving weight of her breasts against his palms.

Bringing his mouth down in kisses across her face to her neck, he said in a husky voice, "Your breasts are beautiful."

Pleasure swept through her. Yes, she thought, my breasts are beautiful, and it had been a long time since she'd remembered that. Bracing her back against the wall, she slanted her hips out to push against his, while he continued to kiss her, at the same time reaching down to pull her work shirt out of her jeans so that he could put his hands up under her shirt.

"Oh, God," he whispered, "oh, God," as he pulled at her bra.

He slid his hands around to undo the snaps and then, groaning with satisfaction, he tugged the material up so that her breasts fell freely into his hands. Still he kissed her, his mouth warm and wet, and she felt how her breasts were too large for his hands, and sensation poured through her veins much as milk had once long ago, pulsing then channeling and gathering and flooding into her engorged nipples. She wanted his mouth on her breasts, she needed his bite to break the tension . . . but suddenly she heard the kitchen door open and Kaitlin called out, "Hello? I'm back!"

Diane pushed Peter away. He stepped back, breathing heavily. Quickly she reached her arms up to fasten her bra and tuck her shirt back in. "Hi, Kaitlin!" she called, her voice unsteady. Then they heard Kaitlin singing to herself as she unpacked the groceries.

"Well," she said, smiling at Peter, feeling desirous and embarrassed and happy and proud.

"Look," he said, smoothing back his hair, "I've got to go to Washington today. I can get back here next week. May I see you then?"

As her blood calmed, she remembered who she was, where she was. A married woman, in her family home.

"I need to think about this," she said, for they both knew what he meant when he asked to *see* her. "Call me," she told him. "In a day or two, when things settle down."

"All right," he said. Picking his abandoned trench coat off the floor, he went to the door and opened it. "I'll call you."

He went out into the afternoon sunlight and Diane watched him walk across the porch, down the steps, and across the lawn to his car.

Going into the kitchen, Diane began to talk casually with Kaitlin about the evening meal, impressed and amused by her own air of normalcy. Then, grabbing her car keys and jacket, she drove into Cambridge. Lisa had taken the afternoon off for a dental appointment, and Diane was glad. She appreciated the silence. Her assistant had piled yesterday's mail on her desk, and Diane began to diligently sort through it.

The American Gem Trade Association wanted her to be on a jury at an international design show for young designers. *Ornament* magazine wanted to interview her. The Rhode Island School of Design wanted her to speak on jewelry design in the nineties. She flipped through a sheaf of telephone messages from sales reps, jewelers, and customers wanting to commission special pieces.

She dropped it all back on the desk. She couldn't concentrate on her work today. Her thoughts were in a tangle: where was her mother, her mother who had had an affair with a spy? What could she do about Julia and Sam—what *should* she do? Oh, surely it was too much to have to worry about her mother and her daughter at the same time! Really, her body informed her, she didn't really want to think about them at all; she only wanted to close her eyes and remember Peter's kiss, his touch, which made her shiver in memory.

She went into her studio. It smelled of warm metal. She picked up the mold she'd been carving, then put it down. Not even this held her interest today.

At five, Diane dialed Jim's office. When he finally came on the line, she said, "Is there any chance you can come home early tonight? I've got a lot to tell you."

"About Julia?"

"No. About my mysterious mother."

"Is she all right?"

"Oh, she's fine. It's me—I can't believe it. It's quite a tale."

"Can't it keep till later? I'm really tied up here."

Diane bit back a bitter remark. She counted to ten.

"How about going out with me for a quick bite to eat?" she suggested.

"I really can't. I'll grab a sandwich here."

"Fine," Diane said, anger edging her voice.

"Are you okay?" Jim sounded wary, defensive, and hurried.

"Yes, Jim. I'm okay. See you later." Diane hung up the phone and put her head in her hands, defeated.

She remained that way for a long while, thinking of nothing at all, letting the tension of the day slide off her shoulders. When she lifted her head she saw that night was falling. The windows were dark and the building was silent, and outdoors horns blared as the traffic moved relentlessly past. The room felt cold. Rising, she shivered a little, wrapped her arms around her chest for warmth, and went back into her studio to turn off all the lights. On her desk, caught in the focused glow of a lamp, lay the sketch pad with the elaborately entwined monograms of the couple about to be married. She saw with her artist's eye that the body of the brooch was muddied, unclear; she needed to draw it again more carefully, making the letters more distinct. She felt an arrow of sadness piercing her heart through, for it seemed to her as she looked at the two letters joined together that it was somehow symbolic of her own life: she had been alone, then for years her life had been truly indistinct from Jim's and also bonded to the lives of her children, but now she was coming out of all that, returning once again to a singular state, separate from her grown children, her distant husband. She was entering a new phase of life, and it frightened her slightly, and yet— Remembering Peter Frost's kiss, she smiled as she turned off the lights, locked her studio, and went down to her car, to drive home.

Entering her house, she noticed how it, too, loomed silent and empty. Instead of continuing through the hall, her mind set on messages on the answering machine and heating dinner and looking through the day's mail, she leaned against the front door and looked down the long passageway from entryway to kitchen. Without trying very hard at all, she found that she could superimpose upon the polished table and clean-swept floor the objects that once had been scattered around the hall: children's raincoats, snow boots, book bags, mittens, basketballs, baby dolls, water pistols, sweaters. So many things had been tossed here, abandoned, as the children raced through the house on their way from one game to another. Now it was all as clean and tidy as a museum.

Yet for her, part of this hallway was dense with a secret richness, and she moved from the door to the spot near the hall closet where she'd stood earlier that day with Peter Frost. Closing her eyes, she felt the memory of his kiss, his touch, his need, his warm, intense, immediate desire rush over her in a flood of heat, leaving her weak-kneed. She thought of the sadness that tinged his eyes when he spoke, so briefly, of his son's problems, and she longed to sit somewhere with him and hear about the rest of his life.

But most of all, she knew she wanted to make love with him.

Drawing her shoulders up sharply away from the wall, she forced herself to head down the hall to turn up the thermostat and glance at the answering machine, which flickered at her. She rewound the tape, then listened to it click on.

"Hi, Mom, it's Julia, I just called to tell you I'm fine. Sam and I will be back Saturday sometime. We've talked to his parents, too, so everything's cool. 'Bye—" A pause crackled along the tape, then in a rush Julia's voice came again: "—Love ya. 'Bye."

Tears stung Diane's eyes. Of course Julia loved her, and of course she loved Sam more and wanted to escape from this house, this life where she was only a child. She sounded absolutely fine. Sane. Safe. That was what really mattered.

Diane went into the living room, fell into an armchair, leaned back, closed her eyes, and instantly fell asleep.

She awoke to the sound of the front door closing. Looking at her watch, she saw that it was almost ten o'clock.

"Hi. Sorry I'm late," Jim said, crossing the room to give her a quick peck on the forehead.

Diane rubbed her eyes. "Have you eaten?"

"Yeah. I had a sandwich. But I'm going to see if there's any pie left. Want some?"

"*Mmm.* I'll join you." She stretched and got up. The house was warm but dark. Moving wordlessly, she turned on the kitchen light and heated up a pot of decaf and cut two pieces of apple pie. Then she sat at the table with Jim and, as they ate, she told him about the discovery in the attic: the locket, the paper, the code, the two scientists working decades ago on the secret of fusion. The discovery that her mother had loved a Russian spy, so many years ago.

"It's astounding, isn't it?" Diane asked when she'd told him everything.

"Amazing," Jim agreed. Something had captured his imagination, and in a quiet voice, as if speaking to himself more than to his wife, he said, "Those poor men."

"Who?" Diane asked.

"The scientists. Brown and—was it Oshevnev? Coming so close to a breakthrough that would change the world, only to have their work cut off."

"Yes, but now that their formula's been found, their work might be a success!" Diane pointed out.

"But they're not alive to see it. They won't know. They died without . . ." His voice trailed off.

Diane studied Jim, who looked very tired, gray with defeat. She hadn't realized that he dreamed of recognition as well as discovery, but of course he did. That was only natural.

"Oh, Jim," she said with a sigh, covering his hand with hers, "you're young. You have years and years ahead of you in which to work. You're bound to have success in your lifetime."

"I hope you're right," Jim said. He sighed. "It's late. I'm going to bed."

"I'll be up in a moment," Diane told him. As she watched him move down the hall, she realized with a pang that for the first time in years he wasn't interested in the news. Automatically she rinsed their plates and set them in the dishwasher, then walked back through the house to the front door. She checked to be sure the front door was locked; it was. Looking out the leaded glass window at the side of the door, she saw a solitary car pass along the street, its lights flashing through the dark night, much like the discontent and desire that flickered and flared within her heart.

Chapter 11

❦ Jean

Thursday was windy and rainy, carrying with it a sharp bite of winter chill. Jean sat in the warmth of her favorite cafe with her kir, a *croque-monsieur,* and a Maigret mystery, and now she paused to rest her eyes. Leaning her chin in her hand, she stared out at the people hurrying past, heads bent against the wind and rain. She was just beginning to feel restless. Perhaps she should move on to Amsterdam before true winter hit, or on down to the warmth of southern France and then to Italy.

A young man entered the cafe, looked around, and came toward her table. His Burberry raincoat fit him perfectly, yet he had the air of a man trying hard to match the perfection of his clothes. This reminded her of her older son as an earnest young naval officer, and so she smiled.

"Excuse me, please. Are you Jean White?" He stood a proper few feet from her table, almost bowing as he spoke.

Later it would occur to her to wonder why she had felt no

dread at the suddenness of his appearance, why she didn't instantly think: Oh, no, a disaster, one of the children—! Perhaps it was because as he approached he was smiling.

"Yes. I'm Jean White."

He held out a card for her to read as he spoke. "I'm Timothy Thompson, an attaché with the American embassy here in Paris. Would you mind if I sat down?"

Jean nodded and gestured toward a chair.

"I've been asked to bring you some news. Nothing bad, I assure you. Something rather marvelous, actually. It has something to do with your life before you were married. It's a bit complicated. Do you have some time now, or would you rather I made an appointment for a later date?"

"Goodness, with an introduction like that, how could I bear to wait?" Jean laughed. "Won't you have a drink?"

After the waiter had taken his order, the young man leaned forward. He spoke quietly, as if taking her into his confidence.

"This is about a locket you once were given," he said. Then he stopped, and he blushed.

This young man could be my grandson, Jean thought, amused, before his words sank in.

A locket she once was given.

It had been years since she'd thought about that gold locket —decades. Now here was this young man seated across from her in a Left Bank cafe, with his hair cut too short for the size of his ears.

"What about the locket?" she asked.

Again he blushed. The tips of his ears turned red.

"It was given to you by a man named Erich Mellor. It contained a paper you had given to Mr. Mellor, a document of possible international importance. Mr. Mellor would like to meet with you to discuss this. He was hoping that you would be willing to come to Helsinki to meet with him—of course all expenses will be paid and all arrangements taken care of for you. It's a matter of convenience and time since he must come from Moscow."

Jean smiled and leaned forward toward the attaché. Any woman in her seventies has sustained all manner of shocks in her life, but the news that Erich Mellor was alive and wanted to see her was moving her in a way she'd forgotten. All of its own accord, her body was trembling, her heart was leaping.

"I didn't know he was still alive. What on earth is he doing in Moscow?"

"Well, he lives there." Timothy Thompson looked perplexed. "You knew he was Russian."

Jean stared at the young man. "Ah, yes, of course," she lied, wanting to relieve him of any more anxiety and very much wanting to keep him talking; she couldn't wait to hear what else he had to tell her.

"I assumed you would be willing to fly to Helsinki. We've been told by your relatives that you're on vacation, so we were hoping your schedule would be flexible enough to let us arrange a meeting very soon."

"Yes. All right," Jean agreed, nodding, thinking it couldn't be soon enough for her. There was so much she wanted to find out.

Erich was Russian! Of course, after he disappeared, she'd suspected that he wasn't an American; in her worst imaginings she'd feared he was German. She'd spent many apprehensive hours during the first year of her married life wondering what the code had really been about, whose hands it had really fallen into, and whether or not she'd stupidly brought about some kind of disaster. But during those long, exciting, exhausting days and nights when her father lectured them during meals about the course of the war, met with other officers in the secrecy of his study, listened to the radio, read the newspapers, and grew pale with worry or effusive with elation over the turn the war was taking, never during all those days and nights did anything happen that even slightly seemed to involve the missing code. And of course after the war, when both her husband and her brother were safely home, and she quickly became pregnant again, she forgot all about the locket and the strip of paper.

Erich Mellor, a Russian! She had made love with him! She was glad her father and mother would never know. And thank God Al was dead. Oh, what a dreadful thought; she didn't mean it, but she was glad he wasn't around to find out about all this. Few things would have crushed him more than to know that Jean had had a lover before him, and that that lover was a Russian. Even during the dramatic events of the past few years, Al had never believed the Russians wanted peace. It would be bad enough if Bert found out. The girls would probably think it was all romantic, and anarchist Art would be simply gleeful.

Timothy Thompson gave her the afternoon to pack her few things at the auberge, then drove her to Orly and put her on a flight to Helsinki, which arrived very late that night. Otto Kaarinen, a kind man in a three-piece suit and a trench coat who looked like an older version of Timothy Thompson, met Jean as she came off the plane. He drove her to the Intercontinental Hotel. She was to order whatever she wished from room service at any time, he told her as he escorted her to the desk and checked her in. They would come for her at noon tomorrow to take her to her meeting with Erich Mellor.

Fresh flowers and a selection of liqueurs, including a bottle of Courvoisier, had been placed in her large, airy suite. She poured herself some cognac and took a long shower, then brought the snifter with her to sip in bed. She was afraid she'd never be able to fall asleep, but as she slid down into the deep covers she found sleep waiting for her there.

In the morning, she treated herself to an enormous breakfast, which she ate in her room next to a window looking out over the harbor. She'd never been to Helsinki before and considered going out for a quick walking tour before lunch. Instead she found herself standing in the bathroom in an idiotic panic, scrutinizing her ancient face and body and desperately trying to think up some way to improve on what she saw.

Erich Mellor. After all these years!

Of course he would be older, too, she reminded herself, and hadn't it been only a few days ago when she'd been preening, congratulating herself on her fine good looks and obvious attractiveness in the Jardin du Luxembourg? She couldn't spend much time deciding what to wear since she'd brought mostly skirts and blouses and blazers, but she did try on her two silk dresses and the tweed suit with the velvet collar. Which made her sexy? Oh, forget sexy. Which made her look as if she still knew what sex meant? But no, she didn't want to look sexy; she wanted to look elegant and unapproachable and serene. He had, after all, dumped her, and she wanted to show him that she'd led quite a successful life in spite of it. He hadn't broken her spirit. He hadn't broken her heart.

Any minute now a knock would come on the door, and she would be ushered off to meet her former lover. Jean inspected every inch of face and hair and bodice. She'd chosen the tweed suit; the jacket slimmed her nicely and gave her another layer over her silk blouse, a purely illusory sense of added protection. She put on her pearls, then took them off. She didn't want to look like some Republican committeewoman.

Oh, why should she care about presenting a pretty picture to this man! He had been a cad. He'd romanced her to get what he wanted, then disappeared without a word of explanation, leaving her heartsick.

Yet he had also been her first lover, her first romance. She had no regrets, really.

She blew a kiss at her image in the mirror and went out to wait for the knock on the door.

The knock came at noon precisely. The same pleasant man who had met her at the airport escorted her to a waiting limousine. As they rode along, he pointed out Helsinki's historic sights. They came to a vast square and stopped in front of a rather dauntingly handsome building. Would Erich come down these marble steps to greet her?

No. The driver opened her door, the official escorted her up the steps, through a massive doorway, down an endless corridor lined with epic-sized oils and bronze statues, and finally, into a private salon. With its thick Turkish carpet, glittering chandelier, red silk sofas, gilt-trimmed escritoires, and Chinese vases, the room was magnificent.

"If you would kindly wait here," Mr. Kaarinen said, gesturing her toward a chair. "Mr. Mellor will be with you immediately."

She didn't have time to be nervous. Only moments after the door closed behind Mr. Kaarinen, it opened again, and Erich Mellor entered the room.

Jean's first thought was: Oh, good! He's kept his beautiful hair!

Erich's hair was white, but it was full and thick and wavy. It offset the appearance of old age that his walk gave him. He moved slowly, bent slightly, leaning on a cane.

My God, Jean thought, rising, he moves like an old man. Why, he *is* an old man! I'm in my seventies. He must be close to eighty!

In spite of emotions so powerful they made her weak at the knees, she stood facing him as he approached. Anger, resentment, pride, curiosity, and also a great whirl of joy at the sight of him buffeted her like gusts of wind. She reached out and rested a hand on the back of a sofa for support.

"Hello, Jean." His voice was deep and sonorous.

"Hello, Erich."

He paused just before her, not attempting a civilized kiss on the cheek. She did not offer her hand. Even stooped as he was, he was taller than Jean, and she had to bend her head back to face him. They stood in silence, studying each other. His suit was immaculately cut of expensive gray wool; there was a patina of wealth and well-being about him. His face was wrinkled and spotted with age, and the bones of his hands showed through skin thin as crepe.

"Shall we sit?" He gestured to the sofa.

Jean sat at one end, Erich at the other. As they turned to face each other, their knees did not quite touch.

"It's good to see you again, Jean," Erich said.

"It's good to see you again, too, Erich. Although the circumstances surprise me. And confuse me." She smiled to offset any disapproval in her words.

"Yes. I owe you some explanations. I think you will be quite pleased once you've heard me out. Shall we have lunch while we talk?"

He was so urbane, it almost made her laugh. He'd always been suave, but the measured courtliness of his words and manners made her feel as if they were in a play.

But of course we are in a play, Jean thought. His play. That's what I've been caught up in all along. But she found she couldn't summon up any righteous indignation at this. She was just so pleased to be with him again.

He turned to press a button inlaid in a table near him. Almost immediately the door opened again, and two men wheeled in a cart. They began to set the table next to the window. Jean saw the black gleam of caviar, the etched glasses, the bottle of Zubrowka.

"Shall we?"

Erich rose, and while leaning with one hand on his cane, with the other he gently took Jean just beneath her elbow, a gentlemanly gesture, to escort her to the table. That simple touch, even after all those decades, made her skin tingle.

She did not turn to look at him. They made slow, stately progress across the room to the table. The waiters had remained to help Jean into her chair, to pour the vodka and remove the silver domes from the plates. Then they bowed silently and left the room.

Erich lifted his glass in a toast. "To our past."

Jean looked at him. "I'm not certain I want to toast to that."

He smiled. "Then, to our future."

"To our future," she agreed, lifting her glass.

The vodka shocked her with its aromatic, dry bite. Their first course was caviar on toast points with slivers of lemon decorating the gold-rimmed plate.

"Whoever you are, you must be quite important," Jean observed.

"Ah, well, I deserve all this. I've devoted my life to my country, you see. I've made more than the normal amount of sacrifices." He smiled, but his dark eyes seemed sad. Then the sadness lifted. "And you, my dear Jean, are quite important, too."

She waited. She kept her hands in her lap and stared at Erich. After all these years, at least she could be dignified.

"All right," he said, nodding, as if having caught her message. "Small talk later. Explanations now." He took another sip of vodka, then leaned back in his chair. "I don't know how much you may have guessed."

"Nothing! Until yesterday I didn't know if you were dead or

alive. Now I know you're alive, and Russian. Perhaps I should have guessed that long ago, but I didn't—though I wondered."

"I was well trained. I'd lived in the States for so many years by that point that my accent and bearing were perfectly American. It says nothing against your intelligence or intuition that you didn't guess that. No, I meant about the locket. Well, I won't speak in mysteries. My dear Jean," he said, suddenly warm and personal, leaning across the table toward her.

"You see, when we met I was working for my country. In short, I needed to get something from your father's safekeeping. The key to a code. When you found what I asked for, a formulalike message on a strip of paper, you assumed you'd found what I wanted, and so did I. I was delighted. I was so young, and I had accomplished a major coup!

"However, when I took it to my colleagues, they began to decipher it and very quickly realized it wasn't at all what we were looking for. In fact, it was a worthless piece of scientific mumbo-jumbo. I was embarrassed. I was immediately sent home—to Russia—and had to work very hard to prove I wasn't the dunce I'd made myself out to be."

Erich paused, took a bite of caviar, touched his white linen napkin to his mouth, and took a sip of vodka. He considered a moment, and Jean sat in silence, waiting.

"I didn't want to leave the country without seeing you. But I was given no choice. The best I could do was to send the locket to you with the strip of paper tucked inside, so that you could return it to your father's safe. In this way I hoped to avert trouble for you."

" 'Avert trouble.' " Jean repeated dryly. This man had broken her heart. She lifted her chin. "My father never seemed to notice that the paper was missing. I was in the house often during that time—I moved back in with my parents. I always knew if my father was in a fury about something. Of course I was afraid he would get into some kind of trouble with the code missing—or that I would get into some kind of trouble. But nothing ever happened."

"Ah. That's probably because the message was considered worthless. At that time. All the papers related to that matter were discarded, thrown away as so much trash. Fortunately, you never opened the locket. You never found the crucial strip of paper and returned it to your father's safe. It's remained in the locket all these years."

"Yes. But, Erich, I lost the locket." Jean leaned forward, suddenly apprehensive. If something significant rested on having the locket, after all these years, he would be crushed to know she had no way of finding it for him.

"But your daughter found it."

"What? My daughter? Which daughter? Where?"

"Diane. In her attic. In the hem of your raccoon coat. It had fallen through a hole in the pocket."

"Good Lord." Jean sat in wonderment, remembering back to those stormy days of her youth, when she'd lost Erich, and married Al, when the globe of her life had turned on its axis. She sipped her vodka. "And this precious piece of paper has been sitting in that locket in my old raccoon coat all these years?"

"Apparently."

"Well, it's a good thing I didn't give that coat to the thrift shop as I'd always intended to. The old rag. But it has such sentimental value for me, and then I suppose Diane thought Julia, her daughter, might wear it for fun. Although it's in terrible shape . . . but I'm babbling. Erich, what on earth is on that strip of paper?"

Erich smiled. "A formula. A formula that might change the world."

"Good heavens. I hope you mean a change for the better."

"I do. The formula is for creating nuclear energy from cold fusion." When Jean tilted her head, looking puzzled, Erich continued. "I'll try to explain. There are two ways to create nuclear energy: by fission, which is splitting the atom, and by fusion, which is combining atoms."

Jean felt impatient. "Well, of course I know something about that, given the atomic bomb, but—"

Erich held up his hand to interrupt. "Fission is unpopular for all kinds of reasons. It's dangerous, and it creates radioactive waste. If science could find a way to create energy through fusion, we could have an inexhaustible source of clean, safe fuel."

"Are you saying the paper in my father's study—"

"—holds a formula for cold fusion? Yes. We think so." And he told her about Brown and Oshevnev, about their code. "But then the war began and Brown was, shall I say, *urgently invited* by your government to stop work on fusion and assist in the work on the atomic bomb. He died during the war. In Russia, Oshevnev lost his lab, and all his communications with Brown were destroyed. Oshevnev did continue working on fusion. He was part of the group of scientists who exploded the hydrogen bomb in 1953. But without Brown and Brown's formula, he never got back on track."

"Why didn't he look for the formula before?"

"After the war, the Soviet Union was secretive about its research, even about what projects it was interested in. Oshevnev died recently, but a colleague of his told us of the importance of Oshevnev's early work. I am on a task force for improved communications between the U.S. and our country. I've always wondered about the code, and when the scientists came to me, I told them about it. I spoke with someone in your government—and here we are."

"And now that you've found Brown's formula?"

"Now scientists—American and Russian scientists working together—will interpret it, test it, and see where it takes them."

"So it could be a scientific breakthrough."

"It could be tremendously important, no question."

"This is a lot to take in," Jean admitted.

"That's understandable. Most people would be surprised to realize that what they think of as an ordinary life has somehow touched history," Erich replied. "If you hadn't taken the code, it eventually would have been destroyed with the other papers in your father's safe. As it is, you've preserved something that might give new hope to the world."

Jean sat quietly in her chair, remembering those days, her brash, eager optimism, her youthful pride . . . her overpowering love. Smiling wryly, she softly concluded, "All this, because I was a fool . . . over you."

"You weren't a fool, Jean," Erich objected, his voice tender.

"I certainly felt like one."

Erich leaned forward. "I never would have left you that way if I hadn't been literally, quite literally, forced to. It was the most I could do to send the locket to you."

"Yes, I understand that. Still—" Jean lowered her eyes, struggling to form her words, and she felt her cheeks flame with humiliation as she lifted her eyes and faced him with the truth. "You used me."

"I loved you, Jean," Erich declared.

Smiling gently, Jean shook her head.

"I loved you," he insisted. "I didn't intend to love you; I didn't expect to. I was surprised by my own feelings." Reaching out, he put his hand gently over hers. "I apologize for lying to you. But I don't apologize for the times I made love to you or the words of love I spoke to you. Those were all true."

Jean studied the man across from her, seeing through the lines and age spots the man she had loved all those years ago. A sudden lump in her throat prevented her from speaking, and she simply nodded her head in acknowledgment.

"I think I've loved you all my life," Erich told her.

Jean felt tears well up behind her eyes. Gently she withdrew her hand, picked up her glass of vodka, and took a sip. "Are you married?" she asked.

He was about to answer when a discreet knock sounded at the door. Erich barked something in another language—Russian? Finnish?—and two waiters entered carrying trays. They cleared the table and set out the main course, plates of poached salmon, boiled baby potatoes, and sliced cucumbers. Erich waited until they had poured the wine and left the room before speaking.

"I was. My wife died several years ago."

"Do you have children?"

"Two. A son. A daughter. My daughter is a physician. My son is—following in my footsteps. I hope you will meet them both."

"You know everything about me, I suppose, with your connections."

"I know you married Al. I don't know if you got my wedding present."

"Wedding present?" Jean tilted her head, remembering. "Of course! The carpet! The mysterious, fabulous carpet! But I had no idea it came from you."

"No. You couldn't have known. It was a romantic gesture. I wanted you to have something beautiful, and lasting. It was a pleasure for me to think you had it in your home all these years."

"That was a clever time to send it. We assumed it was from friends of our parents. I wish I had known it was from you."

"Do you really?"

Jean considered. She and Al had put the carpet in their living room, where it gave the home of the newlyweds an air of permanence and luxury. She'd put her babies down on its velvety surface to crawl. Her family had spent Christmas Days seated on the carpet unwrapping presents. How would she have felt knowing it was from Erich, the lover who left her? She would have felt compromised, confused.

"No. You're right. But I'm glad I know now."

"You had a happy marriage."

"Yes. You know Al died this summer?"

"Yes. I'm sorry."

"He was a good man. A good husband. We had four children. Diane, Bert, Susan, Art."

"Yes. I've met Diane."

"What?" Jean looked at Erich in amazement.

"When she was in Russia about ten years ago. When it was feared her daughter had meningitis. I was able to help her leave quickly. It was a pleasure to see her. She looks very much like you."

"My God!" Jean said. "You were the one who helped Diane. What a lovely coincidence!"

"It was hardly a coincidence," Erich told her.

Another knock came at the door, announcing the arrival of the waiters with a dessert of berries and cream and a beautiful silver pot of aromatic coffee.

When the waiters had bowed and left, closing the door behind them, Erich continued. "They tell me you were traveling and that we interrupted your trip. I wonder if I might persuade you to postpone your journey some more. I would like to take you to Moscow with me. I would like to show you my country."

Jean concentrated on stirring cream and sugar into her coffee. "I don't think I could visit Moscow now. I'd better go home. I've got to spend some time with Diane—I've got a lot of explaining to do. No, I'm afraid I can't go now."

"Perhaps later?" Erich asked. "Perhaps in the spring?"

"Perhaps," Jean replied, smiling.

Erich had to leave after their lunch, but first he returned Jean to Mr. Kaarinen's care. Mr. Kaarinen helped her put through a phone call to Diane. Her daughter's voice sounded so clear that Jean had to remind herself she was half a world away. Quickly she made arrangements for Diane, who was bursting with questions, to meet her plane the next afternoon. Jean smoothly insisted they wait until they were together to talk about it all.

She had three hours before her flight left for London and when she said she wished she could see something of Helsinki, Mr. Kaarinen suggested she visit the famous waterfront. He drove her there, promising to pick her up in two hours to take her to the airport. She thanked him and stepped out by herself for one last, deliciously solitary walk on foreign soil.

It was a glorious day, brilliant with a slanted sunlight that sparkled across the Gulf of Finland and lay warmly on her shoulders like a shawl. An enormous, radiant expanse of water lapped at the clean, modern harbor. Gulls soared and screamed above the fishing boats, launches and trawlers hummed and blared their horns as they set off for other shores, stately cruise ships rocked at anchor, and salt and a tangy foretaste of winter glittered in the air. She enjoyed the mix of people she passed among, kerchiefed farm women and husky fishermen, Gypsy women dressed in bright full skirts, tourists in their sensible sneakers. It pleased her that she could not understand even a syllable of this language. Diane had come here once, she remembered, years ago . . . if she had time, she could look up the jeweler Diane still corresponded with . . . but no, there was not enough time today.

Perhaps if she returned . . . Perhaps if she returned on her way to Moscow.

Wandering through the market set up beside the harbor, Jean admired the plump, glossy vegetables, the vibrant bronze and gold chrysanthemums, and the variety of fresh, pink fish. Herring were marvelous to look at, seemingly made of silver when they were brought up dripping from the water; once smoked, their scales turned into gold. Stopping before a stall of clever wooden toys, she realized that she hadn't bought presents for any of her grandchildren. She'd allocated a certain part of her money especially for gifts—but even if she rushed, she couldn't choose and buy them all now. Well, she would have to come back, if not to Helsinki, at least to Europe. She would have to. She was cutting this trip short.

The delicious aroma of coffee drifted out from a cafe and she entered, glad to sit down. She was tired. She ordered coffee and sweet pastries, then settled back in her chair and simply looked out the window at the passing crowds.

She thought of Al. He would not be amused to see her here —an older, and therefore vulnerable, woman, alone. He'd never wanted to travel through Europe, preferring the more comfortable pleasures of the tried and true. She had never pressed the issue, and they had vacationed in Florida during the winter, where Al played his beloved game of golf, and they had dutifully visited their children and grandchildren during the holidays, and it had all been very pleasant.

She wondered whether or not Al could see her now. Over the past few months, after her husband's death, Jean had tried to be open to the possibility of contact from those "on the other side." Friends of hers, widows, widowers, assured her that they had seen or heard or even been touched by a spouse or child who had died. Al could appear at any time, they told her, as a voice, or perhaps in a dream. She had waited. She had neither believed nor disbelieved. Al had not appeared.

During the last few years of their lives they had lived like friends or comrades rather than man and wife. Finally, theirs had been an affectionate, but not sexual, relationship. Looking back at her life, she was certain that she'd been a good wife to Al. She had made him happy; she had given him four children.

And she had been the love of his life. She knew that.

If he could see her now, would he begrudge her this happiness? She didn't think he would. She hoped not. For in this strange northern latitude, during this chilly season as the year moved toward its winter, she felt strange stirrings in her heart, and an eager anticipation of all that was yet to come. She still had years and years to live, and much to see, and so much she wanted to do. She took a final swallow of the rich, aromatic, dark coffee, then counted out the shining Finnish marks and pennies and hurried back out into the tantalizing bustle of the unfamiliar streets.

Chapter 12

Jean, Diane, and Julia

Saturday morning Jean awoke in the guest room of her oldest daughter's house. For a while she simply lay in bed, collecting her thoughts. The flight from Helsinki to Boston had been interminable, with a long layover in London; and after passing through customs and waiting for her luggage, Jean had wanted to do nothing but take a long, hot shower and stretch out in bed. Diane had been wonderful, understanding that even though it was only noon in Boston it was night according to Jean's body; and while Jean showered, Diane had put a plate of buttered toast and a pot of tea on the bedside table, then left, closing the bedroom door. Jean had crawled into bed, nibbled enough of the toast to settle her stomach, then slipped down into a dreamy sleep. She'd slept straight through the afternoon and night, for almost twenty-four hours.

No wonder she'd slept so late: the sky was dark. Throwing back the covers, Jean padded across the thick carpet to the window. Rain battered the glass, and thunder rolled ominously in the distance. She was glad they hadn't had to endure weather like this during her flight home. Hadn't Diane told her that Julia and Sam would be driving up from Middletown this weekend? Jean had always been edgy when one of her children was traveling on wet roads in bad conditions. But she'd met Sam; she thought he'd be careful.

Now Jean opened her bedroom door and listened, but she didn't hear any voices. Eager to see her family, she quickly washed her face and dressed. As she brushed her hair, she noticed how bright and clear her eyes looked in the mirror. Because of the long sleep? Or because she was so happy? She could see some of her youth shining in her face.

Stepping out into the quiet of the wide upstairs hall, Jean let herself indulge in a moment of nostalgia, and instead of hurrying down the stairs, she went into her grandchildren's bedrooms. Chase's room was so neat that it felt empty, as if it were a photo album he'd arranged and closed and abandoned to a shelf in his parents' house. But Julia's room was a glorious mess, the jumble of a young person metamorphosing so fast that the stages of her life blurred one into the other. Her beloved pink toe shoes hung by their ribbons from the closet doorknob, her windows were swathed with streaked and tie-dyed scarves, her desk was piled with frighteningly fat guides to colleges, and next to her bed stood the white wicker rocker she had sat in as a toddler, now holding her favorite teddy bear. On her dresser was the elaborate musical jewelry box her grandparents had given her the Christmas she was eleven.

"Oh, sweet," Jean murmured, smiling, and crossed the room and lifted the lid of the music box, wanting to hear the tinkling tune, to see the ballerina twirl. And she heard the tune and saw the little doll creak along in its stiff circle, but she also saw, tucked in the bracelet compartment, a bunch of shining foil-wrapped condoms. "Oh, my," Jean said, slamming the lid shut. During their drive home from the airport the day before, Diane had told Jean about all that had gone on with Julia this week; still, the condoms were shocking.

"Serves you right for snooping," she admonished herself aloud and left Julia's room, but still she could not keep herself from stopping at Diane's study. The door was open, so Jean only leaned against the doorjamb and looked in, at the long desk with its computer and phone and copy and fax machines, at the easel with a half-completed sketch of a necklace, at the easy chair and ottoman with the good reading lamp and the basket of trade magazines nearby, at the walls covered with framed ads for Arabesque and photographs of Diane receiving awards. How successful her daughter was, with all these accolades, and a good marriage, and such fine children, too. She hoped she'd told Diane how proud she was of her.

Turning, she went down the stairs and into the living room where a fire of cherry wood and birch blazed behind the brass screen, warming the room. For once her daughter was not sketching or reading or sewing but, instead, sat curled up in an armchair, gazing out into the room as if she'd never seen it before. When Jean entered, Diane looked startled—Jean even thought Diane blushed, although perhaps that was simply heat from the fire.

"Oh! Mother! I didn't hear you come down. Did you have a good sleep?"

"Yes, dear, it was bliss. Just what I needed."

"I've got coffee on, and I'll just heat up some muffins, that is unless you're hungry for eggs—"

"No, that sounds lovely, although I would like a glass of juice. But I can go get it. You don't have to wait on me." She followed her daughter into the kitchen and while Diane heated up the muffins, then spread them with butter, Jean poured herself a small glass of orange juice and fixed her coffee the way she liked it.

"Jim's at the lab," Diane said as they moved through the kitchen.

"He works even on Saturdays now?"

"He works all the time now. He has no life," Diane answered, bitterness tinging her voice.

"Perhaps he's close to a discovery."

"He's always close to one. He's been close for years. Oh, I don't want to waste our time complaining—we've got so much to talk about." Diane turned suddenly and surprised her mother with a look of admiration. "Mother. What's this about a man before Daddy?"

Jean took her breakfast in by the fire and settled onto the sofa. Diane curled up again in the armchair, and they talked as they never had before. Jean started at the beginning, describing her family with an honesty she'd never felt free to express when her parents were alive—they were her children's grandparents, after all, and that was what was important. She described her college days, her pacifist beliefs, and then she told Diane about her love affair with Erich, trying to capture the romance of it all. She didn't say whether or not she and Erich had actually been lovers, and Diane didn't ask. Probably she could guess, Jean thought, for she kept smiling. She told Diane about her trip to Helsinki and about meeting Erich again.

"And that's it," she finished. "Here I am."

"Uncle Bobby will be apoplectic when he hears about this!" Diane remarked with a grin.

"I don't see why he should know about it," Jean replied. "I

don't see why anyone has to tell him. Erich says it will be a long time before they know whether or not the formula is all they're hoping for."

"What was it like seeing Erich again after all these years?" Diane asked.

"It was wonderful," Jean confessed. "He was so elegant, and he had such beautiful manners. And he's such an impressive-looking man—you've met him, you know."

"What?"

"He told me about it. When you went to Leningrad the time Julia had spinal meningitis."

Diane squinted, as if to see more clearly back into her memory. "My God!" she exclaimed. "The official who cut through all the red tape. Wow. He was handsome. Nice, too."

"I gather it's not his particular role in his government to help young American women change their flight schedules," Jean said. "He knew who you were and wanted to see you."

"Because I'm your daughter."

"Yes."

"So he'd been thinking of you through all those years. Mom, that's really romantic. Are you going to see him again?"

Jean tried to maintain some degree of dignity. "Perhaps. I might go back to Moscow in the spring." Then, surprising herself as much as her daughter, she continued, "Perhaps you could go with me. You've never been to Moscow, and we've never traveled together. It might be fun."

"What a good idea!" Diane exclaimed, pleased.

"Would Jim mind if you went off without him?"

"I'm not sure he'd *know* if I went with you." Diane rose to look out the front window, and Jean sensed dissatisfaction in her daughter's face. "Jim's getting to be a real old fogey, Mother. He really doesn't see much past his work."

"That's bound to change," Jean said soothingly.

"Maybe." Diane shrugged and sank down on the sofa next to her mother. "Maybe not. In any case, I'd love to go to Moscow with you, no matter what Jim thinks, as long as everything's settled with Arabesque. And of course, depending on how Julia is."

"I can't wait to see her."

"I can't wait, either," Diane said, and suddenly she turned to her mother and blurted out, "Oh, Mother, I don't know what to do!" Diane was actually wringing her hands. "If Julia were a little girl, I swear I'd spank her! She's put us through such agony, and I'm still anxious about her. Imagine, trying to slit her wrists. Oh, it makes me ill to think of it."

"But she's all right. Sam's with her. And she's coming home today."

"I know. But—getting married! At her age! Tossing away her entire future."

"That wouldn't be tossing away her entire future, Diane. It would only be living her life differently than you'd envisioned."

Diane glared at Jean. She rose from the sofa and paced the room. "I should have known you'd side with Julia."

"She is eighteen. She's always been a good girl, intelligent, responsible. I've always admired her."

"Do you *admire* her now? After all this?"

Jean hesitated, considering. She chose her words with care. "It's possible that this was all she could see to do. Perhaps she felt boxed in. Trapped. Believe me, Diane, she's not the first young woman to go against her parents' wishes."

Mother and daughter looked at each other levelly.

"I just don't want her to get married so young," Diane said.

"A lot of young women do," Jean told her. Then, before Diane could protest again, she hurried on: "But perhaps I can help. I thought I'd ask her to go to Moscow with us. Wouldn't it be marvelous if the three of us all went? We've never had a trip together, just the three of us. It would be something we'd always remember."

"You could certainly ask her, but I don't know if it will do any good. She's so obsessed with Sam."

"We're all obsessed when we're first in love," Jean reminded Diane softly, but she saw that her words didn't smooth the crease between her daughter's eyebrows or lessen the pain in her eyes. Suddenly Jean felt as if she were standing on the heights of a mountain from which she could look down at all the world in its rich diversity, while her daughter was only halfway up the mountain, and from her vantage point she could see only dangers and shadows.

It's always a surprise, it's new each time, and don't you see that's as it should be? Those were the words Jean longed to say to her daughter, along with a jumble of other advice, for she knew Diane was entering a new phase of motherhood now when she would simply have to wait and watch and let Julia and Chase experience their own hardships and bear their own pain. Perhaps this was the most difficult phase of all. For here Jean sat in this really extravagantly beautiful house with her elegant daughter before her, and all Jean could see, *feel,* was the pain in her daughter's eyes.

"I just want her to take a little more time," Diane was saying. "She's so awfully young."

"I'll ask her to come live with me," Jean offered; she would do anything to help her daughter. "There's a second bedroom in the condo. Julia could work. Or even attend a culinary-arts school. There are several in the area." She smiled, pleased with her suggestion.

"Cooking school!"

Jean bit back a sharp retort and quietly reminded her daughter, "When you were a young woman, your father hoped you'd go to law school. For him, in those times, that was fairly radical thinking. But you were his oldest child, and so bright." Now there was impatience in her daughter's eyes, and Jean feared they were headed for an argument, when the phone rang. Diane rushed into the kitchen.

Quickly she returned. "It's for you, Mother. *A man.*"

Ignoring her daughter's wicked grin, Jean hurried to the kitchen. "Hello?"

"Hello, Jean. I wanted to be sure you got there all right."

The sound of Erich's voice took her breath away, and for a moment she couldn't reply. "How nice of you," she said, at last. The connection wasn't perfect, and Erich sounded miles away—as after all, he was. "Yes, I'm safely here."

"How was your flight?"

"Long." She was rewarded with the low, sexual rumble of his laugh.

"I've been thinking," Erich said, "that even if you do come to Moscow next spring, I'd rather not wait until then to see you again. I could come to Washington in about a month, for official purposes. Could I see you then?"

"Why, yes, I suppose . . . Yes, of course you could. Erich, that would be wonderful." If I don't have a heart attack first, she thought, for there was a wild pounding in her chest.

"Good. Well, I'll write to let you know when I'm coming."

"Lovely. Erich—" Jean paused, then said, "Plan to stay as long as you can."

For a moment the line hummed with a mutual and warm satisfaction.

"I will. Good-bye."

"Thank you for calling. Good-bye."

331

Jean hung up the phone and leaned against the wall. Her first clear thought was how glad she was that she'd moved. When Erich came to visit, she would be in her home, not in the house where she'd lived with Al and her family.

Thinking such thoughts, about her house, and her wardrobe, and whether or not to go on a diet, Jean wandered back into the living room and sat down by the fire.

"Who was that, Mother?" Diane asked, smirking.

"Erich Mellor. He just wanted to see how my trip was."

"Oh, really?" Diane pressed, teasingly. "That's the only reason he called?"

"Well, actually," Jean admitted, "he said that he's got to come to Washington next month on a business trip, and he'd like to —see me then."

"Mother, look at you. You're blushing."

Jean smiled at her daughter, pleased by Diane's teasing. Now Jean studied her daughter, thinking how lovely she was, and how much she looked as Jean had when Jean was Diane's age.

"You can get that little mole on your neck removed," Jean advised Diane. "They do it in the doctor's office. It only takes a second, and it doesn't hurt a bit."

Diane flashed her mother an angry look. "I didn't realize it was so noticeable!" She'd chosen a boat-necked emerald mohair sweater with gray silk-and-wool slacks this morning so that she'd look especially elegant for her mother. The sweater had cost a fortune. The pin just below the neckline, a gold twist with emeralds, was one of her newest designs. How like her mother to see a mole instead of the brooch.

"It's not that conspicuous," Jean said placatingly. "I only noticed it because I had one just like it when I was your age. I had it taken off because it bothered me when I wore certain kinds of blouses. It's nothing to worry about, you know."

"I wasn't worrying about it. Really, Mother, do you think I'm thinking about moles right now?"

"No, of course not, I don't know why I even brought it up. I was just thinking how beautiful you are—"

But Diane was irritated, and she got up and began piling the coffee cups on the tray. "Coffee's cold. I'll get a new pot." Chin high, Diane swept off into the kitchen.

Trust her mother to zoom in on any flaw, Diane thought, but as she moved around the kitchen she calmed down and admitted to herself that her sudden pique had been caused by something else. The phone call from a man had been for *her mother,* not herself. She hadn't heard from Peter Frost for three days now, and she wondered if she'd ever hear from him again, and if so, what she'd do. Lucky Mother, her husband's dead, so she doesn't have to deal with a moral dilemma about seeing a lover! Then she leaned against the counter and shook her head and smiled to herself at her own irrationality.

She'd just started a fresh pot of coffee when she heard the front door open and slam.

Julia's voice rang out from the living room: "Grandmother! What are you doing here?"

Diane forced herself to count to ten. She wanted to be reasonable, composed. She only got to six before hurtling down the hall.

Julia was on the sofa, hugging her grandmother. Her hair was clean and wavy, and her face shone. Diane's heart leaped.

"Julia."

As the young woman turned to face her mother, her expression darkened so dramatically that Diane felt sick with guilt and, at the same time, overcome with anger.

"Hi, Mom."

Diane sank down on the sofa next to her daughter. "Show me your wrists."

"Mom."

Diane grabbed her daughter's arms and turned them. Ordinary Band-Aids adhered just below the joint of the hand. Diane's stomach clenched. She peeled a Band-Aid back. The cut was red, only an inch long, and placed toward the outer edge of Julia's arm, so that it missed the radial artery and the deep, navy blue vein.

Julia had never seen her mother's face turn quite so gray, so sunken with grief. All the radiance, all the boldness drained from Diane's face. Her mother suddenly looked old, old enough to die.

"Mom, I'm so sorry," Julia whispered, choking on her tears. "I didn't mean to worry you. It was awful of me. I know that now. I was just so— I didn't think of anyone else."

Diane was still holding her daughter's wrists in her hands, so tightly that she could feel the blood pulse. "Just tell me. Did you really want to die?"

"No!" Julia shook her head in exasperation. "I didn't want to die. I didn't mean to at all. I was just— Oh, I don't know, Mom. I guess I went a little crazy."

"Would you like to see a psychiatrist for a while? Or a counselor?"

"Mom!" Julia laughed. "No!" All at once her mother's concern was annoying. She wrenched her arms free. "Give me a break. I don't need a psychiatrist. I just needed out of that pressure cooker. And I need to be with Sam."

"I hear you want to get married," Jean interrupted, giving Diane a chance to compose herself.

"Oh, yes, Grandmother. I love Sam so much. And he loves me."

"Where is he?"

"He went over to his parents'. We thought it would be better if I talked to Mom and Dad alone, first. I don't mean alone without you, Grandmother. I'm glad you're here."

"If you married Sam, now, what would you do?" Jean asked.

"Well, he'd finish school. He wants to go on to graduate school. He's in chemistry, so he'll be able to get a good job eventually. I thought I'd get a job in Middletown."

"Doing what?" Diane asked, even though by now she could guess.

"Working in a restaurant. Or catering."

Diane stared at Julia without speaking.

"Before you start working, perhaps you could take a trip with me," Jean suggested. "To Moscow."

"Moscow?" Julia's interest was piqued.

"Yes. A very old friend of mine has invited me to visit Moscow in the spring. I've asked your mother to join me, and I'd like you to come along, too."

"Moscow. Wow. I'd love to go. But how do you have an old friend in Moscow?"

"Well, it's complicated, Julia. It's a long story."

"Tell me!"

"Are you hungry, Julia?" Diane interrupted.

"Yeah, Mom, I am."

"I'll make some sandwiches," Diane said and went back into the kitchen. She could hear the rise and fall of voices and laughter as her mother and daughter talked, but at this distance, she couldn't tell whose voice was Jean's, whose Julia's. She leaned her head against a window, grateful for the cold press of glass and the impersonal, buffeting wind. A melancholy weighted her arms and slowed her movements. As had happened many times before, once she knew her child was truly safe, the adrenaline of fear left her, and she sagged with fatigue.

Forcing herself to move, she opened the refrigerator and took out the lettuce, tomatoes, zucchini, broccoli. She'd make sandwiches and slice up fresh veggies to eat with a dip; Julia loved vegetables. Julia did look good. She had to admit it to herself—Julia was absolutely glowing with health. And yet only a few days ago, she had tried to slit her wrists! Diane knew it would be a long time, weeks, months, perhaps years, before she recovered from the agony of that news, before she could hear a phone ring without jumping, before she could trust her daughter to change her life in less dramatic ways.

Just then Julia came into the kitchen in a rush—"I've got to have some juice. I'm dying of thirst—" the young woman said, grabbing a carton from the refrigerator and a glass from the shelf, and Diane wanted to whack the glass from her daughter's careless hand and grab her shoulders and shake her until her teeth rattled. She wanted to scream, "Promise me you'll never do that again! Promise me you'll never again try to die!"

But she knew no one person could make such a promise for all time. And she saw how relaxed Julia was, every molecule of her body fairly beaming, and she remembered how her mother could still make her feel, how her mother had made her feel only minutes ago, so she said, "Julia, you look so beautiful."

Julia responded with a look of pure joy. "Oh, thanks, Mom. I feel beautiful." Then, spontaneously, she went up to Diane and, glass in one hand, carton in the other, embraced her in a clumsy hug. "I love you, Mom," she said, then turned and hurried back to the living room and her grandmother.

Diane stood stunned. Could it be this easy? she wondered. Could she just accept her child? Or should she, must she remain on guard, forever nudging and nagging her daughter toward safety?

The phone rang. Diane picked it up, knowing in advance it would be Jim, calling to see if Julia had arrived.

"Diane? Peter Frost."

"Oh. Hi." Suddenly she was flushed with warmth.

"Did your daughter make it home this weekend?"

"Yes. She just arrived."

"That's good. But I don't want to interrupt—"

"You're not interrupting. My mother's here, too. She got in from Helsinki yesterday. She and Julia are having a little heart-to-heart." Her own heart was racing. "I'm just making lunch."

"So everyone's all right?"

"More than all right. Flourishing. Peter, my mother might start—*seeing* Erich Mellor again. And she's planning a trip to Russia in the spring. She's absolutely glowing." And I am, too, Diane added silently. She leaned against the wall and closed her eyes, the better to soak in the sensation of Peter's voice.

"Good for her. Well, look, I won't keep you. But I've been thinking about you."

"I've been thinking about you."

For a long, delicious moment, she and Peter were connected in a silence so sexually rich it was like a kiss.

"I'd like to see you again. I can get back to Boston Tuesday. Could we have lunch?"

"Yes."

"Then I'll call you when my plane gets in about where to meet. Perhaps we could go somewhere on the coast."

"There's a restaurant I know in Marblehead . . ." Diane suggested.

"If the weather's good, we can take a walk on the beach."

She imagined them kissing at the ocean's edge. "That would be perfect."

"I'll see you Tuesday, then."

"Yes."

"Good-bye, then." He sounded reluctant to hang up.

She didn't want to lose the connection. "Good-bye."

She put the receiver down, then stood staring at the phone. She was going to have an affair, she realized, and she felt completely, utterly, blissfully glad. When she lifted her head, she saw how a cloud had parted, letting a shaft of sunlight streak through her kitchen, so that for a moment all the ordinary appliances of daily life looked magical. The wind gusted, clouds drifted back over the sun, and the kitchen was once again in shadow.

Turning on the overhead light, she set about making the sandwiches, washing and slicing the vegetables. She carried a tray into the living room and put it on the coffee table. Jean was telling Julia about her days as a young woman in Washington, about meeting Erich, and Julia was hanging on every word. Julia had Jean's smile, Diane realized. Diane relaxed in her chair, looking at them, and for a while there was peace in the room.